I0891598

The Unassigned Lands

The Unassigned Lands

THE LEGEND OF BUD DALTON IN THE INDIAN TERRITORY

Ross Callen

Clovercroft Publishing

The Unassigned Lands: The Legend of Bud Dalton in the Indian Territory

Published by Clovercroft Publishing
ClovercroftPublishing.com

Cover and Interior Design by Suzanne Lawing

ISBN: 978-1-956370-91-1 (print)

Printed in the United States of America

Acknowledgements

This would not have been possible without a great deal of help. My first thanks go to Carolee Crider, my first reader, for withstanding the assault of words and pages that was the first draft.

More thanks go to my wife, Dana Callen, and my daughter, Shannon Callen, for proving the thing was readable and to Chris Meadows and Jeffrey Haynes for skillfully pointing out plot holes and irrelevant passages.

More thanks to Oklahoma State University Library for permission to use their digital maps, and to The University of Oklahoma Western History Collection.

Cast of Characters

The James-Younger Gang:
Jesse James
Frank James
Cole Younger
Frank Miller
Roy Baxter
Will Overton
George Overton
Rub Busse
Charlie Jones
"Uncle" George Payne
Zack Smith
Bud Dalton

U.S. Marshals:
Frank Dalton
Henry "Heck" Thomas
William Grimes
E.D. Nix
Chris Madsen
Bill Tilghman

Miners:
Frank Wildman
Elisha Williams
A.J. Meers
Edson Hewes

The Dalton Gang:
Bob Dalton
Emmett Dalton
Grattan "Grat" Dalton
Bill Dalton
George "Bitter Creek" Newcomb
Bill McElhanie
"Black-face" Charlie Bryant
Bill Power
Dick Broadwell
Charlie Pierce
Bill Doolin

Boomers:
David Payne
William Couch
Captain J.B. Cooper
Charles "C.W." Tipton
Thomas Antrim
Elmer Kanable

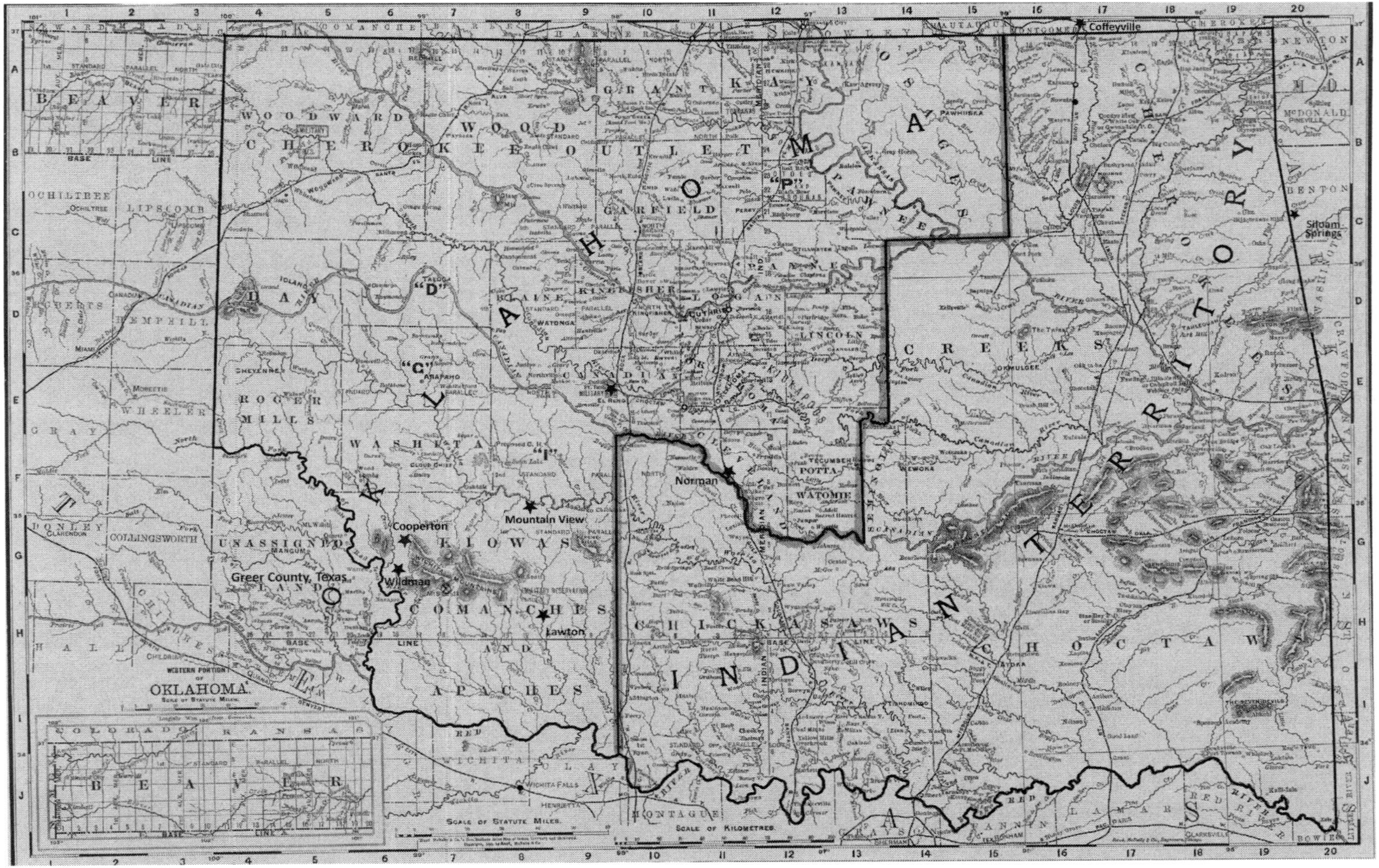
OKLAHOMA
INDIAN TERRITORY
WESTERN PORTION OF OKLAHOMA
Coffeyville
Siloam Springs
Norman
Mountain View
Cooperton
Wildman
Greer County, Texas
Lawton
BEAVER
WOODWARD
CHEROKEE OUTLET
GRANT
KAY
GARFIELD
OSAGE
PAWNEE
KINGFISHER
LOGAN
BLAINE
LINCOLN
CREEKS
CHEROKEE
DAY
ROGER MILLS
WASHITA
KIOWAS
COMANCHES AND APACHES
CHICKASAWS
CHOCTAW
UNASSIGNED LANDS
TECUMSEH
POTTA WATOMIE
OCHILTREE
LIPSCOMB
HEMPHILL
WHEELER
GRAY
DONLEY
COLLINGSWORTH
HALL
WICHITA
CLAY
MONTAGUE
COOKE
GRAYSON
FANNIN
LAMAR
RED RIVER
BOWIE
BENTON
WASHINGTON
CRAWFORD
McDONALD
NEWTON
COLORADO
KANSAS
SCALE OF STATUTE MILES
SCALE OF KILOMETRES

Preface: The First Dots - 1975

I first heard the story of Jesse James and his gang's lost Mexican gold when I was just a kid, maybe eight years old or so. Everyone around this part of Oklahoma knows it and I've even read about it in books: The James Gang was down in Mexico and hijacked a mule train loaded with gold bars. They hauled ass back to the Indian Territory, to what eventually became Kiowa County, Oklahoma. A Mexican posse was on their tail and a blizzard was threatening, so they hid the bars and took off. Hid them here, in these mountains.

My grandparents' farm was in Kiowa County, Oklahoma, in the Wichita Mountains, and if there was gold around there, somewhere, we needed to find it because we surely needed the money. My brother and I figured we knew those mountains as well as anyone, so if anyone could find that gold, by God, we could. We bolted out the door to begin the search.

It only took an hour for two pre-teenage boys to change their minds. There was a lot of territory to cover just on the farm, and the mountains went way past Grandpa's fence line. Way past. Still, we always kept an eye open; maybe something would turn up. No harm in looking and, like I mentioned, we really needed the money.

We weren't alone, either. Searching for Jesse's gold was a real thing because everyone was short on cash and, like I said, everyone knew the story. The 1970s were a tough time to be poor, and pretty much everyone in Kiowa County was poor. Desperation was just an accident, a mistake, or one stupid idea away, and the step after that was robbing a liquor store somewhere. The step after that was prison. Or the graveyard. So, people with a little hope would think about the clues and look for Jesse's gold.

Oh, there were clues, and all common knowledge. After he gave up his outlaw days, Frank James moved to Lawton to look for some of his old scores, but he never found the Mexican gold. Everyone thought that was odd; he was there when he helped bury it, so why couldn't he find it?

Just after World War II, a fellow named Joe Hunter got ahold of a map that was supposedly one of Jesse's. He followed Jesse's old clues and found some stuff that Frank had missed, but not the gold. Joe came way closer to finding it than anyone else, though. Jesse had led Joe to Tarbone Mountain where Joe dug up a brass bucket with some kind of message about gold bars with directions and names scratched on the side of it. Frank and Jesse James, right at the top. Case closed, just follow the rainbow.

That's kind of funny, really, because you never find the end of the thing. Just like leprechaun gold and the rainbow, Joe Hunter's bucket and all its clues never got him to Jesse's pot of gold.

I'd never seen a picture of the bucket, or really even cared what Jesse had scratched onto it. Twelve-year-old brains don't work like that. I'd heard of Joe Hunter, Jesse James, Mexican gold, and the Wichita Mountains. Four dots. More than enough and easy to connect.

As time passed, I slowly tuned into the fact that four dots were not enough; we were going to need a lot more clues to find all the dots. Whoever found them would be able to connect those dots and follow the trail to Jesse's Mexican gold. And those clues had to be in Kiowa County. Maybe even on our farm. Wishful thinking, right?

Looking back, I cringe a little. There was another clue, and a flipping big one. Turns out that key dot was right in front of me the whole time, just waiting for me to pay attention. That dot would lead to all the rest, but I'd never bothered to find out what was scratched onto Joe's bucket.

So, I went the long way. Probably better in the long run, but I think back to '75 and wonder what might have been different.

Part I

Bud's Ride

1875-1876

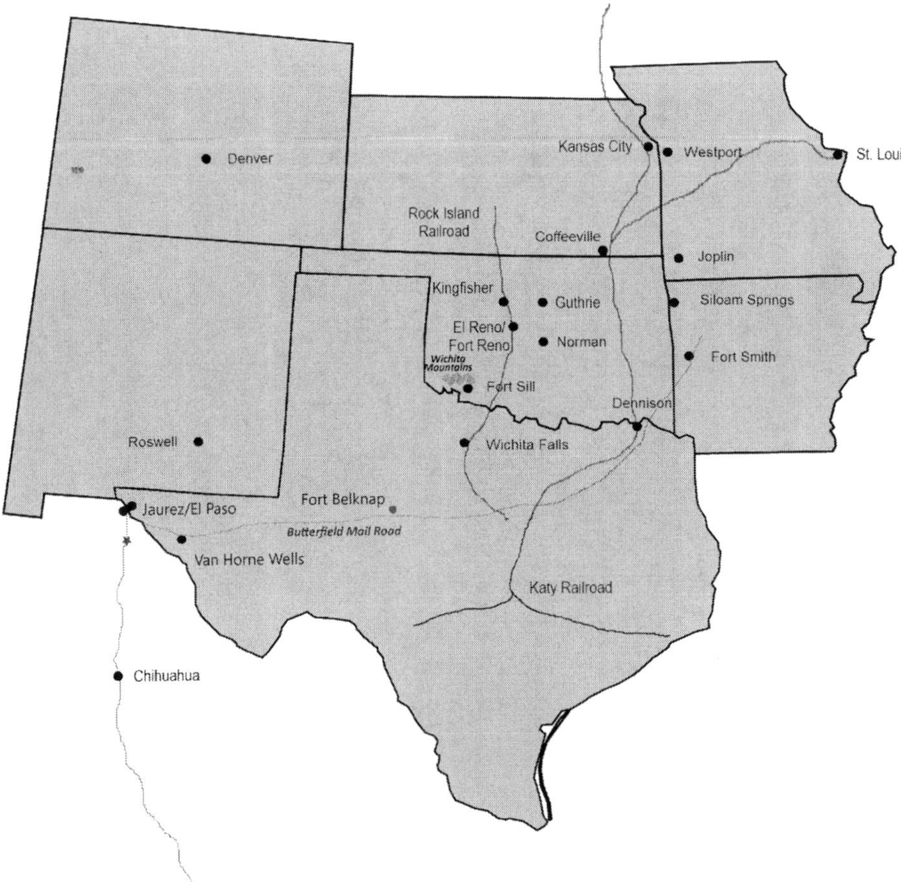
Denver
Kansas City
Westport
St. Louis
Rock Island
Railroad
Coffeeville
Joplin
Kingfisher
Guthrie
Siloam Springs
El Reno/
Fort Reno
Norman
Fort Smith
Wichita
Mountains
Fort Sill
Dennison
Roswell
Wichita Falls
Fort Belknap
Jaurez/El Paso
Butterfield Mail Road
Van Horne Wells
Katy Railroad
Chihuahua

Chapter 1

Bud's horse was tired. He felt the animal gather itself, then lurch up the creek bed in three rough bounds. He would have smoothly climbed the bank a week ago.

We can't take much more of this.

Bud slumped in the saddle. He was tired too.

The mountains were close, he'd caught a glimpse of their silhouette as his horse struggled the last few feet up the steep bank. The sight of the mountains was welcome, but it was his companions that drew his attention.

Bud Dalton was at the end of a ragged caravan of twelve men and sixteen mules. They had barely paused over the previous weeks, but now everyone who had just navigated the creek ahead of him had mysteriously halted. Whatever the reason, it was enough to convince Bud's horse to stop too.

The gang had been pushing the mules, horses, and each other to the very edge of their endurance, those mountains were the goal, and the goal was finally in sight. Yet they'd stopped.

After all this, we stop here? Now?

Bud scanned the scene, wondering what was happening. The leaders had separated themselves from the others and were animatedly discussing the situation between themselves. Bud wasn't sure what the latest situation was, but the weather was turning against them, the temperature dropping steadily and the wind blowing hard from the north. The clouds were dark and low, snow seemed to be a certainty, and they were losing the light.

Bud heard a horse behind him and turned to see George Overton's horse struggle over the creek's bank. George's horse noticed Bud's and stopped alongside, its head drooping.

"Jesus Christ, what's the hold up?" George muttered. "The damn mountains are right there, why aren't we moving?"

Bud tried to straighten up in his saddle, working his head around to stretch the kinks out of his neck and shoulders. He nodded at the three men huddled away from the others, all still gesturing back and forth, and said, "I don't know. Looks like they're tryin' to work somethin' out."

George squinted at the sun through the low, dark clouds, then at the silhouette of the mountains on the horizon. "Hard to tell how much light's left. I reckon they're wondering if we can make the hills."

"I guess. Not much choice, is there?"

George squinted back across the creek, then at the mountains again. "No. This is a bad deal. We need to be moving."

"You reckon they're back there?"

George nodded. "You bet your ass they are. What would you do in their place?"

"Run us to ground. Or die trying."

George mumbled, "That's what I'd do too." He edged his horse forward. "Let's go see what's what." They urged their unwilling mounts to join the men who were not part of the spirited discussion going on twenty yards away.

"Roy, why we stopped?" George asked.

A tall man with an enormous, filthy mustache leaned over and spat a long stream of tobacco juice. The goo streamed through the hairs of his mustache, adding to its filth before flying downwind. Roy sucked the tobacco juice off his mustache and replied, "Jesse wants to make the hills."

One of the arguing leaders saw Bud and George and motioned for them to come over. “Just the fellows I need. George, Bud, you see anyone behind us?”

What a stupid question...

Bud kept his thoughts to himself and simply replied, “Nothing. Yet.” George nodded his agreement.

Jesse James directed his attention back to his brother, Frank, and to Cole Younger. “Dammit, we can’t stop. We have to go right now. We shouldn’t have stopped at all.”

Cole disagreed, which seemed to be the source of the conflict. “It’s a long way, Jesse. We get caught out there and we’re dead. It would be hard to miss our trail and we’re all beat to shit. Christ, my sisters could kill us all and take everything.”

Jesse gestured around, clearly frustrated. “You want to make a stand here?”

Cole pointed to the prairie between them and the mountains. “Better than there.” And then at the sky. “And with that comin’, damn straight, right here.”

Well, that explains all the hand-waving.

Frank jumped in before Jesse could start shouting. “Hold on, wait up a second. How about this: Let’s set up an ambush. We hang around for an hour or two, and if anyone shows then we shoot ‘em up and make them back off. They won’t like it out there in the open any more than Cole does. It’ll take some time for them to figure out how to come at us, and while they do, we run off in a different direction. If they don’t show, then we’ll be right behind you. Either way, Jesse gets movin’ and Cole gets time and cover.”

Cole nodded. “Yeah, all right. That should buy us enough time to get these animals somewhere they don’t leave a trail a mile wide.” He looked back toward the mountains. “How long you think we’ll need?”

“Probably into the night,” Jesse barked. “We’ve been standing here way too long. We need to get movin’. Right now.”

“Whoever stays back is liable to freeze,” George pointed out.

Cole snorted. "Unless they get shot."

Jesse was through talking about it. "Best not get shot, then. Or freeze. Roy! Charlie! Rub! Come on over here. Bud, George, get 'em moving. I want you gone, right now!"

While Jesse explained to the rear guard, Cole started the caravan moving and motioned for Bud and George. "I need you boys to keep your wits about you. That bunch might be comin' up on you fast and you don't need to get surprised and start shootin' 'em. Y'all understand?"

"Hell, Cole," George complained, "you should probably tell them not to shoot us, we won't see 'em coming…"

"If anyone's shooting at you then the ambush didn't work and you can shoot back all you want. Now go, I'm right behind you."

Bud and George nudged their unwilling horses into a trot back to the mule train.

***

Frank motioned for Jesse and Cole to come over as he saddled his spare horse. "Where do you want to meet?"

"You stayin' back too?" Cole asked.

"Yeah, those three will need someone that knows the area if they're gonna find you. And you need to get rid of the mules first chance you get. If it were me, I'd find a good hiding place to wait out the weather and run them off. So, where can I find you?"

Jesse looked toward the mountains and thought for a moment, "Yeah. You remember where we found that Irishman a few years back? With the snakebite?"

Frank nodded. "Yeah, narrow canyon and dry bed, toward the west edge?"

"Right. That would do us."

Frank said, "I think I can find it. Should get us out of the wind, at least. Get a move on, we'll be along directly."

Frank walked his fresh horse over to the three ambushers as Cole and Jesse trotted off in pursuit of Bud and the mules. There were no goodbyes or see-you-soons.

Roy spit another stream of tobacco juice and sucked the mess off his mustache. "So, Frank?"

Frank examined the creek. The mules and horses had carved a gap through the grass and brush, churning up the ground on each side. In addition to being the obvious place the mules had crossed, their trail on the other side was plainly visible, leading from the messy gap in the creek and pointing toward the mountains.

Cole's right, anyone can follow that.

The creek's banks were thickly lined with trees, brush, and dead grass, plus a considerable number of large evergreen trees scattered on each side. Crossing elsewhere would require extra effort, and the gap left by the mule train was obviously the easiest and fastest way across. That's where the posse would cross, too, the perfect spot for an ambush.

"Here's what we're gonna do: Rub, Charlie, spread out on either side of the crossing here, say fifty feet each way. Stay on this side of the creek, find a good spot where you can see across but still be out of sight. Them boys will be comin' hard and are gonna run right through this crossing we made for them. When you hear me and Roy start in on 'em then you pour it on whoever's over there.

"Roy, we're gonna be in here close. When the first one starts up the bank on this side, I'm gonna shoot him and you take the next one. We'll work our way down the line, could be four or five in the creek. The rest should break and run back the way they came. Got it?"

Each nodded his understanding. The men spread out according to the plan. Frank watched as Roy found a large juniper and settled back into its dense foliage for a little protection from the wind. Looking left and right, he saw the others making similar arrangements. Frank followed suit.

The first hour passed and the weather continued to deteriorate. Sleet began to fall, lightly at first, each pellet making a "tick" as it landed on the dead leaves. The sleet gradually fell harder, with larger pellets, the sound of the individual "ticks" merging into a continuous, loud hiss. Snowflakes appeared and, somehow, the wind blew even harder. The sleet and snow appeared to be flying parallel to the ground and not falling from the sky at all.

The ground was gradually covered in a layer of sleet and snow, and the mules' trail was nearly obscured. The second hour was nearly gone and Frank's feet were bitterly cold. He was about to gather up the others to leave when he finally saw movement on the far side of the creek.

Four men approached, moving slowly. They rode in two pairs, the front focused on the ground and the rear spread out slightly left and right, straining to see through the sleet and snow blowing directly into their eyes. All four stopped about fifty yards from the creek, pondering the ground before them.

Frank studied the Mexicans, noting they were lightly provisioned and that they were in no hurry at all. He considered the possibilities as he watched them study the creek.

So much for plan A.

Satisfied with what they saw, the Mexicans carefully approached the creek. Frank slowly raised his rifle and carefully took aim. This was the beginning of plan B; he hoped the others were paying attention.

Jesse was right to be in a hurry. Just four of them, though, and the trail is mostly covered ... Finish off these gents and we might get away clean.

The posse abruptly halted. One of the lookouts apparently did not like what he saw and that made up Frank's mind. He set his sights on the front scout and squeezed the trigger, the bullet hitting him in the chest and tossing him from his horse. Roy shot the second an instant later, but that one managed to remain mounted. Two more shots rang out, but Rub and Charlie had each aimed at the same man and both missed. The remaining pursuers wheeled their horses, spurring them into a sprint. Frank carefully aimed at the center of one's back and gently squeezed the trigger. The rider seemed to twitch, but did not fall. The other shots missed their marks, too, and the riders sped away downwind, chased by the sleet and snow.

"Dammit! Fetch the horses, we gotta get out of here."

They mounted up and fled north to find Jesse and the others. Ordinarily he would believe it impossible for them to be tracked in those conditions, but after seeing the Mexicans in action it was clear that he was wrong. The wind and sleet would erase their tracks, but not soon enough. If the posse regrouped quickly the gang could still be caught.

Frank knew all too well what happened to people caught on the prairie during a blizzard. If he headed straight into the wind, he would be headed due north, and the mountains were due north. The ravine Jesse wanted would provide some cover from the weather; they just needed to get there.

The Overton kid might have been on to something. We're gonna freeze if we're not careful.

Frank buttoned up his coat, pulled its collar up around his neck, and leaned over his horse's neck to present as little as possible of himself to the wind. His men did the same, and spurred their horses into a trot, straight into the blizzard.

Chapter 2

Bud was as cold as he'd ever been in his life. The wind burned any exposed skin, and he was constantly adjusting his hat or coat to cover whatever was exposed, which just exposed something else. He could feel the wind blowing through the stitching in his gloves.

Sleet began to fall shortly after they left Frank. The tiny bits of ice stung Bud's face, and as they grew larger and more painful, he quit looking up altogether. With his hat pulled down as far as he could manage, Bud pressed the top of his head into the wind and tried to keep the last mule in his peripheral vision. Time crawled.

His thoughts drifted back, not even a year ago, back to when he thought he wanted to be an outlaw and to join Cole on one of his "rides." At seventeen, Bud believed he had seen it all and was ready to live life from the saddle.

He was born in 1858, the first child of a moderately prosperous couple in Westport, Missouri. He'd grown into a typical young man, a few inches short of six feet but slightly stockier than most of his friends. While that was an advantage wrestling his buddies or working with animals, he was a little top-heavy on a horse and had to work harder than most to keep his balance. The last few weeks had made that very plain and now he wasn't sure how much more life in the saddle he really wanted.

What he wanted, right then, was to be back in Westport in his parents' warm, dry house. He imagined himself with a haircut and not whatever was under his hat at the moment. His sandy-brown hair was now long, far too long, and was constantly falling into his eyes and leaking from under his hat.

Yes, a haircut, clean clothes, and a warm bath. Westport would be wonderful.

Westport was located on the Kansas border and situated at a convenient crossing on the Missouri river, just across from Kansas City. Settlers had been heading west to Oregon and California for years, and Westport was an excellent place to purchase supplies and outfit themselves for the long, dangerous trip across the plains and over the mountains beyond. St. Louis might have been the gateway to the west, but Westport was the last place to buy food.

Bud's father, Lewis, was originally from Kentucky and settled there to trade horses and run a small saloon. He was always looking for new livestock, and one day traveled a few miles south on a rumor that there might be a few mares for sale. He was denied the horses, but instead he met the fetching Adeline Lee Younger. They courted briefly, and Lewis convinced her to marry him later that year. Lewis and Adeline settled in Westport where Bud was born nine prompt months later.

Things were good for Lewis and Adeline, but Westport, and the rest of Missouri for that matter, could not claim the same.

Missouri had been at the center of the slavery problem from the very beginning, in 1820, when the Missouri Compromise was created. Anxious to maintain its delicate political balance, Congress agreed that states would be allowed to enter the union in pairs – one slave state against one free state. The Compromise also dictated that no state north of Missouri could allow slavery. Missouri came into the Union as a slave state, balanced by the free state Maine.

Thirty-four years later, in 1854, dreams of a transcontinental railroad spurred the government to sign the Kansas-Nebraska Act which would open those territories to settlement and eventual statehood. A provision of the act allowed for the inhabitants of the new states to decide for themselves if they would allow slavery, effectively ending the Missouri Compromise and opening the door for slavery in the north.

John Brown and New England abolitionists flooded into the Kansas Territory along with their southern planter counterparts. Anti-slavery immigrants from Massachusetts and Vermont founded Lawrence just eight weeks after the law was signed, then Topeka shortly after. The pro-slavery faction founded Atchison and Leavenworth at the same time. Each side was determined to control Kansas's future.

Thanks to thousands of Missouri residents who crossed the border to vote in the elections, stuff ballot boxes, and intimidate Kansas voters, the pro-slavery forces controlled the first election. They set up the state legislature and enacted laws targeting the anti-slavery faction, but the abolitionists simply ignored the elections and set up their own legislature in Lawrence, passing their own laws targeting the slavery proponents.

Violence was inevitable. Raiding parties routinely crossed the border to create as much destruction as possible and no one shied away from killing. Kansas was eventually admitted to the Union as a free state with no counter-balancing slave state, setting the stage for the Civil War. By the time the war officially started in 1861, Kansas and Missouri had been fighting for six years.

The Dalton family did everything they could for the Confederates. Lewis never participated in any raids, but he helped with provisions and services. The rebel guerrillas regarded him as a reliable man and each time Bud saw William Quantrill, the Confederate guerrilla leader, shake his father's hand and give Lewis his sincere thanks, Bud's admiration for his father grew. The guerrillas were real-life heroes to Bud.

The war finally ended and peace made for a different life on the border. The relative security encouraged domestic bliss in the Dalton home, Adeline delivering Bud's first brother, Frank, in 1864 and his second, Grattan, in 1865. Lewis and Adeline continued to produce children regularly until Bud's youngest brother, Emmett, was born in 1871. Bud would have eight brothers and sisters.

Adeline insisted that her children be educated. The violence on the border made it difficult to attend school, at least safely, so Bud was taught to read and write at home. Adeline was a strict and short-tempered teacher; he learned early that he should keep his thoughts to himself and to apply himself to whatever his mother commanded. By the time the war ended, Bud could read far better than most men in Westport.

Beyond reading and writing, Bud was a natural artist. He could draw and sketch effortlessly, which baffled his parents because there was not an artist on either side of the family. Bud had an eye for shape and shadow and would doodle on whatever scraps he could find. He somehow learned that charcoal was good for sketching, and would pull bits from the fireplace to play with. Neither of his parents could see any harm, aside from the black smudges he left everywhere, and encouraged him to continue.

The war killed Lewis's horse-trading business, but the saloon had managed to hang on and Adeline declared that it was time for Bud to start pulling his weight, so Lewis enlisted him to help. Bud cleaned and swept and carried boxes to wherever Lewis told him, and was soon a fixture in the background of the place. It was there that Bud began to meet people and hear about what was going on beyond the Westport city limits.

The end of the war had been a mere technicality for Cole Younger and the Missouri guerrillas. Cole and his brothers would occasionally slip in and recount their latest villainy to Lewis. Bud heard it all and young Bud Dalton began to imagine himself an outlaw.

Jesse and Frank James came to the saloon one afternoon accompanied by Bud's cousins Cole and Jim. They settled around a table near the rear, indistinguishable from any of Lewis's other customers. Cole eventually called Lewis over and asked if he and a few of the boys might drop by the house later that evening. Lewis said that was fine, the back door would be open and they could tie up their horses in back.

The gang arrived at Lewis and Adaline's house just before dark and eight-year-old Bud was shooed off to bed.

***

Lewis already knew the James and Younger brothers. Cole introduced Charlie Pitts and Archie Clement, then began by telling Lewis how much they appreciated his help and support during the war. The men all nodded their agreement and Cole went on to say he hoped Lewis could help them one more time.

"I'll do what I can," Lewis said. "What do you need?"

"A place to change horses," Cole replied.

"Change horses? What are you boys up to?"

"We're gonna take a bank. Jesse figures we can get back here all right, but the horses are gonna be spent and the whole world's probably gonna be looking for them. We want to leave some remounts here and scoot on south on the fresh horses."

"All right. What do you want me to do with your old ones?"

Jesse said, "I recall you traded horses before the war. I was thinking you might get back into the business, maybe you could start with those. Get what you can for them, and do it quick. Give yourself a nice commission and we'll settle up later."

Lewis smiled. "That's fine. Any idea when?"

"We have a few details to work out, but we'll let you know. A few days, I reckon." The men spoke for a few minutes longer and then quietly slipped out.

Four days later, Charlie Pitts rode into Lewis's yard leading seven horses. Lewis put them in the small barn behind the house and wished Charlie luck. Lewis then assigned Bud the task of feeding and watering the horses daily, which Bud dutifully performed.

Cole rode into their yard a week later. Lewis met him out in the yard with Bud following behind.

"Good morning, Lewis, Bud. Y'all look well."

"Morning, Cole," Lewis replied. "Early start?"

Cole remained in the saddle. "Yes, sir, early bird gets the worm. Looks like we're going to drop by day after tomorrow."

"That's fine. Everything should be ready for you."

Cole nodded his thanks and trotted out of the yard.

Lewis looked down at Bud. "All right, Bud. Let's take a look at those hooves and make sure the shoes are all secure. You remember how to do it?"

Bud nodded furiously and raced to the barn to prove it.

Two days later the gang thundered into the Daltons' barnyard and dismounted. They were covered in dust, their horses lathered. Each rider pulled his gear from his horse and carried it into the barn where, minutes later, he emerged on a new horse wearing a different shirt and hat. They spoke for a moment, and then sped off in different directions.

The next day the saloon was abuzz with the news that a gang of men had, in broad daylight, robbed the Clay County Savings Bank up in Liberty. They made off with $60 thousand and got away clean, but a young bystander had been killed.

The James-Younger gang had robbed their first bank.

A few weeks later Cole turned up in Lewis's saloon. He bought a beer and paid for it with a ten-dollar gold piece, a denomination usually reserved for major purchases like horses or land. Cole laughed that it was all he had, and asked Lewis to make sure Adeline knew he was all right. Lewis snatched the coin off the bar before anyone saw it; beers only cost pennies.

Just as they had terrorized the Kansas border towns before and during the war, the James and Younger boys now terrorized banks and trains. Jesse advertised that his gang's actions were directed at the North and he liked to write letters to newspapers justifying the robberies. Jesse never mentioned the innocent victims shot during the holdups, or any of the cold-blooded murders he was personally guilty of. That wasn't a problem, though.

John Newman Edwards was an editor for the *Kansas City Times.* Edwards had been an officer in the Confederate Army and was encouraging ex-confederates to get into politics. He believed the James Gang's exploits, Jesse's in particular, were a reasonable response to the North's aggression. In Edwards's mind, Jesse James was balancing the scales of justice.

Edwards portrayed Jesse as a big-hearted and fair man, evoking images of Robin Hood and a happy-go-lucky adventurer. He made no attempt at accuracy, or even to acknowledge that the gang's activities were criminal. Edwards's flowery prose completely concealed the violence, was easy to read, and his bias tapped directly into Missouri's sentiment. The public, Bud included, consumed it with gusto.

***

For the next ten years Bud followed Jesse's exploits through Edwards's editorials, stories, and dime novels that all cast Jesse as hero and savior. Bud learned how to do everything Jesse did in Edwards's stories, to handle horses and to ride, to operate a pistol, to hunt and live outdoors.

Bud was desperate to escape the Dalton house and whenever Cole dropped by Bud hounded him. He was seventeen and, in his mind, a full-grown man. He was not supposed to be helping teach his siblings to read, nor sweep the saloon, shovel the barn, or cater to his ever-pregnant mother. He was supposed to be riding with Jesse, fighting the evil North, and having great adventures across America.

Bud would beg Cole to be taken along, but Cole always laughed, "You don't want to go with us. It ain't your kind of life. Your mama would never forgive me."

In the summer of 1875 Cole made another appearance and Bud pounced. Cole, Jesse, and Frank arrived without warning and none of them was in a good mood. Frank informed Lewis that they had robbed a bank, but something had gone wrong during the get-away and Pinkerton agents were hot on their trail, perhaps less than an hour behind. The gang was making for the Indian Territory and there was no time to lose.

Bud confronted Cole as Lewis was getting three fresh horses ready.

"Take me with you. I can ride and my gear's packed. Please. I got to get out of here."

Cole didn't even look up, "No time for this, Bud."

Jesse overruled Cole, though. He examined Bud and said, "We're a man short and the kid says he's ready. Why not?"

Bud didn't give anyone time to think about it. His gear really was ready, and he'd saddled his horse before Cole could finish his own.

Lewis contemplated Bud for a moment, then said, "Wait here for one minute." He jogged to the house and returned with a small canvas bag and handed it to Bud. "That's an old Navy Colt and reloads. You might need them."

Bud climbed onto his horse. "Don't worry about me, Pa, I'll be fine."

Lewis looked up at Bud and smiled. "Come back when you can."

Jesse, Frank, and Cole rode away with the newest member of the James Gang.

Chapter 3

Bud risked a look forward, clamping his hat firmly to his head. The mountains loomed large, but they were still a mile and at least thirty frigid minutes away. He understood that getting there would eliminate any chance of being caught, but freezing to death in his saddle didn't really appeal to him, either. Those granite hills were not going to produce any heat; he'd have to trust that Jesse and Cole knew what they were doing. Maintaining the firm grip on his hat, he risked a look backwards. Nothing.

Bud leaned back into the wind and thought about his ride. The return trip was completely different from their departure the previous fall.

He'd left Westport with Jesse, Frank and Cole, Jesse keeping up a brisk pace. Eventually the sun began to sink toward the horizon and Frank suggested it was time to find a spot to camp for the night. Bud was relieved because his butt and legs were unexpectedly stiff from his first day in the saddle. Climbing off his horse was a bit painful.

They made camp on a small bluff overlooking a creek. Cole and Jesse surveyed the site and decided they had several good escape routes should they need to leave suddenly in the night. Jesse was convinced they'd lost anyone attempting to follow them, so a fire would be safe.

Frank climbed onto a boulder near the top of the bluff and looked back to the north.

"You make a pretty fine target standing up there like that. I sure hope no one's sneaking up on us," Cole teased.

Frank snorted. "There's no one back there. We lost the bastards before we picked up Bud."

This was the longest conversation that had occurred all day, so Bud listened closely as he pulled his gear from his horse.

Cole gestured to Bud and asked, "Speaking of Bud, Jesse, what's he doing here?"

Jesse lit some dry grass with a match and carefully placed some small dry twigs in the flames. "I was thinking," he replied, "that we need more family. Help move us along a little better. Maybe Tom wouldn't have been shot if he had some kin with him to urge him along."

Shot? Bud wondered.

Frank hopped down from the rock. "Tom got shot because his luck ran out."

Jesse shook his head as he built his fire. "No, he was lagging. He had no one to urge him along. Cole, if Bud were in Tom's place do you think he would he have been shot?"

Cole scoffed, "I reckon so. Could just as easily been you or Frank. Or me."

"Who got shot?" Bud asked.

"Tom was a friend of your cousin John. He got shot after we left town in a hurry."

"What town?"

Jesse blew on the fire, and replied, "Huntington, West Virginia."

Bud had heard of West Virginia and had a vague idea where it was. "So, how did he get shot?"

Cole told the story. "We robbed the Huntington bank a week or so ago. The bank is about in the center of town and we figured if we could make the hills we'd be gone before they could chase us. Once they lost sight of us then we'd have made it – they wouldn't be able to track faster than we could run.

"Jesse and another fellow, Jack Keene, went into the bank. Frank and Tom were keeping an eye on the street from a dry goods store, and I was the other way down the street between two buildings. If things got hot, Tom and Frank would cover Jesse and Jack and I would distract from behind.

"Well, they came out of the bank and jumped on their horses and took off down the street. Frank and Tom were right behind them. The locals came running out of the bank yelling 'They robbed the bank, stop them,' but there was no one to chase 'cuz the boys were already gone. I watched them for a minute then slipped away. Easiest one ever."

Bud finished with his horse and dropped his bedroll near Jesse's small fire. "If you got away, then who shot Tom?"

Frank said, "Well, it turns out we were wrong when we thought we could run faster than they could track."

Cole scoffed and said, "Ain't that the damn truth," but Jesse just snorted.

That seems to be a sore subject.

Cole continued, "Anyway, we had a good map, and we'd scouted the area beforehand. Once we got past the first ridge, there was a creek that would take us where we wanted to go. So, we snuck along that creek, but the going was slow, damn slow.

"What we didn't know was they'd sent out two posses from Huntington. The first was tracking us and wasn't very far behind. The second one never came close, but they'd stayed on the main roads along the rivers and were way ahead of us, and they'd spread the word to be on the lookout.

"The next day we finally got to the Big Sandy River, then crossed it into Kentucky and that's where things went wrong. We'd had enough of riding cross-country, so we took to a main road where we could make better time. That second posse had come down the Big Sandy the day before, and we hadn't gone even a mile when a farmer recognized the horses from the description and took a shot at us. He hit Tom in the back and he went straight down off his horse.

"We chased off the farmer, but there was nothing we could do for Tom, he was already dead, so we had to leave him and hightail it. The other damned posse was right behind us, though, and that damned farmer pointed them right at us. We were riding hard when Jack's luck ran out, his horse threw a shoe. He snuck into the woods to dodge the posse and try for a little town that might have a livery, then meet us in Missouri later. They caught him, though, and took him back to Huntington."

Bud was mesmerized. The tale of the Huntington robbery and getaway was exactly what he'd been reading in the dime novels, although the fact that Jesse came out missing two men didn't register with Bud.

"Shame too," Cole continued. "Tom was a good man and it was just his first ride."

* * *

They were off at dawn. Jesse was headed south to Joplin where they would wait for the rest of the gang.

Joplin had several things going for it. It was a mining town, rich with deposits of both lead and zinc, and several mines were producing marketable ore. A dozen new mines were planned and speculation for a dozen more was rampant. The booming town was dominated by miners spending their pay in raucous fashion, and as long as the profits were coming out of the mines, no one really cared if miners were spending their pay on saloons, gambling, or whores.

In addition to the chaos the miners brought, Joplin housed all the necessities that regular people required: shops, cafés, blacksmiths, hotels, and so forth. What Joplin did not have, however, was a sheriff; the nearest lawman was fifteen miles away in Carthage. All that made Joplin the ideal place for the James Gang to lay low and outfit themselves for whatever came next.

Even though the nearest lawman was miles away, Jesse, Frank, and Cole knew that anyone in Joplin would be happy to shoot them in the back and cheerfully collect the reward, should their identities be learned. Each had an alias and a background story in case anyone asked uncomfortable questions.

Bud, on the other hand, was free to be Bud Dalton from Westport, Missouri. Not needing an alias was a bit depressing because it highlighted the fact that he wasn't really part of the gang yet. He knew he'd get his chance, but he regarded the need for an alias as a symbol of success. He wanted it right then.

Another disappointment was Bud's inability to manage his father's Navy Colt. Bud had explored the contents of the canvas bag in camp the previous evening. He found a wooden box containing the revolver, a pouch full of gunpowder, a brass measuring tube, shot, percussion caps, and a small tub of grease.

The pistol was over a foot long with a smooth wood handle and an octagonal barrel. The cylinder was smooth except for several small notches that would be used to turn the cylinder as the hammer was pulled back. At the end of the cylinder were six small nipples to hold the percussion caps, each above a chamber that would contain the powder and shot. Mounted beneath the barrel was a lever that, when operated, pushed a small ramrod down into one of the cylinder's chambers.

Bud was pleased to hear both Frank and Cole comment that it was a fine weapon. He rested the gun on the ground with the barrel pointed upwards, then poured powder out of the flask into the measuring tube. The powder went into the chamber, then Bud forced a ball down on top of the powder; it was a tight fit and required some effort.

He repeated that process for each of the other five chambers and then, one by one, pulled the lever which forced the bullet all the way into the chamber and compressed the powder underneath. The final step was to smear some grease over the end of each chamber, covering the ball and protecting it and the powder from moisture, dirt, and other contaminants. Finally, he pressed a brass percussion cap onto each nipple.

After five minutes of loading, Bud was finally armed. The pistol felt beautiful in his hand, pride and satisfaction washed over him – he was finally an armed bandit. Well, at least armed, anyway.

He cocked the pistol, awkwardly, with his thumb, and then sighted down the barrel at a tree thirty feet away. He steadied carefully, keeping the front sight just where he wanted it, and pulled the trigger.

Snap.

From behind, Bud heard Cole say, "Probably a bad cap."

Bud re-cocked the pistol, re-aimed, and fired. This time the gun went off with a loud bang and produced a huge cloud of bluish smoke. Bud cocked and fired at the tree again with another bang and cloud of smoke.

Bud fired the remaining loads without another misfire, and then walked to the tree to examine the results. Pride and satisfaction faded as he discovered he'd missed the tree with all five shots.

He retrieved a new percussion cap from the reloading kit, but then discovered he could not get the bad cap off the nipple. The good caps had fallen off after the hammer rose for the next shot, but the hammer had firmly pounded the bad cap onto the nipple. Frustration building, he looked in the reload kit for something to pry off the cap.

He finally got the old cap off and replaced it with another from his kit. He cocked the pistol, aimed carefully at the center of the tree trunk, and gently squeezed the trigger.

Snap.

Composure slipped away to join pride and satisfaction.

"Goddamn it!"

Frank intervened before Bud could throw the pistol to the ground. "There's no telling how old those caps are. Probably a miracle the others worked at all. Pry that one off and I'll get you one out of my kit."

Bud replaced the second bad cap with one Frank supplied, aligned the cylinder, aimed and fired. The gun went off with a very satisfying explosion, but the tree stood unharmed.

"I do believe some target practice is in order," Cole dryly observed.

Bud spent the next day trying to shoot various things as the gang rode south, missing almost every time. The consensus was that Bud was pulling the gun slightly to the right as he squeezed the trigger, but he might eventually overcome the problem with practice.

By the time they approached Joplin, Bud had used most of his shot and all the caps Frank was willing to give him. Between the alias and the pistol, he did not feel much like an outlaw.

Before they rode into town, Cole and Jesse approached Bud.

"Bud, you're going to need some supplies. Do you have any money?"

"Sure, I have about three dollars."

Cole shook his head. "That ain't gonna do it. You need fresh reloads for your pistol, better clothes, and another horse. A rifle isn't a bad idea."

Bud looked surprised and asked, "What's wrong with my horse?"

"Nothin'. You need a second one. It's going to be a long trip. Take this." Cole held out a stack of bills and said, "This is three hundred dollars, it's from Tom's share of Huntington. He can't use it but its more than enough to outfit you."

Bud took the money and, for the first time, seriously considered what he'd brought along. His clothes were thin and shabby, and his boots cheap. The relatively short ride down to Joplin had been easy, but if the weather had been bad, he would have been in trouble. He examined the others' gear and noted that even though they were traveling light, they still seemed to have what they needed and what they had seemed to be of good quality.

Bud pocketed the cash and began making a list of the things he would need, starting with things he could see on Cole's horse: saddlebags, overcoat, blanket, and bedroll.

And a rifle... hope I can shoot it better than the damn pistol.

* * *

They left their horses in a livery stable and checked into a small hotel across the street. Bud dropped his few belongings next to the bed and sat down, thinking about the last two days. Didn't have any gear, couldn't shoot straight, and the damn pistol wasn't even his. Nor was the money he was about to spend on the gear he didn't have. Becoming an outlaw was much harder than he'd expected.

He went back to the livery where he was given directions to the tack shop, dry goods and hardware stores, and a gunsmith. Before long he had saddlebags, along with a box of pencils and two bound journals for sketching, a new pair of good boots, a hat, two shirts, pants, wool blanket, a pocket watch, a nine-inch knife and whetstone, cooking utensils, and a fancy oilskin overcoat the clerk called a duster.

The clerk explained that the duster was made from tightly woven cloth that had been soaked in linseed oil. The oil permeated the cloth and never needed to be resoaked. He claimed that it was identical to the Australian design, was absolutely waterproof, and was suitable in both warm and cold climates. It hung to his knees, but was cut so that it would not hinder mounting or dismounting a horse. All things considered, it seemed to be a quality item.

It was also twice as expensive as other coats in the store. Bud paid the asking price and vowed to himself that if the clerk was lying, he would return and get close enough to use his pistol effectively.

He dropped his new gear in his room and went back out, this time to the gunsmith where he purchased new powder, shot, caps, and a holster and belt for his Navy Colt. He also bought a used Winchester rifle and two boxes of cartridges. Unlike his older model cap-and-ball pistol, the rifle's ammunition was self-contained, the percussion cap part of the cartridge and not a separate component. The rifle could be fired and reloaded in seconds instead of minutes.

Bud also looked at a new revolver, the Colt Peacemaker. Unlike his Navy model, there was no powder or caps to fool with. Colt had wisely chambered the pistol to use the same ammunition as the immensely popular Winchester rifle Bud had just purchased. Like the rifle, it could be reloaded in seconds instead of minutes. Bud really liked it, but decided he needed to be able to use the pistol he had before investing any money in another one.

He returned to his room and packed his new items into his saddlebags where he was delighted to learn he had more than enough space. He rolled the duster around the new blanket and his old bedroll and tied it down with two leather strips.

Perfect.

The last thing on his list was a new horse, but that wasn't a purchase to be rushed into. He'd seen several at the livery, but that would wait until tomorrow.

He wandered down to the hotel's small porch to find Cole lounging in a chair, waiting for him.

"Jesse and Frank have other business tonight. What do you say to finding a saloon? I reckon there's one here somewhere, and besides, I need to talk with you for a bit."

Bud knew there was a large saloon just down the street because he'd seen it on his shopping trip. Bud suggested it and Cole agreed.

The saloon was everything a saloon in Joplin should be. Cole ordered two beers and sipped his while he barman explained the arrangement. The bottom floor was all restaurant and bar, the second floor was dedicated to gambling and, with a wink, the third floor to female companionship. Gambling never held any appeal for Bud, but women certainly did, and Bud's thoughts began to drift in that direction.

Bud asked, "How much on the third floor?"

"Two or three dollars. More depending on your tastes."

A whore in Westport cost less than a dollar. Perhaps these were like his new duster, worth a premium.

Of course, I haven't worn the duster yet, either.

Cole saw the direction Buds thoughts were headed and grinned. "A woman sounding good? Can't say I disagree," Cole said, looking around. "I reckon we'll be here two or three days, maybe not a bad idea."

"What do you need to talk about?" Bud asked, trying to change the subject as his face colored.

"Not here, we need a little privacy. We'll get a table." Looking around, he added, "This is something else, isn't it? Nothing like your dad's place."

"No, not at all."

Cole nodded to a table in the back that had just been vacated and threw some coins on the bar for the beers. They made their way back and sat down.

Cole leaned forward and said, "You need to know what you're getting into."

Bud replied, "I do."

Cole shook his head, "No, you don't. This ain't going to be a Sunday ride. Jesse wants to get down to Texas because it's way too hot up here. That shit in West Virginia was a lot worse than we talked about the other night. Should never have happened."

Cole paused as the waiter approached to take their order. Bud asked for fried chicken, Cole wanted a steak. The waiter wrote it down and hurried away.

"Things are changing, Bud. It's not like it was after the war. Used to be able to run your horses up and down the street, shoot your pistols and the locals would hide like rabbits. The tellers would hand over the keys and open the cash drawers.

"Now the tellers won't cooperate half the time and the locals don't always hide. When that damn farmer shot Tom, that wasn't bad luck. No sir, it was just a matter of time. Things are changing and Jesse's not.

"You probably think you're going to ride into some town, and then ride out rich. Bud, you need to be worried about riding out at all. And if we do get out, the Pinkertons probably won't be far behind us. They were on our ass halfway through Kentucky and all the way through Missouri. And something else you need to think about – they can shoot straight. You won't get three shots at a Pinkerton man; you'd best get the drop on him and down him with the first."

"Cole, I ain't going back to Westport. I'm going to Texas." Bud looked around the dining hall, and continued, "Besides, I owe you three hundred dollars."

"Well, sort of, but judging by those new boots and hat you've used some of it."

"Yeah. I'm gonna buy a horse tomorrow, saw a few that might be good."

Cole sighed and shook his head slowly. "Some of the boys will be in town in a day or so. Jesse left word with your Pa and he'll tell whoever Jesse told him to tell.

"Bud, don't misjudge Jesse, and don't trust him. When he was your age, he was riding with Bill Anderson and rough men twice his age called him 'sir.' He's crafty and he ain't afraid of anything I've ever seen. But when he gets an idea in his head there's no changing his mind. Me and him and Frank have been together a long, long time and we don't always agree, but I can tell you Jesse's not thinking right this time. This is going to be a long, hard ride. Likely to be bloody too."

"Cole, I'm ready. I'll follow orders and stay out of Jesse's way. I won't hold you back."

"No, you won't. Believe that. Now that you're one of us you can't ever tell anyone anything. You don't know who was with you, where you went, what it looked like, or how long you were gone. After we do a job, we scatter for a few weeks till Jesse or Frank sends word. You need to have someone trustworthy that can find you. Your Pa would be good.

"But we're already gone this time, and we probably won't split up if we're way down in Texas. That means you have to keep up. You don't want Jesse thinking you're holding him back, because he will leave your ass.

"The good news for you is you're unknown. If we do separate then all you have to do is get home without getting killed. But eventually, someday, someone will recognize you or your horse during a job. You need to have alibis ready and, for God's sake, learn to shoot straight. We can all handle a pistol with either hand."

Shoot with my left?

Bud gulped internally but maintained his expression. "Should I buy another pistol, then?"

"Maybe."

They paused again as their food arrived. Bud thought for a moment and asked, "What do you think about the Peacemaker?"

Cole swallowed some steak and said, "Frank and I were talking about that very thing not long ago. It sure does reload easy, but the cartridges are expensive. You can always get powder and shot, and get 'em cheap."

Bud nodded and said he'd probably need another three hundred dollars to learn to shoot it. Cole thought that was funny and they spent the rest of the meal discussing weaponry and ammunition.

They paid for dinner and Cole suggested they take a look upstairs.

The second floor was a gambler's paradise; every type of card game and betting contraption ever invented was available. The room was orderly and roomy, and surprisingly tidy considering the loud, rough clientele. A bar at one end served observers and players could get drinks from any number of young ladies walking among the tables.

"Hey, cowboys. Fancy a game?"

Cole and Bud turned to find short, round woman whose enormous breasts were being squeezed from the top of her low-cut dress. She was smiling, with her hands on her hips, looking up at them like a puppy waiting for someone to throw a stick.

Cole laughed, "Yes, I think I do," and offered her his arm. "How about a drink first?"

"Why, that would be nice," she replied, leading Cole toward the bar and leaving Bud standing in the stairway.

Bud watched the odd pair for a moment, then continued up the stairs to the third floor. He had no idea what to expect, and he was nervous.

The room was decorated like a fancy hotel's lobby. It was well lit with padded chairs on either side of the door, a counter on the opposite side of the room, and hallways leading off left and right. A man was sitting in one of the chairs, and behind the counter stood a woman who appeared to be in charge.

"Sonny, you know where you are?"

Bud fingered his hat and replied, "Yes, ma'am."

The woman smiled patiently and said, "I guess you had a run of luck downstairs, did you?"

That sounds reasonable.

"Yes, ma'am."

"Well, how much did you win?"

Bud knew enough to not tell her he had over two hundred dollars in his pocket. Following the barman's advice he replied, "Two dollars."

The woman raised her eyebrows and looked him up and down. "That so? I guess you are in the right place, then." Turning to the hallway on Bud's left she called, "Janie, come on out here."

Janie was a thin, blond woman who appeared to be in her mid-twenties and about five feet tall. She had a terrible complexion, her face scarred from acne she'd endured sometime in her past. Her hair was tied back, and Bud could see more scars on her neck.

She took Bud by the arm and walked him across the room to the opposite hallway and led him into one of the rooms. The room was very small, just large enough for a cheap bed, a small table, and for them to stand.

She closed the door, and Bud was aware of how close she was.

"How old are you?" she asked.

Bud continued to hold his hat. "Seventeen."

Janie began unlacing the front of her dress; Bud stood there with his hat.

"You're gonna need to get out of your clothes. Most start with their boots."

Bud blushed and began to undress.

Janie asked, "Is this your first time?" Bud nodded and she said, "Well, I bet you like it."

* * *

Bud spent the next morning looking at horses. He finally decided on the right one and negotiated an agreeable price, then paid the boy at the livery to saddle him up. Bud went to his room and picked up his saddlebags, Navy Colt, and reload kit.

He spent much of the afternoon out on the prairie shooting and reloading his pistol. He even tried a shot left-handed, only to learn that just cocking the gun with his left thumb was awkward. He was beginning to hit his targets occasionally, though.

He returned to town to find Frank and Jesse lounging in front of the hotel.

"Well, Bud, I hear you had an exciting night in town," Frank teased.

Bud's face flushed red. "I guess so."

Frank and Jesse had laughed long and hard when they learned Bud had paid two dollars for an hour with an ugly whore. Cole had spent three dollars, and he made sure Bud knew that price had included the whole night and several drinks. It seemed that everything in Joplin was negotiable, and Bud began to wonder what sort of deal he might be able to strike.

After the boys finished teasing him, Bud put five one-dollar coins in his pocket and made his way back to the saloon. He passed through the bar and went upstairs directly to the top floor and ambled into the parlor like he owned the place.

There was a different woman behind the counter this time, and she looked up at Bud with some surprise. "You're a bit young to be up here, aren't you?" she asked. "Maybe this is your first time?"

Bud swallowed and shook his head. "No, ma'am, it's not."

She smiled back and said, "All right. How much money do you have?"

Bud was ready this time. Being evasive, he told her, "I have a little, and I think I'd fancy a redheaded girl. Are there a few back there?"

"Why, sure, hon." She turned toward the hallway and called, "Wanda! Come on out here, please."

Wanda's hair was only vaguely red, and she had not even left the hallway before Bud stopped her. "Hold on there, Wanda."

He turned back to the woman at the counter and pulled a dollar coin from his pocket, setting it on the counter. "I want red hair. I think you can get a lot closer than Wanda here."

The woman dismissed Wanda with a wave and frowned at Bud. "Wanda's what you can afford, sonny. We have another redhead, but you'd need at least six dollars to get into the same room with her. One of the regular girls is what you need."

All right, now we're down to it.

"Six dollars! She's just a girl, right? Or do you have the Queen of England locked up back there?"

Being evasive herself, she told him, "Some time back a fellow won big downstairs and stayed with her for two days straight. He paid fifteen dollars. Fifteen! You got fifteen dollars?" she asked, shaking her head.

"Well, hold on there. If fifteen dollars is good for two days, then how come I need half of that just to look at her? Seems like just four dollars would be good till morning if fifteen is two days' worth. And I'm not even saying I'd pay four."

She laughed. "You don't have four dollars so it doesn't matter." She leaned over to call another woman. "Janie will take care of you just fine for your dollar."

Dammit, overpaid after all.

"Maybe I have a little more than a dollar, but it's not for Janie. I'll take your redhead for three dollars."

The woman laughed. "No, you won't. Even if you had it."

"Four dollars, then. Four is more than a quarter of what the gambler paid, and a night is a quarter of two days. That's a damn square deal."

She shrugged and turned away. "Sure, hon. You bring me four dollars in the next two minutes and I'll go get her."

Bud produced three more silver dollars and stacked them on the counter. He straightened the stack into a nice, orderly, column and pronounced, "All right then, we have a deal. Four dollars it is. I like red hair."

I guess...

The woman gaped at the coins and tried to backtrack. "No, no. You'll need a lot more than that."

"No ma'am! We have a deal. What are you, some kind of Goddamned carpetbagger? I offered four, you said yes, and here it is. Pony up your end."

The woman looked at the money, then squinted at Bud. "You're no cowboy."

"Not always, my family trades horses sometimes too."

"That figures. Just wait here and hang on to your money, horse trader. If Kimberly won't bother with you then that's the end of it, Wanda's as red as you're getting. Or we'll figure out another way to spend it." She walked down the opposite hallway and knocked softly on a door, then stuck her head inside and spoke briefly with whoever was in the room. A moment later she returned and told Bud, "She'll be out directly."

Bud was intrigued with how differently Kimberly was treated from Janie or Wanda and wondered what four dollars could be worth.

Kimberly came down the hall, and Bud instantly understood. Kimberly was striking. She was around five and one-half feet tall with slender hips and her hair was a beautiful red, silky and fine. She wore it gathered in the back, tied with a black ribbon. Bud felt his chest tighten and a lump in his throat. She looked like she could indeed be a queen.

"So," Kimberly purred in a deep southern accent, "this is the rich cowboy?"

Bud nodded vigorously.

The madam snorted. "She's talking to me, horse trader. Is he worth four dollars, Kim?"

Kimberly looked at Bud as if she were appraising livestock. "I'm not sure he is, but I am fascinated that he has it. And, it's been slow... so yes, I think four will do for a young cowboy's education.

"Eleanor," she addressed the madam directly, "Would you please have Carl bring up hot water for a bath?"

Bath?

Eleanor nodded and replied, "Yes," then turned to Bud. "I'll have the money, now, horse trader." He scooped the coins from the counter and dropped them into her hand. Kimberly was already gracefully walking down the hall to her room.

She paused and looked back at Bud. "This way, cowboy."

Kimberly's room was much different from Janie's. This room was much larger and decorated as if she lived there, which Bud later learned she did. Just inside the door was a small sitting area with two chairs and an attractive rug between them on the floor. The bed was against the far wall next to a wash basin and a small armoire. Next to the wash basin was a large brass bathtub. Kimberly opened the armoire and produced a robe which she handed to Bud.

"Put this on."

Things were moving a bit fast and Bud was having trouble keeping up. He had never seen a robe before and had certainly never worn one. It felt in his hands like a very shabby coat.

"This?"

"Yes, that. Take your clothes off and put them over there." Kimberly gestured to the corner next to the door.

Bud finally began to remove his clothes, putting them where she had pointed. As he put on the robe, there was a soft knock at the door. A voice from the hallway softly said, "It's Carl."

Kimberly opened the door and Carl, followed by five boys, brought in the water for the bath. They poured the water into the tub and left without a word. Kimberly motioned to Bud and said, "You need a bath before anything else. You're dirtier than old boots."

She handed him a scrub brush and commanded, "Get in. I'll tell you when you're done."

* * *

Kimberly sent him on his way after dawn the next morning. Bud walked back to the hotel, re-dressed in his dirty clothes, smelling of flowery soap and perfume, and his head swirling. He'd gotten a little sleep, but not much. He laid down on his bed, looking forward to some more, when there was a sharp rap on the door and Cole walked in.

"Get up. We're riding out this morning. It's time to go." Cole did not look happy.

This morning? What?

"I thought Jesse said we're leaving tomorrow. What's the rush?"

Cole kept his voice low. "Some of the boys came in with news. The Pinkertons found out we'd ridden south and are tryin' to trail us. If they came straight away they might get here around noon. We'll be gone before then. Gather your stuff, you're getting your ride."

Chapter 4

Bud packed his new gear and loaded his horses. He paid the livery and hotel, then jogged across the street to the general store, which was just opening.

"You're getting a good start today, sonny," the owner said. "Can I help you with something in particular?"

Bud tried to remember what he'd seen in Cole's pack. "I need coffee, some sugar, salt pork, beans and corn meal. Oh, and a coffee cup and frying pan. And I need some jerky or the like. Something that'll store in a saddlebag."

The owner nodded. "Sure thing. Got jerky right over here. A lot of fellows like corn dodgers too. They seem to keep good. You might get some next door."

Bud paid for his items and went to the café next door only to learn there were no corn dodgers to be had. He saw Jesse and Frank across the street with a group of men, and figured it was time to go; corn dodgers would have to wait.

As he approached the group, the men stopped talking and looked at him pointedly. "He's with us," Jesse told them.

One of them smirked openly. "He sure looks like a rough one."

Bud stopped and looked the man in the eye, hoping no one could smell Kimberly's flowery soap. "I reckon I'm rough enough for you, mister."

They maintained eye contact for a moment, and the man spat at Bud's feet. "Maybe you'll find out, runt. Meanwhile you'll be a good enough cook, I guess."

"Leave it, Zack. Bud, meet Zack Smith. Zack, Bud Dalton. Glad to see you boys hit it off so quick. Now, if I'm not bothering you, would it be all right if I finished talkin' to Charlie?"

Charlie said, "There's not much else to tell. We got your message right before the Pinkertons showed up. I don't think they know we recognized them so they'll probably sneak around for a while, but you can bet someone will let it slip and they'll be down this way."

"And it's just you eight?"

Charlie nodded. "Big Tom got the message the same time I did, but I don't know when he'll be in or who'll be with him."

"I guess it's just us, then. We're leaving now."

"We rode most of the night to get here. Can we rest at all?"

"One hour, no more."

Charlie and his group were clearly not impressed with their reprieve, but Charlie just nodded his acknowledgement. Bud was delighted at the prospect of an hour's sleep.

Jesse started back toward the hotel, Bud a few steps behind. Cole approached from the hotel and intercepted Jesse in the street. It was clear that Cole disagreed with whatever Jesse had planned and that Jesse was not remotely interested in Cole's opinion.

The conversation only lasted a moment, but Bud got the gist of it. The friction stemmed from a disagreement over strategy. Cole believed that the gang needed to separate and lay low through the winter, not to gather for a new raid immediately after the debacle in West Virginia, and with the law just hours behind them.

Jesse wanted to ride south through Texas and draw the pursuers out of Missouri and away from the gang's homes and families. The best way to accomplish that would be with high-profile robberies in Texas. Frank had been ambivalent, and so Jesse's decision stood.

One hour later, Jesse trotted out of town, followed by his gang, including a disgruntled Cole. Jesse led them cross-country, heading directly for the Indian Territory.

A few days after they left Joplin they crossed a small muddy river which Frank identified as the Washita. The gang splashed across and in a short time a low range of hills and mountains could be seen on the southern horizon; Frank aimed directly at them.

The individual hills merged into a series of steep cliffs and wooded mountains. The farther south they rode, the more impressed Bud became. Jesse paused, and Bud groped for his sketchbook. An enormous monolith, easily a mile long, erupted vertically out of the ground and rose, by Bud's estimate, hundreds of feet into the sky. Bud sketched furiously, but Jesse got them moving again before Bud could finish. Grumbling, he put his book away.

They continued southward until Jesse found a place to camp. He'd chosen the large creek that ran around the monolith's southern extent and was rewarded with a large clearing bordered with the creek one side and a sheer cliff on the other. Farther upstream was another mountain, the creek running past it through an orgy of rugged confusion.

"Perfect," Frank proclaimed. He swung off his horse and surveyed their new camp. They had a clear view of the valley to the east; anyone approaching from that direction would be seen. Frank climbed up the steep hill at the clearing's edge and looked down the other side. No one would be taking any stolen horses that way.

"What is this place?" Bud asked Cole.

"Still the Indian Territory," Cole replied. "But not by much. A day's ride south and you cross the Red River into Texas. We're on the western edge of these mountains; they go on for about fifty miles and are all pretty much like you see here. It's a good place to hide and lay low if you need to."

"We just spending the night here?" Bud asked.

Cole shook his head. "No, Jesse wants to linger before getting into Texas."

Frank approached. "Cole, I'd like to get a good look around before it gets too dark. We need to scout out the creek a ways up the hill here. Put Uncle George and Zack on that." Cole nodded and Frank continued, pointing, "We're gonna pen the horses over there by the hill. And we need firewood; that's a good job for you two. Get your horses settled with the others and bring up a bunch from the creek over yonder."

Frank handed out assignments and the men negotiated their turns guarding the horses that evening. It would be hard to steal their horses outright, but a handful of braves could potentially sneak up and wreak havoc with the camp. Jesse decided to post two lookouts in order to counter that sort of mischief.

In his time on the trail, Bud had learned that he preferred the last watch, from about four o'clock until dawn. He managed to get it that evening and he settled down with George and a few of the guys he'd become friendly with.

The gang was composed of twelve men. Jesse, Frank, and Cole were the leaders, supported by old outlaw buddies Frank Miller, "Uncle" George Payne, and Rub Busse. The six of them had ridden together for many years and were so comfortable with one another that their tone and mannerisms were very different when they spoke to the younger men than with each other.

Charlie Jones, Roy Baxter, and Will Overton had ridden with Jesse several times in the past, so they enjoyed a level of deference from the older men that the three new guys did not. Zack Smith, Will's younger brother George, and Bud were simply told what to do. No one was interested in their opinions.

While Bud and George were becoming friends, Bud and Zack were not. They had grown increasingly hostile toward one another, occasionally to the point where Jesse or Cole would tell them to shut up. Bud was convinced he could shoot Zack between the eyes and not even feel the slightest twinge of regret, but, potentially, considerable joy.

Bud had cemented Zack's hatred forever when, under Cole's unending cajoling, Bud told the story of how he came to spend six dollars on two prostitutes in Joplin and by the end of the tale he'd convinced half the gang it was a good deal. Bud described, to the gang's delight, Kimberly's skills and maintained that alone was worth twice what he paid. Zack snorted mockingly and Bud, without really thinking, barked, "Shit, you never had any of that. Not from a woman, anyway."

The whole gang, even Jesse, howled with laughter. He could feel the hatred radiating from Zack, but everyone laughing at Zack was simply wonderful.

Hell, THAT was worth it...

Bud lay on his blanket and looked up at the stars, taking stock of his new world. Life in the gang was everything he'd imagined, and he was content. Jesse wasn't quite who he'd expected, Cole's warning seemed to be real. Wild Indians lurking about were an unexpected bonus, these mountains were certainly different, the weather remained mild, and he'd secured the final watch. If Zack could just die in his sleep, then all would be right with the world. Bud closed his eyes and drifted off.

Zack did not die in his sleep. He'd wrangled the watch just before Bud's and he took his duty, and the opportunity to wake his replacement, seriously. When it was time for Bud's watch, Zack unceremoniously tore away Bud's blanket and kicked him hard in the ribs.

"Time to get up, daisy," Zack hissed. Bud gasped and tried to stay quiet. He glared at Zack and cursed him, then stumbled to his post to keep watch till dawn.

He spent the remainder of the night fantasizing about all the painful accidents that could befall Zack on the trail. Arrows, snakebites, and broken bones all played their parts until the sun lit the ridges and Bud was able to get a clear look around.

The horses were all present and unmolested, the area appeared undisturbed with no broken branches or obvious tracks. Aside from his being rudely kicked awake, the night had been uneventful.

The last watch had the unofficial duty of refreshing the fire and starting some coffee. The camp was already stirring, so Bud hurried to gather the remaining coals into a small mound and added fresh sticks to rekindle the fire. It was burning well by the time the coffee pot was wedged into the side to boil – it was a good idea to stay a step ahead of Jesse, and that wasn't always easy.

Jesse was usually ahead of the gang in the mornings, rising and eating quickly. He preferred the men to keep up with him, but since they were in camp he was a little more tolerant. He let the men linger around their coffee that morning, then selected a few men to form a hunting party.

Bud remained in camp, bored. His equipment was still brand new and needed no repair. The horses were fine. His gun was loaded. He was contemplating the wisdom of practicing with his pistol when he faintly heard two gunshots, followed by a third.

Frank was sitting nearby. Bud asked him, "Won't that attract attention? You not worried about Indians?"

"Well, yeah, actually. But the truth is they probably know we're here already. Besides, they should be out hunting, too, and not worrying about us. Winter's going to be here any minute, and we're gonna be long gone pretty quick. Getting into a big fight with us is a bad idea. If it were June, we'd be sitting ducks, but they have their own problems. I reckon we'll be OK."

The hunting party returned with a white-tailed deer which was quickly butchered and put over the fire to cook. There was enough meat to keep the gang fed for two days, but Jesse told the men to eat up.

"We're breaking camp tomorrow morning and riding south. Time to get this show on the road."

* * *

True to his word, Jesse had the gang up and moving after dawn. Everyone quickly cooked a little leftover venison and brewed some coffee, then packed their gear. Two stragglers were still eating when Jesse ran out of patience, pouring their coffee into the fire then kicking dirt over the coals. He tossed their now-empty pot toward the horses.

"Breakfast's over! Let's get a move on."

The mountains were a constant fixture on their left as they rode south, the same rocky chaos broken by occasional gaps and creeks. Bud had gotten used to them when, abruptly, they vanished and before the gang lay a vast grassland. The mountain range angled sharply back to the east, continuing to the horizon, but there was nothing but grass between them and Texas.

After a few hours in the grass, Bud appreciated the mountains—at least they had been interesting. The grassland seemed to go on forever, a constant, boring, seemingly endless expanse broken only by the occasional creek or gully.

Finally, they came upon the bluffs overlooking the Red River, the border between Texas and the Indian Territory. The river's bed was a mile wide and filled, bank to bank, with rust-colored dirt and sand. The river itself was barely a hundred yards wide and a few feet deep, the stream meandering back and forth between the banks and exactly the same color as the dirt that obviously gave the river its name.

Frank nodded at the far bank. "There's Texas."

They forded the river, continuing southwest along a poor but visible trail. They encountered no one for two days before they met four men riding the opposite direction. The two groups stopped to talk and exchange news when, with a start, Bud realized the men were all wearing badges. They were Texas Rangers.

Cole and Frank exchanged pleasantries with the Rangers, claiming they were riding south to find work on a ranch and to hopefully sign on for a cattle drive. A Ranger replied that Charlie Goodnight was said to be gathering cattle for a drive from New Mexico.

They thanked the Rangers and the two groups went their ways.

"You know," Jesse mentioned to Frank, "we've never been to New Mexico before."

"Are there even banks there?"

"Must be. If not a bank, then a train. Hell, that might even be better, something new for the Pinkertons to chase. Yeah, New Mexico."

The gang veered westward, leaving the rolling hills and streams of North Texas for the arid desert of West Texas. They plodded along until they encountered the first significant geographical feature since they'd camped in the Indian Territory. More than just a feature, it was a barrier.

They were still five miles away, but they could clearly see a steep cliff, hundreds of feet high, stretching across the horizon from north to south. Jesse stopped to consult his map while the rest gawked.

"What the hell is that? Where are we?" Roy asked.

Jesse replied, "I think that's the Llano Estacado."

"Well, what's that?"

"It's a line on this damn map," Jesse barked, clearly irritated. "How do I know what it is?"

"Can we go around," Frank asked, "or do we need to climb it?"

Jesse handed the map to Frank and replied, "Pretty sure we have to climb it. That says it goes halfway to Mexico." Frank squinted at the map while Bud sketched the escarpment standing between them and whatever was in New Mexico.

The cliff was everything it appeared to be from a distance, but they finally found a cut where they could make their way up. Once at the top, they discovered a vast and perfectly flat plain, completely different from the rolling hills they'd enjoyed for the past ten days. The cliff was a sharp division between two different places.

Once on the Llano, they made excellent time because there were almost no obstructions at all: no mountains, hills, rivers, creeks, and hardly any trees. After five days of that, George's brother, Will, declared, "We need to get out of here, this ain't natural."

Will's wish was granted a few days later when they stumbled on the Pecos River and discovered they were in New Mexico. The map suggested southward and they plodded into the village of Roswell a few days after Christmas. They'd been in the saddle for four weeks and everyone, even Jesse, wanted to sit on something that didn't move.

Roswell was a small town, but it did have a hotel, a post office, and a saloon. A trading post had been established, then the stage stop, then the saloon and a hotel for stage passengers and travelers. Being a popular camping spot at an easy crossing on the Pecos, there were prospects for much more. Roswell looked like paradise.

Cole learned that a reply to a letter sent to St. Louis could be reasonably expected in a few weeks, depending on the weather, hostiles, and luck. Jesse wanted to know what was going on back in Missouri and decided they would stay until he had some idea what was going on at home.

Bud wrote a note to his parents letting them know he was fine and he expected to be home next summer, perhaps later. A few others did the same, but Jesse wrote over a dozen letters, some in code, asking for information and sending instructions to his agents in Missouri and elsewhere. All the letters went out the next day, and the gang settled down to lounge in Roswell.

It was three weeks before their mail began to arrive, during which time the local Apaches engaged in one of their favorite pastimes - stealing livestock. There was some sort of theft nearly every day, usually a few head of cattle stolen from local farms. It was amusing until the Indians got away with a good number of horses from the livery pen at the edge of town. Two gang members suffered losses—Zack and George lost a horse each.

Bud was delighted that Zack had been victimized and fantasized about the Indians returning for his remount, trapping him, hopefully forever, in Roswell. Cole made sure that didn't happen by moving the horses from the pen to a barn in town.

Jesse's mail informed him the Pinkertons had indeed followed them but had lost the trail in Joplin. The Pinkertons suspected they were hiding near, or in, the Indian Territory and they had spies searching along the border. It appeared that Jesse's plan had worked without killing anyone or robbing anything.

Everyone was relieved that the Pinkertons were not stalking their families, and discussion arose about the gang's next moves. Roswell's comforts had become stale and Jesse had changed his mind about New Mexico. He discovered the Territory was not a good place for a robbery at all, partly because Frank had been correct, there was hardly anything worth robbing. Furthermore, tensions were growing between the cattlemen and merchants in nearby Lincoln. The locals were on edge and there seemed to be a lot of lawmen about, so Jesse was done with the place. It was time for them to move on.

* * *

The gang left Roswell in February of 1876, headed for Mexico. The trail led them into the mountains and over a pass that would send them to Tularosa, where they would cross the desert until they found the Rio Grande and, hopefully, Las Cruces. From there they would simply follow the river south until they got to El Paso.

Bud sketched furiously every time he got a chance—the trees, mountains, streams, and animals were revelations. Even the desert was interesting, although a bit stressful. There was even less water than on the Llano Estacado and by the time they'd made it to the river everyone was acutely aware of how little water they had.

"Let's find a different way home," Cole complained.

Juarez and El Paso occupied opposite sides of the Rio Grande, the towns built on either bank with the riverbed dedicated to agriculture. The two towns had been a single city until Texas won its independence from Mexico and the Rio Grande was deemed the new border. Those battles had occurred five hundred miles away, though, and the new border meant nothing to the locals. Armies and governments respected it, sort of, but everyone else crossed back and forth at their leisure.

"Well," Cole told Jesse, "there's Mexico. What now?"

"It's still winter at home, and we're laying pretty low down here. Let's head down to Chihuahua, spend a week or two, then amble back up through San Antonio to Dallas, then to Dennison and take the supply road home. I guess we could get back in late June or July. What do y'all think?"

The gang was enthusiastic.

"You know," Roy drawled, "I've heard about these Mexican senoritas. I think I like this plan."

"Yeah," Charlie laughed, "maybe Zack can try a girl this time!"

Bud thought that was really funny.

* * *

The gang drifted southward from Jaurez, following the main road which, according to Jesse's map, would lead them all the way to Chihuahua. They would make it in a few days if there was no trouble.

Completely unknown to Jesse, Cole, or most Americans for that matter, Mexico was in turmoil and had been for decades. Back in 1861, the Mexican president, Benito Jaurez, who came to power after a long civil war, suspended Mexico's debt payments to England, Spain, and France. Those payments were for the loans that had financed the civil war which brought him to power to begin with.

The French had been eyeing Central America for years, and decided they would use the debt payments as an excuse to invade Mexico and establish a European-style monarchy there. They successfully invaded and won enough territory to install their puppet emperor, Maximillion, who was the younger brother of the Austrian Emperor.

The Mexicans, naturally, fought back and the war continued until 1866 when the U.S. threatened France with direct military assistance to the Mexicans. France could fight Mexico, but a war with the U.S. was out of the question. The French abandoned Maximillion, who was quickly captured and executed, much to the horror of European liberals.

Jaurez returned to power, the Republic was restored, and everything in Mexico was wonderful again, until the 1871 elections rolled around. Jaurez announced that he would run again, despite the fact he was not allowed to.

When Jaurez won, one of his opponents, long-time politician and French war hero, Porfirio Diaz, refused to acknowledge the victory and mounted a rebellion against Jaurez. Diaz's rebellion dragged on until Jaurez suddenly died and an interim president was appointed.

New elections were scheduled, and Diaz called off the fight while he ran, again, only to lose, again.

Enraged, he retreated to his country estate and began planning yet another revolt that would, hopefully, catapult him to the presidency in the next election, which was scheduled for that very year, 1876. Diaz had been moving pieces around the chessboard for two years, paying off generals and getting them assigned to key stations. He was almost ready.

As the James Gang wandered southward to Chihuahua, Diaz's large payment to General Manuel Gonzalez was headed northward up the same road. Sixteen mules loaded with gold bullion would provide General Gonzalez both the funds to pay an entire regiment and purchase the influence of key politicians.

Diaz's gold was guarded by a squad of Mexican soldiers dressed in civilian clothes. The detachment's leader, Captain Enrique Dominguez, was extremely arrogant and held a much higher opinion of himself than he deserved. His father haunted the periphery of Diaz's world so it seemed natural, to Dominguez, that he would be selected to lead any group of men for an important mission. Gonzalez and Diaz would surely reward him richly for successfully delivering his cargo. He had no idea what his cargo was, but nothing would be allowed to interfere with his mission or his reward.

The road to Chihuahua was mostly traveled by peasants on foot or small groups with a donkey or mule, and all who encountered Dominguez moved to the side of the road to let the obviously official mule train and its clearly armed guards pass. The James-Younger Gang, however, were not Mexican peasants.

Jesse didn't register the approaching mule train as anything other than what it was: another group of men headed in the opposite direction. He edged his horse over so everyone had room to pass, but he did not stop. He evaluated the approaching group clinically, noting the number of riders and that they were armed, concluding they were professionals, if not military. Bud could not see it, but Cole and Frank were doing the same.

Dominguez saw, though, and he was personally offended that the gringos did not move off the road for his team, and he was immediately angry and suspicious. *Those are a lot of gringos*, he thought, *perhaps they are bandits.* Dominguez edged his horse into the center of the road, and stopped. The gringos would yield the way or they would be taught respect.

When Jesse saw the leader stop in the middle of the road, he figured the man wanted to talk, so he walked his horse up to Dominguez's, Frank following a few paces behind.

Jesse removed his hat and wiped his brow with his sleeve. "Hola," he said. "Any of y'all speak English?"

Dominguez was incensed that the gringo would assume they were equals, that it was acceptable to speak first, informally at that, and to make eye contact.

He barked, in heavily accented English, "Get off the road!"

Jesse heard Frank reply, "The hell you say!" He put his hat back on and sat up in his saddle, staring hard at the Mexican, his body language telling Dominguez that he could go straight to hell.

Dominguez read Jesse's reply perfectly and barked something in Spanish. The Mexicans suddenly had rifles out and pointed at the gang.

"I said," he growled in his rough English, "move now or we kill you all."

"Whoa," Frank exclaimed, "we don't want trouble. Come on, Jesse, let's let these fellows pass."

Jesse raised his hand in a conciliatory way and nudged his horse off the road. By then the rest of the gang was muttering, but they followed Frank and Jesse's lead. Jesse gestured dramatically, indicating the road was Dominguez's to ride.

Dominguez felt a flush of satisfaction as he locked eyes with Jesse and motioned for his team to put their weapons away and get moving again. He held eye contact with Jesse as his mules passed. He nudged his horse forward while turning his head, maintaining eye contact with Jesse, explaining to the gringo who was boss. When he finally passed Jesse, Dominguez gave him a slight grin and a scoffing snort, then looked forward again, insulting the gringo further by turning his back to him.

The moment the Mexican broke eye contact, Jesse drew his pistol, turned in his saddle, and shot Dominguez above his left ear. Without hesitating he cocked the pistol and took aim at the soldier beyond the now-dead leader, only about twenty feet away. Jesse shot him in the chest, already looking for his next target.

By then Cole and Frank were shooting, too, as well as the older gang members. One of the Mexicans got an errant shot off with his rifle before he was shot in return, but that was the only resistance the Mexicans could muster. The two guards at the rear of the mule train never even tried to re-draw their guns, they wheeled their horses and sprinted back the way they came.

Bud had been taken completely by surprise and the shooting was over before he even thought to reach for his pistol. Rub chuckled at him.

"You get to know Jesse a little and you know there's no way he's gonna let anyone talk to him like that. That Mexican prick was dead the second he opened his mouth."

Cole dismounted and fumbled with the lead mule's pack. It was just a large pair of saddlebags, but the buckles holding the flaps shut had been crimped closed. "What the hell..."

"Hey, Frank," Cole called, "have a look at this."

Frank fingered the mangled buckles. "Looks like someone wanted to make sure no one could look in here and get away with it." He pulled out his knife and said, "Let's see what the big secret is," as he unceremoniously sliced the leather thongs above each buckle.

He opened the pack and looked inside. "Good Lord."

Cole looked and was also stunned.

Jesse had been watching and asked, "What do you have there?"

Frank hoisted, with some effort, a gold bar from the mule's pack.

It was Jesse's turn to be stunned, but only for a moment.

"Everyone!" he yelled, "On your horses! Let's go. Frank, Cole, let's get these animals moving smartly, we're going back the way we came!"

They had only gone a few hundred yards when Jesse suddenly stopped. "Wait!" He was staring into the desert, facing east, at a barely discernable track toward some distant hills.

"That way!" he commanded.

"Jesus, Jesse," Cole objected, "that's not even a cow trail."

"No, but it's what we have and we have to get off this road. There's going to be a posse coming along real soon, and they're gonna catch us. Unless we leave the mules here and hightail it."

Cole looked at the mules and asked, "How much do you think there is?"

Jesse shook his head. "I can't cipher that. What's it gonna be, Cole? You get to make this call."

Cole looked at the track, then the mules, then back down the road. "God dammit. Let's go."

They turned onto Jesse's nearly invisible path and urged the mules into a trot, directly into the desert.

"I think," Jesse told Cole, "if we can get a mile or two off the road and behind some cover, there's a good chance they won't see us out here. If they miss the trail, and I hope they do, we might get away clean."

Frank caught up and voiced what was on everyone's mind. "Jesse, where are we going? We're gonna die out here."

Jesse shook his head and pulled his map out of his breast pocket. "No we're not. I figure the Rio Grande is about fifty miles due east, maybe a bit less if we edge to the north when we can. It'll be a tough ride, but we should make it – it's only fifty miles. If we can get a good lead, they won't be able to catch us."

Bud heard that and felt his first twinge of doubt.

That's what he said in West Virginia.

Chapter 5

Jesse pushed everyone hard, refusing to stop for any rest at all, even after the sun set. The clear night and bright moon were enough to follow the track eastward, so they pressed onward through the dark. Unfortunately for Jesse, the river was not fifty miles away, but rather sixty-five, and the track he was following would peter out at the edge of a dry lake bed.

The gang reached the dry lake after midnight. They had been riding for ten hours, their path, already faint, had vanished, the moon was setting. The river was somewhere farther into the baking darkness and now there were mountains blocking the way.

Men, horses, and mules all needed rest eventually; even Jesse had to concede it was time to stop. The men pulled their packs off their horses and tied the animals to the scrub brush that was so common in the desert, then collapsed onto the ground. Sleep came instantly.

Jesse rousted men at dawn, no one feeling rested. He was already yelling there was no time for coffee, everyone needed to get moving. Bud rolled over and sat up painfully, trying to find any motivation at all. He took a swig of water from his canteen to rinse his mouth and was about to spit it out when it occurred to him that he was in the middle of a desert. He had another full canteen, but that was all. He swallowed instead.

Daylight allowed Jesse and Frank to get a good look at their surroundings. The mountains would obviously need to be navigated, and the southern peaks were much smaller and the slopes less steep. That seemed to be the best way.

They got the animals moving, Jesse leading the way. Skirting the northern peak, he was rewarded with a low pass featuring a wide, sandy draw pouring out of it. Jesse led them up and when they reached the top they could see that the terrain beyond was no better than what they'd just traversed. Jesse looked back the other way, at the desert basin they'd crossed the night before. He squinted, then asked Frank for his field glasses.

Frank handed over the binoculars and Jesse peered through them, then shook his head. "Dammit."

Frank looked, then handed the glasses to Cole. Cole stared through them for a moment, and handed the glasses back to Frank. "I guess they didn't miss the trail."

"No, and judging from their dust they're coming hard. Probably rode through the night… Let's go!"

The way down the opposite side was obvious. Another draw, much larger than the one they'd followed uphill, led down into a valley and cut through a substantial series of ridges and valleys that, if the draw wasn't there, would have completely blocked them from the Rio Grande. They only had one choice: follow the draw, which quickly morphed into a full-fledged dry riverbed.

They followed the bed for hours, winding, twisting, and turning around peaks, always downhill. By the time they'd traced all bends and twists, they had added another twenty dry miles onto Jesse's original guess. Finally, thankfully, the twisting ended and they were dumped directly into the Rio Grande, which, from Bud's standpoint, could have been heaven.

The narrow floodplain was lined with trees and grasses, some areas were even marshy, ducks floating on the shallow ponds. Evidence of deer was present, as were gnawed stumps proving beaver were nearby.

The most important thing, of course, was the water. Humans, horses, and mules all waded into the river and drank. Jesse, Frank, and Cole discussed the next step.

"The way I see it," Frank started, "is we have three choices: Cross into Texas right now, go upriver, or go downriver. Nothin's jumping out at me."

Jesse and Cole both nodded. "That about sums it up. But," Cole said, pointing to the U.S. side of the river, "I don't really like pushing straight into Texas after the way we pushed out of Mexico."

Less than half a mile across the river, the land piled up into a series of steep ridges, each a little higher than the one before, and several appeared to be vertical. Directly across the river they could see the opening of a large arroyo leading back into the mountains but curving to the north and blocking their view to what might lie beyond. The ridges extended in both directions without a break, perhaps a hundred miles for all they knew.

"Yeah," Jesse replied. "We don't need to go crashing into any damn box canyon with a posse a few hours back." He pointed upriver at a wide, marshy area and continued, "But the river doesn't offer much either. North upstream or south downstream, both look the same."

"Well, we gotta go somewhere," Frank pointed out. "What's it going to be?"

Cole motioned back at the dry bed that had led them to the river. "So, if you were chasing us and ended up here, what would you do? You'd have the same choices Jesse has."

"I'd look for tracks, then follow them."

"What if you didn't find any tracks at all?"

"Then I'd say you're riding in the water. I'd split my posse and go both ways until I found your trail, then keep tracking."

Jesse was nodding. "Yeah. That's what they're gonna do, but we're gonna help confuse them. Get Zack and the Overton kid to push the mules upstream, say a mile or two, but all in the river – they can't leave any hoofprints. Shit, Cole, you better go too, they'll fuck it up.

"The rest of us are gonna haul ass up that draw across the river, then come back and catch up with you. Hopefully they'll just blindly follow the tracks. You're looking for a place with lots of cover. Once you find the spot, have one of the boys keep watch for us so we don't miss you."

"Got it," Cole replied. "I say we go downstream. We've already been north."

"All right, get moving. I bet we don't have two hours."

Cole found George and Zack and explained what they would be doing and that under no circumstances could a horse or a mule step outside the river until they found an adequate spot. Jesse rounded up the rest of the gang and crossed the river into Texas, making sure to leave plenty of tracks in the mud and soft sand on the riverbank.

Cole waded his team into the river until the water was knee-deep and led them downstream where, after a mile, he found the perfect place. Sometime in the past the river had changed course within the flood plain. Its old path had looped around in a long oxbow, almost back to where it started. The ends of the oxbow had been just a few yards apart, but some flood had cut the corner, leaving the old loop outside the stream's new path. The old bed was still lined with trees and now there was a large meadow completely ringed with thick vegetation. Cole nearly missed it.

Cole led everyone out of the creek and into their hiding place. The meadow was covered in Bermuda grass, which was a very welcome bonus for the horses and mules. Cole estimated the meadow was about two acres, all well concealed and far beyond anything he could have hoped for. He sent George down to the river to wait for the gang to show up.

George waited an hour before he saw, and heard, the gang wading down the river. He let them get close before he took off his hat and thrust it through the brush, waving it so the leader, Jesse, of course, could see where he was.

Jesse told Cole and his mule-tenders that it was a good thing they didn't try the arroyo with the mules – after just a few miles it narrowed, then narrowed again into a short canyon, just thirty yards long but only ten feet wide. Beyond the gap the arroyo broke into several draws, each leading straight up the mountain. That way was a trap.

They waited quietly and pondered their next steps. Everyone was prepared for a gunfight, but at the same time wanting to avoid one. The hope was that the posse would waste time on Jesse's ruse and then split up to hastily search the river in both directions. Half the posse should pass them at any moment, then eventually assume they'd gone the wrong way and come back before they ran out of daylight. The gang would rest and then quietly escape downstream before dawn.

The next question was, "Escape to where?" The answer was, of course, the Indian Territory. But how?

Frank, Cole, and Jesse were submerged in figuring out how they were going to get the mule train across four hundred miles of wilderness without getting caught by Apaches, killing any mules, horses, or people, and still avoid a Mexican posse. They were generally pessimistic, but there was, maybe, a way out.

Jesse's map showed the relative locations of the major roads, towns, rivers, and landmarks, and they had a rough idea of their location. According to the map, if they could get to Van Horn Wells, they'd have a chance.

Van Horn Wells was a natural spring that had been a popular watering stop for travelers, stagecoaches, and the mail riders for decades. One of the stage lines that had stopped there was the Butterfield Overland Mail Company, which hauled people and mail between St. Louis and San Francisco. If they followed the old trail back to the east, it would eventually take them all the way to Sherman, Texas, although they wouldn't need to go that far.

Getting to the Wells might be a challenge, though. West Texas was notoriously dangerous and the gang's first problem was their map showed no topography at all – according to it, the whole of Texas was flat as a pancake. The map told them that Van Horn Wells was a short forty miles nearly due east. Reality plainly showed there was a mountain range blocking their way and beyond that, who knew? The map couldn't say, and if the previous few days had taught them anything, it was that nothing around there was flat.

Frank figured they had provisions for about four days, which should be enough to get to the Wells, whatever route they were forced to take. Assuming they did not encounter some crisis on the trail, everyone should get there safely.

That was fine for most of the gang, but George and Zack would be at a crossroads. They only had one horse each, the ones rustled by Apaches in Roswell had yet to be replaced. With a single horse, a dash across the Trans-Pecos in Texas was risky at best, and given their mounts' current conditions, the consensus was suicide.

Thus, Zack and George would ride southeast along the El Paso-San Antonio stage road to Fort Davis, about seventy miles away. Meanwhile, the rest of the gang would ride northeast to the town of Pecos where they would resupply and begin their long, dry ride across West Texas on the old Butterfield track.

The Butterfield would take them to Fort Belknap, just forty miles southwest of Wichita Falls. From there it would be a dash into the Indian Territory and the Wichita Mountains. Jesse made it clear that Zack and George had until Fort Belknap to catch up.

It seemed like a good plan, but they weren't even off the river yet. The sun was setting, and no pursuers had ridden past any of the lookouts, which was puzzling. Surely they had not fallen for the false trail up the arroyo? Whatever happened, everyone agreed they'd caught a break. Perhaps they could get a good night's rest, then slip downstream until they could figure out how to get over the mountains to the Wells.

Jesse had the gang moving at dawn, and no one was dawdling that day. Banking that they had enough of a lead to rely on speedy travel instead of stealth, Jesse made no attempt to cover their trail. He stuck mostly to the level ground at the edge of the river's bed and took the most direct path possible, cutting corners and crossing the stream as it meandered back and forth.

They made excellent time for the first twenty miles, until the riverbed pinched into a series of twisting, narrow gorges. There was still plenty of room to ride, but the cliffs were steep and tall, and it was impossible to see downriver more than a few hundred yards. There would be no escape if they were attacked in the canyons.

The gorges continued for many twisting miles until they crept around yet another narrow bend to discover the riverbed abruptly widening and returning to its previous condition. The narrow canyons were where the river had cut through the mountain range that had been blocking their way, and now they were on the other side.

But still no way out.

"Dammit," Jesse groused. "Looks like we'll be staying in the river for at least one more day. How many more of those can there be?"

They managed to squeeze five more miles out before the light began to fail. Downstream they could see the river pinching up again; another set of narrow gorges would need to be traversed. Jesse decided they'd gone far enough; the gorges were scary enough in broad daylight.

Frank managed the gang while Jesse and Cole tried to figure out where they might be. The map showed the river steadily leading southeast, and now their best guess was the Wells was now north of them, more or less. The map said the river would soon begin curving into a southerly path. If that happened, they'd gone too far. Assuming the map was accurate.

Everyone got another good night's rest and they left at first light, the river indeed contracting into another five-mile stretch of winding, narrow gorges. When they emerged, they found the same pattern as before: The river had cut its way through the mountains, another wide draw was behind the mountains, and the riverbed opened up again with the river making wide, loopy turns between the banks.

This time, however, the draw headed due north, and they could see the river making a southerly bend a half-mile downstream. Jesse looked at his map and declared, "This has to be it," and led them into Texas proper.

Their path was, again, a dry riverbed, complete with banks, thin islands and a shallow channel. The only thing missing was water. And unlike the real river they had been following for days, this one ran straight without any curves or bends. The reason for that was obvious - it had nowhere to go.

When it rained, that riverbed drained the entire valley between the high ridges on either side. Bud estimated the highest peaks to be over five miles apart, and some of those peaks were easily a thousand feet higher than their riverbed.

Jesus, you don't want to be here in a thunderstorm.

Will voiced what Bud was thinking, "How much rain do you think it takes to fill this thing up?"

Rub replied, "Not much, I reckon. Look at all those gullies and washes running out of the hills—they push every raindrop right here."

Everyone looked to the sky, making sure there were no clouds building anywhere.

"Christ," Will said. "We need to get the hell out of here. This whole country is crazy."

* * *

They followed the Green River's bed until it dwindled into a shallow but relatively straight gap leading to level ground. Jesse checked the map, then checked the sun and led them to the right.

They bypassed a group of low hills only to discover another string of low mountains in the distance. There was a large gap that held promise, though, so Jesse navigated toward it. When they got there, they discovered a good road leading through the gap.

"Hey," Jesse exclaimed, "I think we're here."

The road led directly to Van Horn Wells, which was just a few hundred yards beyond the gap. The "well" was a rocky depression with a spring somewhere beneath it that kept the depression full of fresh water. They wasted no time watering all the animals and refilling all their canteens.

"That was the easy part," Cole lectured. "This next leg is a hundred miles long, and the one after that is two hundred and fifty with only one watering hole. We'll camp over there with two lookouts all night. George, Zack, you two take the first watch."

Dawn arrived with no horses missing. All the animals were watered again, and everyone was on the trail as soon as possible. They quickly arrived at the junction with the San Antonio trail, the gang taking the northern fork to Pecos, Zack and George taking the southern leg leading to Fort Davis and eventually San Antonio.

Bud knew this was Zack's best opportunity to meet dire misfortune, and he was sincerely hoping for the worst. That sentiment was tempered, a little, by George's unfortunate partnership with Zack. Whatever befell one would certainly befall the other and George and Bud had become friends by then.

Good luck, George. To hell with you, Zack.

The Butterfield Road was established before the war and was one of the first commercial overland routes to California. The route passed south of the Rocky Mountains so it could be used all year long, at the cost of a long stretch through the desert. Watering stops had been placed as frequently as possible along the trail, but nearly all were manufactured in the form of cisterns and water tanks. Theoretically, there could be plenty of opportunities to find water.

In reality, though, the Butterfield Overland Mail Company had stopped operating when the Civil War broke out and, while the track itself could be followed easily enough, the status of the watering stops was very questionable. Hopefully they would not be forced to ride the full distance between stations, which were army forts, without water, but it seemed unlikely that any of the relics could have much left. They would need to bring all they could when they left Pecos.

Unlike the Butterfield, Zack and George's path was still in heavy use in both directions, they would have no trouble with terrain or water. They set out as fast as their tired horses could carry them.

The pair finally arrived at Fort Davis and wasted no time purchasing new mounts and trading their tired ones. George informed Zack he needed to replenish some food supplies, so they found a store and picked up the stuff they needed, George wanting coffee in particular.

As they were paying, three Mexican soldiers stomped into the store and asked the owner if he'd seen a large group of Americans in the last day or so. There would be perhaps a dozen men and a large number of mules.

The owner shook his head and pointed at Zack and George. "Them two boys is all."

The commander explained to the boys that the men he was searching for were outlaws, and they had stolen the mules and their cargo, which the Mexican Army wanted back. The Mexicans had received permission to pursue the bandits into America, and they were certain the bandits were trying to escape down the old El Paso Road. There was a large reward for good information. Had the boys seen anyone like that? Or any mules?

George shook his head, no, he had not seen any men or mules.

"If you see them, remember, there is a large reward," the commander told them.

As they left the store, Zack told George, "We gotta catch up with the rest."

Chapter 6

General Diaz did not receive the news of the robbery well. He mobilized his entire army in Chihuahua, sending squads to every U.S. Army Fort along the river to question everyone. He had a detachment in pursuit, but Diaz needed to cut the gringos off. He did not want the gold to leave Mexico.

The detachment tracking the gang followed them to the river and was confronted with the choices Jesse and Cole had left for them. They saw the tracks on the far bank and fell for the ruse, following them all the way to the box canyon before realizing they'd been tricked.

They returned to the river and searched for tracks or clues that would point the way. Finding none, the commander elected not to split his detail, but to go north, upstream, toward Fort Quitman. The fort was the closest place where the bandits could receive assistance, and, in his mind, was their only choice.

Fort Quitman was manned by a single lieutenant and cavalry squad, and the Mexicans were the first people to even approach the fort in several weeks. From Quitman the Mexicans continued north along the river, questioning everyone they met in every village they passed. When they met up with the detachments rushing south from Juarez, it was clear the bandits had headed overland into Texas and now had a good lead but also very few choices.

Van Horn Wells, Fort Davis, and Fort Stockton were the obvious places to search because they all had plentiful water and all were on the El Paso Road. The Wells was the best bet as it was the closest place to the downstream path. The bandits were still within Diaz's reach, but the general would have to send his troops deep into Texas.

Detachments were hurried to each place, where one of them spilled the beans to Zack and George. The Mexicans who went to Van Horn Wells found it deserted, but there were many tracks. Fresh tracks, both horses and mules, and their trail was clear, but it headed north.

* * *

Zack and George rode hard until they finally caught up with Jesse, and their news galvanized the gang. Jesse abandoned any ideas of sleep and pressed the gang through the night and into the next day, refusing to rest for more than a few hours at a time. He was certain their trail would be picked up in Pecos where they had spent several hours and were seen by dozens of people.

There was no time to waste.

* * *

The Mexicans followed the mule's trail and found the witnesses in Pecos. They were just a day behind the bandits, and even though the mules left a trail any child could follow, Jesse's mania for speed prevented the Mexicans from closing the gap.

The gang reached the Red River on March 5, after twelve torturous days. The weather had begun to deteriorate, but their goal was in reach, if they could just get there. The posse was behind them somewhere; they didn't know how close.

By the time the Mexican commander realized what was happening it was too late. When the mule's tracks abruptly veered northward off the abandoned road, toward the Red River, he understood: The bandits were headed for the Indian Territory. If they made it, the

Mexicans were finished. While they had papers that would convince the Americans they were permitted to be there, there was no possibility the Indians would tolerate it. He also realized that if he returned to Mexico empty-handed, General Diaz would probably have him, and his entire company, shot.

As the weather grew worse, the lightly provisioned Mexicans grew equally miserable. The company had just crossed the Red River when one of the scout teams came tearing back into view. Or, rather, most of it did. Only three of the four were accounted for, and one of them was injured. They reported that they had been ambushed well inside the Indian Territory and the bandits had escaped.

The mules were gone, but the problem at hand was the weather. There was almost no cover available and by the time the blizzard abated, only fourteen of the fifty-five soldiers had survived the storm. The survivors deserted, discarding their equipment and stripping their dead comrades of their clothes and food before hobbling back to Wichita Falls.

None returned to Mexico and Diaz never learned what became of his gold bars.

* * *

Bud and the other mule-tenders followed Jesse for two frigid hours until Jesse found the ravine he was looking for. It was a massive gap in the mountainside, a creek at the bottom and its sheer sides rising in a steep "V" forty feet from its floor. Unfortunately, it ran north and south, allowing the wind to scream through the gap and, Bud was certain, straight into his bones.

They fought through the howling wind until they encountered a fork and Jesse turned left and was rewarded with some cover. The north side of the ravine merged into the base of a towering mountain that effectively blocked all the wind. Bud could hear it shrieking over the brush and scrub at the top of the ravine, but at the bottom the situation was manageable. Cold as hell, but getting out of the wind made a big difference.

Jesse dismounted. "I guess we're here."

The men dragged their gear off their mounts and looked for a good place for themselves, which there wasn't. Exhausted and sore as they were, the prospect of sitting on the frozen ground while sleet and snow slowly covered them was unappealing.

Bud moved over to the rocky side of the creek, nearest the mountain, searching for a place to at least sit down. A relatively flat rock with a place to lean back was at the far extreme of his hopes. He was finding lots of rocks, but nothing to his liking.

As he edged along the side, he encountered a spot that had no snow or sleet. He inched up and discovered a void in the wall, an area of absolute blackness higher than his head and deeper than he could reach.

An overhang, or maybe a cave?

Bud listened carefully and sniffed the air. Nothing.

He reached into the blackness, hoping to find a rock wall where his wish for a flat rock might be granted. A few inches passed, and then a foot, then two. Bud waved his hand around in the dark searching for the back, or even the top. Still nothing.

A cave...

He carefully dug through his pockets, searching for one of his remaining matches. He found the head and carefully scratched it against the rocky wall, hoping it hadn't gotten wet somewhere along the way. The wax paper had survived and the match flared to life, illuminating a small cave.

It wasn't really a cave, more of a large depression in the cliff's face. It was small, roughly a semicircle ten feet deep with the same sandy floor that made up the creek bed. The old remains of a small fire lay inside; someone had used the cave for shelter before. Bud shook out his match before it burned his fingers, and dropped it to the ground.

Everyone had seen the flare of the match and Cole called, "What do you have there, Bud?"

Bud replied, "Looks like a little cave. It's dry and out of the wind, and there's ashes from an old fire. Seems like a good idea, if we can get one lit."

Everyone heartily agreed and after a few damp matches they were able to find a dry one and get a fire started. The men dragged their bedrolls into the cave and although it was cramped, there was room for everyone to lean against the wall with their feet toward the fire.

Bud was still hungry and cold, but the fire helped. He was out of the wind and sleet, and he was sitting on something that wasn't a horse. Everything considered, things seemed to be improving and sleep came easily.

Bud awoke around dawn to find Jesse and Cole already awake, talking quietly outside the entry. The fire had burned down and there wasn't any more fuel handy, so Bud groaned to his feet to go find some. He searched for the gloves he'd stuffed in his duster's pocket, then went out to find more sticks along the creek bed.

As he was rebuilding the fire, he overheard Jesse telling Cole he didn't think they were in the right place.

"I was pretty sure last night when Bud found the cave, and now I'm positive. This isn't where I told Frank to meet us."

Cole replied, "This is a pretty good hiding place, for now. We'll stick out like a sore thumb if we try to move this bunch, plus we all need to rest."

Jesse nodded. "Two of the mules are almost lame, so we can't go anywhere anyway. I'm thinking we need to hide the gold and slip away. We might as well come back sometime when we're not fighting the weather."

Cole agreed. "Yeah. We need to get back home and dragging this shit along with us is a bad idea. But first we need to find Frank."

Cole looked over to Bud and asked, "Bud, is there any coffee left? Think you could get some going? I don't know about you, but I don't think we should let the first fire we've seen in two weeks get away without heating something."

Bud nodded and began to dig through the gear, looking for coffee and a pot. He didn't bother to check whose gear or whose coffee it was. It turned out that George had never gotten a chance to brew any of what he'd bought in Texas, so there was plenty. Things were getting better and better.

Jesse continued, "I'll take one of the boys and see if we can figure out where we are and then meet up with Frank."

"If he's there."

"Right. I hope they found a place to ride it out—that storm was a bad one. Anyhow, I say we gather them up, rest a bit, hide the loot around here somewhere, and wait for the weather to break,"—Jesse and Cole both looked to the sky, then Jesse continued—"and then get out of here."

"Works for me."

The gang rested the remainder of the morning, drinking George's coffee and feeding their small fire. Jesse drafted "Uncle" George Payne to help him find Frank and they returned a few hours later with Frank and his party.

Frank hadn't been able to find the right place either, and they'd spent a miserable night weathering the storm in a dense growth of scrub oak in the lee of another mountain. The sleet had stopped just before dawn, and when the sun came up Frank was able to navigate to the rendezvous spot where he found Jesse and Uncle George waiting for him.

Frank agreed that hiding the gold was the smart thing to do, but first he wanted some hot coffee and to squeeze in around the fire, which was a delightful surprise. Roy, Rub, and Charlie thought so too.

Later that morning, as the surviving Mexicans were deserting, the gang was discussing their return to Missouri. The weather was clearing, and everyone was ready to be done with that particular adventure. They'd deal with the gold and the mules, and head home.

Zack, however, didn't want to leave the gold and he spoke up.

"I think we should divide it up twelve ways right now and take our chances. There's a million things that could keep us from getting together to dig it up again. I say we do it now."

Bud watched closely. This was the first time he'd seen anyone besides Frank or Cole contradict Jesse, and then it was never in plain view. And Zack was a new guy. Perhaps Jesse would shoot him for his insolence.

That seemed possible. Jesse had become less and less tolerant as the ride out of Texas progressed. He was constantly threatening to leave stragglers to the posse or the desert and he flatly refused to acknowledge the most basic needs of men or animals. Food, water, rest, and hygiene were simply not part of Jesse's plan, nor was tolerating dissent.

So much intimate contact with Jesse had considerably worn away Bud's admiration, and contempt was starting to leak into Bud's opinion of him. Bud knew he wasn't alone; he believed some of the gang might have actually deserted if they hadn't been in the Texas wilderness.

This might be interesting.

"Split it up now? You stupid?" Jesse shot back. "Zack, everyone's beat to shit, the weather's trying to kill us, and we all have somewhere better to be. You're dumb but not that dumb … What is it, Zack? You don't trust me?"

Zack swallowed hard, but held his ground. "No, not like that. I'm just sayin' we're all here now and if we're going to split up then we should split the money too."

When they'd staggered into the ravine, Cole and Frank had pulled the packs off the mules, leaving them in a scattered mess in the creek bed. Jesse found the pack that Frank had cut open in Mexico, then pulled out one of the gold bricks and lugged it over to Zack, dropping it at his feet. The heavy bar landed in the sand with a shallow thud, creating a small crater. "You'll need to carry a bunch of these. Not sure how many."

Zack took the brick and only then realized how heavy the mules' load really was. There was no way he could manage even three. "Maybe if I took one of the mules…"

Jesse nodded his head, mockingly. "Absolutely, you bet. Pick out what you want. You heard those Mexicans are right behind us and now the weather's clearing they're going to be poking around here any time. I'm sure you'll be able to slip past them, no problem. By all means, take all the mules you want. Good luck to you."

Reluctantly, Zack realized Jesse was right. There was no way he could get his whole share home, so the vast bulk of it would have to be hidden anyway. Admitting defeat, he sighed and said, "OK, you're right. So how is this gonna work, Jesse?"

Back in the center of attention and with everyone deferring to him, Jesse was in his element. He looked around and saw a brass bucket that had been tied to a mule's pack. They'd hauled the thing across Texas, and now Jesse had a new idea for it. Never one to miss an opportunity for drama, he picked up the bucket and held it up theatrically.

"Here's what we're going to do. We're gonna make us an agreement. A contract, just for Zack." He took out his knife and began to scratch the brass. "I'm gonna etch our agreement on this here bucket. It's not paper, so it'll last forever."

Jesse scratched each gang member's name onto the bucket along with the date, a cryptic description of the ravine's location, and a message that the gold belonged to the men whose names were engraved on the bucket.

That completed, he outlined what would happen next. "We're going to rest here for another night, then tomorrow we're going to bring the mules away from here into the mountains and let them go. There's a wide valley just to the north, even if them boys behind us find 'em they won't find the gold. Due north is a tall mountain, take a good look at it when we get out of this canyon.

"That's where we'll hide this," he said, holding up the bucket. "This tells how to find the gold. Things will look different in the spring, and we don't want to lose our way. After that, we'll split up and head home.

"I'll send word to all of you, maybe in June or July, and we'll meet up and split this up proper. Do whatever you want with it."

Jesse looked at Zack and caustically asked, "That's how it's gonna work, Zack. That all right with you?"

Zack nodded, at which point Cole sent him to gather what sticks and branches he could find to keep the fire going. Anything that could easily be retrieved had already been collected, so Zack was forced to look farther into the ravine. By the time he had amassed enough wood to keep the fire burning all night he was in a very foul mood.

While Zack was searching, Jesse enlisted four of them to dig a deep, wide hole. When the hole was large enough, the packs were pulled into the hole.

"Cover it all up," he ordered. "It'll be here when we're ready for it."

Bud didn't see any sense in scratching up a bucket and then hiding it on a mountain. Then again, he knew that Jesse enjoyed things like that and had been engaged in similar antics for years. Bud would keep his sketchbook handy, just in case.

The next morning finally brought a break in the weather. It was still cold, but the wind had stopped, the sky a frigid cobalt blue. Tired of lingering, Jesse got them moving early and they cautiously slipped out of the ravine. The prairie was covered in snow and if anyone had been anywhere nearby, they, or their tracks, would have been obvious. There was no one.

Bud finally got a good look at the area. Their ravine turned out to be a very small part of an enormous complex of mountains, sheer cliffs, creeks, gorges, and valleys. He estimated the massif to be at least four miles wide and erupting upwards hundreds of feet, perhaps a thousand. There must be hundreds of ravines right here, Bud thought. No wonder neither Jesse nor Frank could find the right place.

Jesse knew where he was going now, and led them to a gap in the mountains which was filled with in a dense growth of mesquite trees. The trees had long thorns and had to be navigated carefully to avoid deep scratches to hands and faces. After a mile of cursing, the gang slipped out of the gap and into a large valley. The valley floor was rolling grassland and surrounded, of course, by steep stone mountains.

Jesse pointed across the valley where the tops of two mountains could be seen beyond the ridges that defined the valley. One was somewhat taller, and Jesse said, "We go past there, our mountain just beyond. Once we get there, you can't miss it."

Bud drank in the vision of the valley and the mountain, trying to take in as much detail as he could while Frank untethered all the mules. He pulled out his sketchbook and pencil and began rough sketches of the countryside, particularly the mountain that Jesse was using for his landmark.

"How does Jesse know where he's going?" Bud asked Cole.

Cole replied, "He can remember things like this, and we've been through here enough times that I imagine he knows the landmarks as well as any Indian."

Bud closed his sketchbook around the pencil and slipped it into his pocket just as Jesse started talking. "Once we cross the valley we'll be in some rough country, but nothing worse than what we've already seen. Once we're through we'll camp near Buzzard's Roost tonight."

Bud looked to Cole. "Buzzard's Roost?"

"It's a butte a few miles northeast of the mountains here. Good spot to camp."

Jesse left the mules and led the gang across the valley. As they neared the opposite side, Bud saw Jesse was leading them toward a creek bed spilling from between two mountains.

Great. Another damn creek running down another damn mountain. Why can't we have a trail for once?

Jesse led them up and over the pass, and then around the two mountains he'd pointed out from the valley. He headed directly toward a mountain that Bud was certain could not be navigated, but then veered around its wide base and stopped at the bottom of a navigable slope that led most of the way to the top.

How can he know this?

Jesse dismounted, and untied the brass bucket with its cryptic message. "You might be able to ride up there, but I imagine it'll be safer for everyone if we hike. Frank, you mind keeping an eye on things down here?"

"Fine with me. You boys go ahead."

"I'll stay too," Cole added. "I don't need anything up there."

The climb was not difficult, but it was a bit steep and by the time they got to the top everyone was breathing heavily, the frigid air burning their lungs. Above them was the mountain's peak which Bud hoped Jesse didn't intend to climb, but to the north and west he was treated to a magnificent view.

Jesse didn't care about the view; he was looking around for a good spot to leave the bucket. He clearly had something in mind and finally found what he wanted: a flat rock about two feet across.

Jesse dug his fingers under the rock's edge and heaved it up on its side. He used his knife to dig a hole and before long it was large enough to hold the bucket, which he set in the hole and rolled the rock back where it had been.

Jesse then counted the paces from the rock to a good-sized oak tree, where he pulled a mule's shoe and a nail from his pocket and nailed the shoe to the tree using the butt of one of his pistols. He then retraced his steps, back over the rock to a spot almost the same distance as the tree.

Looking around, he began to stack smaller rocks into a pyramid about a foot tall. When finished he looked at the men and said, "Anyone here should be able to find the bucket. Pile of rocks and the horseshoe, halfway the bucket's buried under the rock."

Bud was barely able to conceal his contempt.

Yep. He's completely crazy.

The men all nodded their understanding, Bud not really caring because aside from his name being on it, the bucket was worthless to him. He'd have to rely on Jesse. Or his sketchbook. Probably the book.

"All right, then," Jesse announced, "Let's get out of here."

Chapter 7

They retreated down the slope and gathered their horses. Jesse led them back across the front of the mountain, following the inevitable creek bed at the bottom of every hill. They rode several miles, the terrain steadily falling, until it eventually leveled out and they were ushered out onto the plains.

They followed Jesse about ten miles to a low, round hill topped by a dramatic eruption of stone. The hill sat alone, another island on the prairie. Bud looked closely at the hill and noted that this hill was different. It was not a pile of stones, but rather a smooth mound that, aside from the fifteen or twenty feet of vertical stone at the hill's summit, bore no resemblance to the mountains where they'd waited out the blizzard.

They arrived at the campsite and Frank organized their camp, focusing first on firewood. He had no shortage of volunteers, and the creek had an ample supply of deadwood, so the gang was treated to yet another fire, this one quite large.

No one wasted time and before long everyone had claimed a space around the roaring fire and had something cooking. Jesse agreed that the Pinkertons' attention had been pulled from Missouri, and that it was time to disperse and lay low through the spring. They would slip out of the Indian Territory in small groups and head north. Cole,

Frank, and Jesse intended to pass through Kansas City, so Cole invited Bud to accompany them as far as Westport.

The dawn air was crystal clear and motionless. As the sun rose, it illuminated the mountain where they'd hidden the bucket, tinging it with pale red light. Bud took out his book and began a sketch, regretting he only had a pencil; the reds and purples the sun was applying to the mountains were not making it into the book.

The rest of the camp was moving, gathering and packing belongings for the relatively short ride and trying to get some kind of breakfast going. Bud and George were sharing coffee and the last of their bacon, talking about meeting up at some future time. Bud watched the light change on the mountains as the sun rose and sipped some of George's coffee.

Not too bad.

Bud's mood darkened as Zack plopped down directly opposite him, blocking his view. Bud closed his book and put it away to focus on his bacon and coffee and not let Zack's presence interfere with his mood too much.

Zack had other ideas. Perhaps thinking he may never have another chance, he provoked and needled Bud with whatever insinuations and insults he could concoct. The taunting went on for several minutes, and Bud maintained his composure outwardly, but Zack struck several nerves and Bud was in a furious rage internally.

Zack eventually got bored with Bud and turned to discuss the gold with Rub for a few minutes, but returned to Bud.

"You know, speaking of the bars, we really have old Bud here to thank for all that."

Rub looked at Zack blankly, and several others looked over, too, trying to make the connection between Bud and the bars. Bud and George looked up also, and Zack was delighted to have an audience.

"Yes, sir. Everyone knows Bud's old man tipped off the Pinkertons that we'd gone to Joplin, been doing it for years, I've heard. Oh, yeah, he's a scoundrel, gotta keep a close eye on him. But it all turned out all right, didn't it? Pinkertons went to Joplin, but we'd already headed south. Then Mexico, and now we're all rich."

Cole barked, "Shut up, Zack, you know that's…"

He never finished the sentence. Bud rose calmly and in one motion drew his pistol, cocked it, and pointed it at Zack's nose, mere yards away. Zack's eyes widened as Bud pulled the trigger.

He saw Zack's realization that he'd gone way too far, and Bud felt outright glee as the hammer fell firmly onto the cap. The Colt belched its normal cloud of dense bluish smoke, and Bud stepped through it to view the carnage.

He'd missed to the right. The gun was pointed upward from the recoil and Zack, discovering he wasn't dead, didn't wait for Bud to try again. He launched himself at Bud, clawing at the Colt with one hand and punching at Bud's face with the other.

Bud brought the gun down viciously on Zack's head, staggering him. He took a step back to bring the gun to bear again, but tripped over a stone and fell backward. Zack saw his opening and rushed forward, hoping to trap Bud on his back. Bud hit the ground and rolled over immediately, rising to one knee, turning the gun toward Zack and cocking it as he raised it.

Zack saw Bud bringing up the pistol and reacted instinctively. He took a long step toward Bud, and then kicked at Bud's head with his next step. The toe of Zack's boot struck Bud squarely in the face, just under his left eye, rocking his head back savagely and tossing him backwards. Bud hit the ground and lay motionless. The fight had lasted about fifteen seconds.

Zack regained his balance and was about to draw his own gun when Cole punched him hard in the side of the head. Zack went down, and even though he never lost consciousness, it was several minutes before he could sit up again. Cole relieved him of his gun and went to check Bud's condition.

He was breathing, but Zack's boot had gouged a deep and jagged cut through Bud's cheek and the wound was bleeding heavily. Cole found a relatively clean shirt in Bud's roll and used it to stem the bleeding. Bud was still unconscious, and Cole had to enlist George to hold the shirt against Bud's face.

Jesse was beside himself. "Damn it, Zack, what the hell was that? You know his Pa didn't tell anyone anything. He's probably the only reliable man left in Missouri. You could see he was wearing his gun and you started in on him like that? Why didn't you just call his mother a whore? You Goddamned fool. I wish he hadn't missed. Maybe I'll fucking finish the job."

He called over to Cole, "How's Bud? He alive?"

Cole answered, "Yeah, for now. I hope this doesn't addle his wits."

Jesse cursed again and looked Zack over. Bud hadn't completely missed, his bullet had grazed Zack's left ear, cleanly notching a perfect semicircle from it. The wound wasn't serious, but it was bleeding. The back of his head was also bleeding from the blow Bud scored with the gun, and the right side of his head was bruised from Cole's punch.

Jesse's words clearly hadn't registered. "That little shit nearly shot me!" Zack complained, gingerly exploring his head.

He discovered his notched ear. "Ouch! What the hell? He did shoot me! By God, I'll kill that son of a bitch!"

Zack tried to stand and find his pistol, but hadn't quite regained his balance and was staggering back and forth. Cole reached over and roughly pushed him back to the ground.

"Agh … My damn ears are ringing," Zack complained, pressing his palm to his forehead.

Cole wasn't listening, but rather looking pointedly at Jesse. Jesse glanced over to Frank, who just looked disgusted. Frank looked at Zack, then to Jesse and motioned "Away" with his head.

Jesse nodded. "Right. We're splitting up right now."

He looked around for Charlie and Rub, both of whom were still holding their coffee.

"You two take Zack. Get him out of here. Now. I don't want to see that stupid fucker until summer."

Rub and Charlie glanced at each other and sighed. They took one last sip of their coffee and tossed the rest onto the ground as they stood up to gather their gear. The rest of the gang followed suit, no one wanting to linger a moment longer than necessary. Cole made sure Zack's party was the first to depart, the rest just behind them.

Bud began to regain consciousness after Charlie and Rub had led Zack away. Cole examined the wound and was disturbed to see it went clear into Bud's cheekbone. The cut was "V" shaped, with the point on the cheekbone and the legs extending upwards, left and right, almost to his eye. The pointed part was largely detached from the flesh below.

Cole pushed the flesh back to where it was supposed to be and bound the wound as best he could with what he had. The bleeding had slowed, but Bud's eye was black and swollen, along with the entire side of his head. It took a while for Bud to remember what had happened and Cole had to explain his injuries. Bud seemed to understand, but was obviously in pain and couldn't talk or stand without holding onto something.

Jesse's patience was completely exhausted and he nearly washed his hands of Bud, but Frank insisted on staying with Cole, and Cole refused to leave Bud, which only served to frustrate Jesse further. Jesse eventually refused to wait any more and demanded that Bud had to ride, and do it right then.

Cole managed to get Bud onto his horse and it was all Bud could do to hang on to the pommel. Cole tied Bud's reins to his own horse and they rode to one of the supply roads connecting Fort Sill and Kansas. They turned northward and followed the road.

Fort Sill had been established as a permanent base to control the Indians and to replace a string of smaller forts constructed to support the various Indian agencies. Their official purpose was to keep the Indians in line, but they never could prevent the Indians from leaving to raid Texas and Kansas throughout the summer and fall months and were deemed failures.

Being deep in Indian Territory, Fort Sill required a constant stream of food, forage, ammunition, horses, and construction supplies. Civilian contractors and drovers delivered most of the supplies, and a few small outposts had been established to protect the supply lines. There was a lot of traffic along the roads between the forts, so four riders would not draw undue attention.

Speed was on Jesse's mind that day, but even on the road Bud was holding everyone back. Jesse's irritation was growing, and grew further when Cole ordered a stop to check on Bud.

What he found was bad. The flap of skin had worked its way back toward Bud's eye, exposing the tissue below to constant rubbing from the bandage. Although the bleeding had stopped, the wound was oozing. On the positive side, Bud could keep his balance and appeared to be steadier on his feet.

"I've seen worse," Cole told him. "But not much. Can you open your mouth to eat? Or talk?"

Bud shook his head. He had tried earlier, just moving his mouth was too painful to repeat. Chewing was out of the question.

Cole rebandaged Bud's face and they continued on, still too slow for Jesse. Bud wasn't the only thing bedeviling Jesse, though. The temperature had inched up enough to begin melting the ice and snow, and now their road was a muddy slop.

They managed another mile when they came across an army detail headed to Fort Sill. They were having trouble with the mud, too, and were attempting to free a stuck wagon. Frank, Jesse, and Cole waved and exchanged pleasantries as they passed, but when the captain saw Bud he exclaimed, "Good God! What happened to you?"

Cole explained that it was just an accident—Bud had been kicked in the face by his horse. They were hoping to get him some treatment once they were out of the Indian Territory.

The captain turned back and called, "Dr. Sullivan, I believe we have a patient for you."

Once again, Bud's bandages were removed and Sullivan poked at the wound. "Yep. That's a kick all right, looks like he got you with the tip. Awfully ragged and deep, though." He fingered the loose part at the tip, "I don't like the way this bit flops around, either."

He rummaged around in a canvas bag he'd brought and pulled out what looked like a sewing kit. He called to two privates that were idling, "You two! Lower the gate on that wagon."

Sullivan led Bud to the wagon and had him lie down on his back. He opened the sewing kit and extracted a long, curved needle and a small spool of thread. Bud saw the needle and attempted to get up, but Sullivan put a hand on his shoulder.

"Son, you won't like this but you need it. That bit that's flopping around needs to be sewed down so it can heal. If it doesn't heal it'll turn bad and when that happens we try and cut off the green parts, but most of the time it ends up being the whole arm or leg. We can't cut off your head, though, so we need to get this fixed right now."

There had been a small battle in Westport during the war, and Bud had seen men missing arms and legs after it was over. He recalled the stench of some of the wounds and the pile of arms and legs outside the makeshift hospital tent.

Bud glanced over at Frank, Jesse, and Cole. They appeared to be casually interested in what Sullivan might do to their partner, but Bud could tell all three were tense, Jesse as tight as a fiddle string.

We need to get away from here. Can't hurt much worse, let's get it over with.

Bud nodded and Sullivan had Frank and Cole hold Bud's head. "Try not to move too much," Sullivan admonished. "You're getting the last of my silk. Usually save that for officers, but it's all I have now."

The captain asked Jesse, "What brings you through here this time of year?"

Jesse didn't look up from Bud and casually said, "Spent last year punching cows down in Texas, and thought we'd try to get home for a spell. Couldn't afford a railroad ticket, and thought we'd save time passing through the Territory. Figured we'd make good time along the trail, but then got caught in the weather. Bud getting kicked isn't speeding us up any, either."

"No, that's poor luck. Where you headed?"

"Just north of St. Louis."

Bud let out a muffled shout as Sullivan pushed the curved needle through the loose flesh and pulled it tight, deftly tying the silk thread into a knot. He repeated the process on each side, making sure that both sides of the cut were aligned, more or less, and cinched together.

"If you put some bacon grease on it you might be a little more comfortable," Sullivan advised as Bud slowly climbed to his feet. He'd put clean rags over the newly bleeding wound, then secured them by tying a long strip around Bud's head to hold it on.

"You look like an outlaw," the captain observed. The irony was not lost on Bud.

Cole thanked Sullivan and the captain. "How much do we owe you? We don't have much, but we're willing to pay," he lied.

Sullivan waved his hand and walked away. "My pleasure. This one is courtesy of the army." Then calling back to Bud, he ordered, "You take it slow, sonny. You don't want to tear those out. You'll thank me twenty years from now."

Cole told the captain, "Much obliged to you. If it's all right, we'd like to move along."

The captain said, "Yes, yes. Don't dally. The weather could turn poor, again," then went back to yelling at the soldiers who had stopped pushing to watch Bud get sewn up.

The outlaws didn't waste any time leaving the supply train behind. After a slow mile of silence, Cole told Frank, "It's been a hell of a winter. Summer has to get better."

* * *

Unfortunately, winter wasn't through with them yet and their journey back to Missouri only grew worse. Bud's wound became infected and although the stitches held the pieces of flesh together, his face had swollen more, pulling the skin against the stitches. Pus oozed from the wound, and the margin began to turn yellowish-green which clashed with the purple of his bruised head. The overall effect was gruesome.

He began to run a fever, and could barely ride. After three days of very little progress, it was clear that Bud would not make it home without a long stop. The nearest place to leave him was Fort Sill's cousin, Fort Reno, which was just a few miles to the west.

Jesse was all for leaving Bud and flatly refused to ride anywhere near an army fort. Cole maintained that Bud would be the focus and no one would notice the outlaws if they behaved themselves. Jesse didn't care; he refused to go. Frank elected to stay back too.

They arrived at the fort and Cole led Bud's horse across the parade ground toward the building that seemed to be the most active. A sergeant got a look at Bud and immediately sent a soldier for the post surgeon and another for the commander.

By the time the doctor arrived Cole and the sergeant had pulled Bud off his horse and had laid him on his back. The doctor pulled off the horrid bandages and recoiled.

"Jesus. What happened here?"

Cole told how Bud had been kicked in the face by his horse the previous week and was stitched up on the Fort Sill supply road by Dr. Sullivan. The post commander, Colonel Park, arrived and ordered Bud taken to the infirmary immediately, but he held the doctor and Cole back.

Both the doctor, whose name was Ebbs, and Park had seen severe infections before. Although no one understood precisely how they occurred or why some men recovered, infections like Bud's were often feared far more than the injuries that preceded them.

"This boy is in bad shape," Ebbs gravely told Cole.

"Is there anything you can do for him?"

Ebbs shook his head. "I can give him some laudanum for the pain, but he's on his own. It probably wouldn't hurt to get some clean bandages on it, though."

Park turned to Cole. "We'll do what we can for him, but he can't stay here."

Cole was taken aback. "You're going to let him die?"

"No, no," Ebbs interjected, "you misunderstand. There's no treatment for his condition. We can change his bandages, and we'll do that, but it could take weeks for him to recover, if he does. He just can't stay here at the camp.

"Colonel," Ebbs continued, "perhaps Lieutenant Marchant's wife could lend these men a hand."

Park nodded. "That we can do."

Ebbs explained to Cole, "One officer's wife was a nurse during the war. She has accompanied him here and should be able to attend to your friend here. I'm sure you can work out an arrangement. Meanwhile we'll clean this up as best we can."

Ebbs removed the filthy rags covering Bud's wound and carefully wiped away as much dirt, dried blood, and pus as possible. He replaced the dressing with a new clean one, and expertly tied it to Bud's head.

Army outposts were virtually always accompanied by a civilian settlement comprised of army families and the various people necessary to maintain the outpost. Fort Reno's settlement was small, but there was a shack available to house Bud during his potential recovery. Cole installed Bud there and the lieutenant's wife, Harriett, acquainted herself with his condition.

Harriett dutifully kept Bud's bandages clean and changed, but he began to deteriorate immediately. Bud became the primary interest among Fort Reno's civilians, and there were numerous theories on the best treatment, as well as wagers on his recovery.

An ex-Confederate named Ellison Pausley approached Harriett with a suggestion. He told her that during the war his medical officer had routinely used maggots from the common green bottle fly to clean wounds. Pausley had personally seen men recover from infections far worse than Bud's.

Disgusted, but at a loss for anything else, Harriett dropped a small piece of meat into a jar, which attracted flies in very short order. She allowed the flies to crawl over the meat for an hour or so, then shooed the flies away and covered the jar. The next day revealed a dozen small maggots crawling on the scrap.

Harriett scraped the tiny worms off the meat and, with Pausley nodding helpfully, dropped them into Bud's wound and covered it with a clean bandage. Pausley encouraged her to leave the bandage on for at least two days, perhaps three, without changing it. He explained the maggots would consume any dead flesh and keep the wound cleaner than she could, if she would just let them do their work.

Harriett was skeptical and was quietly certain that Bud would die, but followed Pausley's advice anyway. More wagers were made.

Two days later, she pulled back the bandage and was amazed at what she saw. The maggots had tripled in size and had completely cleared Bud's wound of dead flesh, leaving it clean and pink. The yellowish tinge on the gash's margin was still there, but Harriett thought maybe it wasn't quite as bad as before.

A week later the swelling had subsided and Bud was looking, and feeling, much better. Everyone was amazed how the maggots had worked and the consensus was they had probably saved Bud's life. Harriett picked the now fat and squishy larvae out of the wound and reverted to a more traditional approach.

Only three people had bet on Bud's survival and they were rewarded with winnings in excess of five dollars.

Jesse had fled the moment Bud was lodged in the shack, claiming he and Frank had business that needed attending. Jesse urged Cole to come with them and let Bud recover by himself, but Cole elected to stay with Bud.

When it was clear that Bud would survive, Cole left too. "I gotta catch up with Jesse," he told Bud. "And I've hung around here too long. I figure another week or so before you'll be ready to travel, so try to rest up and heal. I think it'll be July or August before you hear from us again, so stay handy. I've settled up with Harriett, and you can square with me next time you see me. You did pretty good, and I reckon Jesse's gonna call your name at some point. Take care, Bud, I'll see you around."

Bud stayed in the shack for another week, and Harriett concluded that his gash had healed sufficiently to remove the stitches. They came out much less painfully than they went in, and Bud finally finished his trip home in April 1876.

Part 2

The Unassigned Lands

1876-1889

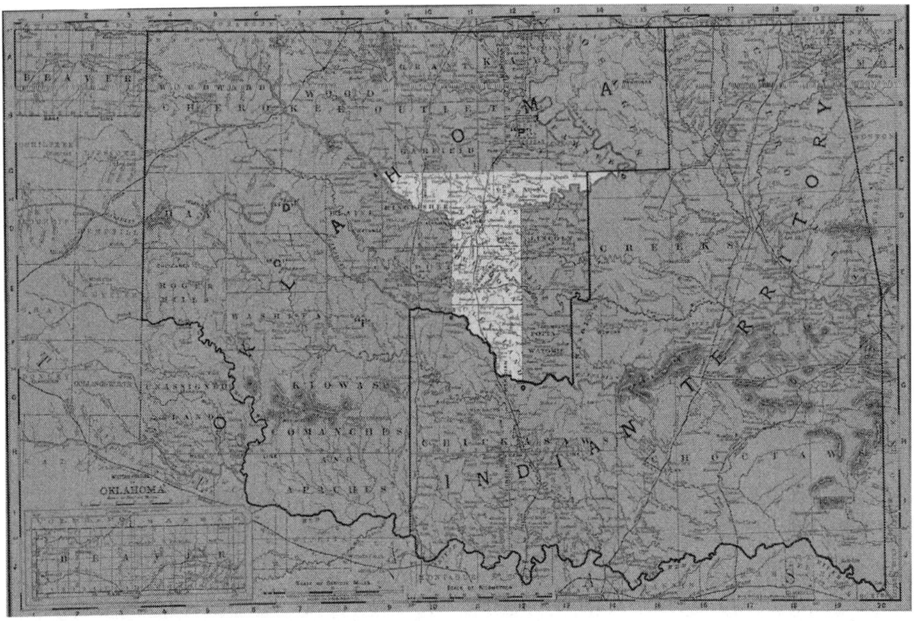
OKLAHOMA
INDIAN TERRITORY
CHEROKEE OUTLET
CREEKS
KIOWAS
COMANCHES
AND
APACHES
OKLAHOMA
BEAVER

Chapter 1

Bud had been gone for eight months, and it was instantly obvious to him those months had altered his course. He could just barely tolerate being in his parents' house, the domestic routine so comfortable before was now completely alien to him, and more than a little repulsive. The noise, children, and sharing confined spaces were all grating, but what really bothered him was that he was no longer in control of his day-to-day activities – his mother was.

Jesse, at least, had simply told him what to do and left him to do it. If he did it wrong or badly, Jesse would bitch at him for a while, but Adeline would let nothing go. She had very particular ways of doing things and she expected her family, including Bud, to comply. Now that he was aware of it, he didn't like it at all.

Bud began to consider his options. While ugly, his wound was mostly healed. He still had both his horses, gear, and about one hundred dollars of Cole's money left. Leaving Westport forever seemed like an excellent first step in whatever would happen next, and his mother sealed the deal two days later, announcing that she was pregnant—again. Bud's vague ideas crystallized into an escape plan.

He informed his parents that he would be heading south immediately. Privately, he told his father that he would be in Joplin, and that he was expecting Jesse to be looking for him around July. Once Jesse surfaced and Bud was settled, he would let Lewis know how to find him.

Bud's brother, Frank, the eldest behind Bud, had been forced into the role of policing and nannying the younger siblings in Bud's absence. Frank didn't care for the job any more than Bud had, and when Bud announced his impending departure Frank was aghast at the thought of owning it again. Frank followed Bud's lead, announcing that he, too, would be leaving the house to work in Kansas City.

* * *

The ride down to Joplin was uneventful and, Bud thought, quite pleasant. Unlike the James Gang, Bud did not avoid people and traveled on the main roads to take advantage of what civilization there was on the Kansas-Missouri border.

Bud ambled into Joplin, left his horses at the same livery he'd used the previous year, then walked across the street to the same hotel. The innkeeper discreetly examined Bud's scar as Bud filled out the register.

The clerk cleared his throat and asked, "How long will you be in town?"

"A month or two, I guess. I was actually hoping you could give me some advice. I don't think I can stay here that long."

"No, you would not be comfortable at all. You'll need to be looking for a boarding house. There are a few in town, the best is just down the street, run by a woman named Amy Lins. If she has a room available, you'll be comfortable there. Are you looking for work too?"

Bud hesitated for a moment, "No, I'm waiting to meet up with… family. We're heading south."

"I see. Mrs. Lins should be able to oblige you until they arrive."

The man gave Bud directions to the Lins Boardinghouse. Bud left his gear in the room and walked across town to see if there was a room available.

Mrs. Lins, a plain and slightly dumpy widow in her late forties, looked Bud up and down, lingering on his scar, and informed him that she did have a room, and he could have it in the morning. He would pay weekly and he could share meals with the other boarders in the dining room.

Bud moved into his new room the next morning. Mrs. Lins usually had eight to ten boarders, each with their own small room and furniture. Meals were served at the same time every day, and there were strict rules about alcohol and noise. All in all, it was very much like a family, just not the Dalton family. Mrs. Lins's boarding house was much better.

Bud spent the next weeks doing little besides sketching. He filled pages with everything from small doodles to carefully made drawings of people and the view from Mrs. Lins's porch. He had explored most of Joplin by then, and had a good idea where to find everything he needed.

He had told Mrs. Lins and the other boarders that he was waiting for his family to meet with him to settle down south. Since this was a common occurrence, everyone accepted his story and it wasn't long before that was what Joplin's rumor mill, which was often piloted by Mrs. Lins, reported about the young man with the bad scar.

One afternoon he was stopped in the street by a matronly woman he'd never met. She was well dressed and Bud estimated her to be about forty years old. Her manner hinted that she was used to getting her way.

"Why, you must be young Mr. Dalton. I understand you're an artist?"

Bud was baffled.

Who the hell is this woman? And how does she know my name? Who's an artist?

He tried to stammer something, but she interrupted him.

"My goodness, where are my manners?" she said. "My name is Lois Abernathy." She held out her hand for Bud.

Bud snatched his hat off his head and shook her hand politely. "I'm pleased to meet you, ma'am." As he replaced his hat, he asked, "How do you know me, ma'am?"

Lois replied, "I am very close friends with Amy Lins. She told me all about you, and I recognize you from her description."

Right, scar.

"Oh, yes. Mrs. Lins is a nice lady, but I think she might be stretching the truth about me being an artist."

Lois put on a stern look. "Amy Lins does not stretch the truth, young man. Amy is very impressed with the pictures in your book. She's of the opinion that you could capture an excellent likeness of anyone."

Bud had shown Mrs. Lins his sketches, and had not hidden the fact he could draw, but he'd never tried to pass himself off as an artist. He certainly didn't consider himself one.

"Oh, well, maybe, ma'am, but I'm no artist."

Lois didn't care. "That's not what Amy says, and I'd like you to give it a try. You'll draw a portrait of my daughter. I intend to put it into the post and have it sent to her grandmother in Boston. They have never met, but my mother is growing old and infirm. I do not want her to die without ever seeing her granddaughter. So, you'll do it?"

That's crazy...

Bud was back to stammering and couldn't manage either yes or no.

Which was good enough for Lois. "Excellent. Mrs. Lins can give you directions to my house. I'll expect you on Saturday after lunch. Thank you, Mr. Dalton, good day."

Lois turned on her heel and walked away.

An artist... Sure, why not?

* * *

Saturday arrived, and Bud followed Mrs. Lins's directions to the Abernathy's large house. Bud had learned that Lois's husband owned several local mines and had done quite well. He was respected because of his success, but he had a reputation for being ruthless, sometimes more ruthless than necessary. Mining, he claimed, wasn't only dangerous below ground. There were many dangers above, and they all needed to be dealt with swiftly, completely, and permanently.

Lois met him at the door and led him into the drawing room, a comfortable room filled with pretty and, seemingly, expensive things. They chatted for a moment, then Lois fetched her daughter, Emma.

Emma Abernathy was pretty. At nineteen, she was a year older than Bud, slender and about five feet six inches tall. Her hair was dirty blonde, she wore it shoulder length and behind her ears. Bud made Emma's portrait with charcoal on some fancy paper that Lois had acquired for the event. Emma sat patiently and after several hours Bud had produced an extraordinary portrait.

Lois was delighted with the results and paid Bud a dollar for his work, which was a full day's wages in the mines. Bud was a bit surprised she paid him and he hadn't even considered asking for a fee.

The dollar was very welcome, though. Although he was careful with his funds, there was a constant trickle of expenses and he knew that he could not stay in Joplin indefinitely. He could manage through the year and Jesse should turn up long before then, so Bud calculated that he would be able to manage.

Inevitably, Lois showed Emma's portrait to everyone she knew and Amy Lins began referring to Bud as "her" artist. By the end of his second month in Joplin, Bud had been approached twice more to produce portraits for local women. No one wanted Lois Abernathy to have her own, unique prize.

Shortly after he finished the second portrait he was greeted with a knock on his door, where he was surprised to find a deputy sheriff and an extremely pleased Amy Lins. She breathlessly explained that the county judge in Carthage, fifteen miles north, needed someone to produce sketches for wanted posters and the like. Lois Abernathy had somehow learned of the opening and had "persuaded" the judge that Bud was the perfect man for the job. The deputy was there to somehow evaluate Bud's talent. Five minutes with Bud's sketchbook was more than enough for the deputy.

Thus, Bud became employed. He didn't want the job, but it didn't seem wise to turn Lois down. But the money was certainly welcome and he discovered that he enjoyed the work. While nothing in the league of what he'd done with Emma's portrait, dashing off rough, but good, sketches in just a few minutes was almost a game.

July was on the horizon and Bud was on the lookout for a message from Jesse. Jesse James did materialize on the ninth, but in an entirely unexpected way. Jesse and Frank, along with Cole, robbed the Missouri-Pacific Railroad near Otterville, Missouri.

They simply stopped the train in a steep canyon that had been carved through a mountain and took about $14 thousand. The robbery itself was uneventful, but one of the robbers was apprehended. A young man named Hobbs Kerry, on his first ride with the James Gang, was captured with some of the stolen money and interrogated by the authorities. Kerry buckled and confessed to his role in the robbery and named his accomplices: Jesse and Frank James, Bruce and Cole Younger, Charlie Pitts, William Chadwell, Clell Miller.

The episode made headlines, which was how Bud learned of it. Jesse, never one to miss an opportunity, responded in kind. He wrote a letter to the paper's editor claiming he had nothing to do with the robbery and offered up an alibi, complete with the names of Missouri's most well-respected citizens. The paper, naturally, printed the letter along with an editorial comment supporting Jesse's statement. Not much had changed.

The robbery's publicity, however, ultimately forced the James Gang away from Missouri again. Jesse and the newspapers could claim whatever they liked, but the law had a confession and many lawmen, particularly Pinkerton Agents, were adopting a "shoot first, ask questions later" philosophy toward Jesse and Frank James.

Bud was certain that there would never be a better time to call the gang and retrieve the bars they'd left in the Wichitas. Jesse would certainly need to hide out and lay low, and Bud went so far as to warn Lewis to expect a message at any time. Bud was ready and the time was at hand.

***

Bud was wrong and Jesse refused to lay low. Jesse reenacted his plan from the previous fall, trying to pull authorities and attention away from Missouri. This time he went north to make a ruckus and he succeeded.

On September 7, the gang rode into Northfield, Minnesota, with the intention of robbing the bank there. Northfield was a small town in southern Minnesota, about fifty miles south of Minneapolis. The bank was an easy target, and the newspapers in Minneapolis were sure to make a lot of noise about the James Gang robbing and stealing in Minnesota. The law would be drawn north, the gang would sneak away, and Jesse's game of cat and mouse would continue.

Jesse, Frank, and Charlie Pitts casually walked into the First National Bank while the rest kept an eye on things outside. The plan was to simply rob the bank and make a big scene during the getaway, something dramatic for the newspapers, but things went wrong right away.

A local, J.S. Allen, was suspicious of how Clell Miller was blocking the bank's front door. Allen tried to look inside, which prompted Miller to draw his pistol and chase Allen off, cursing him as he left. Allen sprinted across the street and raised the alarm.

Cole and Miller mounted their horses, attempting to clear the street by shooting their pistols into the air and running their horses back and forth. The dismounted outlaws were doing their part, yelling and threatening to shoot anyone who didn't hide, but none of it worked.

The locals picked up their own weapons and attacked the gang in the street.

Miller was the first one shot, blasted off his horse by a shotgun. Cole rode over and leapt off his horse to discover Miller was just injured—the shotgun had been loaded with birdshot. Cole was trying to wrestle Miller to his feet when he was shot in the leg. Cole fell away from Miller, who was then shot again, fatally this time. Bill Chadwell, fighting from the middle of the street, suffered the same fate moments later.

Nothing was going right inside the bank, either. The bank tellers, Joseph Heywood, Frank Wilcox, and Alonzo Bunker, flatly refused to open the safe. Jesse pistol-whipped Heywood, demanding he open the safe or be killed, which created enough of a distraction for Bunker to make a run through the back door.

Cole, bleeding, hobbled to the bank's front door and informed the robbers inside that everyone outside was getting shot, and they were leaving. Right then. Jesse was furious, but the gunfire could not be ignored and he relented. Before he left, though, he made good on his threat to Heywood, executing him as they departed.

The surviving gang, six men on five horses, fled town as fast as they could. The robbery had lasted just seven minutes and netted the gang $26.70.

An enormous manhunt was mounted, but the gang could not be caught despite several excellent opportunities. Over the course of two weeks and over four hundred miles, the gang rode desperately and the posse pursued relentlessly. Finally, on September 20 near Madelia, Minnesota, they discovered the gang's camp and quietly surrounded them.

Realizing they'd been caught, and under the impression they were going to be lynched, the gang elected to fight and came out shooting. Tremendously outgunned, they were decimated. Remarkably, when the posse searched the camp, they found that Charlie Pitts was the only fatality. All the others had been shot, some for the second time, but all survived and were taken into custody where they would eventually recover.

What the posse did not find, however, were the James brothers. They had separated from the rest at some point, and the Youngers refused to talk. Detectives learned that neither Jesse nor Frank had been wounded and managed to get away clean, their whereabouts unknown. Frank and Jesse had escaped, but the James-Younger gang was broken forever.

***

The details of the gang's previous murders, already reported everywhere beyond Missouri, were suddenly published in Missouri newspapers without any counterpoint at all, not even from John Neuman Edwards.

Bud noticed the tone of all the articles suddenly portrayed the James-Younger gang as a band of villains who had been terrorizing the Midwest for more than a decade. Words like "bloodthirsty" and "cruel" were used instead of descriptions of Jesse's happy-go-lucky demeanor or carefree lifestyle.

Bud's opinion of Jesse, already low at a personal level, wilted further. The Pinkerton Agency's accounts of Jesse were particularly harsh and while Bud took those reports with a grain of salt (they had not caught Jesse, after all, and he was still on the loose), one observation resonated with Bud: Pinkerton claimed nearly everyone the James Gang murdered had southern, not northern, ties. Pinkerton unflinchingly disputed Jesse's public persona and maintained that he was simply a mindless killer. The sooner he was put down, the better.

One of the robberies the papers rehashed was the Huntington robbery from the previous year, the one Bud heard about on his first day with the gang. It turned out that Cole had omitted a considerable piece of the story, and the reason was obvious. It was impossible to tell the unvarnished truth without making Jesse look very bad.

The gang had not dashed from West Virginia to the Dalton's house; they had lingered in Kentucky where Jesse had engaged in a war of words through the newspapers.

A detective named Bligh was in charge of the investigation and pursuit after the robbery, and he managed to generate considerable personal attention during the episode. He enjoyed seeing his name in the paper and being interviewed by reporters and the implied authority it all conveyed. He could go where he wished, whenever he wished, all in the name of the "official investigation."

In the course of one of his interviews, he made a mistake by claiming that the robber who had been killed was none other than Jesse James. Bligh claimed he had identified Jesse's body personally, which was duly reported in Nashville's paper.

The fiction was exposed several days later when Jesse took the opportunity to pummel the detective in a letter of his own. Jesse wrote that not only was he alive and well, but he and Frank were being falsely accused. Bligh, he wrote, held a grudge against the James brothers because of their Civil War activities, and was engaging in little more than wishful thinking. He teased that Bligh was unfit to be called a detective since he had never actually found anything or caught anyone.

Bud then read something that struck him as odd.

> *"I and Cole Younger are not friends, but I know he is innocent of the Huntington robbery, and I feel it my duty to defend him and his innocent and persecuted brothers from the false and slanderous reports circulated about them."*

The comment was in the context of Bligh's incompetence, and the whole world knew the Jameses and the Youngers rode together. The casual reader would take the comment as simply providing an alibi for his partners.

Bud wasn't so sure, though. The remark about Cole and Jesse not being friends seemed a gratuitous slap at Cole and rang a bit true to Bud. The unspoken acknowledgement in the gang was that Cole was the brains but Jesse was the leader. It seemed that some animosity might have seeped into Jesse's letter.

Cole had warned him not to trust Jesse, and although he hadn't elaborated, Bud now understood why. Jesse had said Tom McDaniels was lagging when he was killed, and Bud remembered perfectly well Jesse's displeasure with Bud's slow travel out of the Indian Territory and his threats through the Texas Badlands. It was clear that Jesse would abandon people, and it had happened again at Northfield.

Wait, he thought. Maybe they'd agreed the wounded men would make a stand so the others could escape. But Charlie Pitts had not been wounded at all, and yet he stayed with the Youngers only to be killed. Charlie had remained loyal while Jesse had left two of his oldest "friends" behind to die.

Bud recalled how the Pinkerton Agents had been mere hours behind Jesse when he'd stormed into the yard after Huntington, and the reason they were so close was now clear. Jesse had lingered so he could play games in the papers, then the Pinkertons nearly caught him and chased him to Westport, and then Joplin, and then southward, catching one robber and killing another.

Bud rubbed his scar, entertained at the irony of Jesse James being the one to lag.

He should have been running, but instead he was screwing around with that detective and nearly got caught… then I stepped right into the middle of it. I wonder what Ma thinks about Jesse leaving Cole like that … I reckon Pa isn't going to messenger for Jesse anymore if Ma has any say in it. No more waiting … I'm done with that bastard.

Chapter 2

Bud had received a letter from Lewis about the time the news of the James Gang's destruction was reported. The gist of the letter was to inform Bud that Adeline lost the baby. Bud was sorry to hear that, but also grateful not to be there in person. He much preferred Joplin and had decided to stay.

Bud pulled Mrs. Lins aside to talk.

"My mother was expecting another child, but I've received word that she lost it and her health is poor. Our move south is delayed; no one knows how long."

Mrs. Lins was appropriately concerned. "I am very sorry to hear that. Will you be returning home, or will you remain in Joplin?"

"I'll be staying, ma'am."

"I think that's good," she replied. "Will you stay here, or do you intend to find a permanent residence?"

"Well, as long as the work at the courthouse holds out then I should be able to manage here. I don't believe I'll be able to afford anything permanent, unless it were near the camps, which I don't want. A few more portraits wouldn't hurt, but I think I can manage if you'll have me."

"Excellent. I'd think there would be plenty of work at the courthouse for an energetic young man who reads and writes as well as you can. Perhaps I'll inquire on your behalf."

Bud imagined Mrs. Lins and Abernathy politely raising hell in the county clerk's office until they got what they wanted. He wasn't sure why, but both women seemed to be protective of him and he was certainly grateful for that now.

"You don't need to do that, ma'am. I'll be fine."

"Nevertheless, you are a fine young man and I should not like to see you leave. I'm very sorry to hear about your mother. I'll include her in my prayers."

* * *

Mrs. Lins immediately conspired with Mrs. Abernathy who, through her husband, was indeed able to convince the county clerk to get Bud steady work at the courthouse. The situation there was complicated, but it turned out that Bud was the man for the job.

Bud grasped their system and fit in quickly. The ride to Carthage and back was not onerous, and he was soon a fixture, flitting around town bringing documents from one place to another or dashing off sketches for the marshal. The judges and clerks all liked him, which made Lois and Amy very happy. Between the judges, the sheriff, and the marshals, Bud stayed busy.

It was in the Carthage courthouse where Bud's real education began. For the first time in his life, Bud began to see connections between the things he had always taken for granted. Some were obvious, like Kansas, Missouri, and the war. Others, like Indians, cattle, and Texas were not obvious to him at all, and had to be explained.

The distance between Missouri and Texas was geographically small, but was huge culturally and politically. The differences began with the defeated South, in Missouri, and the still-wild South, in Texas. The border war, and then the Civil War, had taken a terrible toll on Kansas and Missouri. Texas, on the other hand, was vast and relatively untouched by the war. And while post-war Missouri had focused on rebuilding and recovering, post-war Texas focused on different things entirely: cattle, land, and Indians.

The war's most tangible impact on Texas was to deplete the territory of white men, which was perfectly fine with the Indians. A somewhat less tangible effect, but one that came to have an enormous impact, was that without any limiting influence by white men, the wild cattle herds in Texas and New Mexico, sizable before the war, grew to enormous levels.

Those cattle were valuable. A three-year-old steer that could be purchased in Texas for $9.50 could be sold in New York for an astounding $70.58. Anyone who could get Texas beef to market could get rich. The fastest way to market was by railroad, and the closest railheads were just across the Indian Territory in Kansas, where they could be shipped to Chicago, New York, and Boston.

A man didn't even need to purchase the cattle, either, because they were literally roaming the countryside. The first northern cattle drive out of Texas occurred in 1866 and was so profitable that an entire industry was instantly born.

The wild cattle were dubbed "Mavericks," supposedly a jab at a San Antonio man named Samuel A. Maverick. It was said that Maverick had accepted four hundred of the wild cattle as payment for a debt. Not being a cattleman, he never bothered to claim them by branding them, thus all unbranded cattle on the range were "Mavericks" and free for the taking.

Ranches were established to manage the cattle and organize the drives, and to house the men who dealt with the animals, a sturdy new creature dubbed a "cowboy." Cowboys would round up wild cattle, brand them, and eventually drive them to market, which were the Kansas railheads in Dodge City, Abilene, Hunnewell, and Caldwell.

Land should have been easy to understand, but Bud had never considered how anyone came to own land. He'd assumed one just built a house on an unoccupied spot, but he never thought about "unoccupied." Turned out nothing was unoccupied.

Just after the war started, Abraham Lincoln signed the Homestead Act into law. That law allowed almost anyone over twenty-one years old to claim one hundred and sixty acres of public land. All they had to do was live on the land, farm it for five years, and pay land filing fees totaling $18.00. In the years following the war, every hundred-and-sixty-acre plot that could be farmed, ranched, or built upon had been claimed.

Bud grasped that, but the Indians, of whom Bud was completely ignorant, and their land had to be explained twice.

Bud learned that most of the Indian tribes had sided with the Confederacy in the war. When the South lost, the North punished all the southern allies, including the Indian tribes. Each was forced to surrender part of their reservation land in the guise of a sale. The Creeks "sold" three and one-quarter million acres to the U.S. for thirty cents an acre, and the Seminoles were forced to sell their entire holding of over two million acres for fifteen cents per acre, only to "buy" the Creeks' just-sold parcel for fifty cents per acre. The Choctaws and Chickasaws sold their holding of seven million acres for just $300 thousand, or just over four cents per acre.

The Cherokees came off slightly better than the rest because they renounced their treaty with the South. Their holding was known as the Cherokee Strip, and also "the Cherokee Outlet," because it occupied the "strip" of land from the Kansas border south for sixty miles. That land would remain theirs on the condition that other Indians were allowed to relocate there too.

Calls to open the Indian Territory for white settlement came from every direction, and the army, marshals, and Indian agents were constantly escorting white trespassers off Indian land. The government ignored the calls, pointing out that a multitude of treaties governed which tribes owned which lands, that none of it was public land, and that was the end of it.

Except that it wasn't. Bud's favorite part of the tale was how the "reassignment" of the Indian lands after the war had created a problem.

The bureaucrats who consolidated the Indian Territory either did not consult a map or didn't care that their new tribal boundaries left a relatively large "hole" in the very center of the Indian Territory. Since that land was specifically excluded from the Indian reservations, then it stood to reason the Unassigned Lands must be part of the public domain and therefore available for settlement as provided in the Homestead Act.

The Indians and federal government disagreed with that analysis. The Indian Trade and Intercourse Law of 1834 made it illegal for unauthorized people to cross the Indian lands and provided the army, Indian agencies, and law enforcement officers the authority to escort interlopers back across the boundary.

The potential settlers, who had branded themselves "Boomers," were determined. One Boomer in particular, Captain David Payne, was determined to see the new territory opened and had organized to that end.

Payne had dubbed the disputed territory "Oklahoma" and he was filling the papers with stories of clear streams, plentiful timber and game, and deep fertile pastures. Those stories grabbed the attention of every dirt-poor farmer from Indiana to south Texas.

Payne's organization was named The Oklahoma Colony. The Colony's mission was to collect as many would-be settlers as possible on the Kansas border and to settle the Oklahoma Territory en masse. Payne was fond of claiming that the first school would be running within the first three days of settlement. The Colony was small, but there was a great deal of interest. Payne was tireless in traveling the border towns and promoting the idea, particularly in Coffeyville, Independence, and Wichita.

Everyone wanted Oklahoma, but for the first time ever, the Indians held all the cards. Those fabulously profitable cattle drives needed the Indian grass to fatten the herds before they were sold in Kansas. The Indians were perfectly willing to make a deal for the grass and the cattlemen were more than happy to take them up on it.

The Indians would make money, the cattle would get fat, the cattlemen would get rich, and Washington would protect it all by keeping white settlers out.

No wonder everyone's going to Texas. There's nothing left here and they can't have the Indian land. Crazy.

* * *

Bud was surprised one day when Lois Abernathy tracked him down at the courthouse in Carthage. Her husband had come on business, something about testing a new mine. Lois was uninterested in that, but took the opportunity to check in on Bud and to give him some news.

One of Lois's friends in Kansas City wanted a portrait and she'd promised Bud would sketch it. He complained that Kansas City was a very long way to go for a dollar, but Lois waved that away: Charge her five; she will expect to have to pay more.

Bud would have ridden anywhere for five dollars, so Lois helped him make arrangements and he went to Kansas City for Warda Swensen's portrait. Warda had curly hair, so Bud elected to use pencil to better capture the detail. He spent a long time, constantly grinding the pencil lead to a sharp tip to get the shading and detail just right. Like Lois, Warda was delighted and, also like Lois, she showed it to everyone she knew.

Soon, Bud was riding up to Kansas City about once a month for another portrait. That was all right, though, because it gave him an opportunity to visit with his parents.

They were closely following David Payne and his Boomers. Adeline, in particular, was determined to move south. They would never have another opportunity for 160 acres of prime land, and Westport was grating on her. Bud had to remind her that it could be years before the land opened, and one of the judges in Carthage claimed it would never open. Best not to do anything rash.

Adeline's hopes were raised in April 1879 when two officials wrote a lengthy article claiming it was impossible to keep Oklahoma closed. That spurred a rush to the border that would have included Adeline if Lewis had not prevented it. As a compromise, Bud agreed to ride down and have a look.

Bud had an ulterior motive – he had begun thinking about the bars they'd left in the creek and when Lewis asked him to check out the situation in Coffeyville, it clicked. He'd check out the border, and then he would continue on south.

He pulled his old and weathered sketchbooks from under his bed and flipped to his drawings of the mountains, particularly the one he'd dashed off as they left the canyon. It was rough, but Bud thought it captured enough of the geology to narrow down a search.

Bud pulled out his trail gear, too, sorting through it, figuring out what should be replaced and what was still usable. He would definitely need a pistol, and new clothes. The old mess kit was fine, as were the duster, bags, and bedroll. His rifle appeared to be in good shape, perhaps a little oil might be in order, and he was sure the ammunition was still good. He wondered if he could hit anything with it.

Bud went and bought a new Colt Peacemaker along with the gear he needed to replace. The papers told him that the border was crowded with Boomers, so he packed his horse and let everyone know he'd be back in a few weeks and trotted down to Coffeyville, Kansas.

The papers were correct; Coffeyville was packed with Boomers. What the papers neglected to mention was the Boomers had sprinted to the border expecting that it would open and they were not prepared for a lengthy stay. It was instantly obvious that Bud and Lewis could set up a trade in the border towns. Horses, food, clothes ... they needed everything.

Bud was not the only person to perceive an opportunity on the border, and from what Bud could tell, servicing the homesteaders was now Coffeyville's primary industry. Moreover, the towns were engaging in a fierce rivalry to attract as many hopeful homesteaders as possible.

Bud dashed off a note for Lewis and put it in the post to Westport. It was then he discovered there were absolutely no lodgings available anywhere in Coffeyville. Tents were by far the most common dwelling in town, and unless he planned on sleeping in the open, he'd need to find one.

With little other choice, Bud purchased a one-man tent at a grotesque premium and tried to blend in with the Boomers. Since he was alone, without wagon or livestock, he was able to squeeze into a small spot on the south side of town, near the river and just a few hundred yards from the border. He managed to pitch his tent and scrounge up some firewood, looking exactly like a Boomer.

David Payne visited Coffeyville the next day, expounding on the virtues of the Oklahoma lands and lecturing how the government had no standing to prevent them from settling there. He encouraged everyone to join his colony and reap the benefits of an organized push to open the Territory, and he carefully and clearly explained why the Oklahoma lands were available for settlement.

Payne could see that Washington was dragging its feet, and he hinted that he intended to defy the government and create a small settlement on the Canadian river, right in the heart of Oklahoma. His main goal was to prompt the entire party's arrest and to initiate a legal action to solidify Oklahoma's status as public land. If the government would not do the right thing, perhaps the courts would.

The southward flow of people continued. Space was now at a premium and, like everywhere else, the good spots were gone. The new arrivals had to eat, so there was a constant stream of people in the streets buying whatever food and supplies were available. Nearly everything was in short supply and, like Bud's tent, selling at a premium.

Lewis arrived a few days later with Bud's second brother, Grat, leading a string of good ponies and carrying a small supply of beans, flour, and bacon. The food was sold by noon the following day, but the horses, being costlier, were out of reach for the impoverished Boomers. While there was considerable interest in the animals, Lewis could not find anyone able to meet his price.

The horses wouldn't sell, but everything else would, so he and Grat immediately headed back to Kansas City to dispose of the horses and purchase more food staples. They would make four more exhausting trips to the border that spring and would realize a handsome profit as the events on the border unfolded.

A few days after Lewis and Grat departed, the government tried to rein in David Payne. Carl Schurz, secretary of the interior, called upon President Hayes to intervene and Hayes posed the question to his cabinet. They quicky recommended the president take swift and deliberate action.

Hayes obliged by issuing a proclamation stating that no land ceded by the Indians was in the public domain, none was open to settlement, and that any interlopers on Indian land would be expelled by force. The secretary of war, George McRary, confidently advised Schurz that the army had more than enough troops to keep the Boomers out of the Indian lands.

The announcement was not well received at the border. One of Payne's contemporaries, Charles C. Carpenter, openly agitated for defiance. He, like Payne, had founded an organization to settle the Indian lands and was very noisy about it.

Carpenter, while energetic, had a bad reputation. In a similar scenario, Carpenter had organized settlers to immigrate to the Indian Lands in South Dakota following the discovery of gold in the Black Hills, despite the fact the land was set aside for the natives. Carpenter's "invasion" was successful in that the government eventually gave up trying to dislodge the settlers, but the war it started with the Sioux made settling the land quite dangerous.

An editor in a Topeka newspaper described Carpenter as "a scalawag of the worst type, a burly, swaggering, reckless character who would have been lynched by the men he fooled in the Black Hills if they could have caught him."

Now Carpenter was in Kansas, where no one was trying to kill him. He and his wife, conspiring with merchants and businessmen in Independence, moved their headquarters there and urged Boomers everywhere to join them.

The flood of would-be settlers intensified in Independence. Carpenter then made a serious miscalculation. He called for a mass settlement, like in South Dakota, and identified the iron bridge over the river at Coffeyville, mere yards from Bud's tiny camp, as the key crossing point.

Bud had been regarding Carpenter as an amusement up to that point, but the prospect of thousands of illegal homesteaders drawing the army directly to Bud's jumping-off point, at the exact moment that Bud was about to jump, was not amusing at all. Bud simply wanted to slip across the border and make his way along the cattle trail toward Texas, not get swept into whatever Carpenter was up to.

The authorities took Carpenter seriously and dispatched Inspector John McNeal, who knew Carpenter from the war, to confront him in Independence. McNeal explained that the authorities were aware of his intentions and that McNeal was authorized to arrest Carpenter and march him to jail. Or he could depart the Territory, right now. Carpenter departed.

Carpenter's retreat relieved the tension at the border, the troopers returned to their barracks. Bud decided to leave before anyone kicked the hornet's nest and quietly slipped across the border just after midnight. He made his way as fast as possible, keeping to the tree lines and creeks as the sun began to rise.

His maps told him where he needed to go, and he arrived without misfortune. Bud snuck past Fort Sill and after putting a few miles between him and the soldiers there, he found a secluded spot in the hills to make a camp.

He built a small fire to cook some beans and pulled out his old sketchbooks, turning to the pages from the ride south with Jesse. He grimly noted that his sketches closely matched virtually all the terrain he'd seen over the previous twenty-four hours. Specific features were not going to be easy to spot.

Unless they're huge…

It occurred to him that the gap with the thorny mesquite trees was the landmark he should be searching for, not a specific creek or mountain top.

Morning came and Bud made his way south, into the grasslands. He eventually had an excellent view of the mountains and as he continued westward he could make out what appeared to be a huge massif just to the west of a pass between two mountains.

That one.

He kicked his horse into a trot and headed for the gap.

By the time he got there the light was fading and there would be no time to scout that day either. He found a nice spot on the eastern edge of the gap, which, he was pleased to see, was full of mesquite trees. He had just enough time to set up a small camp before the light faded. He dug a shallow hole for a small fire and soon had a small dinner heating.

Aside from insects and a light breeze through the tall grass, the night was nearly completely silent. Bud thought about Payne and his Boomers and considered what he'd seen in Oklahoma. Everything, including Payne's Oklahoma lands on the Canadian River, appeared to be highly desirable. The Kiowa and Comanche land upon which he was currently trespassing was a perfect case in point: unlimited grass and water, plentiful game, and abundant timber. It seemed that Payne's claims about the Indian Territory were true, and he wondered who in their right mind would hold this back from Americans.

The sun came up the next morning, and the sky was perfectly clear and calm. No bears had mauled his horse in the night, so it seemed safe to stoke the fire and make some breakfast. He gathered some sticks and twigs and was about to drop them onto the surviving coals when he chanced to glance toward the west.

A thin finger of smoke was rising straight up into the motionless morning air. Someone was camped on the other side of his gap, hiding in the mesquites. Bud stood next to his un-stoked fire with his handful of sticks and thought about his next move.

Well, let's go meet the neighbors.

Chapter 3

He tossed the sticks aside and kicked some dirt onto the coals, then repacked his gear on his pack horse and leisurely rode toward the other camp. It was situated in a small clearing in the mesquites, which was good for concealment but hid Bud's approach.

Bud peeked through the mesquite leaves to see two men sitting at a small fire, each with his back to Bud. They had quite a bit of equipment stacked about, accompanied by two mules to haul it around. Bud stepped into the clearing, and called out, "Hello, camp!"

Both men jumped like they'd been electrocuted. They whirled around to see who'd snuck up on them so completely, just to find Bud waving to them.

"'Morning! I saw your smoke and came over."

"Jesus Christ," one of the men huffed, "You scared the hell out of me. Who are you, what are you doing here?"

"My name's Bud Dalton. I'm from Missouri."

"Well, he's not the army or an Indian," the second man told the first. "Probably not an outlaw, either. I guess if we're to be snuck up on, we're lucky it was him."

The first man waved Bud into the camp, "Well, come in, Bud Dalton. Have a seat while my heart slows down. I think we have some coffee. You out here alone?"

Bud tied his horse to one of the mesquites and walked into the camp.

"Yes sir, just me. What are you fellows doing out here? You know this is Indian land, right?"

"We do. My name's Elmer, Elmer Kanable." He pointed to the second man. "And that's Bart Richards. We're here to look around a little."

"Well," Bud needled, "if you keep building smoky fires, I don't imagine you'll get to look very much."

"That ain't fair," Bart complained. "If there had been any breeze at all then you'd have never seen us. That's probably the first time in five years the air's been still around here. Hell, the breeze is already picking up."

"I'm just kidding you," Bud laughed. "I'm doing the same thing, and I don't really want any attention either. When I saw the smoke I figured it was best to just come on over instead of running into each other in the brush."

Elmer and Bart were prospectors. They worked together and had been partners for years, both in California and Colorado. They were on their way to Tennessee when they stopped in the Wichitas to prospect for a few days and then move on.

"You think there's gold here?" Bud asked.

"Oh, I'm fairly certain of it," Elmer replied.

"Why?"

"Well, the geology of the area heavily suggests deposits here."

Bud looked around. "Really?"

"Yes, indeed." Elmer warmed to the task of educating a new pupil. "Gold deposits are formed deep underground and over time they're heaved to the surface as mountains are formed. The mountains eventually wear away and the gold is exposed and washes downstream in creeks. The gold is heavier than the rocks and gravel and grit in the stream bed, so it sinks and washes downstream much slower than the other stuff. It often gets stuck under things that don't wash downstream at all, like a boulder."

Elmer pulled a wide, shallow, steel bowl out of a pack and continued, "You use one of these to search. You dig down into the stream bed, then wash away the dirt and rocks. Hopefully you'll find flecks of gold, or if you're lucky maybe a nugget. You keep searching upstream until you find the source. Then you dig it out."

Bud motioned around them. "How do you know which creek to start in? There are probably thousands."

"Good question. It turns out that we often find gold, and silver for that matter, in layers of quartz that form in the margin between two layers of hard rock. Quartz is fragile, though, as far as rocks go, and breaks up quickly when it's exposed. Any gold it's holding can start its way downhill, usually to a creek, where we can find it."

Elmer motioned over his shoulder toward the mountains in the background. "So, if you explore over there, you'll see long sections of rock—hell, they're whole mountains—that are plainly two different kinds of stone. They're different colors and you can see the line where they touch. If you find quartz on that line there's a good bet it'll be loaded with gold. If your creek is running out of a formation like that and is showing color, then that's where you start your mine.

"Then there are rocks that hold gold inside them, but not like how quartz holds nuggets and strands. The gold is part of the rock. For instance, there's a kind of sandy gravel called magnetite. It's unusual because it's black, so if you see a stream bed with black sand, then you need to scoop some of it up and send it to a smelter. If it's magnetite, you might get gold out of the sample."

"Wait, how much gold can be in a grain of sand? Not too much, I guess."

"No, not much at all. We call that ore. It's possible to separate the gold from the rock, and magnetite is one of those rocks. The magnetite comes from veins, too, and washes downstream like any other mineral. You find the vein of magnetite and haul that ore straight to the smelter."

"What's a smelter?"

Bart chimed in, "They crush the rocks up and add some other things that help separate the gold from the rock. When they heat it all up and as it melts the gold separates from the other stuff. Tons of rock goes in, globs of metal come out. Once they get enough, they melt the globs and pour it into a brick-shaped mold."

Bars. You don't say.

"And you say all that's here? On Indian land?"

"Probably. We would need to spend several weeks here to confirm it, but I doubt we could hide that long. Just the geology is enough to warrant a good look, though."

"What about you?" Bart asked. "What are you doing here?"

Bud put down his coffee and returned to his horse where he pulled one of his sketchbooks from the saddlebag. He opened the book and handed it to Bart.

"You're going to laugh, but I'm here to make drawings."

Bart flipped through the pages. "Impressive."

Elmer looked at the sketches and said, "You're risking getting arrested just to draw the countryside?"

Bud nodded, "Yep. I'm pretty sure they'll just run me off; I don't have anything to confiscate. Besides, this is kind of fun, isn't it? I think you two are risking a lot more than me."

"That's probably true. You're not going to turn us in, are you?"

"No, I was actually hoping you'd let me camp here with you."

Elmer and Bart looked at each other and shrugged.

"I guess that would be all right," Elmer replied, then gestured to Bud's horse. "Is that all you have?"

"That's all."

"Well, all right then, let's get you unpacked."

* * *

Bart helped Bud pitch his tent, and they got Bud situated. Once the chores were completed, Bud grabbed his books, a few pencils, his rifle, and picked his way through the mesquites toward, he hoped, a large valley. If he was in the right place, then the mountain in his sketch should be clearly visible once he cleared the thicket.

Ten minutes later he was proven correct. The valley was spread out before him and the tall mountain was exactly where it should be.

All right, this is where we let the mules go. The creek should be a few miles west.

He turned his horse around and picked his way through the mesquites back to the prairie, then trotted westward. He was looking for a large creek with a gorge, and he came upon one in less than an hour.

Bud eased the horse into the creek bed and headed into the gorge, everything unfolding as he recalled. The creek forked, the left branch led to the canyon, sandy creek bed, and the little cave. The main difference, now, was water running directly over where the packs were buried.

He dismounted and walked to the stream's edge and stared into the water. The creek was relatively wide at that point, but the clear water was only inches deep. Was it possible to dig a hole in the bed of a running stream?

He reached down and scooped a handful of sand out of the stream. Within seconds it was impossible to tell where he'd dug.

Nope, I'll have to come back when it's dry … in the summer, I guess. Hadn't counted on this.

Bud looked at his handful of sand and was about to drop it back into the creek when he noticed many of the grains were black, the rest red or light grey. He recalled what Elmer said about black sand being associated with gold and looked closely at the black grains.

Just looks like sand to me.

But it might not look like sand to Elmer. He dropped it back into the creek and washed off his hand. Elmer wasn't the first prospector to poke around the mountains and he certainly wouldn't be the last.

What if they actually find gold?

That gave him pause. Just over a week ago Charles Carpenter made a nuisance of himself attempting to repeat a trick he'd already pulled off in South Dakota: Leverage a gold strike to settle Indian land against government and Indian wishes.

The only thing missing here was the gold strike, but Elmer and his ilk would fill that blank. The same thing would happen as in the Black Hills: a massive influx of prospectors, miners, merchants, and settlers, Indians be damned.

Hell, this is barely a day's ride from Texas – they could turn up overnight. These mountains will look just like Coffeyville in forty-eight hours. Either Elmer or Payne is going to get the wheel turning, and when it starts, it ain't gonna stop. I gotta get this shit out of here before it's too late.

He looked around, imagining dozens of Boomers camped along the creek, then back to the running water. Bud hadn't really considered anything beyond finding the packs, but now the implications of gold in the Indian Territory were beginning to sink in. The longer he thought about it, the more certain he became that he needed to do something.

Bud rode back to camp, thinking. He came to a creek he'd passed earlier. It was too small and there was no gorge, so he'd dismissed it and ridden on. But now he was interested, and paused in the creek bed. The sand appeared to be a dull tan color, just regular gritty sand. He dismounted and dug a handful of sand from the bed, picking through it carefully. Not a black grain anywhere, not a single one.

I wonder where it all came from in the other creek? If Elmer finds that one, he's gonna dig up the whole creek bed ... but this one is invisible. Wouldn't get a second look.

Bud remounted and detoured upstream, back into the mountains. There was no gorge or canyon; this creek simply ran between two hills and there was plenty of flat ground on either bank. About two hundred yards upstream, it curved to Bud's left. Bud rode to the curve and looked around.

The right-hand bank had been widened by the water flowing outward around the curve, creating a sand bar between the stream and the bank itself, perhaps eight feet wide. Trees lined both banks, mostly the scrub oaks common to the area but also a few cottonwoods. Looking back toward the prairie, Bud discovered that the curve, the hills, and the trees completely obscured that location from the plains.

Bud slid off his horse and squatted down to scoop up a few handfuls of sand from the bar. Still no black grains.

This is the place.

He climbed back onto his horse and returned to the prairie, burning the landmarks and landscape into his brain as he dashed off a sketch of the creek and its surroundings.

As he trotted back to Bart and Elmer's camp, he built a timeline in his head. At some point, the creeks would dry up. He would bring a wagon and team to move his gold the short mile to its new hiding place. Sometime in late summer felt best. Then it would be safe to wait and see what happened with the land.

Bud spent the next days scouting and sketching and listening to the prospectors. Elmer and Bart were scouting, too, chipping away at rocks, panning in the streams, and filling small wooden crates with dirt and rocks. They hadn't found anything definitive, but Elmer was very confident. Bud didn't mention the creek with the black sand.

Bud finally packed his gear, said his goodbyes to Bart and Elmer, and headed back to Joplin. He stuck to the cattle trails, traveling briskly and making no effort at stealth. He was approached by the army on several occasions but had no trouble convincing them that he was riding the supply roads bound for Kansas, not invading the Indian Territories. He was scolded a few times, but sent on his way.

The rest of the spring and summer was spent trying to save his pay. He purchased a serviceable buckboard and Lewis lent him a good horse. The wagon was a no-frills affair, basically four wheels, a flat platform, removable sides and tailgate, and a seat. But it was sturdy, low maintenance, and could carry a very respectable load.

The calendar turned to August and Bud decided it was time to try again. That summer had been very hot, so if the creeks were going to dry up at all, they should have by then. He let Mrs. Lins and the marshal know that he would return in a few weeks, and departed the next day.

That was Bud's first experience driving a wagon more than a mile or two. The buckboard's ride was very rough, any speed over a trot was nearly unbearable. Like everything else, the road had been baked mercilessly, every rut, mound, and bump was rock-hard and capable of tossing a wheel into the air if it was rolling too fast.

Certain that he'd be questioned, particularly since he was moving at practically walking speed, he planned to tell the soldiers he was heading for Red River Station, which was where the road, originally part of the Chisolm Trail, crossed the Red River. Since he was lightly provisioned and traveling on the main road, he didn't expect any trouble and that proved to be the case. He was repeatedly stopped and questioned, but always sent on his way.

He crept past Fort Sill four days later and snuck off the supply road, flanking the mountains as the wagon rattled over the prairie. He noted his new creek was bone dry, as were most of the rest. After another mile of bouncing, he found the creek leading to the cave, running just a slight trickle. He turned the wagon up the dry creek and drove it directly to the cave. Aside from the lack of water, it was as he'd left it in the spring. Bud was elated.

He unhitched the horse and tied it to one of the scrubby bushes lining the creek and quickly made a small camp in the cave. Once he completed his housework, he began what he'd come there for. He pulled his shovel off the wagon and walked to where he thought the gold was buried. In minutes his shovel struck something solid, which turned out to be one of the packs.

He widened the hole to expose the packs and wiped away the sand until he found a flap. Without any ado, he cut the straps to the flap and pulled a gold bar out of the pack. He sat back on the edge of the hole, holding the heavy bar in his lap.

Hell, that was easy.

He climbed out of the shallow hole and went to the wagon. He pulled the tailgate off and fashioned a ramp, then tied a rope to the horse's halter and looped the other through the pack's center strap. The horse easily pulled the pack up the makeshift ramp, Bud cut the flap and removed the bars. He repeated the process with the rest and before long all the bars were tidily stacked into a small block. The empty packs went back into the hole where they were reburied.

He pondered his stack of gold, 192 bars, just twenty-one inches long and wide, and fourteen inches high, but weighing over two tons. Theoretically, the horse and wagon might manage the whole load, but Bud was skeptical the horse could pull that much through the loose sand. Furthermore, he was intimate with the wagon by then and was certain that even if the horse could pull the load, the rough ride would tear the wagon to pieces. He would need to make several trips.

The next morning he loaded forty-eight bars into the back of the wagon, about twelve hundred pounds if he figured correctly. Sure enough, the horse struggled to pull the wagon through the sandy creek beds, but had more success over the hard-baked prairie. And, exactly as Bud feared, the rough ride threatened to break wheels, axles, and even the bed itself. He looked around as he crept along, wondering what he should do if the army materialized.

The army didn't show up and he made it to the new creek undetected. He dug a hole in the sand that would accommodate his stack of bars, then unloaded the first batch into the hole. He hurried back and forth between the creeks, loading and unloading as fast as he, the horse, and the buckboard could manage. He unloaded the final batch that afternoon and buried the bars in their new hiding place.

Bud hadn't intended to bring anything back with him, but he succumbed to temptation and held back two bars. He had no idea what he was going to do with them, maybe something would present itself. Just having them was satisfying.

Morning came and Bud leisurely broke camp for the slow ride home. He drove the wagon back onto the prairie and turned east toward Fort Sill, but hadn't gone a quarter mile before the cavalry squad he'd feared materialized and forced him to stop.

"You're quite a ways off the beaten path, sonny," the lieutenant in charge said. "What are you doing here?"

"Just passing through, sir," Bud said. "I'm headed for Missouri and need to go this way to get to the supply roads. This wagon is beating the hell out of me."

"I bet it is. Climb on down. Sergeant, see what he has there."

Bud climbed down and the sergeant rummaged through his pack, pulling out his sketchbook and handing it to the lieutenant, who flipped through it. The sergeant looked through Bud's gear, confiscating his rifle and pistol, and gave some cursory attention to the tent. He ignored Bud's duster, which was rolled up tightly and lashed under the seat. Bud had rolled the bars into the center of the heavy coat, figuring no one would pay any attention to it in the heat. He thought he might puke as he watched the sergeant paw at the tent.

"Nothing," the sergeant reported. "Trail gear is all. Looks like he's just passing through."

"Any whiskey?" the lieutenant asked the sergeant.

"No."

The lieutenant turned to Bud and scolded him, "Son, this is Indian Territory and you're not allowed to be here at all. If you were carrying any liquor or homesteading gear or heavy equipment, we'd confiscate it all and take you to Fort Smith. As it is, we're going to escort you to Fort Sill and make sure you find that supply road. The sergeant is going to hang onto your firearms till you're where you're supposed to be. You gonna behave yourself?"

Bud gulped. "Yes, sir. I sure will, sir."

The army escorted him to the same supply road where Dr. Sullivan had stitched him up and he wasted no time, creeping north as fast as the road and his rickety wagon would allow. He was harassed daily by what seemed to be every army officer in America. No one else searched the wagon, but by the time Bud reached the Kansas border his nerves were completely shot. He was very happy to finally depart the Indian Territory where he would only need to worry about robbers.

Chapter 4

Several days after Bud's return, Jesse James made the papers. Jesse had assembled a new gang and robbed the Chicago, Alton & St. Louis Railroad of $40 thousand. Details were sketchy, but it was suspected that the James brothers had been hiding out in Tennessee and had now re-emerged.

As Bud read the newspaper account of the robbery, he felt vindicated in his decision to move the bars. After the Northfield debacle and then hiding out for over a year, Jesse had robbed another train instead of recalling the surviving gang and dividing the loot. Jesse was clearly uninterested in the bars, or perhaps was afraid of being captured by the army in the Indian Territory. Bud thought that was unlikely but, either way, he felt no remorse about moving the bars.

He managed to surreptitiously weigh one of the bars and confirmed it weighed about twenty-five pounds. He then went to the bank and simply asked how much an ounce of gold was worth. The cashier humored him and informed him an ounce of gold was worth $20.65, then shooed him away. It took Bud a few minutes to do the arithmetic, but he finally calculated that each bar was worth about $7,500.

Fine, but how do you explain where you got them?

Bud scoffed to himself. The answer was, obviously, that he'd stolen them because there's no way a twenty-year-old artist from Missouri, who lived in a boarding house, could ever legally acquire a gold bar, and certainly not two.

That was a problem for another day. Bud rolled the bars tightly into his duster and pushed the heavy wad under his small bed. Based on what he had seen on the border, and how well Lewis had done the previous spring, Bud would need to spend his time and energy acquiring things Boomers could buy. David Payne was still noisy, and was promising more.

He looked around the small room and wondered how much stuff Mrs. Lins would let him store there. It turned out he could store quite a bit, which turned out to be fortunate.

President Hayes had written a memo to Congress that he didn't see any way the Oklahoma lands could be kept closed. Payne used that to promote membership in The Colony, which doubled in new membership. After all, if the president agreed, then it must be so.

Payne announced he would personally lead an invasion of Boomers into the Oklahoma Territory in March. The border towns filled again and Bud was back in business. He and Lewis sold anything that could be eaten or worn. They made good money right up to Payne's threatened invasion date when President Hayes dispatched the army with orders to clear the area and find David Payne. The Boomers trickled away from the border, but Payne was nowhere to be found.

After weeks of silence, he turned up in the *Kansas City Times.*

> *To the Kansas City Times:*
>
> *Please say to any that may wish to know that the public lands in the Indian Territory are not only open to settlement, but settled. We are here to stay; are building houses and making homes. Brought with me 153 men, all of them with good teams. Will have one thousand people here in thirty days. Yours truly*
>
> *D. L. PAYNE*

Payne and a small group had evaded the army and built a settlement on the Canadian River. His claim of having 153 men was a distortion, another unsuccessful attempt to provoke the authorities. He did manage to provoke Adeline, who was ready to join the Boomers at the border right then, but Lewis managed to convince her to stay home and watch what happened.

The army found Payne eventually. After some debate, the entire party was arrested and hauled to Fort Reno where they received a healthy finger-wagging. Payne complained bitterly, but the commander was unmoved. He had orders; Payne and his Boomers were headed back to Kansas.

They had nearly arrived when a courier breathlessly intercepted them. Upon reading the dispatch Lieutenant J.H. Pardee suddenly ordered the entire party to halt and make camp. It didn't take long for Payne to learn the army had delivered him a beautiful gift.

A judge in Kansas had issued a writ of habeas corpus, instructing the army to bring Payne's group before him and to show cause for detaining them. Pardee's new orders were to avoid being served, then get the Boomers back to Kansas undetected.

Once delivered to Kansas, Payne held more, and larger, rallies to tell the tale, emphasizing how the army had proved his point: If the government was right, then they would have had nothing to worry about from a Kansas judge. They obviously knew they were wrong and the Unassigned Lands were in the public domain.

Payne continued: He'd done precisely what he'd threatened to do. He'd invaded the Oklahoma lands, staked claims, been forcibly removed by the army, but was never charged with anything despite the fact he'd warned everyone in advance. The federal government knew it had no case to prevent the settlement of Oklahoma and was using the army to illegally prevent the Boomers from exercising their rights under the Homestead laws.

Thus, to Bud's surprise and delight, Payne announced that he would return to his Oklahoma settlement immediately. The *Kansas*

City Times printed Payne's announcement and the Boomers returned in force. By the time Bud returned with his load of supplies, the towns were as full as they'd been in March.

Determined to keep his promise, Payne led his party over the border. The army met them at their settlement, arrested everyone, and dragged them back to Fort Reno.

First-time offenders were sent back to Kansas, but repeat offenders would be sent to Fort Smith to deal with Judge Isaac Parker. Parker had earned the nickname of "The Hanging Judge" from an episode where he had five convicted murderers hung at the same time. Judge Parker's court had jurisdiction over the Indian Territory, so any crimes committed there would be handled in Parker's courtroom.

President Hayes, hearing of the second invasion, instructed Attorney General Charles Devens to charge Payne and the other repeat offenders of conspiracy to violate the Indian Intercourse Act of 1834. Thus, Payne's wish was to be granted – the courts would decide the fate of the Unassigned Lands.

The Boomers were charged per Devens's instructions. Judge Parker heard the case, and ruled against Payne. He ruled very specifically on a particular claim Payne had staked, craftily avoiding the controversy of the Unassigned Lands. Parker noted that Payne's claim was larger than 160 acres, so even if that land were available, the claim would still be invalid.

Guilty of violating the Intercourse Act, Payne was informed by Parker that he was subject to the penalty spelled out in that statute. That's when the government discovered their mistake: The Intercourse Act offered only one penalty.

First-time offenders were sent away with a warning, repeat offenders would pay a one thousand dollar fine. Unfortunately, Payne didn't have a thousand dollars, nor did he have any property to confiscate. Prison time was not an option and with collection impossible, Judge Parker, ever the pragmatist, simply set Payne free and adjourned court.

While a setback for the Boomers, it was a catastrophe for the Indian agents. They knew that no Boomer could pay the fine either, and Judge Parker had just set the precedent that the fine would be ignored if it were uncollectable. The government's primary legal weapon, the Intercourse Act, was not a deterrent at all.

* * *

Back in Westport, Adeline was about to have her wish granted – Oklahoma was in her future. Or rather, the Indian Territory was. Lewis had become acquainted with a cattleman who needed supplies hauled from Kansas to his ranch in the Cherokee Strip, twenty-five miles south of Coffeyville. Lewis's experience hauling supplies around the border made him an excellent choice for the job and he was quickly hired. Adeline was delighted, too.

The existence of those cattle ranches made the Boomers furious. They claimed the ranches were illegal, but Congress said the transient nature of cattle herds made the question moot. Since the cattlemen were not settling in the Territory, it was not a fair comparison. The Boomers countered that the buildings, barns, and fences were permanent, not transient, but it didn't matter. The cattle lobby was just too strong.

Lewis would be the beneficiary of that strength. He and the family would move to a ranch near the village of Nowata where he would manage the cattleman's shipping. His employer's agreement with the Cherokee Agent ensured that Lewis could come and go as he pleased and could continue supplying Boomers at the border.

Everything was fine until Lewis pulled into their new yard. Adeline had been focused on moving south, closer to Oklahoma, and never even asked about their new quarters. Their new home was considerably smaller than their house in Westport, yet they still had the same number of children and the same belongings they'd just hauled south.

That provoked a spirited discussion, but in the end, there was nothing to be done. Much of her furniture and belongings went into the barn for storage and Adeline made certain that Lewis understood this to be a temporary arrangement. When the Oklahoma lands were opened, she explained, Lewis had better be prepared. Then she told the boys they would be spending a lot of time outside.

Shortly after they moved in, a letter from Frank found its way to them. Frank was moving to Arkansas where he would be a Deputy U.S. Marshal in Fort Smith. He would be tasked with hunting down criminals attempting to escape into the Indian Territory and attending to whatever business Judge Parker deemed appropriate. By the time they read the letter, he wrote, he would probably be there.

* * *

As the rest of his family was relocating, Bud remained in Joplin. He had a good reason – he'd met a girl.

Angela Wood lived in a shack with her parents and brother on Joplin's east side, very close to the mining camps. Her father and brother worked in the lead mines while she and her mother worked in the saloons in town. Between the four of them they were just barely getting by.

Bud met her one afternoon when he decided, uncharacteristically, that he would splurge and have lunch at one of Joplin's taverns instead of at the boarding house. Angela was clearing a table as he walked in, and Bud noticed her immediately. She was slender, just taller than five feet with blonde hair and freckles on her cheeks. She wore her hair tied back and when she looked in Bud's direction her green eyes seemed to sparkle.

Goodness, who is that?

She had some quality that attracted him, although he could not put his finger exactly on what that quality was. He had seen prettier girls, but there was more to this one than just her looks. She moved with efficiency and precision, all of which seemed to accentuate her figure which, while average, was still irresistible to Bud.

Bud discreetly approached the table to get a closer look at her. She brushed past him without a glance and he watched her carry the dirty plates and bowls back to the kitchen. Bud sat at the table and motioned the waiter over and asked what her name was and if he knew anything about her. The waiter said only that her name was Angela and she had worked there for several weeks. Bud saw him talk to her a few minutes later, and saw her glance in his direction.

Bud finished lunch, but lingered with his dirty plate, hoping Angela would come over to clear it. He didn't have long to wait, and as she approached, he stood and picked up his hat. He had no idea what to say.

She stopped at the table and looked at Bud, her bright eyes completely befuddling him. All he could manage was, "Uh, well, um, Miss? Will you be here tomorrow?"

Her eyes drifted over him, pausing on his scar, before she told him, noncommittally, "I'm here about every day."

He nodded, "All right, um, good. I guess I'll have lunch here about every day too. I'll see you tomorrow."

She gawked a little, and responded, "Well, it's a free country."

Bud could feel his face and neck coloring and scurried away before she could ask what was wrong with him.

He kept his word and ate lunch there for the rest of the week. After the third day she asked some people about the boy with the scarred face and learned that he stayed at Lins's and occasionally did a little artwork around town. He was no one dangerous.

Bud finally screwed down his courage and, heart pounding, he asked her if he could walk her home after work. To his astonished delight, she agreed. They worked out the details of what time and where to meet, as well as where he would take her. He left the tavern walking on air.

The walk from the tavern to the edge of the mining camps should only take about fifteen minutes, but the area grew increasingly worse as one approached the camps. Murders and beatings were not uncommon around the camps, so Angela was usually accompanied on her walk back to the shack, usually her mother.

As luck would have it that day, Angela's mother finished her work much earlier and could walk back in daylight while Bud accompanied Angela that evening. Everything was working out nicely. Given the situation near the camps and the time of day, Bud elected to wear his pistol, just in case.

He met Angela at the back door of the saloon and they walked down the street, getting to know each other a little. They managed to turn the fifteen-minute walk into a thirty-minute stroll, in which time Bud learned that her family, which consisted of her, her parents, and her brother Arthur, had moved from a worthless farm in Arkansas to work in the mines, that she had some schooling, and that she didn't care much for Joplin.

She learned he was from Missouri, just across the river from Kansas City, had moved to Joplin to escape his mother, had been kicked in the face by a horse, was an artist, and worked at the Carthage courthouse as much as he could.

Angela's mother, Sarah, was waiting for them at the shack. Bud took off his hat and introduced himself. He saw her eyes linger on his cheek, and then on his pistol.

He told her preemptively, "There's trouble out here sometimes, ma'am. I guess you know that. I think it's best to be careful."

She nodded and said, "Yes, it is. Good evening."

Mrs. Wood ushered Angela inside and left Bud in the dusty street.

* * *

Jesse James robbed another train in September.

Bud didn't care. He was spending as much time as possible with Angela, although it seemed that circumstances were conspiring against him. His working in Carthage limited their time together, and his preparations for Boomers didn't help. When they were together, though, social expectations were their main obstacle. A young woman's reputation was to be protected at all costs, and it was not unusual for a chaperone to watch over unmarried, and even engaged, couples. Public touching between unmarried people was scandalous, and a public display of affection was virtually criminal.

But the rules in Joplin were not as hard and fast as they were in New York or Philadelphia. Their walks from the saloon to the Woods' shack, while technically inappropriate from etiquette's standpoint, merely reflected the reality that Angela needed to get home and it wasn't safe to walk alone. Nevertheless, they were not married and while their unchaperoned walks were tolerated without much judgment, they were rarely really alone.

Neither Angela nor Bud had much of a reputation to damage, but neither wanted to be the subject of rumor or gossip. Both understood that Joplin, or rather the women of Joplin, would not hesitate to repeat, embellish, or even fabricate a juicy story just for the fun of telling it. Still, Bud could occasionally steal a kiss without risking Angela being reported as a prostitute the next day.

Angela could read and write almost as well as Bud. She was an avid journalist, jotting down her thoughts, feelings, and observations much the same way Bud would sketch whatever caught his fancy. She was articulate and her mind was quite sharp, particularly where people, relationships, or motives were involved. She would ask probing questions until she understood the details and personal connections surrounding an event, and was very adept at noticing small gaps or inconsistencies. Joplin's rumor mill had taught her well.

As summer turned into fall, then threatened winter, Bud's feelings for her grew. He had gotten to know her family, her mother and brother seemed decent, but the more Bud got to know Angela's father, the less Bud liked him.

Jediah Wood was a bitter man, blaming his tenuous situation on his wife, children, the mines, his luck, or Arkansas bankers. He was often drunk when Bud brought Angela home, and Bud knew the money he'd used on the bottle would have been better spent on food or clothes. Bud avoided Jediah as much as possible, but he figured dealing with her father was a small price to pay for Angela.

Chapter 5

As Bud was courting Angela, Payne and his Boomers did their best to distract him. Payne had snuck into the Territory with a small team and remained there for several weeks undetected.

That by itself was a victory, but while he was gone, Federal Judge George McCrary of the U.S. Eighth Circuit, in a completely unrelated matter, ruled that the recently adopted Revised Statues of the U.S had nullified Section I of the Indian Intercourse Act, and Section I was where the borders of "Indian land" were defined.

McCrary urgently wrote that based on current law, it was impossible to define any land as Indian land. The press gave the McCrary decision wide circulation and Payne returned just to announce he would lead another invasion in July.

On the heels of the McCrary ruling came news that Jesse James had been shot and killed in Missouri. Bud read about it and shrugged.

Just a matter of time. The son of a bitch had it coming. The world is a better place.

The Boomers cared nothing of Jesse James. McCrary's ruling, however, put another crack in the government's contention that the Indian Territory was off-limits. Payne pointed out that if the whole Territory could be abolished by accident, then surely laws passed intentionally should hold sway. Payne kept fanning the flames and Bud and Lewis kept selling to any farmer who moved to the border. They had their best year yet.

One reason for his success was Bud had noticed people were having a hard time finding firewood. Earlier Boomers had stripped the creeks and now there was very little to be had. While he was falling in love with Angela the previous year, Bud hired several boys to gather wood from the creeks around Joplin, cut the sticks into consistent lengths, and deliver it to Bud. Bud stored the ever-growing stack of wood behind Amy Lins's small barn until he was ready to haul it to the border. Bud and Grat sold tons of wood to the Boomers, all at a tremendous profit.

* * *

Depleted of firewood and needing a break, Bud returned to Joplin and Angela. He met her at the tavern to see if she wanted any company on the walk home that night. She did indeed.

When they arrived at the shack, they discovered her father, rather than her mother, waiting for Angela. Wood wasn't quite drunk, but close, and there was a man waiting with him. Angela's mother was standing in their doorway and appeared to be near tears.

What the hell is going on here…?

Bud pulled Angela up short, keeping several yards between themselves and Wood. Bud wasn't sure what was going on, but Zack's boot had taught him that a little distance was often a handy thing. He nodded to Mrs. Wood and touched the brim of his hat, then spoke to her husband.

"Good evening, Mr. Wood."

Wood ignored him and slurred to Angela, "Angela, gather your things, we've found you a husband. This here is Arkady Arturovich. He wants to marry you, and we've made a deal."

Arkady appeared to be about thirty-five and while not particularly tall, perhaps a little taller than Bud, he appeared to be quite fit. He was standing with his arms crossed and Bud could see his muscular arms and thick neck. It was his dark eyes and dead expression that drew Bud's attention, though.

Angela was dumbfounded. "I'm sorry, what … you've done what?"

"You're gonna get married," Wood slurred. "Arkady is going to be your husband. We've worked it all out."

Angela disagreed. "No, he isn't. You don't get to pick my husband!"

Wood took a wobbly step toward the shack's door and pointed. "Go on, girl, get your things. Arkady has agreed to pay us fifty dollars and get me a better job at the mine if you marry him. It's best for everyone. We need the room and the money, plus you should already be married by now, anyway. Arkady is better than anyone you're going to get here, so it's best for you too."

The last remark irritated Bud considerably.

No one better? I'm standing right here!

Wood slurred on, "So that's what's going to happen. Come on. Let's get this over with; it's best."

Angela was angry by then, shouting, "No! You can't do this, you can't choose! You can't make me and I won't go!"

Mrs. Wood began to sob in the doorway, and Wood advanced a step.

"Yes, you will, damn it! Right now!"

Nope, this is bullshit.

Bud put his right hand on his pistol, stepped in front of Angela, and held up his left hand to stop Wood. He felt very calm.

"Get back, Wood. No one's marrying Angela."

Wood froze. The other man, Arkady, had never moved, not even a little, through the entire exchange. Angela's shout had attracted attention, though, and people were coming outside to see what was happening.

Watching Bud, Arkady said to Wood, in heavily accented English, "You not tell me other man want her."

"Forget about the kid. We have a deal."

Just as Arkady said, "Hmm. Kid have pistol," Bud drew the .45 and cocked it, pointing it at Wood's chest.

"You can't sell your daughter, Wood."

To his credit, or perhaps the alcohol's, Wood didn't flinch.

"Dalton," Wood sneered, "you've just made a bad mistake. Arkady here is an important man at the mine. He gets what he wants, and he wants her."

Bud scoffed. Keeping his gun on Wood, Bud said, "Well, Mr. Arkady, I'm not an important man, like you, but my brother is a deputy U.S. marshal. Plus, I work for the federal judge and the marshal in Carthage, and we're on pretty friendly terms. So, even though I'm not important, I think I can make a few things happen too.

"I bet I can telegraph Fort Smith, calling my brother here to look for you. I reckon he can be here in a few days. I'll bet you the same money you're buying Angela with that I can get my brother to drag your ass to Fort Smith and keep you there till next Christmas. You still going to be important then?"

Arkady was unmoved. "Few days long time."

"Let's try this, then. The next time I see you, I'll kill you."

Arkady spit into the dusty street. "You not see me, kid."

Oh yeah?

Bud shifted his aim from Wood to Arkady and tightened his finger on the trigger.

"I see you now, you piece of shit. We don't sell women in Missouri, and this one is not for sale anywhere."

That comment attracted the attention of the women in the crowd, one asking, "What did he say about selling women?"

Arkady didn't like the way the situation was unfolding, and his stone-like expression was beginning to crack. Still, he maintained his control. Bud was about to press him when Wood, now that he didn't have a gun pointed at him, reinserted himself.

"Calm down, Dalton, this has nothing to do with you. You—"

Bud barked at him, "Shut up, Wood. You're going to get what you want, but right now Arkady and I are talking."

Wood shut up.

"Mrs. Wood," Bud called to Angela's mother, "please gather Angela's things and bring them out."

Angela didn't like that. "Bud?"

Bud turned his head slightly, keeping his eyes on Arkady the whole time, and replied quietly, over his shoulder, "Trust me."

Mrs. Wood returned a few tense minutes later, carrying a small bag. Jediah was seething by then, but Arkady had re-solidified his visage.

Bud told Angela, "Make sure everything you need is in it."

She dug through the bag, noting that her mother had included her journals. Sarah obviously believed that whatever was about to happen was going to be permanent.

Angela confirmed she had what she needed, so Bud told Arkady and Wood, along with the considerable crowd that had gathered, "All right, here's my offer: Mr. Arkady, you get to keep your fifty dollars and be an important man at the mine. Wood, you get to live. In exchange, Angela is coming with me."

Arkady didn't even twitch, but Wood couldn't stand it anymore and tried to rush Bud. It was pitiful. Bud waited patiently for Wood to get in range, then swung the heavy pistol as hard as he could, aiming for Wood's head. The pistol's long barrel caught Wood in the temple.

He went down, but was not unconscious. Bud stepped to his right, away from Wood, and snapped the pistol back to Arkady's chest. The crowd behind Arkady dove to either side, out of the potential line of fire.

"Huh, I'm surprised it didn't go off. You have one second to walk away, because when he comes at me again, I'm going to shoot you both. You first, then him."

Arkady raised his hands and stepped back, his expression finally morphing into an unmistakably evil smile. "OK. Have it your way. I see you later, kid." He walked backwards several steps, then turned around and sauntered away like he was going to the store, his hands in his pockets.

Jesus. Watch out for that guy.

As Wood was trying to get to his feet, Bud told Sarah, "You need to take him inside, Mrs. Wood. I don't want to shoot him, but if he tries to touch me or Angela, I'm gonna. Angela is never coming back here."

Bud yelled at Wood, "You hear that, Wood? Angela is not coming back here. I don't want to hear about you or that Arkady asshole sniffing around or bothering her anywhere in town. You hear me?"

Wood was holding the side of his head. "To hell with you kid, I'm going to kill you."

"Uh-huh, good. We understand each other, then. Angela, we're leaving now."

Bud began backing away, the gun still pointed at Wood. The people who'd gathered behind them stepped away so they could pass. When they had fifty or sixty feet of separation, Bud holstered the pistol and turned around to walk normally, checking behind him every few steps.

Bud's calm disintegrated once the confrontation was over. His heart was racing, his pulse thundering in his ears. Angela was clinging to his arm with both hands; he could feel her shaking.

"Bud, what are we going to do?"

"We'll figure something out. It'll be all right."

Maybe.

Bud wasn't so sure. He was certain Mrs. Lins was not going to permit Angela to stay with him, and he was right. There was no scenario where she would allow Angela into Bud's room.

As Amy was detailing her outrage, Bud had a thought.

"Mrs. Lins," he interrupted, "do you have a vacant room? Is there a room she can rent?"

She paused. "Well, yes. Yes, I do."

"Well, that solves the problem, doesn't it? Can't she be just another border?"

"I'm not sure it does. It seems to me that having you two in the same house is nearly the same as being in the same room. People will talk. I won't have it."

"No, ma'am," he argued, "Angela was being forced into an arranged marriage – her father had agreed to fifty dollars to let a foreigner marry her. Mrs. Lins, she was being sold! Angela is a victim and she has nowhere to go, so you'd be providing refuge. It all happened in the middle of the street in front of a hundred people!"

Angela's pending sale did not sit well with Mrs. Lins. She considered Bud's words as she examined Angela, standing to the side, clutching her single bag with both hands.

The older woman's face softened and she sighed. "All right. She can have the room but I want your promise that you'll behave yourselves."

Angela gasped and began to sob with relief. "Oh, yes! Yes, ma'am, I promise. Thank you."

Bud agreed too.

Mrs. Lins looked back and forth at them, and sighed again, this time in a heavy, what-have-I-gotten-myself-into way. "It's all right, dear. Come with me, and I'll show you your room. Everything will be fine."

After Angela was settled in her new quarters, she sat down and opened her journal.

> *Had a horrible night. Pa tried to make me marry someone from the mine, a Russian, I think. He seemed terrible, I can't imagine what it would be like to be with him. Ma couldn't do anything but Bud stopped it all. He had to hit Pa with his gun, and threaten to shoot the Russian. Then brought me to the boarding house. I don't know what I'd have done if he had not been with me. Mrs. Lins is nice, but she didn't want to let me stay. I want to be with Bud, but if he doesn't want me then I don't know what I'll do. I think he does, but I'm still scared.*

At the same time, Mrs. Lins went to see Bud and inquired as to his intentions, and Bud told her that he would marry Angela if she would have him. Beyond that, he had no idea. Mrs. Lins approved of an engagement, but informed him that it was time for him to find his own place. She loved him like a son, but she wasn't wild about the huge stack of firewood behind her barn, nor the large pile of stuff in his room, and now Angela's presence was a long step over the line. Time to go.

After breakfast the next morning, Bud hitched his wagon, strapped on his pistol, loaded his rifle, and took Angela with him to Carthage. As they trotted out of Joplin, Angela slid over next to Bud, put her hand on his thigh, then leaned over and kissed him on the cheek, precisely the scandalous behavior Amy Lins had been concerned about.

The point of the trip to Carthage was exactly what he'd threatened Arkady with. He made his way to the telegraph office and had a message sent to Fort Smith requesting his brother Frank to come to Joplin right away, Bud was having a problem with a local. They received a reply within the hour.

Leaving immediately. Two days most.

Bud and Angela took their time returning to Joplin. Bud told her that even though he didn't have fifty dollars, he hoped she would marry him instead of Arkady, which made her laugh.

"Your credit is good with me. You I'll marry."

Two days later, Frank Dalton rode into Joplin and was directed to Amy Lins's boardinghouse. Bud and Frank caught up for a while, then Bud explained the situation with Arkady and Wood. Frank asked a few questions, then brought a small stack of wanted bulletins for them to search in the hope that Arkady was wanted somewhere.

Arkady was not wanted, but Frank had a backup plan. He rode out to the Wood's shack first thing in the morning and questioned

Wood on Arkady's whereabouts. Wood refused to cooperate at first, but Frank explained that it had been illegal to sell human beings for several years now. Since the transaction was not concluded, Frank wasn't sure if Wood, while still a detestable worm, had done anything illegal.

However, Wood's customer, Arkady, had offered money and was guilty of conspiracy to engage in slavery, which was definitely a crime, at least crime enough for Frank. Wood's degree of complicity in that charge would depend on his behavior in the next two seconds. The worm turned and Frank was shortly on his way to find Arkady.

Arkady, predictably, was unmoved by anything Frank had to say. Frank told him that if he wouldn't talk now, Frank would have no choice but to take him to Fort Smith and work it out in front of Judge Parker.

Arkady replied that he wasn't going anywhere and that Frank should go back to wherever he'd come from or he would suffer the same fate as Bud. The last syllables were hanging in the air as Frank hit Arkady, hard, in the center of his face.

Arkady staggered, but didn't go down. Frank followed up with his favorite tactic, a firm kick to the crotch. That worked perfectly and Arkady went to his knees. Frank hit him in the face again, then cuffed the helpless man's hands behind his back and dragged him, bleeding, into the street.

Frank tied Arkady's feet to the stirrups to prevent him from attempting to jump from his horse, then tied the reins to his own saddle, and trotted to Carthage where Arkady was thrown into a cell. No one at the jail asked about charges; a deputy U.S. marshal with a trussed prisoner was more than enough. Frank would have him released on his way back to Fort Smith.

By the time he returned to the boarding house, the day was mostly over. Bud was incredulous at Frank's story—he'd had no idea that his threat to Arkady could actually be carried out.

Angela felt like a weight had been lifted from her shoulders. Frank told her that he didn't think she'd hear from her father again, particularly when he learned what had happened to Arkady. Mrs. Lins was horrified when Angela grabbed Frank around the neck and kissed him on the cheek. That sort of thing simply didn't happen on the porch.

Chapter 6

The immediate problem had been dealt with, but finding new quarters was still a concern. Neither Bud nor Angela had any idea where to start, but Mrs. Lins, ever connected to Joplin's nervous system, was there to help. She introduced Bud to a young man named Alex Keyworth whom Mrs. Lins had known since he was born. Alex's mother had recently died and Alex had convinced his father to return to Texas with him.

They were very anxious to be on their way but needed to dispose of the small farm on Joplin's north side before they left. Mrs. Lins thought perhaps Bud and Alex could reach a mutually beneficial arrangement.

The farm was small, only forty acres, but the house, while old, was structurally sound and accompanied by a small barn. Angela was very enthusiastic; the four-room farmhouse was a mansion compared to the shack she had shared with her family.

Bud pointed out that it was considerably larger than what they needed, it was definitely more than he could afford, and it came with forty acres he had no intention of working. He told Alex that he could not pay anywhere near what it was worth.

Alex wanted to get his father to Texas as soon as possible and countered that if Bud could pay cash, he could have the place for one hundred and fifty dollars. His parents had originally claimed the land and built the house, then sold the other 120 acres to a mining company years ago. Alex told him his father was not losing any money and getting on the road immediately was worth whatever the difference a better offer might bring.

No one could come up with a reason not to conclude the sale, so a few days later Bud delivered fifteen ten-dollar gold coins, the bulk of his net worth, and Alex delivered the deed to the farm. They took the paperwork to the land office in Carthage and registered the deed in Bud Dalton's name.

Never one to miss an opportunity, Angela teased Bud, "And you said you didn't have fifty dollars!"

Two days later, on October 17, Bud and Angela married and moved into their new home. Since neither of them owned anything, there wasn't much to move beyond some personal effects. Angela immediately made a pallet in the center of the bedroom floor. Her intentions were clear as she pulled her dress over her head.

"We're married. Get over here!"

After a few days of marriage Bud began to suspect he knew what the intangible quality that originally drew him to her might be.

Angela continued to work in the saloon. Beyond the slight income she earned, the job allowed her to stay in contact with her mother without having to go to the shack. Mrs. Wood missed Angela, and was disappointed she missed the small wedding, but Wood refused to allow her to go.

Wood, already bitter, had begun drinking more. The confrontation with Bud, and then his brief visit with Frank, had proven just how little control he really had, so he compensated with more whiskey which he could not afford. Angela was worried for her mother and brother, but there was very little she could do. Just as Wood prevented her mother from attending the wedding, Bud refused to allow her to return to the shack for any reason. The saloon was the only way Angela and Sarah could speak in person.

The effort and expense necessary to get their house running surprised Bud. While he didn't have to pay Mrs. Lins anymore, he did have to purchase food, housewares, and furniture—everything from knives to blankets had to be acquired. He was able to get an old bed, a side table, and some miscellaneous items from his parents' barn, which helped, but it seemed his world was now a never-ending stream of expenses.

As the rooms required furniture, the fireplace required wood, which in turn required an axe and saw. Thankfully, he had a horse and wagon to haul the wood, but the horse would need hay for the winter. He suddenly knew exactly how the Boomers felt, needing to purchase every vital item to simply get through the week.

A few exhausting weeks later, they were sitting in front of the fire when Angela offhandedly asked him if he'd heard about Frank James.

"Everyone has heard of Frank James."

"No, no. Of course, you've heard of him—I asked if you'd heard about him. In the paper."

"Oh, no, I didn't. What happened to Frank? Was he shot too?"

"He's about to go on trial for murder. He turned himself in a few weeks before we got married."

Bud had been spending every moment cutting and hauling wood and hay, and outfitting their house, so he'd spent very little time at the courthouse and was not privy to the latest scuttlebutt. He had not heard anything about Frank James.

"Murder? Huh. Jesse was the one prone to killing. I wonder what happened. And you say Frank turned himself in?"

She was looking at him strangely. "Yes, to the governor himself. Why do you act like you know them personally?"

Oops...

Bud nearly deflected her, but reconsidered.

"Well, I do know them personally. Or did, I suppose, with Jesse killed. Frank, Jesse, and all the Youngers."

"You're pulling my leg now. How in the world could you know them?"

"It's true. My mother's maiden name is Younger, and Cole Younger is my cousin. My father used to help out Quantrill's and Anderson's boys during the war; that's how we came to know Jesse and Frank."

Angela was astonished. "You're teasing me!"

"Nope. It's all true."

"Oh, my goodness. I can't wait to tell Mother!"

Whoa, hold on, there.

"No, no, please don't tell anyone. I don't want, hell, we don't need that kind of attention. Jesse James was a bad man and an unbelievable asshole. We don't want to be associated with any of them at all, even by accident. Please, let's keep that to ourselves?"

"All right. But it's very exciting. I've never met anyone famous before."

Bud snorted. "You still haven't."

* * *

Their conversation sidetracked Angela throughout the next day. She went through it in her head, over and over again. The more she thought, the more she wondered about her new husband. Bud had gone to Carthage, and by the time he returned she had some questions for him, and she cornered him after dinner. She was ready.

"Bud, where were you when you got kicked by the horse? When you got your scar?"

Eh...what? Where was I?

Bud had never considered any detail behind his scar. Kicked in the face had always been more than enough explanation.

Bud's mind was blank, nothing was coming to him. "Well, it was south of here in the Indian Territory. An army doctor stitched me up on the supply trail to Fort Sill."

"You told me you got kicked when you were seventeen. So, you were in the Territory when you were seventeen? What were you doing there?"

Running from the Mexican Army...

Bud tried to think fast, but he had nothing and fumbled, "The truth is I was down there when I shouldn't have been, and this scar is what I have to show for it."

Angela was having none of that. "Bud, honey, I asked what you were doing there, not if you were where you should be. How did you get kicked by the horse? Was it your horse?"

"Why is it important how I got kicked? Or which horse did it?"

"Because I've been thinking about it all day. I think you know Frank James a whole lot better than you told me last night, and I think he was mixed up with your scar somehow."

How the hell did she come up with that?

Bud gawked at her. "Why in the world would you think that?"

"Because of the way you handled your gun when you dealt with Pa and that Arkady man. Not that many people even have a gun. But you seemed to know what you were doing, and now you're friends with the whole James Gang. You got your scar when you were seventeen, and that was just a few years ago, and now you just told me it happened in the Territory, which I didn't know before. You just mentioned, 'which horse,' so you weren't alone. The timing works too … it all seems to go together. You were in the James Gang then, weren't you? But you got kicked and missed everything after."

He stared at her, wide eyed, slack jawed, and absolutely astounded. He shook his head. "Well, I'll be damned. All right, then, I'll tell you all about it. It's not exciting, but here's what happened."

They sat at their flimsy kitchen table and Bud told her how he'd pestered Cole and how he finally barged his way into the gang. He described the ride down to Texas and the Indian Territory and told her about the tension between Cole and Jesse and how Jesse's tactics were ultimately adopted. He omitted the parts where he'd been to Joplin before, the weeks they'd spent in Roswell, or riding into Mexico, but was detailed about what he saw both in Texas and the Indian Territory.

She re-examined his scar as he related the fight with Zack, his fever, recuperation, and his decision to leave Westport for Joplin.

When he finished, she said, "Goodness me, I guess you do know the James brothers."

He replied, "A long time ago. That's why I tell people I was kicked by a horse. I don't want to be lumped in with them even though I never did anything."

She looked at him sternly and said, "Now, that's a big lie, and stop saying it was a long time ago. Who did you rob in Texas?"

Bud was about to object, but before he could make it worse, she pointed out the gap his omissions had created.

"Jesse sent y'all south to make a lot of noise and bring the Pinkertons out of Missouri. You had your fight with Zack on the way back. So, you robbed someone in Texas. Who?"

Bud stared at her, flabbergasted again.

Christ almighty, don't ever try to keep a secret from this woman. Time to fold.

"Sit here, I'll be right back."

He went to the tiny closet where his trail gear was stored, unrolled his duster, and pulled out one of the bars. He lugged it into the kitchen and set it on the table, which creaked ominously.

"Not Texas, Mexico. We robbed Mexicans. This is part of what we got."

"Oh, my dear Lord Jesus. Is that gold?"

"Yes."

"Can I touch it?"

"Sure, it won't bite."

Angela tried to pull the bar toward her, then put some effort into it as she realized how much the small bar weighed. The table creaked and swayed, but didn't fall down.

"How much is this?"

"About twenty-five pounds. Somewhere short of eight thousand dollars, I think. I don't really know for sure."

"And this is just part?"

"Yes."

"How much more is your share?"

He sat back in his chair, which also creaked ominously, "Well, all of it, I guess. There are almost two hundred more buried in the Indian Territory. I don't see any reason to share it, to hell with Jesse James."

"Well," she replied, "he's dead and doesn't get a vote. The rest of the gang, though … what about them? Aren't they going to want their share?

Bud pictured Zack, and smiled. "Probably. It wasn't easy to find, but if they do manage to find the creek they won't get the bars because I moved them."

"Goodness." Angela's mind began to get traction again. "Wait, why we are tight on money if there's a brick of gold on the table?"

"That's the problem. You can't spend a brick, and if you take it to the bank they want to know where it came from."

"Oh ... Right, I see. So, we need to figure out how to turn this into money without raising suspicion."

Jesus, she's smart.

"Yup. And we gotta to eat in the meantime. So, you carry dishes, I ride to Carthage, and we sell stuff to the Boomers. We'll figure something out, but for now we need to keep on."

Chapter 7

Down at the border, Payne had become tied up in legal shenanigans as both plaintiff and defendant, but none of that meant the invasions would cease. While Payne was tending to his legal problems, he handed control to his vice president, William L. Couch, who immediately organized a new invasion.

Couch led a small group south in early August. They were intercepted and sent to Fort Reno where they were held for a week, then first-time offenders were sent back to Kansas. The repeat offenders were sent south, this time to Texas.

The troopers escorted Couch and his team southward where, upon crossing the Red River, the Boomers simply turned around and returned north with the troopers who had just escorted them south. The troopers' orders had been only to escort the Boomers across the river and, having completed that, they were happy to ride with the Boomers on their return.

The two groups were apparently quite friendly, sharing their camps and supplies with no hostility at all. The Boomers said their goodbyes to the troopers at the North Canadian. The troopers returned to Fort Reno and never said a thing about the Boomer's return, only that they'd followed their orders and had escorted the illegal squatters to Texas.

The Boomers returned to their Oklahoma settlement and spent the next week unmolested, staking claims and surveying before riding leisurely back to Kansas. No one knew they'd been sent to Texas, only that they'd gone to Oklahoma and returned on their own terms.

* * *

Angela quit the saloon to help Bud with the Boomers and discovered that she enjoyed it immensely. She loved chatting with the women and found the whole experience quite sociable. Both she and the Boomers knew the prices were high, but under the circumstances a premium was to be expected.

For commodities like flour, bacon, and corn meal, Bud's prices were inflated, but negotiable. A bag of flour that would cost ten cents in Kansas City went for fifteen cents at the border, but Bud would ask for twenty. The Boomers would always negotiate and meet somewhere in the middle. Angela and Bud were not the only outfitters in town and if they could not agree on a price, then their prospective customer needed only to walk down the street to find someone who would. Angela occasionally recommended particularly disagreeable people do just that, but more often she would shave off a penny or two for friendlier women or those who badly needed that extra penny.

Prices on things like firewood, however, were rigidly set because there was nowhere else to find it. To avoid haggling, Bud sold the wood in stacks of fifty pounds each for fifty cents, and estimated each bundle cost him about five cents to gather, cut, bundle, and haul to the border.

Bud and Angela finally exhausted their inventory and hustled back to Joplin and their snug farmhouse as quickly as possible. In six weeks of hard work they had each earned more than most Joplin residents did in a year. Angela confided to her journal:

> *I'm glad to be home, Caldwell and Coffeyville were a lot of work and it was so very hot. But, it was wonderful! Bud says we did*

well this year. He said that every stack of wood makes half of what a miner earns every day, and we sold 400 stacks! I loved the people, they are not so different from Ma and Pa, and truth told some of their tents look to be much better than our old shack. I think about them a lot now, I didn't know how unhappy I was. Without Bud I would still be there, or with that horrible Arkady. I suppose that's how the girls end up selling themselves, no other choices. I am truly blessed.

* * *

Angela's brother and mother were not blessed and probably would have described their situation as more like cursed. The curse was, of course, Jediah. While Angela and Bud were at the border Arthur and Sarah weathered the storm. Angela's next entry was somewhat grimmer:

Mother went through hell while we were away. Apparently, Daddy was spending all their money on liquor and hasn't been sober for months. Last week he tried to hit Mother but Arthur stopped him and threw him out of the house. They had another shouting match in the street, then Daddy went to the camps to keep drinking. The next morning the Carthage Sheriff brought his body to the house so Mother could claim it, seems he was knifed trying to steal a bottle. They buried him day before yesterday and Bud says the world is a better place now. That made me mad at first, but I think Arthur thinks so, too. Mother claims to be sad, but she seems relieved. Bud reminded me who tried to sell me to a Russian, and says me being mad is really me feeling guilty for not feeling bad. I think Bud's more perceptive than I give him credit for.

Jediah's demise opened the door for Angela and Sarah to see each other as often as they wished. Bud reminded Angela to keep their secrets and she agreed not to tell anyone anything. She did not tell Bud that she often confided those secrets to her journal, and would do so for her entire life.

* * *

Word of Couch's successful incursion spread across the border towns and Boomer enthusiasm raced to even higher levels. Payne and Couch fanned the flames through the summer and fall, helped by their friends in the press, and expectations were very high. Many people believed 1884 was the year the Boomers would prevail.

The Daltons worked continuously all the way to early November. Bud and his team of wood cutters furiously grew the stack behind the barn, Angela packed and stored dried beans, peas, cornmeal, and anything else that would keep, plus tarps, tack, buckles, and leather to repair harnesses, and so on. The Boomers needed everything, and there was no time to waste.

They were convinced the next year would be a huge year on the border, and they were determined to take advantage of it.

* * *

It proved to be exactly that. The border towns were overflowing and several papers estimated the number of wagons in Coffeyville alone to be well into the thousands. The Daltons worked night and day, selling tons of goods to the Boomers for as long as they stayed.

Spring of 1884 sent Payne to Washington while Couch led the largest invasion to date into Oklahoma. Even as that convoy left, the number of wagons at the border grew larger and new arrivals rolled into town every day. Bud, Angela, and Grat worked long days, selling anything the Boomers could pay for while Lewis frantically drove his team between Nowata, Coffeyville, and Kansas City over and over again.

News floated north that Couch's invasion had been halted, but the tide of humanity washing into Coffeyville and the other border towns only rose. Families from Ohio and Kentucky were arriving and inquiries from Virginia, Maryland, and New York were received at the Boomer headquarters.

The Daltons were exhausted but doggedly continued their cycle of delivery and sales until June when Payne, back from D.C., led an enormous wagon train over the border. Bud and Angela had been working without a break, were out of almost everything, and were bone-weary.

Angela was very convincing. "Payne's left and Couch is arrested. Let the damn border take care of itself. Let's go home; it'll be here when we get back!"

They spent the summer and fall tracking Payne's adventures in the news. Things felt like they were building to a climax, and they were.

Despite the size of Payne's wagon train, the army failed to intercept them. Payne had taken a new route and founded a new town, named Rock Falls, out on the prairie. This time, though, the Boomers prepared defenses and by the time the army arrived, they discovered they were outgunned.

Reinforcements were called and the commander informed the Boomers that they would get the gunfight they were asking for. That unnerved many of the Boomers, who packed their wagons and fled with the army's blessing.

No longer outgunned, the army rounded up the rest and sent them to Fort Smith, which began the chaos.

Another Kansas judge had dispatched another deputy sheriff to serve a warrant on the squad escorting Payne to Fort Smith. This time the deputy prevailed, sneaking into the army camp and serving the papers to the captain in charge.

The big news was that the army ignored it, sent the deputy away, and dragged the Boomers before Judge Parker. The deputy returned to report that the army had clearly been mistreating the prisoners and had refused the judge's warrant. Tempers were flaring everywhere, but Judge Parker dodged it all by simply sending everyone back home.

September delivered Payne a gift – one of his lawsuits would proceed, and it was the most important one. Judge C.G. Foster agreed to hold a trial in Topeka to resolve the status of the Unassigned Lands. Payne had finally gotten his wish and the trial would proceed in November.

On November 18, 1884, Judge Foster ruled that the Unassigned Lands fell squarely into the public domain and the Boomers could not be prosecuted, regardless of how the army chose to read the law. All charges and indictments against any Boomer were quashed and Foster ruled the army had no standing to remove any Boomers from the Unassigned Lands.

It was an enormous victory for Payne and the Boomers, and the festivities were nonstop for a week. Then, nine days after Foster's ruling, they suffered a blow equal to their victory. While he was having breakfast with his wife and Boomer leaders, Payne suffered a massive heart attack and died in the dining room.

The Boomers' grief was profound, and his death created a brief period of chaos in The Colony. Order came quickly, however. Couch immediately took control and was elected president of The Colony, and thus the de facto leader of the Boomer movement. He vowed to continue what Payne had started and would eventually open the Territory, much to Bud and Angela's relief.

Payne's death came at a very bad time for the government, it turned out. His dreadful treatment the previous summer had people wondering if perhaps that had contributed to his death, and Judge Foster's latest ruling caused some of his detractors to reconsider their opposition completely. One of Payne's most vocal assailants had been the editor of *The Wichita Beacon,* who characterized Payne as a boozing swindler attempting to steal the last thing the Indians had left.

The episode outside Fort Smith, particularly the army's refusal to turn Payne over to an authorized deputy with a warrant in hand, had served to change the editor's mind. Perhaps Payne was right. Perhaps the government was indeed acting tyrannically and dishonestly, as

Payne had claimed all along. The editor finished a long piece by comparing Payne's efforts in Oklahoma to Daniel Boone's in Kentucky.

The tide was turning.

* * *

Couch went to Washington after Payne's funeral. Against advice, he set a meeting with Lucius Lamar, the new secretary of the interior. When asked the reason for the appointment, Couch inquired of the government's stance on the Oklahoma Lands. Lamar replied there was no change, no Boomers allowed. Couch countered with a challenge regarding Judge Foster's ruling and the cattle ranches dotting the prairie, to which Larmar replied they were not allowed either.

And yet, there they were, the hypocrisy in plain sight. Couch squeezed, challenging Lamar to explain.

Newspapers across the country took up the fight and began a smear campaign against Lamar. With Payne's memory fresh, editors across the country accused Lamar, in milder editorials, of insincerity. More often he was referred to as a hypocritical, underhanded, lying bastard.

The Senate took note and established a subcommittee led by Senator Henry L. Dawes to study the situation of Indian lands and cattle grazing. Couch repeated Payne's challenge and demanded that Dawes convene a hearing at Caldwell. Couch promised detailed evidence of the cattlemen's underhanded agreements with the Indian agents and the army.

Senator Dawes had no choice but to agree to the meeting and scheduled it for June.

* * *

Dawes convened his hearing and Couch held up his end, testifying in detail and producing documentation and affidavits of bribes between Indian agents, cattle ranchers, and politicians. He provided specific details about ranches, fenced pastures, herd sizes and locations, then identified their owners by name.

The subcommittee returned to Washington to write their report. Virtually overnight, all white opposition to opening the Unassigned Lands vanished. The commander of the Department of Missouri, Gen. Nelson Miles, referred to the Indian lands as "a block to the pathway of civilization" in his annual report, and he recommended Bud's original solution: that Indian lands simply be abolished everywhere.

The government voided all contracts between the Indian tribes and the cattlemen, then dismissed all the Indian agents who had been involved with their creation. The Indians could still lease their grassland, and the cattle could still cross, but the cattlemen's ranches, barns, and fences had to go. Permanent structures were to be destroyed and fences cut down. It was the cattlemen's turn to howl in protest, but to no avail.

In December, the president directed Congress to appoint a commission whose mission would be to consolidate the Indian lands.

But first the Unassigned Lands needed to be dealt with. The die was finally cast— Payne's Oklahoma Lands would be opened.

Chapter 8

Lewis and Adeline were very quickly evicted. Since Lewis was merely an employee, he convinced the lieutenant to allow him to remove their property before the house and barn were burned.

They pulled into Coffeyville the next day, looking very much like Boomers, and Adeline declared it would be their new home until they settled a claim in Oklahoma. She directed Lewis to secure them a home immediately, which he was eventually able to do since there were no Boomers on the scene.

Frank surprised them with a visit, and Bud and Angela were called to Coffeyville to get the entire family together for the first time in years. Frank entertained them with hair-raising tales of chasing and capturing villains, shootouts, and wild rides through the Indian Territory.

The younger boys were spellbound, and Bud recalled his own infatuation with life in the saddle. Frank eyed Grat and Bob, then mischievously mentioned that the deputy marshals always needed posse men. They were old enough to come along if they wanted, and the pay would be good enough for them. Was that something they would be interested in?

The answer was a resounding, "Yes." The boys were ecstatic, and Frank kept his word, deputizing them for the first time just three weeks later.

Frank's tendency to deal with conflict physically and abruptly must have been genetic because both Grat and Bob behaved the same way. Both seemed to carry chips on their shoulders and inclined toward fighting when talking would work. But both were good posse men, unafraid of hard riding or rough conditions. Both were good shots with pistol and rifle; Grat could shoot with either hand and Bob routinely showed off with his Winchester at several hundred yards. It looked like they might follow in Frank's footsteps.

Which was fine with Grat. He detested driving to Kansas City and back, haggling with destitute Boomers, and being out in the weather. He would much rather ride in Frank's posses, flirt with the girls in Coffeyville, and raise hell in the saloons.

All that hell-raising had made it clear to Adeline that it was time for all four boys to start making their own way. The younger children, mostly girls, didn't need that sort of influence, plus, Adeline declared, there still wasn't any room in the house.

Grat, Emmett, and Bob intended to stay in the area, punching cows and waiting for posses with Frank and the marshals. Bill had been seduced by stories of California and elected to leave the Territory completely. He had joined a company of migrants headed for California and would be leaving any day.

* * *

The gold bars drifted through Bud's mind a few days after they returned from Coffeyville and, with nothing to do, he impulsively asked Angela if she'd like to sneak down into the Kiowa Territory and see the mountains, and the gold's location, for herself. She thought that was a marvelous idea.

Bud inventoried their gear and concluded they would need some equipment for Angela. After a trip to town she was the proud owner of some sturdy clothes, a pair of lace-up boots called "packers," a poncho, a knife, a blanket, a bed roll, and a tremendously ugly hat.

"Function," Bud told her, "not fashion."

Bud elected to leave the tent because when the army saw it, that would certainly end the trip. Being summertime, it was a safe bet there would be no rain.

Angela insisted on learning to shoot before they departed. The Peacemaker was far too big and heavy, but she could manage the rifle well enough, particularly if she could rest the stock on something. Just an hour of practice was enough.

They were ready to leave, needing only to replace the ammunition they'd used practicing and to pick up a few things they'd forgotten. At the gunsmith's, Angela noticed a smaller version of Bud's rifle.

The gunsmith explained that it was indeed a Winchester rifle and used the same ammunition as Bud's full-sized model. The short-barreled version was less popular because it was considerably less accurate at distance, but in short-range situations it was a handy tool. Angela enthusiastically claimed it.

They packed the wagon and left at first light the next morning. They crossed the border and were instantly harassed by the army, but Bud's old explanation of "just passing through to Texas" was accepted.

After they crept past Fort Sill, they were able to sneak off the supply road without being seen. Familiar with the route now, Bud had no trouble finding the landmarks leading him to the canyon. He nudged Angela as they crossed through the creek hiding the cache. "It's just up there."

They pulled into their creek and took the left fork into the canyon, but as they approached the cave Bud pulled the team up short and stopped. Piled next to a shallow hole in the creek bed was a stack of rotted leather packs.

Bud picked up his rifle and jacked a round into the chamber, thoroughly alarming Angela.

"What's happening?"

"Shhhh. Someone's been here that knew where to dig."

Angela pulled out her rifle and cocked it as well. Bud hopped out of the wagon and scanned the banks over the creek bed, but they were far too steep for anyone to hide without falling. The cave was vacant, too, but showed evidence of recent occupation.

"Ah, shit." Bud began to look around for some sort of clue as to who had dug up the packs.

"Bud, what's going on?"

"Well, I left those packs buried and someone's dug them up. They were obviously looking for the bars."

"Oh, God. Who?"

"Who do you think? Come on down and let's make sure we're alone."

Angela climbed off the wagon and they searched another fifty yards upstream for any signs of occupation. There was none.

They returned to the cave and looked around. There was a pile of horse manure near the cave, and what were obviously wagon ruts in the sand.

"Christ, they were just here," Bud declared. "That turd isn't three days old."

"Bud, what should we do?"

"Get the hell out of this canyon. And never come back."

They wasted no time in leaving. Bud turned back to the east and they made their way to the mesquite-choked gap leading to the central valley. He pulled the wagon into the thicket where it would be hard to see, and dismounted.

Angela climbed down, too, and asked, "What now?"

"Well, I think we should stick to the plan. Let's look around a little bit and head back in a few days. Watch out, these bushes all have thorns."

"Oh, yes they do... What about the gang?"

"Well… Keep your rifle handy, I guess, but we'd best not run into them."

"Who do you think it could be?"

Bud thought for a moment. "Well, eight of the twelve aren't dead or in prison, and one of them's me. It could be one of seven guys." Bud ticked them off on his fingers. "I don't think it would be either Will or George, so that leaves Charlie, Zack, Rub, Roy and Uncle George. Zack didn't want to bury it to start with, so I'd bet on him. But could be more than one."

"Isn't Frank out of prison now too?"

"Oh, yes. So, him, too, I suppose."

"And now they know someone's beat them to it. Do you think they suspect you?"

"I don't think I'm the first person they'd track down. I was in pretty bad shape when we split up, so they'll probably look to someone else first. I didn't even think to take those packs with me. If I had, they'd still be digging holes and wouldn't know anything."

"Well," Angela replied, "they returned the favor by leaving them laying there for us to see. Now we know they're looking."

Bud looked at her. "Right. But the gold could be anywhere. They need to find who took it, and like I said, there's only a handful that could have done it. They're eventually going to come looking for us. Of course, we can find them too."

"What good does that do?"

"Well, say we find out that only two or three of them have been around in the last month or so. That'll narrow it down pretty well, right?"

"I guess it would. But how would we learn that?"

"Oh, that's easy, I'll ask Pa. He was one of Jesse's messengers for years. He'll know who knows about each one of them."

Angela looked irritated. "Lewis was close to the James gang too? Why don't you tell me these things? What else should I know?"

Bud put on his most apologetic expression. "Well, I did tell you he helped out during the war."

"Helped out?" She slapped his shoulder. "Jackass."

"Sorry."

They fought their way through the mesquites and emerged into the central valley. Bud turned left, to the west, looking for a sheltered and level spot near a stream to park the wagon.

He found a perfect location about a quarter mile into the valley. A large outcrop of solid granite protruded from a small knoll, forcing the creek at the bottom to curve around the outcrop and creating a small shallow pool at the base of the stone. Large trees grew on either side of the pool, and the banks of the creek were very level. It was a perfect place to camp. Or live.

They picked a concealed spot near the pool and unpacked their gear. Their bedrolls and blankets were spread under the wagon's bed and Bud dug a small pit for their fire. The horses had abundant grass.

The top of the knoll was just a few steps away and afforded an excellent view of the valley. Angela joined Bud at the top and asked, "Is all this Indian land?"

"Yes. If I read the maps right it belongs to the Kiowas and Comanches. The territory the Boomers are agitating over isn't anywhere near this lush. If the Boomers can get that, then I don't see the Indians keeping this."

"Good."

* * *

Angela thought about Bud's idea overnight and by the time they had coffee brewing the next morning she had some serious doubts.

"Bud, I don't like this plan, it's going to lead to trouble."

"How?" he asked, slurping his hot coffee.

"Well, what are you going to do when, say, this Rub character gets word you're looking for him and shows up in our yard? Are you just going to tell him, 'Never mind' and send him on his way? Isn't he going to want to know what you want?"

"I hadn't thought about that," he admitted.

"Well, how about this?" she declared. "How are you going to explain looking for Zack at all? If you two hate each other like you say, then just trying to find him is suspicious."

"Yeah, that's true too."

"And now that I think about it, why do we need to know who is around and who isn't?"

"Well, so we know who to look out for."

"No, we don't! Bud, what does it matter? They've got about as much business looking for you as you for them. If you see any of those boys, then you know that's who did it."

"So, you think we should let them come to us?"

"I do! Let's not tip our hand; let them tip theirs, and they will."

"All right, so what do we do if Rub shows up in our yard? Just shoot him?"

"Well, nothing that severe, I hope. Do we need to do anything at all? Our business with the Boomers is no secret … what if we let him talk and then tell him you're not interested, no matter what he says?"

Bud took another sip and nodded. "That's good. Tell him we're doing just fine right here, and unless he's planning to dig up the bucket we've nothing to talk about. That will work."

"The bucket? What's the bucket?"

"After we buried the gold, Jesse scratched a message and all our names on a bucket, along with some crazy instructions on how to find the canyon."

Bud pointed at the mountain they'd buried it on, its summit just visible over the valley's rim. "Then we buried it on that mountain, the one just sticking up there. About halfway up the back side, under a flat rock between a tree and a pile of rocks Jesse made. The idea was the canyon would be too hard to find, but the bucket would be easy and would show the way."

Angela was incredulous. "A damn bucket? Buried on a mountain? That's Jesse James?"

Bud nodded, "Yup, that's him exactly. He loved doing stuff like that and was always making elaborate codes to find places where he hid things. Mean and crazy at the same time."

"Do you think anyone dug up the bucket?"

"Hell no. If you don't know where that canyon is then the bullshit on that bucket won't be any help. But if anyone from the gang turns up, that bucket is where our story starts."

"How did you find the canyon?"

"I made a sketch of the mountain after we left the ravine. Remember the thorn bushes? That's the place I sketched it. I found the gap with that view of the mountain, then backtracked from there. The maps at the courthouse gave me a good idea of the general area, but you saw how many little creeks and canyons there are out there. Just wandering around won't work very well."

"But anyone could find it?"

"Eventually, yes. Just have to find the right creek and remember the way. I made the first move."

"I guess they were going to do the same thing."

"Or just pack it all up and head south into Texas. It's barely a day's ride away."

"Oh. I hadn't thought of that. Why didn't you do that?"

"I only had one horse and this little buckboard. To haul that much, I imagine you'd need a whole team and a heavy freight wagon. It took me four trips and a whole day just to move it a mile."

"How long did it take you to dig them up?"

"Not an hour."

"They probably weren't there very long at all, then. I bet it was just one of them, they dug up the packs, then left. I wonder what they'll do now."

"They're going to come looking, that's what they're going to do."

* * *

They camped and explored undisturbed for three days. By the time they broke camp Angela was convinced there was no way the land would, or should, be held back for Indians. She told Bud that they needed to be on their toes when it was opened for settlement. She wanted her 160 acres right there, right where they'd camped.

They loaded the wagon and made their way back through the mesquites and turned east toward Fort Sill. They bypassed the fort well to the south and got on the Kansas supply road to make their way back home. Aside from the army patrols pestering them every day and the wagon getting stuck during a creek crossing, the ride north was uneventful.

That changed when Bud turned their wagon into the lane leading to their farmhouse and they found a rider coming from the opposite direction. From their house. The rider reined in his horse and waited for the wagon.

Bud told Angela, "Son of a bitch, I surely didn't see this coming. You best keep your rifle handy."

They pulled up to the rider and stopped the wagon.

George Overton said, "Hello, Bud. Been a while, hasn't it?"

* * *

Bud pulled into the yard and told Angela, "I'll unhitch the wagon and talk to George here. See if you can rustle up a bite to eat. I'll be in shortly."

Angela nodded and climbed off the wagon, making a show of keeping her rifle with her.

George watched her walk to the house and asked, "Is that your wife?"

"Yep. What can I do for you, George?"

George was staring at Bud's scar. "I didn't get a good look at you when that happened, but I tell you, you were in bad shape. Cole was worried you might be dead."

Bud rubbed his cheek, the smooth scar tissue plain against his fingers, and replied, "Yeah, it was touch and go for a while. An army doctor sewed me up north of Fort Sill, but I couldn't ride. Had to wait in the Territory to get better before I could get home."

"Damn. Well, I'm glad it worked out. I guess you're wondering why I'm here?"

No, actually not. We were talking about you just the other day.

"Well, yes. I am. I have a suspicion, but it's your game."

George looked around and said, "They told me you and your dad were doing pretty good down here. I didn't know you'd got married, though."

"We're doing all right. Let's get on with this, George. What's up?"

"Well, we're trying to get down south and split up what we got in Mexico. I'm here to bring you along."

"I thought Frank was laying low and leading an honest life. He's gathering us up to go back?"

George looked at his feet. "No, Frank doesn't know anything about it yet. Zack's trying to pull this together."

Zack. I knew it.

"So, Frank's not involved and Zack's in charge? Forget it, not interested. I guess you can hold Frank's, and Cole's shares, but I ain't going. Just let me know where I can pick up my share and we'll all part friends. Is that why Zack sent you? 'Cuz he knew I might shoot him?"

George looked uncomfortable and mumbled, "Something like that."

"Speaking of shares, how's Frank going to get his if he's not coming?"

"I don't know. Zack just sent me here to get you."

"Well, George, I'm sorry, but you can tell Zack he can kiss my ass. He's welcome to dig up that bucket and fool around in the wilderness all he wants. But you let him know that if he tries to screw me, Cole, or Frank, it'll start going bad in a hurry."

"You're not going to go?"

"With Zack running it and Frank on the outside? No fucking chance. Y'all go right along. When can I expect to hear from you?"

George had no idea what to do. "Bud, you know Zack ain't gonna split it with anyone that isn't there. You have to go."

Bud stood there, pretending to think. "You know what? I'm not going to get crosswise with Frank or Cole. If Zack thinks he can steal from them, well, then good luck to him. I'm staying away from that shit, but I'll make certain that Cole knows Zack's in the middle of it."

"So, you're not coming?"

"No, I don't trust Zack. Dig it up, bring my share, do whatever you want with Jesse's cut. I ain't riding with Zack."

George mounted his horse. "OK, I'll tell him. You take care, Bud."

"You too, George."

* * *

Angela took the opportunity to gloat about being right – whoever took the first step would tip their hand. Zack had tipped his by sending George. Bud pointed out that, according to George, they hadn't gone yet, so Zack hadn't tipped anything. Neither had a good idea of what would happen next. Angela hoped that Zack might just let it drop in the face of Bud's threat, but Bud knew better. He was sure that Zack would make an appearance eventually.

It was Bud's turn to be proven correct just over a month later. Zack Smith, George Overton, and Roy Baxter walked their horses into Bud's yard as he and Angela were eating lunch on their rickety table. The group reined in and Zack called out for Bud.

Bud got up and glanced out the window. Seeing who was in his yard, he went to the closet holding their trail gear. He pulled his rifle from the closet and jacked a round into the chamber.

"Well, here we go."

Bud stepped through the door and into the yard. The rifle was hanging loosely in the crook of his arm, his finger near the trigger. He made sure it was pointed in Zack's vicinity, then spoke directly to him.

"Get the hell out of here."

Roy said, "Easy, Bud, we just need to talk."

"We went down into the Territory," Zack said, "but we didn't find the bars."

"Well, that bucket didn't make much sense to me when Jesse scratched all that shit on it. That what you came to tell me?"

"No, I mean the bars wasn't where we left 'em."

"You sure you were in the right place?"

"We're sure," Roy replied. "Took us a while to find it, but yeah, canyon, little cave, dry creek."

"Or," Bud deadpanned, "you found it just fine and are trying to keep it. Who all went looking with you? George, you're not in on this, are you?"

George said, "No, Bud, he's telling the truth. We found the place we buried them, but the packs were laying there in the creek bed. Empty. Someone had already dug them up and carried off the bars."

"Who could have done that?" Bud asked.

Zack leaned forward in his saddle. "I'm thinking you did."

Bud kept calm. "That's because you're a dipshit asshole."

George said, "Bud, there are only four of us left, and we're all here right now. You were the only one that wasn't there when we found the place."

"What about Frank? Was he there?"

Zack leaned back and George replied, "Well, no..."

"No. And neither was Cole. There are more than four of us left, George. I told you before, I'm not getting crosswise with either Frank or Cole. You get Frank involved and then you can count me in."

Zack shook his head. "You don't seem to understand, you're already crosswise with me. Frank has nothing to do with it. I know you dug up the bars—you're the only one that could have. Where are they?"

Bud scoffed, "You think if I had a fortune I'd be here, selling beans and firewood to farmers? Look around, is this how a rich man lives?"

Roy looked around. "He's got a point."

"That's horseshit. Just means he's hiding them somewhere."

"You really are an asshole. I don't have them and don't know what happened to them. Add in the fact that Frank's not involved and it makes me think you're trying to set me up for something." Bud became less vague with his rifle. "So, get the hell out of here. Roy, George, this bastard is up to something, you best watch your backs."

Roy and George glanced at each other, neither sure what to do. Zack did, though. He touched his cheek under his eye, and began to needle Bud.

"You know, that looks good on you. I have to tell you, I sure enjoyed that. I think there might still be a little piece of your face stuck in those boots. Yes sir, that was a good day."

Zack carried on, "I'm going to give you a matching set if you don't come clean. And maybe I will anyway. I'll tell you another thing, you best listen hard. George told me that you have a pretty gal for a wife. You don't get right with me and she'll have a set of her own. You can remember me every time you look at her."

Son of a bitch...

Roy started to warn Zack to back off a little, but it was too late. Anger and hatred washing over him, Bud shouldered his rifle and pulled the trigger.

Zack didn't get lucky that time. The bullet hit the center of his chest and pushed him backwards in his saddle. The gunshot startled all three horses, and Zack rolled backwards off his horse as the animal jumped. He landed face down in the dirt and didn't move, an ugly exit wound in the middle of his back.

Roy and George regained control of their mounts and stared at Zack's body as Bud jacked another round into the chamber.

"Jesus Christ, Bud," George exclaimed, "you shot Zack. What the hell are you doing?"

Bud kept the rifle pointed toward the pair and replied, "He should have been dead the first time. The piece of shit had it coming."

Roy dismounted and rolled Zack onto his back. "Well, he got it now. Bud, I swear I'll never say a thing against any of your kin folk."

"That son of a bitch was up to something," Bud insisted. "I didn't steal any gold, and if something happened to it, I bet he was behind it."

Roy looked at Bud and the rifle and asked, "What now?"

Bud lowered the gun. "I don't have a quarrel with you two, do I? Was he telling the truth about the bars? Someone already got to them?"

Roy nodded and said, "Yeah, it was like George said. The packs were laying there in the creek bed."

"So, he convinced you that I must have done it?"

"Yeah," George replied. "He said you were the only one unaccounted for and was sure you had the bars hidden here."

Bud scoffed and turned to George. "So, where's Will?"

"He's down in Texas."

"Jesus Christ, George! How can I be the only one missing when your fucking brother's in Texas?"

"Well, Will wouldn't take them. Zack said we could trust him."

Bud was amazed. "Zack said…? Roy, did Zack say anything to you about Will? Or about Charlie or Rub or Uncle George for that matter?"

Roy glanced at George. "No, he didn't."

Bud walked toward Zack's body. "That bastard. I don't have any gold. I bet he dug up the bars, and left the packs laying there so he could bring you boys down there to find them and then pin it on me. I'm glad I shot him before he convinced you two to hang me."

Roy spit tobacco juice through his mustache and said, "That subject did come up."

Bud shook his head in disbelief. "I'm sure it did. So, where are we? Do you still think I stole the gold?"

George said, "I guess not. But how do we know for sure?"

Bud was exasperated. "Because I didn't shoot you, George. If I had the bars, why would I want any of you sniffing around for the rest of my life?"

"You wouldn't shoot me, would you?" George asked.

Angela's voice came from behind them. "I would."

They whirled around to find the muzzle of Angela's rifle pointed at them, held steady against the side of the house.

"Holy shit," Roy exclaimed, "where did she come from?"

Bud called over, "It's OK, hon. We're done here."

He looked back at the two men and said, gesturing around him, "I don't have it. I didn't take it. Zack was playing you for fools, I'm sorry to say."

George gestured to Zack's body and asked, "What are you going to do with him?"

"Well, I don't think the law needs to get involved, does it? What are you two going to say if anyone asks about him?"

Roy looked down at the body and replied, "I don't believe I've seen him."

"What about the gold?" George asked.

"If it's not in that canyon," Bud lied, "then I don't know where it is."

* * *

The ground behind the barn was soft, so Bud was able to dig a nice, deep grave for Zack's body. George and Roy left with Zack's horse, which was fine with Bud. He didn't want any evidence of Zack anywhere near him.

"So, is that it?" Angela asked. "They think the gold is gone and suspect Zack?"

"I think so. If Zack didn't dig up the packs then whoever did might turn up, but we need to lay low and go get it whenever we can."

"Is there any chance they'll turn you in?"

"No."

"How long should we wait?"

"Let's see what happens with the Boomers. They're gonna open Oklahoma, and there's a particular claim we want."

Chapter 9

Bud was nearly right, but not quite. As Roy and George led Zack's horse away from Joplin, George asked, "Roy, do you think Bud is right? Zack was playing at something?"

"I don't know, but something ain't right. I just can't put my finger on it."

"Well, everything he said makes sense, doesn't it? If he had the gold, then they would have had to shoot us all. But Bud hated Zack really bad. Looking back it seems like we should have known one of them would start shooting. Zack shouldn't have come."

"Yeah." Roy nodded. "But do you remember how Zack was when we finally found the packs? He wasn't pretending to be surprised. Or angry. And I don't think he'd been in the canyon before – remember how hard it was to find? We wandered around there for a damn week."

George nodded, remembering the dozens of creeks they'd searched. When they finally found the correct spot, Zack was as excited as the rest of them were.

"So, if Zack didn't get them, who did?"

Roy nodded. "Yeah. So, let's see ... if it wasn't Bud there's only Charlie, Uncle George, Rub, and your brother left. And Frank."

"Will's still down in Texas."

"OK, if we leave Frank and Will out, it's down to three, then. Let's see what Charlie, Rub, and Uncle George have to say."

"What are we going to do with Zack's horse?"

"Take it to Zack's family, I guess."

"What are we going to say happened to Zack? That Bud shot him?"

"Yeah, I guess so. If they want to get the law involved then it's up to them."

* * *

Roy and George delivered Zack's horse to his nearest relative, his brother. Abraham Smith lived in Siloam Springs, Arkansas, just twenty miles south of the Missouri border and directly adjacent to the Cherokee Nation. Abe did not receive the news of his brother's death well.

Roy told him that Zack had been in an argument with a man named Bud Dalton, and Dalton had ended up shooting Zack, who was now buried in Missouri. It appeared to be a fair fight, and since Dalton had no quarrel with Roy or George they had been permitted to leave with Zack's horse and saddle, which they turned over to Abe.

Abe Smith had much of Zack's temperament, but none of his brains. Abe raged for a few minutes, vowing revenge on that Dalton bastard, and thanking Roy and George for doing the right thing. Abe did not ask any interesting questions, such as where Dalton could be found or what he looked like. The barest fool could have found Bud with those two pieces of information, but Abe didn't measure up to that standard. Roy and George were allowed to depart without having to share the key information and, disliking Abe immediately, neither felt obligated to share it.

Abe had an idea, though. He was acquainted with a newly hired deputy marshal that was building a reputation as a determined man-hunter, and Abe would set him to work finding this Dalton character. The deputy's name was Henry "Heck" Thomas.

Thomas had first made a name for himself in 1878, working as a messenger for the Texas Express Company. The train he was assigned was stopped by the Sam Bass Gang, who generally terrorized North and Central Texas at the time. Thomas secured the doors to the express car and then moved the contents of the safe to a small iron stove. He doused the lights and waited for the robbers to come.

Thomas was about to open fire through the door, but the conductor and several passengers shouted that they were being used as shields. If he shot, he would hit them. Thomas told the gang he would open the doors and they could have whatever they wanted if they agreed not to shoot anyone. Bass agreed, and Thomas opened the door and surrendered the key to the lockbox.

Finding the box empty, the gang quickly departed. Thomas was given a two-hundred-dollar reward for his quick thinking, saving twenty-two thousand dollars from the robbers.

Thomas later worked as a detective in North Texas until he went after the notorious Lee brothers, Jim and Pink. The Lees had shot up a posse and killed a U.S. deputy along with several posse members. The father of one of the dead men offered a large reward for the Lee brothers, dead or alive. He posted the reward in Denison, Texas, which got Thomas's attention.

Thomas partnered with U.S. Deputy Jim Taylor and they set out to track down the Lees. Taylor and Thomas found them hiding at a relative's ranch, and then ambushed the Lee brothers as they were setting up an ambush for the bounty hunters.

Both bodies were delivered to Fort Smith, where the reward was verified. Impressed, Judge Parker offered Thomas a job as a U.S. deputy. Thomas accepted, which was how he became acquainted with Frank Dalton.

Thomas proved to be proficient at delivering fugitives back to Judge Parker, although he also gained a reputation for "shooting first and serving papers on the corpse." Siloam Springs was a convenient stop on the way back to Fort Smith, and that was how Abe Smith's acquaintance had originally been inflicted upon him.

Heck passed through Siloam Springs in July, a few weeks after Roy and George had left. Unfortunately for him, Abe saw him as he was dismounting in front of the town's saloon. Abe didn't even let him get indoors; he dove straight into his unprepared speech. Thomas certainly didn't consider Smith to be a friend, but listened politely to the story of how Abe's brother had been killed.

Abe finally took a breath, giving Heck the opportunity to ask the questions that Abe did not ask Roy and George. Upon learning that Abe had no information beyond the story, which was little more than an accusation, Heck vaguely dismissed him.

"I'll see what I can do."

A few days later in Fort Smith, Thomas ran into Frank, the only "Dalton" Thomas knew, and off-handedly asked Frank if he had any relatives named "Bud." Surprised by the question, Frank informed him that his older brother was Bud Dalton.

"Why do you ask?"

"Well, a shifty fellow named Abe Smith told me that his brother, Zack, had been shot by a man named Bud Dalton. He wants me to track him down."

"Well, I can tell you that Bud lives on the north side of Joplin, Missouri."

"Smith said his dead brother was buried in Missouri."

"Is that so? Well, Bud's pretty easy to find. You should go talk to him."

Thomas snorted. "Missouri? Ha. There's no reward, no warrant, and it's outside our jurisdiction. Not interested. Mr. Smith and the law in Joplin will need to handle that."

So, the law was involved, sort of, and that was how Heck Thomas first became entangled with the Daltons.

* * *

After leaving Abe to stalk Heck Thomas, George and Roy rode back to Kansas City. George wondered where the remaining gang members were, and they spent several hours discussing the topic.

Will was still in Texas, Cole was in prison, Zack and Jesse were dead, Bud was in Joplin, and Frank was trying to be an honest citizen, but Uncle George, Charlie Jones, and Rub Busse were unaccounted for. Why didn't Zack try to find them too? Or maybe he couldn't. Or maybe he did.

The more they talked about it, the more they convinced each other that until they'd heard from everyone else, they couldn't really know if Zack was right about Bud. They would need to track down their missing friends and figure out what happened.

Uncle George was easy to find, living right there, outside Kansas City, under his real name, George Payne. George had given up his life of crime after the James-Younger gang was destroyed at Northfield, and now he ran a small shipping business with his brothers. He had given up any hope of ever seeing the gold after Jesse was killed, but was delighted to see his old friends.

He had no idea of anything that had transpired, but was very irritated to learn that Zack had pulled together part of the gang to retrieve the gold and he had not been invited. He was not hiding, or even laying low, and would have been easy to find, as George and Roy had just proven. As they listened to Uncle George, Bud's story seemed plausible; perhaps Zack was playing at something after all.

Uncle George told them that Rub was punching cows, last he heard, but he hadn't heard Charlie's name in years. He thought Charlie had a sister who lived in Liberal, Kansas, but that was a long time ago too.

They left Uncle George, vowing to keep up with him, and thought about how to track down Rub. If he was punching cows, then he'd have to turn up at one of the rail heads, and maybe someone knew him. Roy wanted to head south right then, but George demurred. He had things here at home to deal with, so they would have to wait until next spring, when the grass was growing.

* * *

Heck Thomas was living up to his reputation as a man-hunter, disappearing into the Indian Territory for weeks at a time and returning with six or eight prisoners destined for Judge Parker.

Thomas would pass through Siloam Springs occasionally and was nearly always accosted by Abe Smith. Abe wanted to know how the investigation into the Dalton bastard was coming and Thomas kept telling him it was ongoing. Judge Parker had other assignments that took priority, so if Abe wanted to find a detective with more time, then Heck would understand.

No, Abe trusted Heck. He'd be patient.

* * *

Bud and Angela were keenly watching Washington, waiting for the announcement opening Oklahoma. But the same senator who had obliged Couch with the subcommittee hearing and had cleared the way for Oklahoma's opening, Senator Dawes, had authored legislation that accidentally stopped the opening dead in its tracks.

The Dawes Act would eliminate Indian reservations and essentially treat Indians like White Americans: They could claim 160 acres each, the rest would be made available for settlement. But there were some details that had to be worked out and the law couldn't be passed yet.

In January of 1886 the Boomers officially complained that the Dawes Act had nothing to do with them and Oklahoma should be opened now. The land was not the Indians'; it was in the public domain and should be open for settlement. They were different issues and Congress should get to work.

Washington hemmed and hawed, but didn't do anything.

* * *

One afternoon in February, Angela had Bud hitch up the wagon to drive her the short distance to downtown Joplin. They went every month to stock up, and she'd told him several times they were getting low on everything, so Bud didn't think anything about it when she demanded to be taken right away.

Her favorite store was owned by a friend's husband. Amy Lins had introduced Angela to Agnes Wilmenz and recommended her husband's store. They occasionally ran into each other there, so that's where Angela preferred to do her shopping. Any opportunity to chat with her friends took precedence over nearly everything.

Another thing she liked was that Agnes's husband was willing to order almost anything. He kept a vast array of catalogs for companies in Kansas City and St. Louis, but also some as far away as Chicago and a few from New York and Boston. If one were patient and could afford it, nearly anything could be had.

It was also Bud's favorite general store—not that he actually liked any store or would ever admit he did—but Wilmenz's store was less offensive because Wilmenz subscribed to a magazine named *Harper's Weekly*, and Bud enjoyed it immensely. He would peruse *Harper's*, taking in the art and skimming the essays while Angela waited for her order to be assembled and she perused the catalogs.

This trip was no different. Bud scanned *Harper's* while Angela managed their order. He was closely examining the magazine's front cover, a drawing depicting Indian scouts helping the army track down Geronimo. He didn't think the detail was particularly good, and the Indians seemed cartoonish, but then again he had no idea how such a thing could be copied a hundred thousand times and shipped to every corner of the nation. Perhaps the printing process diluted the feel of the drawing.

He stared at it, pursing his lips and wondering if he could do better, publishing challenges notwithstanding. Angela saw him and ambled over, leaning over to see what had him enthralled. She knew, of course, because she'd witnessed that scene a hundred times before.

"What do you have there, hon?"

Bud didn't look up, but replied, "Just looking at this drawing. It's interesting, is all."

"I've seen better in your sketchbook."

He looked up to reply, "Well, maybe, but that's open to debate. None of mine have been copied a few thousand times and printed, either. How do you think they do that?"

"No idea, but I know you can do better than that."

Bud scoffed, "No time soon, and probably never."

Angela giggled. "Well, we'll just see about that. Mr. Wilmenz, that package, please?"

Wilmenz reached under the counter and produced a small package, then handed it to Angela. He was smiling broadly too.

Bud looked back and forth. "What are you two up to?"

Angela pulled *Harper's Weekly* from his hands and replaced it with the package. "Open it, have a look."

Bud untied the string holding the paper wrapping and looked inside to find a dozen small glass jars containing colored powders, several brushes, and a small booklet on the basics of watercolor paints.

Once Bud figured out what he had, he was astonished. He couldn't recall ever telling Angela about colored art or his even being interested in experimenting with it. Of course, he must have, or she figured it out, because here was everything he needed, straight out of the blue.

She cocked her head and asked, "Do you like them?"

"Honey, I don't know what to say … I love it! Thank you! How did you know?"

Angela giggled again. "You've only mentioned it offhand a few thousand times, so I asked Lois Abernathy about colored paintings, and she told me that watercolor is quite the rage these days. Mr. Wilmenz found all the pieces in his catalogs, so we made the order and everything finally arrived. Now you can draw in color."

Wilmenz leaned over the counter and said, "Look underneath, there should be some pens and ink too. For something called 'washing.' Apparently, you can draw with the ink, then color with the paints. You're the artist; you'll have to let us know how it works."

"I don't know what to say. This is the finest gift anyone's ever given me. Thank you both."

Wilmenz replied, "You're welcome, Bud."

"Once you've unloaded the wagon," Angela teased, "you can play with your new toys."

* * *

Bud did play with his new toys. The booklet explained how to wet the pigment powders to produce paint, rough guidelines on mixing the powders to produce new colors, how to treat and clean the brushes, and some basic techniques of watercolor painting, including the "wash" that Wilmenz mentioned.

Washing was simply using watercolor to paint over a drawing, either to add color or shading to the sketch or to soften or blur details. It seemed obvious to Bud and he understood immediately, but the ink and the pens were a revelation.

Pencil and charcoal were never perfectly black, nor made a perfectly sharp line. The pens and India ink produced both, and combined with washing could produce exquisite precision and detail. The downside, which he quickly learned, was that once an ink stroke was made, it was permanent. The slightest mistake could ruin everything, including one's clothes.

Angela designated the ink-stained shirts and pants as his "work" clothes and warned him not to do it again. By summer Bud needed Wilmenz to order more pigment powders and ink, some additional brushes, some high-quality paper, and new nibs for the pens, particularly a needle-sharp one that Bud already had plans for.

He spent several hours a day sketching, painting, and experimenting with various combinations of paper, ink and pencil, and techniques. The only things that distracted him were the day-to-day chores necessary to keep the place functional and the occasional social engagements Angela arranged. By fall, Angela, and everyone else, thought Bud was possibly the best artist in the west, probably the best in Missouri, and certainly the best in Joplin.

By the end of the year, Bud's small reputation had grown considerably, mostly because of the portraits he'd done for some of Joplin's ladies as practice. Lois Abernathy owned an excellent example of Bud's work and she showed it off regularly. She wanted everyone to remember that she had found Bud first.

"Bud, I believe you could make a living at this."

"You're very kind, Mrs. Abernathy, but I think there's a reason you don't see artists out here."

"Oh, why's that?"

"They all had to find real jobs before they starved to death, I think."

* * *

Roy and George reunited in Kansas City about the time Bud received his gift. They headed south to track down Rub, but he turned out to be much harder to find than Uncle George. Cowboys were ephemeral, never in the same place for long and often off the map entirely. Roy and George spent the entire spring and summer riding back and forth between the railheads searching for someone who knew or knew of Rub. There were thousands of ranches in Texas and not all of them drove their herds to Kansas. When August arrived, they were about to give up and head farther west when, finally, they found a cowboy who knew Rub Busse.

Rub was a trail boss for the Crazy Snake Ranch, located outside San Antonio, and the cowboy used to work for the same outfit. He'd made several drives with Rub, and he thought the herd should show up in Abilene any time. All they needed to do was wait there till the Crazy Snake herd ambled out of the Indian Territory.

George and Roy hurried to Abilene and only had to wait a week before the Crazy Snake's herd arrived. They found Rub easily; all the cowboys knew the trail boss.

Rub was delighted and surprised to see his old outlaw buddies. He listened to their story with interest, but he didn't know anything about the bars, either. The Chisolm Trail ran on just past the Wichitas and he thought about them on every drive north, but there was no way he could stop to search for them, and certainly not to run off with them. George asked him if he knew anything about Charlie, but Rub hadn't heard from him for years. He also thought he recalled Charlie having a sister in Liberal; she would be their best bet, assuming she still lived there.

Liberal was another border town in far western Kansas. George and Roy trudged into town in late October. They learned they should ask the postmaster if they were looking for anyone in Liberal, and so they did. Of course, he knew Miss Jones, now Mrs. Perkins, and he gave them directions to her house.

Sally Perkins played dumb at first, not admitting that she knew a Charlie Jones; it was just a coincidence of names. Roy was able to convince her that he really was an old friend who'd ridden with Charlie and she finally admitted that she was indeed his sister.

Did she know where he was?

It was hard to keep up with Charlie, he moved a lot, but she thought she recalled him living at a place named Sapulpa Station, just south of the Osage Reservation. That was over a year ago, though, and she wasn't exactly sure where it was.

No problem, Sally, we know exactly where Sapulpa Station is. Thank you very much.

It was almost November and they hadn't been home for almost a year. Both were ready to call it a day.

"Let's meet in Coffeyville," Roy suggested. "Say, mid-January, if the weather allows? We can sneak down to Sapulpa and see if Charlie's there."

"Sounds good. He's our last hope, it seems"

"Yeah, I'm starting to think Bud was right."

* * *

George and Roy met in Coffeyville, then made their way to Sapulpa where they found Charlie pretending to be named William Goldthwait. Charlie had been smuggling liquor into the Territory, but that was dangerous work and he didn't like it.

He had recently had a very close call, escaping a U.S. deputy by the narrowest of margins, and it was time to move on. He wanted something else, preferably something with little risk or effort. Charlie had never forgotten the bars and when Roy asked about the gold, Charlie was willing to talk.

Jesse's death and the inevitable demise of the Indian lands prompted Charlie to return to the canyon and grab the gold, or at least some of it, before it was too late. With Jesse dead, and Frank and Cole tied up with the law he didn't see any reason to bother with the others. He'd spent years in the mountains and could find the canyon on memory alone.

So, he stole a wagon and snuck into the Territory, intent on digging up and taking as much of the gold as he could carry. He would head south, into Texas, leaving Missouri behind forever. But, when he dug up the packs, the gold was gone. Someone had beaten him to the punch.

"So you were gonna cut us out?" Roy exclaimed. "What the hell?"

"Sorry, boys. I was short on time and money. Wasn't gonna take it all, but like I said, didn't matter. Someone already got them.

"And that's how I ended up in this whiskey mess. Since I couldn't get the gold, I had to do something...didn't have anyone to work with, so I couldn't take a bank or a train. That left me stuck selling whiskey to Indians. But now I'm caught and you can bet Parker's going to be on my ass any second."

Roy and George absorbed that, then Roy told him of how Zack had attempted to gather the gang and retrieve the gold, too, only to find the empty packs. They promptly headed to Bud's place in Joplin where Bud shot Zack off his horse. It seemed they had missed each other by weeks.

They had no idea that Bud and Angela had also found the packs mere days after Charlie had dug them up and left them, but once the stories were put together two things were perfectly clear. Someone had taken the gold, and that someone was probably Bud Dalton. There were an uncomfortable number of loose ends and unanswered questions, but Bud was the prime suspect.

"But why didn't Bud shoot us?" Roy asked George. "He didn't have any problem shooting Zack, and if he took the bars he'd need us gone too. And why would he even live there at all? Remember what he said about not living like a rich man? There's no reason to stay in Joplin if he had that much gold, but he lives in that little farmhouse."

"Yeah. I don't know, something still ain't right," George replied.

"Well, whatever it is, we need to have a long talk with Bud," Charlie decided. "But first, I gotta get the hell out of here."

* * *

Charlie snuck south, to Texarkana, to let the Goldthwait alias die a quiet death while he built up a new one with an alibi that placed him well away from the Indian Territories for at least a year. Selling whiskey to Indians was dangerous enough, but gunfights with Judge Parker's deputies was volunteering for a noose. Parker never forgot.

George and Roy accompanied Charlie to Texarkana and stayed several weeks there. They eventually got bored and returned to Missouri. Charlie had to remain in Texarkana until he could safely get within twenty feet of a lawman. Fort Smith and Judge Parker were not that far away.

Their path home hugged the Indian Territory's border and after a week's rough travel Roy and George wandered into Siloam Springs. Neither of them gave their previous visit there a second thought until they encountered the same misfortune that Heck Thomas had endured. Roy and George were tired. They wanted a hot meal and a dry room more than anything else in the world, but Abe recognized them and plopped down at their table.

The years since Zack's shooting had completely erased Abe from their memories, but just a few minutes with him brought it all back in vivid detail. They were forced to endure Abe's random conversation until the waiter brought out their food, but Abe didn't mind talking while they ate. The boys politely nodded and grunted their agreement with whatever Abe said, until they finished and stood up to leave.

George shook Abe's hand and lied that it was good to see him, maybe they'd pass this way again. Abe thought that would be great and finally left, thinking what great guys Zack's old buddies were.

George and Roy each got a room at the saloon and as they climbed the stairs to get some sleep, Roy looked back and told George, "You know, that guy's a good reason to never come back here, ever again."

Chapter 10

Heck Thomas was dispatched to the Indian Territory to capture and return a dangerous whiskey runner named Goldthwait who'd shot his way out of an arrest earlier that year. Thomas searched for four weeks, from Sapulpa Station all the way up into the Osage Nation, but had no luck. The trail was too cold.

Siloam Springs was directly on the way home, and Thomas's first instinct was to bypass it. But he'd just spent weeks roughing it in the Territory, he was tired, and he needed whatever civilization was available, not just for him but for his horses. Siloam Springs was it, so he'd stay overnight and take his chances.

He managed to avoid Abe until breakfast the next morning. He was just about to finish when Abe wandered in and saw the deputy sitting alone and sat down uninvited.

"Howdy, Marshal, how long you in town?"

Heck swallowed some coffee and replied, "I was just leaving, actually. Been in the Territory for a few weeks and I'm headed back to Fort Smith."

"You made any headway on that Dalton bastard?"

"No, I haven't. Like I told you before, I'm pretty busy being a deputy marshal," he said, stressing deputy, "and don't have time for detective work. I can tell you that he probably lives in Joplin, Missouri, but like you said, that was a while back. You might hire yourself a real detective."

"So, you ain't gonna help me? Just let Zack's killer get away with it?"

"Mr. Smith, that's not how it works. I don't get to do whatever I want. I work for Judge Parker. There are plenty of lawmen in Missouri; you need to make a complaint there. They'll listen to your story and track down the witnesses, and if there's evidence of a murder, then they'll get a judge to write out a warrant. A deputy or the sheriff will arrest him, and you'll have your trial."

"Witnesses? I'm the witness, dammit. I'm telling you he did it!"

"Mr. Smith, I recall you told me someone else told you about the shooting. Those are the witnesses, not you. Tell your Missouri lawman where they are and he'll question them."

Heck stood up and dropped some coins on the table. "I need to leave, Mr. Smith. Good luck to you. Help yourself to some coffee if you want."

Abe sat at the empty table for several minutes.

Witnesses?

* * *

In November, around the time that George and Roy were encountering Abe in Siloam Springs, the Daltons received dreadful news. Frank had been killed in a shoot-out while attempting to apprehend another whiskey runner in the Indian Territory.

Adeline and Lewis were devastated, but Grat and Bob were enraged. Grat immediately rode to Fort Smith and requested his brother's old job. Bob followed suit a few weeks later, and both were granted deputy marshal commissions. Emmett was deemed too young, so he remained at the ranch and served as a posse-man as often as possible.

Heck Thomas eventually learned who the new deputies were and introduced himself to offer his condolences. It didn't take long for Thomas to realize that Frank's younger brothers didn't share many of

Frank's good qualities. They appeared to be rash and impulsive, preferring action over thought, and, even then, very questionable action. They might be good deputies, but Heck wasn't sure he'd want either one as a neighbor.

Probably best to keep his distance.

* * *

Around the same time, Couch and a delegation of Boomers traveled to Washington where they delivered their resolutions detailing their stance on the Oklahoma Territory and the Dawes Act. Unexpectedly, the resolutions were favorably received by everyone who saw them, which completely unnerved the Seminole and Creek's agents, who, regardless of what the maps showed, claimed much of the Boomer territory. They had assumed the Unassigned Lands would be subject to the Dawes Act, but now the Indians weren't so sure. Things were moving much faster than they'd hoped.

Things began to move faster still. The government was on the verge of clearing up the ambiguous parts of the Dawes Act, the survey was completed, and the details of allotting the land to Indians had been agreed upon. The Creeks and Seminoles would need to make some kind of deal if they were to get anything at all, so they started moving too.

Bud and Angela followed the Boomer's visit to D.C. closely. As the years strung out and the Oklahoma land remained out of reach, the tone around the border had turned ugly. There were loud discussions in saloons everywhere about new invasions, not as settlers, but rather as military invaders.

Bud told Angela, "I hope Washington can get this moving—these fellows are out of patience."

Washington was indeed listening and the noise at the border was one of the main reasons the Boomer's demands were being so well received. Bud and Angela were convinced that if it didn't happen next year, there would be an actual uprising.

"Maybe we should start selling bullets," Angela quipped.

"That's not a bad idea."

* * *

Bob and Grat were proving their worth as deputy marshals, each producing prisoners for Judge Parker and accepting assignments with other districts and marshals. Both received high marks as lawmen, and Emmett seemed to be in line for a commission when he was deemed old enough.

But things started going wrong that summer, about the time when Couch presented the Boomer proposals in D.C. Bob was sent on a routine job to arrest a small-time horse thief and whiskey peddler named Charley Montgomery. Bob had no trouble finding him, but Montgomery refused to be arrested and attempted to pull his gun. Bob shot him and then hauled the corpse back to Fort Smith.

Unfortunately for Bob, Montgomery was not wanted dead, just alive. Judge Parker refused to pay any bounty, then when no one claimed the body Parker forced Bob to pay for Montgomery's burial. To add insult to injury, he also refused to pay Bob's traveling expenses.

Bob's attitude disintegrated. He was still owed pay and expenses from his assignment to the marshal in Kansas City, four months' worth, and although he'd done everything he'd been assigned he still hadn't been paid. No explanation or apologies, and the episode with Parker made him paranoid, believing he was being singled out.

Grat had no problems with his pay, although he'd also been assigned to Kansas City. As the months wore on, Bob's patience, already thin, wore down completely.

Part 3

Oklahoma

1889-1897

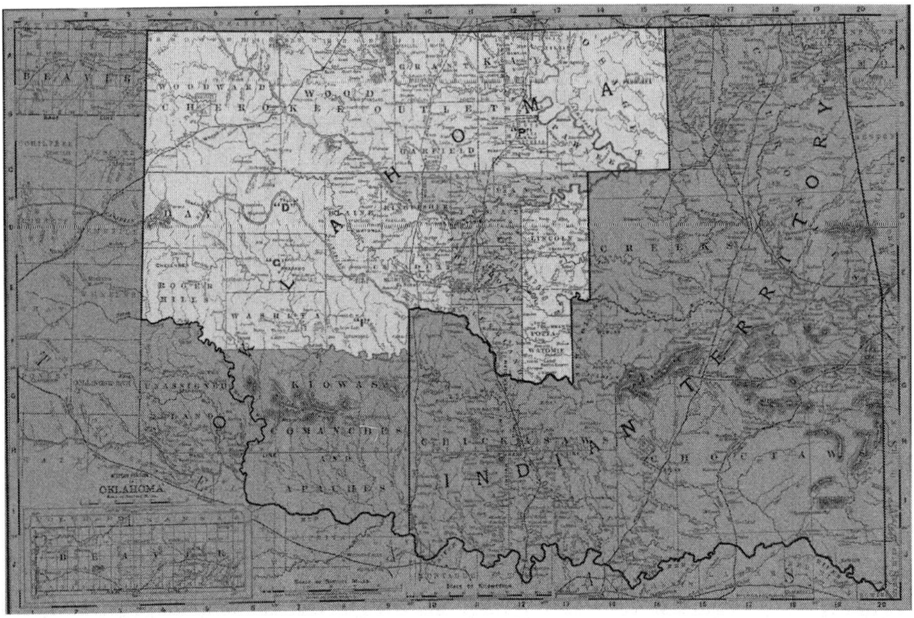
OKLAHOMA
INDIAN TERRITORY
WOODWARD
CHEROKEE OUTLET
GRANT
GARFIELD
LINCOLN
CREEKS
KIOWAS
COMANCHES
AND
APACHES
WASHITA
ROGER MILLS

Chapter 1

Angela's bullets might have been a good idea. Everything went smoothly at first, the details were finally worked out and the governmental wheels began to turn in spring of 1889. The Creeks submitted a proposal for the U.S. to purchase its "unallocated" Oklahoma lands, which was followed by a similar proposal from the Seminoles. Both tribes had always denied the land was "unassigned," but between the Boomers' persuasive resolutions and the Dawes Act ready to crash down on Indians everywhere, they elected to try and get something for the land that was obviously, one way or another, about to be taken.

The proposals were submitted to Congress and both had enough support to pass, but, as usual, there was a new problem. November had hosted elections. Grover Cleveland was out, Benjamin Harrison was in, and there would be considerable turnover in the next Congress. The current Congress was set to adjourn without accepting the Indian proposals.

The Boomers were rightly concerned, but Illinois Representative William Springer came to everyone's rescue. He added both bills as riders to the pending Indian Appropriations Bill, which was further amended to allow the president to establish two land offices and to open the unallocated lands under the terms of the Homestead Act. Congress passed it on February 27, 1889, the Senate approved the bill four days later, and the outgoing president signed it into law that very afternoon.

After twelve years of agitation, Payne's Oklahoma land was to be opened in just weeks. President Harrison proclaimed that the entire Oklahoma district would be thrown open to settlement at high noon on April 22, 1889, just four weeks hence, in a land run.

The border was stunned, but not for long. Enormous celebrations erupted and a storm of settlers thundered in, not just from the north and east but also from the southern border through Texas.

Bud and Angela were gearing up to supply the huge gathering when Lewis suggested a different plan. The Territory was to be opened at once, and the people with the fastest horses would get the best claims. Everyone needed to eat, certainly, but the weather in mid-April would be mild and no one would have to camp for an uncertain time period. After noon on April 22, the Boomers could come and go as they pleased. No, a good, fast horse was not a luxury, but a necessity this time. The Daltons could sell food, but they needed to sell horses too.

Bud immediately procured the best string of ponies he could. Lewis drafted one of the girls, fifteen-year-old Leona, to accompany him to Kansas City in hopes of finding additional livestock.

In four days, Bud managed to acquire thirty-six quality mounts. He headed directly to Coffeyville to await Lewis, who arrived five days later.

By then there were more Boomers gathered than ever before with more arriving each day. They were as poorly provisioned as ever and all of Angela's basics sold as they always had. Bud also noticed there were very few decent horses in the crowd, and those were generally ridden by army officers and were not for sale. Lewis's observation was spot on and Bud knew the horses would sell briskly.

The tone was different this year too. The crowd was boisterous and excited, but now Bud noticed many men wearing guns. Reports of shysters and swindlers were rampant and Coffeyville averaged a shooting death per day while Bud awaited Lewis. Bud took to wearing his pistol and carrying his rifle everywhere he went.

When Lewis and Leona arrived in Coffeyville, they discovered Adeline packing their belongings. Asked what she was doing, she curtly told Lewis that the time had come and they would also be heading south into Oklahoma.

Bud wondered if his house was being packed up too.

Lewis's prediction of the necessity for fast horses was proven correct. There were over one hundred thousand people surrounding Oklahoma, but there were only twelve thousand tracts to be claimed. Speed would be vital if one were to acquire a choice claim, and speed demanded a choice mount. If one wanted a good claim, price was not a factor where horses were concerned and the person with the most money typically got the best horse.

An interesting wrinkle developed when Payne's Oklahoma Colony investors and members learned that claims they had staked during the invasions would not be recognized under the preemption laws, despite Judge Foster's ruling that made them legal. There was not enough time to litigate, so they would have to run like everyone else. They had a slight advantage in that they knew in advance where to go and how to get there, but they still had to get there first and put down their stake. With everything they had already invested in Oklahoma, Payne's Boomers were very motivated to acquire the fastest mounts available too.

Lewis and Bud traveled back and forth between Baxter Springs near the Missouri border all the way to Arkansas City, due north of the Oklahoma Territory and the nearest jumping-off point on the border. Arkansas City was an excellent place to sell horses in April of 1889. Lewis and Bud made their largest profits ever, more than doubling their money on each horse they had purchased. As April 22 approached, horses would sell for even more.

The stage station of Kingfisher and the rail stop of Guthrie had been designated as land offices, and the lots in and around those places would be particularly valuable as there was no doubt towns would be founded there. The railroads believed the same would happen at their watering stops at Norman and Edmond, and they'd surveyed streets and lots at both places. A building boom was expected everywhere, the materials that would become houses, stores, saloons, and hotels were already stacked on railroad sidings and freight wagons all along the border.

Lewis had no interest in claiming and farming a quarter-section, but residing in one of the new-to-be towns showed promise. He and Adeline set their sights on Kingfisher and began preparations for their run.

When they were finally packed and ready, they made their way to the Boomer's rally point at Arkansas City. There were thousands of like-minded families, so the road was crowded and the going was very slow. To make matters worse, heavy thunderstorms turned the track into a nearly impassable bog and the endless wagon train slowed even more. Lewis spent hours in the rain with a shovel, digging out stuck wheels and inching the heavy freight wagon along as the children followed in the covered wagon.

They finally arrived in Arkansas City a week before the run, Lewis and two of the children sniffling from the wet and cold. The place was more crowded than Coffeyville had ever been and thoroughly infested with con men trying to sell tickets for the trains that would take Boomers to the border. Not that there were any scheduled.

Their stay in Arkansas City was brief, as the army had received permission to escort the Boomers across the Cherokee Strip down to the official starting line. The road had not improved, and there were certainly no fewer wagons on it, so Lewis and everyone else picked up their shovels again and inched their way south.

When they reached the line after nearly a week of exhausting travel, Lewis was officially sick and coughing steadily. He was able to organize a camp but as they ate their cold dinner huddled in the covered wagon, Adeline grew concerned. Lewis ate only a small amount and immediately rolled himself into a damp blanket to sleep. She checked on him later and found him feverish and breathing coarsely. The run was just two days away.

The next morning Lewis was burning with fever and refused both food and water. The Boomers were spreading out along the line, but Lewis was clearly incapable of participating. Adeline decided she would leave Lewis in the care of the children while she and Leona sprinted the short distance to Kingfisher and a choice claim. Then she would register the claim and hustle back to see to Lewis.

They got the buckboard hitched to their two fastest horses, then Adeline checked on Lewis again, finding him completely unresponsive. A doctor was fetched.

The doctor spent a few moments examining Lewis, then dispassionately told Adeline the worst: Lewis had contracted pneumonia and his prognosis was not good. Unless Adeline could get him indoors, warm, and dry, Lewis was unlikely to survive. Even then, it looked bad.

Lewis deteriorated as the day wore on, his breathing growing more and more ragged and his color fading to a pasty grey. He finally died around four that afternoon.

Adeline was frantic. She could not leave Lewis's corpse unattended with her children, but she had no time to attend to the details of his burial. The children were completely distraught, incapable of caring for themselves.

A marshal heard there had been a death and came to investigate. Upon learning the situation, he made her decisions for her: She would not leave the corpse unburied, nor would she leave the children unattended. If she wanted to leave the freight wagon, that was her business, but the body would be buried and the children would go with her.

The grief and panic that had been threatening to break her finally did as the marshal dictated her future. Not knowing what to do next, she sank to her knees and sobbed in the mud with her frightened children.

Two Irish women took pity on her and bullied their husbands into lending a hand. The women attempted to console Adeline while their husbands unwillingly dug a shallow, but adequate, grave for Lewis's body. As the sun sank to the horizon, the men proclaimed their good deed done and went back to their own camp for their own run.

Adeline was on her own.

* * *

The morning came and the sky was completely clear for the first time in a week. Preparations were completed, and everyone on the line tensed for the coming rush. At exactly twelve o'clock noon there would be a gunshot and the race would be on.

The moment finally came and it was pandemonium. Individuals riding Bud and Lewis's fast horses streaked into Oklahoma like bullets, fanning out as they sped away from the line. Fast wagon rigs trailed behind, but every stream crossing was an adventure and the leadership positions changed hands from moment to moment. Once a satisfactory tract was located, it must be claimed immediately.

The original Boomers exercised their advantage fully. A few actually set out on foot, carrying a few days' provisions and tools on their backs, and successfully claimed the tracts they had located during the Boomer invasions.

Adeline, however, did not know the land and was very heavily laden. She and the children did the best they could, but it was hours before they covered the few miles to their destination. Adeline was certain, beyond doubt, that it could not get any worse and her nightmare would end soon in Kingfisher.

She was wrong. Kingfisher had already been claimed, and had been claimed before the gunshots that started the run. Bud later learned that there had never been any city claims available at all.

Two different groups of men had snuck in from the western boundary, just a half mile away, and laid out the town and claimed the choice lots for themselves before the run. Each group had different opinions on where the town should be located, so there were two separate sets of plots and claims, each with its attendant tents and wagons on opposite sides of Kingfisher Creek, each claiming to be "Kingfisher." There wasn't anything left worth having on either side.

Adeline wandered along the creek, stunned, searching for a claim, wondering which version of Kingfisher was the best choice. She was nearly ready to give up and return to Coffeyville when Leona saw a group of people looking at a few available plots on the creek bank.

None of them were desirable, and it was possible that none of them were even safe. The only positive aspect was they all were immediately adjacent to the creek, so water supply would never be a problem. It was clear, however, that the recent rains had raised the creek well into each lot's interior. All of them would flood when it rained.

The other families were debating how high the water might get and where a safe place to build a cabin might be versus the possibility of finding something less objectionable later on. Emotionally drained, and with no other options, Adeline trudged down and stabbed her stake into the ground, claiming the lot she thought had the most potential. Leaning against the wagon, weeping again, despair overwhelmed her.

Oklahoma had destroyed the Daltons, completely and thoroughly, in mere hours.

* * *

Bud received a letter from Leona in May. Lewis's death was, of course, the main topic but Leona also described the situation in Kingfisher and their mother's seemingly impossible situation. He and Angela hastily made their way to Kingfisher along the new and well-traveled roads through what used to be Indian lands.

The weather had returned to normal – hot and dry. The thunder clouds cleared away, the mercury rose, and by the time Bud and

Angela reached Guthrie all the traffic on the new roads was churning out clouds of fine, choking, red dust. The frantic development of building around the town ensured the red clouds were produced day and night.

The small creek running past the new city could not possibly support Guthrie's needs, even if it ran consistently. Wells and cisterns were being dug, but water was a valuable, and scarce, commodity. It was certainly too valuable to be used for bathing or laundry, and by the time Bud and Angela passed through town it was impossible to determine the color of people's clothes under the red dirt.

They trotted into Kingfisher to find Adeline and the children attempting to build a dug-out into the upper bank of Kingfisher Creek. Bud quickly set up his own camp and set to work helping with the digging, sawing and cutting of lumber, and the hiring and supervision of what little help was available for the construction. After two weeks he was satisfied his mother and siblings were reasonably safe, if not comfortable.

Bud and Angela returned to Joplin, back through Guthrie and straight through the Cherokee Strip. No army scouts pestered them about their business, brand new roads and tracks crisscrossed the Territory, and there was lots of traffic in every direction.

"This will be next," Bud told Angela. "It's practically open now. Mark my words: this will be part of Kansas soon."

"Bud, what do you think about moving south, into Oklahoma?"

"Well, I'm not very impressed with what I've seen so far. It's going to take a while before they get the problems worked out."

"I was just thinking if this is next, then the Kiowa and Comanche lands can't be far behind. If we were south, it would be easier to, um, keep an eye on things?"

Bud nodded. "If that turns out to be anything like this was, we'll be some of the folks in before the gun. Maybe Grat and Bob could help us there. But yeah, maybe we should think on that."

* * *

Bud was more accurate than he knew. Congress's new commission, not very subtly named the "Cherokee Commission" and ultimately known as the "Jerome Commission," had already begun approaching the various tribes to "negotiate" land "sales." The grand prize, greedily eyed, was the official title's namesake holdings which Bud was riding over and bordered nearly the entire Kansas border.

The Commission's intention was to use the precedent the Creeks and Seminoles had set when they accepted the individual 160-acre allotments and sold the rest in lieu of having it confiscated. The Cherokees were not being cooperative, but the numerous smaller tribes around Oklahoma were "cooperating" nicely. Even at that early date, June 1889, the next Indian land opening was being contemplated and planned.

* * *

As the details of the run's corruption finally emerged, Bud could not believe what he read. Even his mother's experience paled compared to what happened everywhere.

Across the new Territory, Boomers had arrived only to discover the land occupied. Thousands of people had entered the Territory before it was opened and illegally claimed the choicest tracts and lots before the gun had even sounded. Kingfisher's settlement was the rule, not the exception, in the 1889 Oklahoma Land Run.

The Boomers named the illegal settlers "Sooners." Some were simply settlers who slipped across the line in the dark, evaded the army scouts, located a choice claim, and waited for noon to stake their claims. The most egregious Sooners, however, were the deputies, railroad workers, and surveyors who had been allowed into the Territory to organize its opening.

Weeks before the run, hundreds of deputy marshals had been employed to keep the peace in the Territory and government surveyors had been employed to mark the 160-acre homestead tracts the settlers would race to claim, and the railroad's surveyors laid out new towns and marked streets around its existing water stations.

After the towns had been surveyed and marked, the deputies and railroad workers simply selected the claims they wanted. By the time the Boomers raced into Guthrie, the deputy marshals charged with maintaining order had already selected at least one claim each, and were daring anyone to try and take them.

Thus, the first Boomers riding Bud's fastest horses were infuriated to discover Sooner wagons and tents well into the Territory's interior, some claims already under the plow. There was tremendous anger and frustration across the new Territory.

By the end of the month Oklahoma City's population had grown from zero to over seven thousand. The first weeks and months were spent sorting out conflicting claims and leveling accusations at Sooners. The courts would be clogged with land disputes for well over a year, one case being decided by the U.S. Supreme Court, and hundreds of others by violence.

W.L. Couch, Payne's right-hand man, was elected the first mayor of Oklahoma City, and prominent Boomer D.B. Dyer elected to the same office in Guthrie. They both took immediate action to establish law and order in the new cities and, to their credit, schools, churches, and various civic organizations were founded and immediately flourished.

Even after land disputes were officially concluded at the land offices, conflicts between people remained. Oklahoma City's new mayor was embroiled in his own land dispute with a man named J.C. Adams.

Adams was a determined trespasser and Couch a determined settler. Their dispute finally led to a gunfight where Adams was killed and Couch badly wounded. Couch died from his wounds a year later, leaving his Oklahoma City claim to his wife and children.

Shortly after his death, the Supreme Court ruled that Couch's claims, along with those of his party and hundreds of others, were invalid and could not be kept. When the run had commenced, Couch was employed by the railroad to build roadbeds in the eastern section of the Territory. On April 22 he and his entourage had left from the railroad, not from the starting line, to claim their land. The Court held that this constituted an illegal entry into the Territory, and the claims were forfeited. If only Couch had been a surveyor or deputy.

In an irony that Adeline would have bitterly appreciated, Couch's family, after more than ten years of waiting and maneuvering to open the Territory, was forced to abandon Oklahoma penniless while the deputies and railroad men got away clean.

Oklahoma ultimately destroyed the Couch family too.

"Bud," Angela exclaimed, "this is unbelievable! They openly stole land, and got away with it!"

"Yeah, I don't think anyone saw that coming. No one likes it, but no one's doing anything about it, either. Something to think about..."

Chapter 2

Oklahoma's birth closed the 1880s, and the 1890s opened with the Dalton brothers embracing their fates, although none of them saw it coming. It started quickly, in February, when Judge Parker dispatched one of his deputy marshals, Bob Cox, to Claremore, Indian Territory, to arrest Alex Cochran. Cochran was a whiskey peddler who had been very active in selling to the Indians and didn't bother to keep a low profile.

Deputy Cox and his posse man arrested Cochran at his house without incident, and tied Cochran to a chair while they searched for the contraband whiskey. While Cox was searching, Cochran's neighbor slipped in and cut him loose. Cochran retrieved his rifle, then shot Cox as he returned from the barn with the whiskey. Cox's partner exchanged shots with Cochran, but neither scored hits and Cochran escaped.

Deputy Cox died the next day. When word of Cox's death reached Judge Parker, he immediately had his two roughest deputies assigned to bring Cochran back to Fort Smith for a trial and subsequent hanging. Bob and Grat left for Claremore immediately.

They were nearly there when they encountered a rider approaching from the opposite direction. When the rider noticed the deputies, he turned around and kicked his horse into a trot back toward Claremore.

"By God, Grat, I think that's Cochran himself," Bob exclaimed.

"You might be right." The description matched both rider and horse. "What do you say we go take a look?"

They, too, kicked their horses into a trot and Grat called out, "Ho, mister, we're deputy marshals. We need to talk with you for a minute."

The rider spurred his horse into a full sprint away from the deputies.

"Son of a bitch." Bob pulled his horse to a stop and leapt from his saddle, pulling his rifle from its scabbard and jacking a round into the chamber. Resting the rifle across his saddle he carefully put the fleeing man's back in his sight.

"How far away is he, you think?" Bob asked.

"At least two hundred yards, two-fifty by now. You better hurry."

"Don't weave, you bastard," Bob muttered as he pulled the trigger.

The bullet struck the rider between his shoulder blades, throwing him from the horse. Bob and Grat raced up to the man to discover that, first of all, he wasn't Cochran and second, he was dead. It was Cochran's son who had been riding Cochran's horse.

Judge Parker was not happy. Not only had a deputy's murderer escaped, but the men sent for him had killed the fugitive's son instead, on the open road, in broad daylight. That sort of thing could not be tolerated, even in the Indian Territory. The fact that the deputy in question had already killed another suspect who did not need killing did not help Bob's cause.

Bob and Grat tried to explain, but Parker was unmoved and sent Bob packing. Grat could keep his job, but Bob had pulled the trigger, again, and his deputy U.S. marshal career was over.

Bob was furious. It was a justifiable mistake, particularly in light of Judge Parker's instructions when he'd ordered them to Claremore. Bob's feelings of persecution from the Charley Montgomery shooting, coupled with his missing pay from Kansas, fully consumed him as Parker fired him. He would get even, somehow.

Bob packed his belongings and lodged with Emmett near the Bar-X Ranch. Bob fit in with Emmett's rough-and-tumble cowhand friends easily enough, but he didn't like working cattle. He put up with it for a few weeks before he managed to hire on as a deputy in the Osage Nation, which was managed from the Indian Affairs agency in Wichita instead of Judge Parker's Fort Smith court.

Bob had few responsibilities in his new job, so he spent most of his time loitering near the Bar-X and hanging around with Emmett. Neither Dalton had much money, but it wasn't long before they hatched a plan to get some. It was the same plan everyone eventually came up with: They would sell whiskey to Indians. Emmett would do the actual selling while Bob made sure he wasn't caught.

Their plan worked briefly, until a beautiful day in late March 1890. Emmett was selling to a relatively large group of Indians and his first customers uncorked their bottles and got to work immediately. By the time the last Indians got their bottles, the first were half-way through theirs and already getting rowdy. The last recipients, in a hurry to catch up, quickly became incoherent and a loud, raucous Indian celebration ensued. Emmett wisely left the scene as quickly as possible, but the noisy Indians attracted attention. Eventually the drunken Indians were rounded up and locked in the jail to sober up.

The decisive question to the now-hungover Indians, of course, was, "Where did you get the whiskey? Who sold it to you?" Eventually Emmett and Bob's names bubbled to the surface. Word was sent to Wichita and Bob's new boss, Commissioner Fitzpatrick, personally came down to manage the situation. Once he learned the details, he called Bob into his office and sent deputies to arrest Emmett.

Fitzpatrick took Bob's badge and officially arrested him. He and Emmett would be charged with "introducing intoxicating beverages into the Indian Territory" and would be held until trial, then sent to prison.

Grat was still on good terms with the court and managed to convince Fitzpatrick and the judge to allow him to post bail for his brothers. Emmett and Bob were released into Grat's care until their upcoming trial.

The boys returned to the Bar-X, Bob raging that he had quit the service, again, because they refused to pay him what he was owed, again, and he vowed revenge, again. He would take what he was due, and he didn't care who he took it from. The Bar-X cowboys thought that was a swell idea and, like the ill-fated venture that put Bob into his present situation, it would be far superior to punching cows.

Over the course of the next few weeks a notion percolated through Bob and Emmett's brains. They decided they would escape to New Mexico instead of standing trial in Wichita. Three Bar-X cowboys, George "Bitter Creek" Newcomb, Bill McElhanie, and "Black-face" Charlie Bryant decided they were through punching cows, too, and would ride to New Mexico with the Dalton boys. The brand-new Dalton Gang fled the Indian Territory in June and eventually turned up in Silver City, New Mexico.

They hadn't been in town longer than an hour before they sat down at a faro table and, naturally, began to lose heavily. Bob was convinced the game was rigged and pulled his gun to retrieve his lost money. Emmett and the others followed suit, cleaning out the entire game, then raced out of town in a cloud of dust. The Dalton gang had committed their first robbery.

Bob and Emmett's departure put Grat in a bad situation. Not only was he out their bail money, but he'd lost his credibility with every judge and marshal in the Territory. His own position was uncertain and, like Bob, he was growing angrier by the day.

* * *

In June, about the time Bob's new gang was robbing card games, the Sac and Fox, Potowatomie, and Iowa tribes reached a settlement with the Jerome Commission. Although the Cherokee holdings were still the prime target and the Commission was strong-arming all the tribes, these smaller tribes' lands were important because all were immediately adjacent to the eastern boundary of Payne's Oklahoma lands. Each tribe had accepted their individual land allocations and the land would be made available to settlement the next year.

Not coincidentally, in May of 1890 Congress passed the Oklahoma Organic Act. The Act officially designated the area as a U.S. Territory, authorized the creation of a legislature, authorized the survey of all lands, and made it possible to organize towns. Organic Acts were typically the first step toward statehood and the Oklahoma Organic Act would be the driving force behind the Jerome Commission's activities over the next decade. Oklahoma would become a state; the only questions were "when" and with "what boundaries."

The Commission interpreted its charter as a mandate to separate the Indian tribes from the land, and the Dawes Act, which deemed land belonged to individuals and not tribes, would be the mechanism. Jerome and his commissioners, in very unsubtle terms, explained that the tribe members could either select their allocations and sell the remaining land or have the allocations selected for them and the land simply taken.

That worked fine on the smaller tribes, but the larger tribes fought back hard.

The Cherokees understood exactly what was happening and insisted on standing by the treaties, refusing to delay any of their demands for later consideration. The main point of contention was the Cherokee's demand that the U.S. be responsible for removing white trespassers from the land, a problem that predated Payne's Boomers and had grown obscenely since the land run. The Commission would leave the bargaining table empty-handed twice before eventually reaching a settlement with the Cherokees.

The Commission also encountered an able adversary in the form of Quanah Parker. Parker, representing the Comanches, dismissed the Commission's opening speeches and refused to even discuss terms until a sales price was agreed upon. The Commission tried to brush aside his objections and Parker turned the tables, delivering some bullying of his own.

Parker told Jerome that his Commission was greatly confused if they believed they were making a deal. In fact, he told them, there was no Comanche support for any type of agreement at all, and this meeting was about the Commission presenting its preliminary offer. In the absence of an offer, there would be no discussion. The Commission left there empty-handed too.

The Cherokee and Comanche, however, were the exceptions.

* * *

Bob and the gang robbed their way northwest and finally turned up on Bill's doorstep in California. Bill wrote to Bud, reporting Bob and Emmett's location and assuring Bud that everyone was fine.

The same day Bud received the letter, Grat inexplicably stole, and then tried to sell, a string of ponies in the Indian Territory. He was easily caught, arrested, and thrown into jail.

The next day Grat was pulled from his cell and delivered to Judge Parker. Parker officially fired him, but mysteriously didn't send him back into his cell. Perhaps Parker thought Grat would wait for his trial, but Grat proved him wrong by bolting the Territory before anyone changed their mind, fleeing to California to catch up with his brothers.

Bud and Angela had started kicking around the idea of moving south when they learned about the second Oklahoma land opening. They weren't really very serious, but with Adeline already in Kingfisher, the Boomers gone, and all his brothers hiding in California, there was nothing keeping Bud there. Sarah and Arthur were still in Joplin, though, and leaving her mother wasn't Angela's first choice. But it was still fun to think about.

* * *

As Bud and Angela contemplated Oklahoma, the Dalton brothers were corrupting the previously upstanding Bill. Bill's ranch had been involved in one of the Southern Pacific Railroad's constant and ruthless land grabs, and Bill was vocal and tireless in his criticism and opposition to the railroad.

In February of 1891, Bill let Bob convince him that legislation alone was not sufficient to protect California from the railroads. Something tangible was necessary, so Bill crossed the line and agreed to help his brothers rob a Southern Pacific train.

Grat had arrived by then and the four brothers selected a train bound for Los Angeles. The town of Alila was just a few miles away from Bill's place so they decided to stop it as it slowed before entering town.

They took control of the engine and forced the fireman, George Radcliff, to show them the express car containing the cash. The express car, as usual, had a guard who elected to fight instead of surrendering the money. The gang returned fire through the car's door and sides, but the guard refused to surrender. At some point during the gunfight Radcliff was shot in the back.

After thirty minutes of foolishness, the gang gave up and rode away empty-handed, leaving Radcliff bleeding in the dust. Word was sent to Alila where a posse was raised and sent out in pursuit of the robbers.

Radcliff died two days later. Soon after, the sheriff stumbled across Grat and arrested him for the attempted robbery and for Radcliff's murder. The evidence was circumstantial at best, manufactured at worst, but was enough for the D.A. to convince a grand jury to indict Grat.

While Grat was being held in Visalia, another Southern Pacific train was robbed at Ceres. The Daltons were immediately suspected and the sheriff arrested Bill on general principle and threw him into jail with Grat. The district attorney got an indictment against Bill for the Ceres robbery.

Things getting uncomfortably hot in California, Bob and Emmett decided that they'd had enough of the west and headed back to the Indian Territory with the rest of the gang.

Grat went to trial in May. During his trial, the Dalton Gang surfaced in the Indian Territory where they made the news by robbing a train at Wharton and getting away with $1,700. Grat didn't get away with anything and was sentenced to twenty years in Folsom Prison.

Days later, as Bill's trial was about to begin and Grat was about to be sent to Folsom, the Dalton Gang materialized again. This time they robbed the Katy Railroad near Wagoner, Indian Territory, with new members Bill Power, Dick Broadwell, Charlie Pierce, and Bill Doolin. They stole $2,500, and as the gang made their getaway in Oklahoma, Grat made his own from the Visalia jail.

The jail was constructed in a way that the prisoners would spend the nights locked in their cells, but during the day their cells were open and the prisoners could mingle inside a larger area. The cell doors could be locked with a lever located outside the main cell block and the jailer rarely entered the inner cell block; he preferred to let trusties, low-risk prisoners the jailer trusted with basic tasks, do most of the work. Prisoners spent most of the day playing cards on a wooden crated covered with a blanket. Security was lax.

Grat convinced one of the trusties to smuggle a hacksaw blade into the cell block and was able to recruit two other prisoners to join him. The rest would only agree to look the other way when the time came.

Grat found a spot on the outer cage that was not visible to the guard if he were to glance inside. It was a small window connecting the cell block to the basement where the jail's firewood was stored. Sticks were pushed through the bars into the cell block where the prisoners were expected to manage their own fire. If one short iron bar were removed, Grat could get into the basement.

The prisoners pulled their card "table" in front of the window, completely obscuring it, while Grat hid behind the crate, patiently cutting away as the other prisoners loudly played cards.

After three days of tedious sawing, Grat finally cut through both ends of the bar and removed it. He replaced it with a piece of broom handle cut to the same length and blackened with soap and charcoal from the stove. The dummy bar would pass a casual inspection, not that there would be one. Grat and his cohorts waited for that evening's command of "everyone inside."

Instead of entering their cells, Grat and his accomplices wedged their cell doors closed and hid behind the crate. When the jailer glanced inside, he saw the cell doors closed and the common area empty. He threw the lever to secure the cell block doors and then sent the trusty in to check the individual cells.

The trusty dutifully looked the other way, leaving the escapees to their own devices. Grat removed the broom handle and squeezed through the narrow space, lowering himself to the room's floor as quietly as possible. He looked around as the others quietly squeezed their way in too. The place was quiet and empty.

Grat replaced the broom handle and then used the iron bar from the cage to pry open a window grate, which led into an alley. The three prisoners quietly crawled out of the jail and into the street, stole a buggy, and left town completely undetected.

The men were not missed for a full twelve hours. Their locked cells were discovered empty the next morning and the entire cell block undamaged. It was hours later, after a determined search was finally conducted, that the broom handle was noticed and the escape route discovered.

The escapees split up and went their own ways. Grat simply found a train station and purchased a ticket on the next train south. By the time Sheriff Kay learned the prisoners were missing, Grat was well over one hundred miles away and getting farther every minute. He would get off the train somewhere in Kansas and go find his brothers.

Bill, awaiting trial, was housed on the floor above the convicts and was able to plead complete ignorance.

His trial finally started the following week. The prosecution produced thirty witnesses and the trial lasted nearly three weeks. When the case was given to the jury, they deliberated for just thirty minutes before returning a "Not Guilty" verdict.

Unfortunately for Sheriff Kay and the District Attorney, the real robbers at Ceres had been caught. Furthermore, all the evidence against Bill was not even circumstantial, it was nonexistent. There was absolutely no evidence against him and the jury set him free. Bill went home to his wife.

All the Daltons were loose again.

* * *

Back in Kansas, the gang's California antics were causing lawmen and detectives to look at Bud. The gang's activities in the west made for fun reading, but when they rematerialized in the Indian Territory at Wharton, that was practically in Bud's backyard. It was no secret Bud was related to half the gang and the law was suspicious that Bud knew something.

Bud and Angela received their first visit from a railroad detective just days after the Wharton robbery. Like Bill's ignorance of Grat's escape in California, they knew nothing of the gang's whereabouts and they cooperated freely. The detective left satisfied that Bud was not involved at all.

But then Heck Thomas showed up. He had been assigned to bring in two ex-deputies and a posse-man—all were named Dalton, and Bud was their brother. Since the robbery had occurred in the Indian Territory, Thomas had all the jurisdiction he needed. Furthermore, a man by the name of Bud Dalton had been unofficially accused of killing Zack Smith and burying the body in Missouri, and here he was, in Missouri, standing on Bud Dalton's tiny front porch.

Bud and Angela told Thomas the same true story they had given the railroad detectives: They had not seen the Dalton brothers since they left for California, nor had they heard from them, either by messenger or mail.

It seemed to Thomas that they were telling the truth, so Heck took them at their word. He got up to leave and Bud walked him to the door, Angela trailing a step behind. As they ushered him outside, Thomas paused and turned to Bud.

"Say, one last thing. A man named Smith approached me a while back and told me a story about his brother being killed in Missouri by a man named Bud Dalton. You know anything about that?"

Bud was taken entirely by surprise, and it showed.

"What Smith? I—I don't know any Smith."

Thomas was watching Bud closely, eyes squinting under bushy eyebrows.

Angela came to the rescue. "Are you saying Bud's brothers killed this Smith person and are blaming it on Bud?"

It was Thomas's turn to be surprised. He had only been fishing for a reaction and had not considered the possibility of Angela's perfectly reasonable suggestion.

"Well, no, ma'am."

"So, you're asking about something different from the train robbery?"

"Yes, ma'am. I'm just following up because your husband has the same name."

"Oh. And who asked you to follow up?"

"A man named Abraham Smith. Claims a man named Bud Dalton killed his brother in Missouri, and—"

Angela didn't let him finish. "And Judge Parker asked you to investigate this? When did Judge Parker talk to this Abraham Smith?"

"Ma'am, Judge Parker isn't involved in this—"

"Parker's not involved and this Smith man has nothing to do with the robbery? You're doing this on your own! All right, so how do you know that Bob or Grat didn't kill this Smith person? Or anyone else in their gang, for that matter?"

She was getting angry and raised her voice.

"Deputy, you have some nerve. We have nothing to do with that robbery and we told you so. If you don't believe us, talk to that railroad agent that bothered us yesterday. What was his name, Bud?"

"Farraday."

"Yes, that's right. You find him, Deputy Thomas, and you ask him what we told him yesterday and it'll be the same thing you heard just now. But you don't want to do that because you know we're telling the truth, so now you have to make something up to bring in a Dalton, even if you have to frame him to do it! I see what you're up to, Deputy! And don't think for a moment that I won't complain to Judge Parker. You have not heard the end of this. You'd best leave now."

Angela's outburst shocked Thomas and had given Bud a chance to recover.

Bud said, "Easy there. Deputy Thomas is just doing his job."

And to Thomas, he said, "Deputy, I don't know anyone named Abraham Smith, and I've never killed anyone at all. I don't know where you heard this story, but it's a lie."

Thomas backtracked, "Ma'am, I didn't mean to upset you. Your husband is not suspected of anything, I was just curious about the coincidence."

"There's no coincidence," she barked. "It's an opportunity for you to look like you're getting somewhere with the Dalton gang when you're not." She looked Thomas straight in the eye and pointed toward the road leading away from their house.

After Thomas had left, Bud told Angela, "Maybe I should have shot George and Roy after all. Abraham Smith must be Zack's kin, and those two fools must have told him about it. This is getting complicated."

* * *

The encounter with Heck Thomas offered a completely different viewpoint for Bud and Angela. Leaving Joplin suddenly seemed like an excellent idea, and perhaps the sooner the better. The second land opening would be a way to put distance between Bud and his brothers before he and Angela were pulled into a bad spot, either because of the gang or because of Zack and Heck Thomas. Even if they didn't claim any land, Bud was quickly warming to the notion of leaving Missouri and all its complications behind.

A brief look at a map led them to one of the railroad's watering stops, the town of Norman. No sooner had they selected Norman when the gang pulled off the second robbery, the train at Wagoner, with Grat escaping his California jail cell at nearly the same time. Marshals, Pinkerton Agents, and railroad detectives descended on Bud and Angela, demanding to know the gang's whereabouts and if they had any contact with Grat, who was expected to return to the area.

Heck Thomas also showed up again, now officially interested in everything associated with the name Dalton. Once again, Bud and Angela had no information to provide and their questioners eventually left them alone, even Thomas, who carefully avoided the subject of Zack Smith's alleged murder.

Angela was very worried that Grat might appear in their yard at any time, though.

"Bud, he knows where we live. What do you think he's going to do first after riding from California? He's going to need food and money and he's going to come here for it."

Bud nodded. "I imagine so."

"You can bet those deputies and detectives imagine so too."

"I hope he's smart enough to realize he won't get past the yard before they shoot him or arrest him. I wonder if someone's watching our place."

Angela, alarmed, squinted through their kitchen window, looking in all directions. "Watching us? Bud, I don't like this."

He sighed. "No, I don't either. It's just a matter of time before we get caught up in their mess. I have no idea why those boys are screwing around here. They were better off in California."

"From what I hear they're not very good outlaws."

"Well, they've got a long way to go to catch up with the James Gang, that's true."

"Right, and see how that ended? Bud, I'm afraid Bob isn't right in the head. I'm sorry, but there's something wrong with that boy."

Bud closed his eyes and rubbed his temples with his fingers. "I guess we need to go before there's a shoot-out in our front yard. What do you say we bundle everything up here and make sure the water down in Norman is good."

"I say, yes. Why are you frowning?"

Bud had opened his eyes and motioned to the small closet where he kept his saddle and trail gear. "I wouldn't be surprised if someone were to go through our house if we're gone very long. I'd hate for them to find anything valuable and take it."

The likelihood of surveillance, followed with the possibility of burglars, upset Angela considerably. "What? In the house? Would detectives do something like that?"

"Maybe, but if Grat shows up he certainly will."

"Bud? Do you think they'll break anything? The furniture or dishes?"

"No, I don't think they'd gain anything from that. Detectives would be looking for clues, or evidence, or something."

"Bud! I don't like this, not at all! Do you really think someone will go through our things?"

Bud shrugged. "Yeah. Probably, so."

"Bud! No, I hate this! What are we going to do?"

"We'll hide the bars somewhere safe, and leave everything else where it is. Should all be here when we get back. I hope."

The next morning, Bud went behind the barn and shoveled away an edge of the dung heap, which also happened to cover Zack's grave, then dug a small hole for the bars. He and Angela each carried a bar to the hole and dropped them in. Bud covered the bars with dirt, then covered the top of the hole with dung. He then cleaned out the barn, shoveling the fresh manure onto the bars.

"I doubt that would be the first place anyone would look," Angela remarked.

"Should have come up with it years ago."

They quickly packed and loaded the wagon, then headed into town to tell Amy Lins that they would be gone for a while and asked her to check on their place once or twice. She naturally agreed, and the Daltons headed south.

The Oklahoma Territory was growing larger even as Bud and Angela were headed there. Oklahoma's second land opening was occurring, absorbing the Sac-Fox, Iowa, and Potawatomie lands. While much smaller and less dramatic, the run would open four new counties and expand Oklahoma's boundaries to the east.

When Bud and Angela arrived in Guthrie, they found it to be crowded, hot, and still dusty. Since no new land offices had been authorized, Guthrie was the nearest land office to the new counties and the new Boomers were all headed there to register their new claims. Without a pressing reason to stay, they pushed their way southbound through the flow of northbound Boomers, all hurrying to Guthrie to stand in line in the heat.

They arrived in Norman two days later and found the town bustling with activity. Located just north of the South Canadian River, Norman's primary use had been a water stop for the railroad. Named after Abner Norman, a railroad surveyor who laid out the town, Norman officially sprung into existence when one-hundred-and-fifty people planted their stakes and erected tents in the '89 run.

Both Bud and Angela were impressed, or at least more impressed than they had been with Guthrie, and began looking for a place they could rent or buy.

Angela discovered that two people had reportedly made new claims in the run, and their town lots might be available. One had a small shack erected on it, but the second plot's occupant had only a lean-to erected and appeared to be living in tents. Angela directed Bud toward the lot with the shack.

Tracking down the owners, however, proved to be very difficult. Since both had just made new claims, they would either be on their new land or back in Guthrie standing in line. The shack's owner was nowhere to be found.

The other lot, with the tents, was owned by a fellow named Thomas Ransom. He had left his wife, Claire, and son, Jeremy, in Norman while he tended to the paperwork in Guthrie. Angela learned the reason they were still living in tents was because they had never even wanted their Norman claim. Instead of spending what they had left to build and live there, they had clung to the hope that more land would be opened, and their patience had paid off.

That made sense to Angela, although she could not imagine living in a tent for two years, even a large and sturdy one like the Ransom's had. Many settlers in their position had elected to abandon their claims, but Angela could see that, while relatively small, their location was actually quite good. Angela noted their tattered clothes and equipment.

They're still Boomers, aren't they? I wonder if they'll sell?

She began her proposal by saying, "We're hoping to find a place here in Norman. This is a little small for us, but would you consider selling?"

"Whoa, there," Bud interjected. "I thought we wanted the one down there?"

"Well, Claire's here now and who knows when the other man will turn up. I'd just as soon take less now than wait."

Claire jumped at the opportunity. "We'll sell it to you. You bet."

Bud scoffed and turned back toward the wagon to leave. "I don't want it. Let's go."

"Bud, wait." Angela looked to Claire. "We can give you ten dollars right now. Please, take it. If he gets on the wagon I have to leave."

"Ten now?"

Angela smiled inwardly.

I knew it.

"Yes, right now."

"Done," Claire said.

Bud returned and reluctantly pulled a ten-dollar gold coin from his pocket and handed it over to Claire.

Bud looked back and forth at the women. “I don’t like this but if we’re going to do it then I have some conditions. First, we put this in writing, and second you let us stay here until your man gets back and we make it all legal.”

Claire held out her hand. “Absolutely, yes.”

Chapter 3

After questioning Bud and Angela the second time, Thomas returned to Fort Smith, reluctantly, via Siloam Springs. As Bud and Angela drove to Norman, Abraham Smith cornered Heck Thomas again.

Smith sat down uninvited at Thomas's table in the cafe. Thomas had been looking for some peace and quiet, along with some beans and cornbread, and Smith was not part of that plan. Perhaps he could be dispensed with quickly.

"Smith, right? What can I do for you? I'm eating."

"That's right, Marshal. Did you learn anything about my brother's killer? That Dalton bastard? I found your witnesses. You should have everything you need."

Thomas shook his head and collected a spoonful of watery pinto beans. "I'm not a marshal, I'm a deputy. And all I know about Dalton is that he lives outside Joplin, his brothers are criminals, and it's likely that they killed your brother."

"No, that's not right. It was Bud Dalton. I know it."

Thomas put his spoonful of beans back into the bowl and leaned forward, toward Abe. "Mr. Smith, my business is not in Missouri. Furthermore, Dalton is not a suspect and there's no paper out on him. From what I can tell, his only problem is that his brothers are train robbers. If you have a complaint, then you need to go handle it with the authorities in Missouri. We discussed this. Several times, as I recall."

"Murder is a crime, dammit!"

"Then go to Missouri and file a complaint. I'm eating, so please be on your way."

Abraham stood up and stormed off, to Heck's relief.

Smith's insistence that Bud killed his brother made Heck want to ask why he was so sure, but having that conversation wasn't convenient. Or even pertinent. Or was it?

Smith had brought Bud's name to Heck. Bud was known to be the brother of the Dalton Gang's leaders, and they were definitely pertinent, Grat especially so. What if Dalton's wife was right? Did someone in the Dalton Gang kill this Zack Smith character and then feed that to Abraham so Bud could take the blame?

Heck chuckled at that. Pretty clever, if it's true. But it would also tie Abraham Smith to the Dalton gang, and Smith had approached Heck to start with. He can't be that stupid, can he? Well, maybe. Who the hell was Zack Smith, anyway?

He shook his head and got back to his beans. He only had paper on the Dalton Gang, and so long as he worked for Judge Parker he would focus on the man on the paper because that's how he got paid. Bud Dalton was just barely attached, a potential witness at best, and his wife was not worth the trouble. Let it be.

* * *

Abe left Heck, seething. He would handle it, all right. If Dalton was in Joplin, that's where he would go, but there would be no official complaint because the law didn't seem to care. Yes indeed, Abraham would handle it himself. Joplin was an easy ride, due north. He could be there in a day or so if he hurried.

* * *

Bud and Angela made camp a few yards from Claire and Jeremy's tents while Claire rushed off to purchase some badly needed supplies. By the time Ransom returned four days later, Angela and Claire had gotten to know each other fairly well and Angela had learned their story.

The Ransoms entered Oklahoma from the south. Thomas had a good, fast horse and intended to open a store in Norman. He negotiated the Canadian River better than most of his competition and while he wasn't the first to arrive in Norman, he was near the front of the pack.

Like everyone else, he was unprepared for the fact that deputy marshals and railroad men had already claimed the prime locations in town and the Boomers who'd just arrived had claimed the few remaining valuable sites. So Ransom, like Bud's mother, had reluctantly claimed an inferior lot. The Boomers behind him got nothing.

The Ransoms elected to bet on more land opening soon and hunkered down in Norman to see what might happen. They were rewarded with the latest run.

Claire was delighted to learn he'd secured a prime location in Tecumseh and Ransom was delighted that Claire had gotten something for their old lot. He produced the deed from a strongbox stored in their tent and the deal was concluded in just a few minutes.

Bud left the next day to stand in line at Guthrie and the Ransoms left on their short journey east to Tecumseh.

Bud returned five days later with his deed. Since he was not filing a new claim he did not have to stand in the sun as the line slowly snaked through the streets. He was concluding a transaction on a piece of settled property, so he merely had to pay the fee to have the new deed recorded. The line for that transaction was very short.

Two more Daltons were going to try Oklahoma.

* * *

Bud and Angela started back to Joplin the next day and by the time they arrived home they were determined to leave Missouri in the spring.

Angela went inside while Bud tended to the horses and wagon. She looked around the house; everything seemed to be as she'd left it.

She glanced in the small closet in the bedroom and was about to close the door when something stopped her. Her old packers sat in the back of the closet along with a few other items that were in good enough condition to keep, but were not used on a daily basis. She'd put them back there months before, and had seen them without really paying attention to them every time she opened the closet. In her mind's eye, she could see the boots sitting there, tidily, next to each other.

That was not what she saw in real life. The left boot was lying on its side, the right boot standing up like it should.

She carefully searched the little house, looking for anything out of place. Sure enough, she found a few things in cupboards and closets that might have been moved, but nothing as obvious as the boots. Bud was right, someone had picked through their house.

She was standing in the kitchen, seething, when Bud came in carrying a short leather band. He held it out. "I think someone was rifling around in our barn while we were gone."

"Why? What is that?"

"I think it's a hat band. I found it under the loft. I think someone was up in the loft and lost their hat, and this fell off when it hit the ground. They probably didn't notice in the dark."

"I found a few little things out of place in here too. I guess the Pinkertons came by after all."

"Bastards," he snorted.

Angela motioned to the tiny closet where Bud kept his old trail gear. "Did you look in there?"

Bud opened the door. "Looks all right. No, wait. It doesn't."

Angela came over. "What?"

"The duster is poking out from under the saddle. I roll it up tight and tuck it underneath, out of sight."

He pulled the old saddle up with one hand, and reached down for the duster in the other. It was rolled up, but messily, and Bud shook it open.

"It's a good thing you thought of that before they did."

"I suppose." He put the saddle down and draped the duster over it, then went in and sat down at their rickety table. "You think we can get our money back for this place?"

Angela sat too. "More than that, I think. The farmers have it hard, but the mines and the railroads are getting richer and richer. Mamma told me that they're planning two more mines east of town, plus some up in Carthage. There are more miners than ever, and they're leaving the farms to come find work. Just like Daddy did."

"I'm not sure those folks are going to have any money."

"No, but there are always people that do. Talk to Mrs. Lins, she'll know someone. Or at least know someone that knows someone."

"Yeah, good idea."

Angela shuddered, then blurted out, "Bud, let's just leave. People going through our things, Grat and Bob up to God knows what, it's just a matter of time before something happens and we're stuck in the middle of it. Can't we leave right away?"

"Just abandon the place? I guess if we traveled light, we could go anywhere the weather lets us. But we'd be spending the winter in a tent, and I'm not too keen on that. Besides, we need the money from the house. It isn't going to break us, but we've been living off the Boomer money for years, and that's never coming back."

"But there are going to be more openings, right? Didn't you tell me they're already talking about a third one? Can we try to supply it?"

Bud shrugged. "I'm not sure we can. We were in the right place for the first one, and it took ten years for them to pull it off. This last one all happened in the space of a few months, plus we don't have Pa or

Grat to haul the goods. We're going to need to figure out something else."

"So, we're stuck here? With the agents and detectives and whoever's digging around in our house and looking through our things?"

"I think so. It's already October, we'd need to be situated before December and that's risky. I don't think we could ever get moved and settled in two months."

"I say we try."

"Even if we did, we won't have a house. We need to wait till spring, like we talked about."

Bud and Angela rarely quarreled, but he could see this one coming. She was already angry, and now she was getting frustrated with him, but he was certain they were jumping the gun and had decided he was not going to budge.

"Dammit, Bud! I am not staying here."

"So, we're going to live in little tents like the Ransoms? Hell, maybe they left theirs and we can just use those. Use your head, we can't just cut and run."

"We're not running away, we are getting OUT of the way."

"You won't think that in January when it's ten degrees, sleeting, the fire won't stay lit and the tent's falling in."

"The Boomers did it."

"Every Boomer would trade places with us in a heartbeat. Every single one of them."

Angela stood up. "Well, we have a hundred times what the richest Boomer had and by God we're going to make it work. I'm talking to Amy Lins tomorrow morning and if anyone's interested in this house we'll know in a few days. And you mark my words, Bud Dalton, when that man shows up, you're going to take his money, buy whatever we need, and we are leaving here. Right now."

Jesus, she's serious about this.

"And another thing: I don't care if we do abandon this place. We are leaving."

"Angela, this is a bad idea."

"I don't care. I won't stay, and that is that."

* * *

The intruders were not Pinkerton Agents.

Charlie had had enough of Texarkana and judged it safe to meet up with Roy and George. They had endless discussions of how to extract information from Bud, everything from torture to simply asking for their shares and letting bygones be bygones. George was certain that merely confronting Bud and Angela with the facts and simply demanding their shares would work. Charlie disagreed, maintaining that Bud's bad faith justified him losing his entire share. He had to be punished.

They did agree that searching the house was a good idea, regardless of which approach they adopted for Bud. They saw Bud and Angela ride out of town in the wagon and knew they would not have a better opportunity. They quickly searched the entire house, from the root cellar to the attic, hoping to find some hint that Bud had moved the gold.

Their search yielded nothing. With no other choice, they elected to discreetly hang around Joplin, which was very easy to do. Joplin was still a good place to lay low.

* * *

Abraham arrived in Joplin at dark the next evening. He took a room at the first hotel he saw and left his horse in the livery stable, a beer very much on his mind. He wanted to find Dalton, but he was tired from the ride and he didn't know where to look. So, he'd find a saloon, have a beer, and ask around. Dalton would be dealt with the next day.

A beer turned into four beers, and Abe, being the man he was, began to get loud about finding this Dalton character. George heard the name Dalton come from the front of the room and was shocked to see Zack's brother getting drunk at the bar.

"What the hell…?"

Charlie asked, "Who is that? Is he talking about Bud?"

"Shit. That's Zack's idiot brother. What the hell is he doing here?"

"He's making a lot of noise about the guy we're waiting for. Call him over here and shut him up. How does he know Bud? What the hell is going on?"

Roy stood up. "George and I told him about Bud after Zack was shot and we took his horse back."

Roy forced a smile onto his face and called across the room, "Abraham! What are you doing here, partner? Get on over here so we can buy you a beer. How are you, boy?"

Abe squinted in Roy's direction. "Oh, yeah. I know you." He began negotiating his way through the chairs and tables to sit with Roy, Charlie, and George.

Two more beers and Abe was officially drunk and loud enough for the bartender to throw him out. George apologized for their friend and the three of them escorted Abe into the street, then into a dark alley where they pushed him against the wall.

Roy got into Abe's face. "What are you doing here, and why are you yelling about Bud Dalton?"

Abe pushed back as best he could, and slurred, "I'm here to kill that Dalton bastard. The law doesn't care what he did to Zack, so I'm doing it tomorrow. He lives around here somewheres, and I'm going to find him and kill him."

Charlie asked, "What do you mean, the law doesn't care? What law?"

Abe looked Charlie up and down. "Who're you?"

"He rode with us and Zack too," George explained. "He's a friend. His name's Charlie."

"A friend. OK."

Charlie tried again, "What law?"

Abe explained, "I told a marshal that Bud Dalton killed my brother, but he told me I'd have to come here and he wasn't interested. Well, dammit, I'm here and I don't need the fucking law. I'll find this Dalton bastard and set it right."

Roy looked away from Abe, over to Charlie, "A marshal?"

Charlie shook his head, half in pity and half disgust. "Swell. Abe, why do you want to kill Dalton?"

"Didn't I just say? He killed my brother, and I'm going to kill him because that damn marshal doesn't care."

Charlie said, "Abe, look over here. Look at me."

Abe turned to Charlie. "Yeah, I see you."

"You don't have to look for Dalton."

"I don't? Why not?"

"Because he isn't in town right now. He and his wife are gone on a trip, or something. But here's the deal – we need to talk to him. If you kill him, we can't very well do that, can we?"

"Hell, no you can't! Dead guys can't talk, and I'm going to kill that bastard. Make him dead. No talking after that!"

Patiently, and painfully, Charlie persisted. "After we're through talking to him, you can do anything you want to him. Hey, I have an idea. Abe, where do you live?"

"Siloam Springs," he slurred. Nodding at George, Abe added, "He knows where. Was just there."

"How about we deliver Dalton to you in Siloam Springs when we're through talking to him. How about that? You don't have to wait here or track him down. You can sleep it off in your room and just ride back home tomorrow. You have a room, right? Where's your horse?"

"Of course I have a room, it's over there."

Charlie smiled, "Well there you go, then. What do you say, how about you take it easy and we'll give Dalton to you on a big silver platter. What you do to him don't matter a bit. But tonight, you get some sleep and tomorrow you ride home nice and easy. I'll take care of the rest, and we'll all get what we want."

Abe smiled and slurred, "Bring Dalton to me. Yeah…I like that. You are a friend, aren't you? Sure, bring him to me."

* * *

After they got Abe into his room, the gang found another saloon to discuss Abe's appearance. Charlie was very irritated with George and Roy.

"What the hell were you thinking? You told him that Bud shot his brother? And you returned his horse?"

"And saddle," George added. "It seemed like the right thing to do."

"So now this fool is looking to shoot him and doesn't seem to mind who he tells. And a deputy marshal may or may not be looking for him too—that's just what I fucking need. And we still don't know what he did with our … stuff. Either dead or in jail we still never find out."

"We didn't know he'd talk about it," George said defensively. "We were just giving Zack's horse to his nearest kin."

Charlie sighed. "Yeah, yeah, I know. I can just tell he's gonna fuck this up. Maybe he'll stay in Siloam Springs, wherever that is, and keep his mouth shut."

Roy said, "That was some quick thinking, telling him we'd bring Bud after we talked to him."

"Well, maybe we'll do that after all. Meanwhile, we need to track Bud down so we can have our talk with him."

Roy said, "I'm sick of Joplin. Let's meet back here in a month or so. There's no telling how long he'll be gone."

Charlie agreed. "Yeah. He'll be here when we get back."

* * *

No, he wouldn't.

A week after the gang intercepted Abe and then went home, Bud and Angela returned from Norman and had their argument. There was absolutely no convincing her to stay, and Bud finally caved. She eventually confessed that the intruders who searched their house completely unnerved her. They might come back any time.

True to her word, Angela went to see Amy and explained that they'd acquired a place in Norman and Angela wanted to move before winter. They needed to sell their little house as soon as possible. Could Amy help? Amy promised to tap into her network and see if perhaps there was a need for a small house.

To Bud's horror, a buyer materialized that very day. It was none other than Emma Abernathy's husband, a man named Parker Hicks. Hicks worked for Emma's father as a foreman in one of the mines. Emma was expecting her second child and their current living situation was unacceptable to Lois, and when Amy told Lois that Bud was moving south and his little farmhouse was available, Lois leapt into action.

She pulled Parker away from the mine two hours later and headed for Bud's house. At about four o'clock that afternoon, Parker drove Lois into Bud and Angela's front yard and Lois got straight to work.

"You see, Parker, this is perfect. Small barn, nice sized yard, four rooms – there are four, right Bud? Of course, there are. See how well built it is? Amy knew the man that originally claimed the place, Keyworth was his name. She says he was a stickler for details and would never tolerate sloppy work. This house is exactly what you want: plenty of room, well built, near town. Perfect for you and Emma and my grandchildren. I suspect we could have you moved this week. Oh, yes. This is perfect."

It had been a while since Bud had seen Lois in action, and while she had aged, she was no less of a bulldog. He glanced at Parker, whose expression was an unmistakable plea for help.

Bud showed Parker around the place, Lois helpfully providing narrative the entire time. When Lois began negotiations with Bud, however, Parker asserted himself.

"Now, Lois," he began.

"Please, call me Mother, Parker."

Parker's face darkened, "Yes. Mother. I think Mr. Dalton and I can manage from here."

"Yes, of course, you can. I'll be right over here if you need me."

Parker and Bud stepped a few paces away in an attempt to at least pretend to speak alone.

Parker sighed. "Have you known Lois long?"

"Yes, actually. She, uh, convinced me to make a portrait of Emma to send back east before her mother died."

"Really? The charcoal?"

"Yes. You've seen it?"

"I certainly have. You're quite talented. Did you do the colored one of Lois too?"

Bud nodded and Parker cleared his throat. "Very impressive. Well, I guess I'm buying your place. What are you asking?"

Lois called across the yard, "We'll pay any fair price, Bud. Don't be shy."

"We're doing fine over here… Mother," Parker called back.

Bud glanced at Angela, who was standing with Lois. She made eye contact and held his gaze, daring him to screw it up.

Shit. Shit, shit, shit…

"One-fifty is what we paid. How does that sound?"

"It sounds painfully fair."

"Then I guess we have a deal," Bud sighed. He held out his hand and they shook on it.

"You don't look very happy, Bud."

"No. I don't actually want to move."

Hicks nodded ruefully. "Yeah. I don't want you to either."

* * *

All the women were very happy, though. Lois decided that Bud and Angela should move out immediately and Angela enthusiastically agreed. Bud pointed out they had nowhere to go, nor a place to store their belongings, when Amy offered to let them have one of her vacant rooms and use her barn as storage for a few weeks. She wouldn't even charge them.

Bud could not believe his ears. No, Mrs. Lins didn't like giving rooms to couples, but she'd softened over the years and, besides, it was Bud and Angela. It would be fine.

Things are moving way too fast, Bud thought. *I was forced to buy a place in Norman that I don't want, now I'm forced to sell the place I want to keep. Amy Lins is letting us stay together, but nearly refused when we desperately needed help. The world is going crazy.*

Events only accelerated. Angela had their personal belongings packed in less than a day, then decided their furniture, what little they had, could simply be sold since there was not going to be a place for any of it in Norman. It was all hauled into Amy's barn and dutifully advertised throughout Joplin and Carthage. The last was sold six days later to a young man who clearly didn't want it but couldn't say no to Lois.

"Well," Bud told Angela, "we're homeless and have almost no possessions. The good news is we have plenty of cash. When do we leave?"

"Actually, Mrs. Lins had a thought about that."

Oh, Great Jesus Christ, what now?

"I'd love to hear."

"She suggested taking the train. All our things will fit on the wagon. She thought we might simply load it all up, drive it onto a rail car, then ride down to Norman and then drive it off. With stations in both Joplin and Norman it would be silly not to consider it. We could be there in a few hours."

Of course. The brilliant idea that makes the plan I hate work perfectly. Shit. Shit, shit, shit.

"I think that's a great idea. I guess we better find a new tent?"

"Don't we have one already?"

"Yes, but we can't live in that. It's barely big enough to sleep in."

"Hmmmm. I didn't think about that."

"And you still sold our house. Good thinking. Let's go find a damn tent."

* * *

They ended up having to go to Kansas City to get what they needed. Still a popular departure point for the long and dangerous trek to Oregon, Westport boasted many merchants with tents. After some debate, they elected to purchase an older style of tent called a Sibley.

It was cone-shaped, like an Indian teepee. The base was a tripod which held up the central pole, both made of iron. The pole was composed of two pipes that fit together and then fit into the top of the tripod. Around the pole was a ring, about a foot across, that attached to the canvas at the top of the tent. When the ring was hoisted to the top of the pole, the tent was raised.

The sides of the tent were stretched away from the center pole and staked to the ground with pegs. There was also a muffler to cover the hole in the top of the tent and prevent rain from entering but still let smoke escape. When erected, the tent would be a cone twelve feet tall and eighteen feet in diameter.

They bought a small iron stove and enough stove pipe to run up the entire length of the pole to vent the smoke. They also purchased a large canvas tarp to use as flooring since the tent was designed to be set up over the open ground. Satisfied they understood how it worked, they loaded their new tent and stove onto the wagon and returned to Joplin.

Being as prepared as possible, Bud was ready to get it over with and leave. One of the last things he did in Joplin was dig up his two bars and wrap them tightly in his duster, which was lashed under the buckboard's seat. It was virtually invisible on the packed wagon.

They'd taken Lois's advice and purchased cargo space and two tickets to Norman on the train. They said their goodbyes to Amy and Bud drove the wagon to the station. They were directed to the correct box where their wagon and horses would ride, then to their passenger car.

They arrived in Norman six hours later and made their way to their lot.

"Well, we're six months early," Bud grumbled, "but by God, we're here. I don't want to mess around with that damn tent in the middle of the night, so I think we'll be under the wagon tonight."

Angela shivered and complained, "It's a little cool to sleep outside, don't you think?"

Bud's expression screamed, "See? I told you!" but he managed a calm, "Well, it seems we had to leave the house in Missouri."

"Under the wagon should be fine…"

* * *

Charlie, Roy, and George met back in Joplin that December, only to discover Bud and Angela no longer lived in their little farmhouse. They asked the new occupants where Bud had gone, but "somewhere down south" was as specific as they could get. When one heard the phrase "gone south" in Missouri, it usually meant "Texas."

Bud had slipped through their fingers.

Chapter 4

The morning after they arrived in Norman, Bud got to work setting up their new living arrangements. After some initial mistakes, they were able to get the tent raised and most of their belongings inside. The remainder of their first week was spent preparing for the winter that Bud was certain would be horrible.

While Bud was busy digging a latrine, building a simple shelter for the horses and wagon, and gathering wood, Angela spent her time learning her way around town. Norman boasted nearly every convenience Joplin did, but did not include the raucous bars, saloons, and brothels that serviced the miners. It would be a nice place to settle down, and she was feeling a bit smug.

Just as Bud predicted, winter made its first appearance a few weeks later. The wind came out of the north and a hard, cold rain fell for two days, soaking everything and making large puddles in the low spots of their lot. As the puddles grew, the water eventually found a path leading somewhere else, and a small stream ran steadily into the street.

As she watched the tiny lakes and rivers form in her yard, Angela began to appreciate how comfortable their old farmhouse had been, and just how challenging their new tent might become. The ground was completely saturated and their tent's canvas floor only held back the water for a short time. Anything on the floor, such as their bedding, was getting damp.

They lit their small stove, which warmed things up but burning the fire, of course, depleted their fuel and Bud began an ongoing cycle of finding and cutting more firewood. Angela's quest was to keep their belongings dry, either by getting them off the floor or by preventing water from getting into the tent.

By the time Charlie and the gang learned that Bud had left Joplin, Bud had scrounged enough planking to floor their tent, and dug a shallow trench around the perimeter to divert runoff around, instead of under, its floor. By the time the first winter storm arrived near Christmas, Bud had their quarters prepared, more or less, for winter.

* * *

Bud's brothers and their gang had prepared for winter, too, but they were spending it in a snug farmhouse in the eastern part of the Cherokee Strip. The bad weather kept them indoors, too, so Bob had plenty of time to think. Their relative success in robbing trains, in his mind, was pointing to bigger and better things. One night he threw out the idea of robbing a bank, pointing out that the James Gang had robbed banks, too, and had done pretty well at it. Bob was clearly unaware that the James Gang had been decimated attempting to rob a bank.

Bob was adamant that anything Jesse James could do, Bob Dalton could do better. And bigger. They debated and argued through the winter, and by the time the weather began to settle, the whole gang was tired of talking about it. The only thing they could agree on was they needed cash and robbing a train was the path of least resistance. Banks could wait.

March found Bud and Angela nearly frantic to build a permanent place to live. While their Sibley tent had survived the winter quite nicely, Bud had been proven correct about living in a tent, even a large one. Since the first storm that had moistened everything they owned, it seemed like there had been some minor crisis nearly every day. The worst problem, which Angela had never considered, was cooking in the tent when the weather prevented cooking outdoors. Their stove was designed for heating, not cooking, and there were two long periods where the only time either of them left the tent was to visit the latrine. Both lost weight over the winter.

Now that spring had arrived, Bud's thoughts were turning to the thunderstorms that were an absolute certainty. He already knew how the tent handled heavy rain, so he'd made a list of chores to better deal with the vast amounts of water that would fall and rewet their belongings. He was also concerned about high winds, but the tent had weathered everything so far and there wasn't anything he could do beyond adding more stakes, which he added to his list.

The expenses attached to dealing with all their daily challenges was also a problem. Norman boasted all the resources and tools he needed to deal with the day-to-day problems, but living in the tent had begun a constant drain on their cash and Bud wasn't sure what to do about that. He was confident they could get through the year, but building a house and furnishing it would deplete most, if not all, of the remaining funds they'd made back in the '89 land run.

They needed a new source of income, and since he was only good at one thing, he set up a small studio in Norman. A university had recently been established in town, and Norman was growing and looking for respectability. Art was respectable; perhaps there was money to be made.

Bud acquired the basics for his studio: paper, pencils, charcoal, watercolors and brushes, more ink, an easel, and some advertising in the local paper, the *Norman Transcript*, which had sprung into existence at roughly the same time as the university.

A few weeks after his studio opened, the Jerome Commission announced that it had concluded negotiations with the Arapaho and Cheyenne tribes, and their land would be opened in a run that would occur in just seven days. Angela wanted to gather a wagonload of supplies and head for the starting line, but it was happening too fast. It would be impossible to provision any settlers even if they elected to take the risk.

Missing the Arapahoe run turned out to be good luck; they would have made no money because there were very few participants. Some sites were taken, mostly in the new county seats, but the majority went unclaimed.

The short notice before the run was certainly a factor for the low turnout, but the larger problem was the land was very desolate and only suitable for cattle ranching, which required considerably more than 160 acres. One observer noted it was easier to find a rattlesnake than water on a typical quarter section. The few settlers who foolishly attempted to farm gave up before summer's end.

Along with the announcement of the Arapahoe run was an update on the status of the major tribes' negotiations. An agreement had been made, in principle, with the Cherokees and a new proposal was about to be formally submitted to the tribe. Progress was being made in the Comanche negotiations, too, but nothing as promising as with the Cherokees.

While the future held some promise, their current situation had Angela concerned. She wanted, more than anything, to get a house built and to get out of the tent. She was skeptical that Bud's studio could fill the gap, although she kept that to herself. Bud had submitted some samples to the university, but even he believed that was a long shot.

The note about the Comanche lands got her thinking about their gold bars, still buried in the Territory, and she brought it up to Bud. If the land was going to be opened, they only had two options: To move the bars again, or to claim that location themselves. Adeline's experience in Kingfisher, together with the Ransom's stories from Norman, had convinced Bud the only sure way to get a good claim was to be a Sooner, not a Boomer. And based on his earlier experience moving the bars, it seemed obvious that taking the land would be the safest and easiest approach. They still didn't know how to capitalize on the bars—that would have to get solved later. They had to get their hands on them first.

They spent hours debating how, and when, to enter the Territory in advance and how to remain concealed until the run commenced. Bud thought that coming from the west, instead of past Fort Sill, would be the best approach. Once they got there, hiding would be easy. The challenge would be, again, getting to the right place.

Bud would make a scouting trip as soon as possible. If the Arapaho run was any indication, the land could be opened at any moment and with no warning. Unfortunately, committing to the bars also meant putting off a permanent house. If the land opened quickly, they would not need a permanent house in Norman. If the land didn't open, they would build later. Either way, Angela resigned herself to living through the summer, at least, in their big round tent. She understood exactly what the Ransoms had gone through.

Bud's scouting trip was delayed when Bud received the first of three commissions to make portraits. The first was with the university, who wanted portraits of two college deans, the other two for prominent locals.

Bud arranged the sittings with the professors and made their portraits with ink and watercolor which he would varnish. Both were large pieces, meant to be hung in large rooms, but Bud thought they were boring. There was very little color, the theme being that these were serious and important men. Both were dressed in dark suits against dark backgrounds, and Bud had them finished in two weeks. It would have been sooner, but one of the professors, Dr. Haynes, was a bit heavy and wished to appear fitter in his portrait, so Bud had to rework that one to satisfy the ego. He needed more work from the university, so he accommodated the vanity silently.

Bud put off the other two commissions, informing the businessmen that he had to leave town for two weeks, possibly three. He made sure Angela had everything she would need in his absence, then prepared his gear. He intended to travel lightly, carrying only essentials. Food, clothes, sketchbook, and basic equipment like a compass were packed into saddlebags; he didn't even bring a weapon beyond his knife.

* * *

He was gone for sixteen days, and the trip was very productive. He made dozens of sketches, and a crude map that, even though it wasn't to scale, noted many landmarks and their relationships to one another. Finding his creek from the west had proven to be a challenge. Bud didn't appreciate how far it was from the western side, and he had no landmarks to guide him. It took several days and a dozen false leads before he finally recognized the gap full of mesquite trees, then backtracked from there.

He'd seen several groups of riders, including cavalry detachments from Fort Sill, and he easily evaded all of them. He could do this.

Bud trotted his horse up the street that led to his lot and its tent. He was anxious to tell Angela what he'd seen and learned, but he hesitated as he swung out of the saddle outside the tent. There was an odd sound, a slow grinding noise, coming from inside.

What the hell is she doing in there?

He ducked into the tent, and was taken aback at what he found. Angela was sitting in front of an old grinding wheel, the sort that someone would use to sharpen an axe or a knife. It was operated by a foot crank, and Angela was pumping the pedal as fast as she could.

Beneath the wheel she had spread a page from Norman's new newspaper, and in front of the spinning stone she'd placed a small table. Angela had one of their gold bars resting on the table and she was pressing it against the spinning grindstone. Bud had heard the sound of the bar being slowly ground away.

"What the hell are you doing?"

Angela jumped, startled. "Oh, Bud! I didn't hear you. I had a brilliant idea while you were gone. Look!"

Bud looked. She had ground off a corner of their gold bar, perhaps a quarter of an inch.

"I see. Why are you doing that?"

"No, no," she motioned to the sheet of paper, "look down here."

Bud didn't see anything at first, but then he saw it – a faint gold stripe under the stone.

"Gold dust?"

"Yes! We can spend that! Watch."

She carefully picked up the paper and took it to their table where she raised the edges and tapped the fine dust into the crease in the center of the page. She then emptied the dust into a small glass on the table. There wasn't much, but enough to be visible.

"I'll be damned."

He looked back at the bar, and asked, "Where's the rest?"

Angela beamed at him. "Right here." She held out a small leather pouch with a drawstring at the top and handed it to him. He could feel the weight of the dust inside, maybe an ounce, perhaps two.

"This should set us up pretty well," Bud said.

"And we can build a house and get out of this damn tent."

"Out of the tent, right. Good idea."

* * *

The same day Bud discovered Angela making gold dust, the Dalton Gang robbed a train, sort of, in the Indian Territory. They forced a train to stop near Red Rock and while Emmett and Dick Broadwell robbed the passengers, Grat and Bob kicked their way into the express car where they found a single, unarmed clerk. Fearing for his life, the clerk opened the small safe and allowed the robbers to take the fifty dollars inside.

Bob was seething as the gang scurried away with its fifty dollars and small bag of pocket watches. He vowed the next train would be flush with cash and he would take it all.

He made good on his vow a few weeks later. The gang snuck into the small town of Adair where they patiently waited for the Katy #2 to arrive at its scheduled stop there. The plan was to simply get on the train and rob the express car as it sat at the station.

When the train finally pulled into the station, two members jumped into the engine's cab to make sure it stayed put while two others tried to force their way into the express car. As usual, the door was bolted from the inside and the express agent refused to open it.

The bandits threatened to blow up the express car if the agent didn't let them in. Believing they were sincere, he unlocked the door. He was quickly tied up, relieved of the key to the safe, and pushed into the corner. When Bob got the safe open, he was delighted to discover the train was carrying $17,000 in cash. The gang simply needed to carry it away.

The train was also carrying a detachment of armed guards tasked with guarding the express car. The guards, however, did not want to ride in the uncomfortable express car with the express agent and the money, but rather in the lounge car where they could relax, drink, and smoke cigars.

Adair was a very small town, and the train usually stopped there for the few minutes necessary to take on water. One of the guards wondered why the stop was taking longer than usual and joked it was probably a hold-up. The evening was warm and all the windows were lowered, so he stuck his head out the window to see what was happening.

He looked out just in time to hear Bob threaten to blow up the express car. He shouted an alarm, only to be rewarded with gunshots by the gang members on the platform who were now aware of him and his worthless partners.

Shattered glass and wood splinters showered down on everyone hiding in the lounge car. A few tried to shoot back, but the gang was doing a fine job of shooting at any gun, hat, or head that exposed itself and the guards were forced to hunker down in the rain of debris.

With the agents pinned down in their lounge car, there was nothing to inhibit the emptying of the express car. After just a few minutes the gang rode away from the station with all the cash.

When the gang stopped shooting up the lounge car, the agents, keenly aware of their utter failure, could safely shoot back. They fired desperately at the retreating gang and while they did not hit any of the thieves, they did manage to shoot both of the town's doctors on the other side of the square. Dr. Goff died at the scene and, since there was no one left to treat Dr. Youngblood, he was expected to die too. Fortunately for the town, and the doctor, Dr. Youngblood ultimately survived.

Bob and his gang had finally made the big haul they'd been dreaming of and were validated with a $6,000 reward for their arrest. The gang split up to lay low and would reassemble a few weeks later.

When Bud read about the robberies, he was very glad that he and Angela were nowhere near the Indian Territory. No doubt lawmen of all types were descending on his old home, wishing to interrogate him on his brothers' whereabouts.

Sorry about that, Hicks.

* * *

Back in Norman, Bud visited the bank one afternoon and asked to see the director. The clerk frowned and complained that was very irregular; why would he need the director? Bud explained that the matter was very sensitive and required the utmost discretion. The bank's director would certainly need to be involved.

The clerk fetched the director, a plump and pink man in a nice suit named Samuel Deskin. Deskin seemed cordial enough, although Bud noted how Deskin sized him up and saw the irritation on his face at being summoned by the likes of Bud. Deskin managed to control it, though, and invited Bud back to his office anyway.

Introductions were made, and Bud saw outright annoyance when Deskin learned that Bud simply wanted to open an account. The banker, forcibly maintaining his cordial expression, informed Bud that the clerks in front routinely open accounts; the bank's director doesn't need to be involved. Was there something that did require the director's attention?

Bud smiled thinly, knowing that accentuated his scar, and dropped the leather pouch on the banker's desk. "Don't spill any."

Deskin's demeanor changed dramatically when he opened the pouch and Bud explained that he would be depositing gold.

"This is a sample. Will you be able to assist me in this or do I need to go somewhere else?"

"I see. Yes, we certainly can. You were right to speak with me directly; we will need to arrange for you to make deposits. We must also have it assayed so that we can accurately determine its worth and credit your account appropriately."

Bud nodded. "Great. I assume you have an associate that can do that?"

"Yes." Deskin smiled, suddenly Bud's best friend. "I know a jeweler in Oklahoma City who is very reasonable. I'll send for him and tell him what we need. Tell me, how did you come by this? How much do you expect to deposit?"

None of your damn business.

Bud smiled at him. "We've discovered what should become a very productive claim. I'll leave it at that."

The banker raised his eyebrows. "Is that right? Well, I'm pleased to be your banker, Mr. Dalton. Please call me Sam."

* * *

The jeweler, a foreigner named Chaim, arrived a week later dragging a bulky case. Bud met him in Deskin's office and watched him unload a collection of boxes onto the banker's desk. Several of the boxes had glass beakers of clear liquid packed in straw, some contained odd little tools, others recognizable items like hammers, chisels, and a scale.

Bud could not resist. "Jewelers use hammers and anvils?"

Chaim did not look up. "Yes."

He finished unpacking his equipment and held out his hand. "I'm ready for your sample."

Bud handed over the pouch.

After twenty minutes of analyzing and experimenting, Chaim rendered his verdict.

"Ach. I've seen it before, but only once or twice. Definitely gold, and very pure."

Deskin asked Chaim, "Are you sure? How pure?"

"Between ninety-five and one hundred percent. Only coins can be one hundred, and even then, not quite. I think ninety-five is fair for you both."

"Both of us?" Bud interjected.

"Yes," Deskin replied. "Handling your gold creates risks and costs for the bank. Chaim believes that paying you ninety-five percent of the pure price gives you a fair price but also covers our costs. I'm willing to accept his recommendation if you are."

"Fair enough," Bud nodded.

Chaim had poured the dust onto the scale and was weighing it. "Two-and-one-eighth ounces," he announced.

Deskin did arithmetic on a small pad. "Your opening balance will be $41.68, Mr. Dalton. Chaim's fees and expenses come to four dollars, netting you $37.68. Do you require any cash? Or letter of credit?"

"Not now, Sam. Thank you."

* * *

Bud and Angela began building their new house immediately. Oklahoma was booming, structures of every sort being erected in every town. Bud had no trouble hiring carpenters or acquiring lumber—all those things were still littering railway platforms everywhere.

Angela was very happy at the prospect of leaving the tent and explained to her journal.

> *They started work today and seem to be getting quite a bit done. The lean-to is already gone and the framing for the house and barn begun. We should be indoors for good soon, thank God. I'm starting to believe there might be something wrong with me, or maybe Bud - we should have had children by now but we haven't. I know women who've had children late, maybe I'm one of them, but if something finally happens I sure don't want it to happen in that tent. Bud says I'm enough for him, which is sweet, but if we were going to have any it probably would have happened by now. Still, you never know. Out of the tent is for the best.*

By the time September arrived, their new cottage was completed and their bank account flush. Angela had been outfitting the house with furniture and unpacking the few things they'd brought from Joplin. Although neither Bud nor Angela knew it, they had earned quite a reputation in Norman and were a common topic of gossip, courtesy of the clerks at the bank.

It was highly unusual for someone to deal exclusively with Deskin, and the clerks figured it out immediately. They noticed the extra security associated with gold transfers and put two and two together: Bud Dalton obviously had interest in a producing gold operation. But where?

He was never away for long, and claimed his occupation as an artist. To be fair, his abilities were no secret, and his advertisements were in the *Transcript* for all to see, but that didn't explain the mysterious gold deposits.

Adding to the intrigue was the fact that there wasn't a working gold mine within hundreds of miles. There had always been rumors and stories of rich ore and lost mines in the Indian Territory, though, and the army often ran prospectors off the Indian lands. Perhaps Bud had struck pay dirt and was quietly depositing Indian gold.

By the time Bud's small house was completed, most of the town believed that Bud was extracting gold from an illegal mine in the Wichita Mountains.

On October 5, however, another theory emerged.

That morning the three Dalton brothers, along with Bill Doolin, Dick Broadwell, and Bill Powers, quietly rode toward Coffeyville. Bob had come up with a scheme that would top anything Jesse James had ever done and bring unheard-of notoriety to the Dalton gang: They would rob two banks at the same time, and they would do it in their hometown of Coffeyville so the whole world would know who did it.

Just like the James Gang's undoing, Bob's plan started badly. Bill Doolin's horse lost a shoe on the way into town and was forced to hobble back to their hideout. The rest continued into Coffeyville, sneaking into an alley near the town square where both their targets were located.

Unknown to them, Bob was recognized as he and Emmett nonchalantly headed toward his bank, The First National. When the rest of the gang veered toward the other bank, The Condon, it was clear what was about to happen. The locals grabbed their guns and waited for the bandits to emerge.

Bob and Emmett made short work of their bank, emptying the cash in the safe into a burlap bag and tying up the cashiers. When they tried to leave the bank, the locals started shooting. Fortunately for the outlaws, they missed and Bob and Emmett were able to dive back into the bank and escape out the back.

The gunfire alerted Grat's team that the alarm had sounded, and they elected to leave with what they had through the front door. Both teams fought their way back to their horses, killing several residents and the town's marshal in the process.

They were about to escape when the end came. In addition to the hail of gunfire shrieking through the narrow alley, one of the locals snuck around the side and began shooting the bandits. Bob and Grat were both killed, but Emmett and Broadwell managed to mount their horses and escape.

Broadwell was fatally shot as he turned the corner but Emmett, unharmed at that point, was going to get away. Or he should have. When he saw he was alone, he returned to the alley to help his brothers where he, too, was shot three times even before taking a load of buckshot in the back.

Although he had over twenty wounds, Emmett was not dead. The buckshot, while impressively gory, did not penetrate enough to damage any vital organs. His other injuries, in his arm, leg, and hip were far worse, but Emmett Dalton would be the sole survivor of the Coffeyville Raid.

To Bob's credit, his fight in Coffeyville had lasted longer than Jesse's in Northfield – the Daltons had managed an entire fifteen minutes.

When Bill Doolin learned that the gang had been exterminated in the alley, he scoffed. "I knew that dipshit plan wouldn't work. Glad they went on without me." Doolin then snuck away to begin his own crime spree.

In a final and personal insult to Bob, the federal judge decided all rewards outstanding on the Dalton brothers would be paid, even though the bounties were for their arrest and capture, not their death. The technicality would be overlooked—just dead was good enough for the Dalton Gang.

Chapter 5

Bud was staggered when he learned the full account of the raid, torn equally between grief for his brothers and anger over their absolute stupidity. He received word that Bill was coming from California and that Adeline would meet him in Coffeyville to collect Grat's and Bob's bodies and to see to whatever defense Emmett could mount.

Which was none. As soon as it was clear Emmett would survive, the town began clamoring for his immediate execution. The sheriff squelched that, but still moved him to the jail in Montgomery as soon as possible. Emmett would convalesce there until he could stand trial.

Bill arrived in Coffeyville to discover that not only had everything been stolen from the dead bandits' pockets, but the survivor's belongings had also been appropriated. Emmett's horse and guns were missing, even though they should be in evidence for his upcoming trial. Having recently survived a show trial, Bill was having none of it.

The guns had been taken from Emmett by the *Coffeyville Journal*'s editor, a man named David Elliott, in the alley while Emmett lay wounded. Elliott's absurd contention was they had been "given" to him, as a gift, and he was under no obligation to return them. As Bill slowly worked through the legal machinations to get Emmett's belongings returned, Elliott roasted Bill daily in his paper.

Eventually the court forced the editor to return the property, at which point Elliott wrote a long editorial extolling his own virtues while continuing to demonize Bill. Elliott's comments were echoed, debated, criticized, and denounced by other editors attempting to sell their own newspapers.

Roy, Charlie, and George naturally heard about the botched robbery and realized Bud would certainly head to Coffeyville. Thus, the three of them hustled down to Coffeyville to pick up Bud's trail.

Bud did not disappoint. After securing a room, he made his way to the sheriff's office to find out where Emmett was being held and where his brothers' bodies were located. It was there he ran into Heck Thomas.

Thomas was conciliatory and made some small talk with Bud. Where was he living now? Did he need help with arrangements? Did he know where Bill and Adeline were staying? Bud suspected, and was correct, that Heck was only sorry he hadn't shot them himself.

Bud didn't know it, but he also ran into George at the sheriff's office. George suspected Bud would go there and patiently waited across the street. George spotted him approaching, then waited while he conducted his business inside.

After Bud left, George discreetly followed him until he returned to his hotel. He waited fifteen minutes and then casually walked into the hotel lobby and asked to see the register. Halfway down the page he found "Bud Dalton, Norman, OT."

George found Charlie and Roy and told them what he'd just learned.

"We need to get down there right now, before he gets home," Charlie exclaimed. "We can find his place and be there waiting for him and make him give up the bars!"

Roy wasn't so sure. "What if they're not there? They weren't at his place in Joplin; why would he have them here? And then, what if he won't give them up? We gonna just kill him and never get them, ever?"

"We'll have to make him tell! Threaten the woman—that'll loosen his tongue!"

George and Roy glanced at each other, and George shook his head. "You try that and he'll make you kill him. Or he'll kill you. Either way you won't get your bars."

Charlie looked back and forth at them and said, "All right, then what? Whatever it is, we need to do it right now."

George said, "Why can't we just follow him? He has to go to them eventually. Follow him to the spot and take them."

Roy shook his head. "How do we follow him without getting seen?"

Inspiration struck George. "Zack's brother! Abe! Let's cut him in and have him follow Bud. We could set him up in Norman and Bud would never know. Hell, we wouldn't even have to tell Abe exactly what we're after, just that it's Zack's cut and Bud has it. Once we get what we want, Abe can have him just like Charlie promised."

Roy leaned back, clearly not enthusiastic about the idea.

Charlie seemed to feel the same way. "Didn't strike me as a very reliable fellow. There has to be someone else."

George stuck to his guns. "Not with this little time. What other choice do we have? Me and Roy can fetch Abe. Charlie, you get down to Norman and see what you can learn about Bud."

Without a better alternative, Roy reluctantly agreed. "All right…I guess. Abe's place isn't too far out of the way, I reckon we'll be a day or so behind you."

Charlie heaved a sigh and shook his head. "This is a mistake, but let's get on with it."

* * *

Charlie rode hard and arrived in Norman well ahead of Bud. He found a small hotel room and livery for his horse, then headed for a saloon to discreetly ask about Bud. Maybe someone would know him. It turned out that everyone knew the guy with the ugly scar, even if they didn't know him personally.

The town of Norman had also discerned that Bud Dalton was indeed related to half the gang that had just been wiped out in Kansas, and the whispers around town intensified. The men in the saloon were more than happy to gossip with the new stranger.

"He has plenty of money, probably from a mine."

"A mine? What kind of mine?" Charlie asked.

"They say he struck gold in the Indian Territory."

What the hell?

The bartender leaned in and said, "But some say the money isn't from a mine. Maybe he was tied to that gang up in Kansas." He raised his eyebrows and nodded knowingly at Charlie.

Charlie slid a nickel across the bar and told the bartender, "This is a friendly town; I like it here. How about another beer?"

* * *

Being the center of all that gossip, it was inevitable that some of the talk would get back to Angela, and it did. She scoffed at the notion of Bud being an outlaw and told her friends, who would certainly repeat it, how the railroad agents and marshals had lined up outside their house in Joplin to question them. If Bud were tied to the gang, then the authorities would be in Norman too.

She also pointed out that the gang got their start in California, not Kansas, and it was the gang's return from California that ultimately convinced Angela and Bud to flee to Oklahoma in the first place. And finally, if Bud were mixed up in the Dalton Gang, why wasn't he lying dead in Coffeyville instead of arranging his brothers' burials?

Angela's gossipy response made its way around Norman's quilting circles and card games. Bud's outlaw reputation faded and his illegal miner reputation regained its momentum.

Just a week after the Dalton Gang was exterminated, while Angela and Charlie were attending to the local gossip in their own ways, the Jerome Commission announced that it had finally concluded negotiations with the Kiowa and Apache tribes. The tribes would accept an allotment and their lands would be opened too. The date was forthcoming. Many eyes glanced toward Bud and Angela, and more rumors were exchanged over beers.

Bud's old outlaw buddies were up to speed on everything Norman knew about the Daltons. Abe was very excited to be part of the gang and to finally be able to exact his revenge on Dalton. Charlie, George, and Roy had done their best to impress upon Abe the absolute need for secrecy. He should not even bring up Dalton's name, only keep an eye on his comings and goings, and report those to Charlie. Under no circumstances, ever, should he approach or speak to Bud or Angela.

Abe was not happy about any of that, but Charlie made clear that if Abe ruined the plan, he would receive neither Zack's share (share of what, Abe still didn't know) nor Bud Dalton when it was all over. Abe reluctantly agreed and settled into stalking the Daltons around Norman.

Abe learned where Bud and Angela lived, what their horses and wagon looked like, where they went and who they were friends with. All was dutifully reported back to the gang. Charlie continued to quietly tap into Norman's rumor mill and made sure to avoid any of the places where Bud was likely to appear.

After a few weeks of watching and listening, Charlie was forced to agree that Bud did not have the gold bars stashed in Norman. Furthermore, neither Bud nor Angela seemed to be trying to hide anything. They were clearly well-off, and George reminded them how well Bud and Angela had done in the Boomer camps. They probably had plenty of money left and no reason to hide it.

Charlie would just have to keep listening.

* * *

If Charlie was listening, then someone had to be talking, and it finally got back to Angela again. One of her friends, Janet Monroe, casually mentioned that she expected Angela to be preparing for a move soon.

"Why would I move? Bud just finished the house."

"Well, with that Indian land opening soon we assumed Bud would be taking a claim."

"'We'? Who's talking about us?"

Janet's cheeks colored. "No, it's not like that. Everyone knows Bud has business down in the Territory, and it seems logical that when the Territory opens Bud will go down there."

Oh, dear God.

Angela remained calm and, very carefully, relaxed her face into what she hoped was a puzzled expression.

"What business is everyone talking about?" Angela asked.

Janet leaned in conspiratorially and lowered her voice. "Angela, everyone says Bud has a gold mine down there."

Angela felt her eyes blink twice and knew she'd just confirmed the rumor. Her mind raced as she stared at her friend.

Angela finally sighed and sat back. "Well, it wasn't a very good secret anyway. Truth is, this is a relief."

Janet gasped. "It's true?"

Angela shook her head. "No, but close." Then she set the hook. "I'll tell you, but please keep it to yourself?"

"Oh, yes! Of course!" Janet nodded vigorously, nearly salivating at the thought of breaking possibly the juiciest gossip in Norman's short history.

"When Bud was younger, he spent a lot of time down in the Territory, even before the Boomers opened any of it. I'm sure you've noticed his scar? Right, well, he got that in the Territory when he was seventeen. He was kicked by a horse."

"I'd wondered about that but thought it would be rude ask."

"Yes, and the fact it happened in the Territory is one of the reasons he doesn't like to talk about it. Bud doesn't want people to think he's been scrounging around the Territory for the last eighteen years."

Janet, who was just in her twenties, registered the fact that Bud Dalton had been scrounging around the Indian Territory for most of her life.

Angela continued, "So, about two years ago he and his partners were panning in a creek and found gold. Not a lot, but enough to warrant a closer look. They discovered that many creeks showed gold, two of them enough that just panning could pay. That's where our share comes from.

"But that's still Indian land, and there's no way they can do anything except pan and try to locate the source. Digging an actual mine would attract the army's attention and give away the location. Then no one would have anything. Lord knows the army has run them off enough already."

"So, there's no mine?"

"Not yet, but Bud and his partners are pretty sure they know where to look." Inspiration struck, and Angela added, "He says there's probably a lot more in those mountains than what he's found."

Janet asked, "But you're not going to try for a claim?"

Angela replied, "Bless your heart, of course we are. I just didn't know it was such common knowledge. It doesn't change anything, but at least we don't need to worry about it anymore. Thank you for listening to me, Janet. I feel much better with that off my chest."

* * *

Angela went straight home after her confession to Janet and told Bud the entire story. After they'd talked for a while, Bud suggested they do nothing.

"Let everyone think that, now we don't have to explain where our money comes from. Meanwhile, we wait until they announce the run and then grab the claim just like we planned."

"Bud, I don't think you can just wait in Norman. Everyone's still watching you and if you don't give them something to talk about pretty soon they're going to make up new ideas."

"So what?"

"Well, don't we want them to stick with the idea they have? If they all know for sure, then there's nothing to talk about. Since people like to talk about new things, they'll move on to something else."

"Hmmmm. So, make everyone think we're getting ready to make a move?"

"Yes! Janet Monroe is probably telling the quilting circle about promising creeks right now. I think you should ride down there again, soon, and make sure a few people know you're going and see you leave.

"When you get back, take another sack to the bank and let someone overhear you telling Deskin that your partners aren't sure how the opening is going to play out. Production will slow, and if you can't get the right claims … well, tell him you might have to buy someone out."

"Yeah, now we're waiting like everyone one else … that should put a lid on all this. I think I'd like to dig up another bar anyhow. I wonder how many we could get back before the run?"

"I expect not very many. Wouldn't you need the wagon for more than one or two?"

"Yeah. And we don't want to be stopped with a wagon full of gold bars. I got awful lucky last time. Besides, the run won't happen till spring at the earliest. They'll need to survey, and winter will slow that down. Maybe in May? We'll be ready well before then. Yeah, I'll leave in a day or two."

"Good. I'll give Janet another tidbit and that should set the table."

* * *

Janet did her job, and the Norman rumor mill did its. Before long it was common knowledge that the Wichitas were the rich mountains they were always rumored to be and that Bud Dalton was the man who was going to break it open.

That information confused George, Roy, and Charlie considerably. George asked the obvious question.

"What if we have this wrong and he really doesn't know where the bars are? He's got a mine, why would he ever bother with that if he already had a big stack of gold bars?"

Roy agreed. "Yeah, that doesn't make any sense. If so, then who moved the bars to start with?"

Charlie slowly asked, "Is there any chance Zack was playing at something? Maybe he'd already moved them before I dug up the emp ty packs?"

Roy and George glanced at each other, and Roy nodded. "Well, that's what Bud claimed when he shot Zack. And what he said made a lot of sense at the time. But I still don't think Zack could put on an act like that. Besides, if he had the bars, why bother with the act at all?"

"To frame Bud and keep it all?"

Charlie was at a loss. "Zack definitely hated him. And he didn't want to bury them to start with, so maybe … I guess. So, what do we do? If Bud really doesn't know where they are then we're just pissing up a rope. Unless Jesse's back from the dead or Cole is out of prison ... Wait, Frank is out of prison."

Roy shook his head. "I don't think so. He can't make a move without the law watching. I heard he has five Pinkerton men assigned to him."

George chimed in, "Yeah, Frank's got nothing to do with any of this. Bud is still the most likely person to have dug up the bars, even if he doesn't need them anymore because of that mine. I'm telling you, we need to just put it all in front of them: We know he has the bars hidden somewhere, we know he has an illegal mine, and we don't care that he shot Zack. We just want our share of the gold and we'll call it square. Bud won't care."

George's timing was unfortunate.

"By God, I care! And gold? What gold? You saying that Dalton bastard killed Zack to steal his gold?

All three turned and saw Abe standing in the doorway, completely wound up.

Charlie spoke first. "Calm down, Abe. If you were listening then you know we're not really sure what Bud did..."

Abe pointed at Roy and George. "They said Dalton shot Zack. Is that true?"

"Well, yes."

"And now you say that Dalton has some gold that belonged to Zack?"

"Uh ... well, maybe. We don't know for sure."

"That's enough for me. I'm going to kill that bastard right now."

"No, you're not. We want the gold, but we need Bud to find it. If you do anything to him before we find the bars, then you're going to answer to the three of us. So just calm down. Anyway, what are you doing here? What's happening?"

"I heard Dalton is leaving for the Territory tomorrow."

"So?"

"So, now's the time. We follow him and he leads us to either the mine or the gold he stole. That, or we make him tell us. And then I shoot him."

Charlie shook his head. "Things are different now. We don't want any part of his damn mine, and that's probably what he's up to. George might be right—the more he makes off that mine, the less important those bars become and maybe he'll be willing to deal. Or maybe he really doesn't know anything. No, we need to keep watching. Now's not the time."

Abe glared at them. "Won't get a better chance."

"We will if you don't spook him," Charlie barked. "You need to trust me. I want the same things you do. Just keep watching him."

Abe scoffed and stormed away without another word.

No one will do anything to this guy—first the marshal, now these three. To hell with them all.

* * *

Bud left the next morning, but not too early. He went out of his way and rode past both the bank and the courthouse, pausing at each to make sure as many people as possible could see him and anyone interested could take note of his departure.

He left town heading southwest, crossing the South Canadian River just outside of town. He'd ridden that trail many times and allowed his mind to wander as his horse walked leisurely along the track. He was still grieving for his brothers and worried about the one who had survived. Emmett would be spending a long time in prison.

He thought back to his own youth and his ride with Cole and Jesse, and how he thought he had wanted to be an outlaw. How things change.

Cole warned me, and he was right. Jesse James was an untrustworthy piece of shit, the locals will always fight back, and the cashiers won't open the safes. Hell, there won't even be an Indian Territory to hide in much longer. Every damn bit of that just happened to Bob and Grat ... and Cole too, for that matter.

The old notion that Zack's boot had altered the course of his life for the better once again crossed his mind.

Isn't that something? The guy I hated more than anyone might have saved my life by nearly killing me.

Visions of Zack coming at him through a cloud of blue smoke, Sullivan and his curved needle, and disconnected memories of recovering at Fort Reno drifted through his mind.

I never told Grat or Bob about any of that. I wonder if that would have made a difference to what happened to them?

He was being so negligent that his horse turned off the track and stopped to graze on some grass. As Bud urged his mount back onto the trail, he happened to glance behind him. There was another rider about a quarter mile behind him, which was not unusual, but this rider wasn't moving. He'd halted his horse when Bud's had gone for the grass, and he appeared to be waiting for Bud to ride on.

Bud gave his horse a gentle kick, urging him into a trot. People behaved strangely on the trail sometimes, and it was possible the man behind him was concerned that Bud was an outlaw and simply didn't want to get any closer. Bud didn't want company either, and decided to focus and make better time.

He kept up the trot for about twenty minutes until he came to the crest of a small hill and took the opportunity to look behind him. The rider was still there and still about a quarter-mile back.

That bastard is following me, and badly at that. What the hell does he want?

Bud shook his head and spat to one side.

I should have seen this coming. He thinks he can follow me to the mine or take me on the trail and beat it out of me. I'm surprised no one's tried already.

Bud trotted his horse down the hill. At the bottom he inspected the small draw where runoff would go during a rain. It was bare, with no cover at all, not even any scrub oak.

That won't do. Let's check the next one.

He continued trotting along the trail until he finally came across a small creek that would suit his needs. There were small trees and bushes lining each side, not enough for protection from bullets but plenty to hide behind. Bud figured he had about five minutes before his pursuer caught up.

He splashed through the slight trickle in the creek bed and turned to the right, tracing the bank until he came to a juniper tree large enough to hide his horse. He slid out of the saddle and secured the horse behind the tree, then pulled his Winchester from its scabbard. Crouching down, he watched through the brush.

***

Abe didn't like Bud riding so quickly. Each time Bud rode over a hill and Abe lost sight of him, Abe got nervous. He felt his chest tighten as Bud crested the latest small ridge and forced himself to calm down. He would get up the hill and Dalton would be riding steadily along the trail.

Except this time he wasn't. Abe paused and looked both left and right, standing up in his stirrups for a better view. *It's all right,* he thought. *He's down there. Just keep on.* He trotted down the hill, trying to regain contact with Bud.

***

Bud watched Abe stand and look around. He instinctively noted how Abe was dressed, his hat, boots, and horse, that he was armed, and that his ruse had worked. He would wait there for fifteen minutes or so before continuing, giving his pursuer plenty of time to get out of the way.

He lounged in the shade, letting the horse drink from the creek and graze on whatever grass he liked. When the time was up, he loosened his pistol in its holster and made sure his Winchester was in easy reach, then prodded the horse up the hill.

He was surprised to meet someone coming in the other direction. He reined in and stopped his horse, waiting for the rider.

The other traveler reined in, too, and said, "Howdy."

"Howdy. I'm trying to catch up with a fellow on this track, maybe you've seen him? Tall fellow, black hat on a roan gelding? I hope he's just ahead of me."

The stranger snorted. "Yeah, I saw him. He's on top of a hill about a mile back, looking for someone and talking to himself. I guess he's looking for you."

Bud laughed. "Yeah, that's him all right. I thank you. Good day."

Bud spent the rest of the afternoon carefully stalking Abe, doing all the things that Abe should have done. He stayed out of sight, moved carefully and deliberately, and stayed off the trail.

Abe made it easy, though, never moving very far and tending to stay on the high ground where he could see better and, naturally, be seen. Bud had a long time to watch and decide whether or not to confront him.

This guy's a fool. We should have a talk, and now's as good a time as any.

Bud carefully moved to the downwind side of the track, eliminating the chance that Abe's horse might smell his own. He tied up about a hundred yards off the trail, again behind some foliage to screen his horse from view. He checked both his pistol and rifle and quietly approached from behind.

Abe was sitting on his horse, positioned so he could watch the track in both directions by simply looking back and forth. He was obviously upset and the possibility of someone sneaking up behind him never crossed his mind.

Bud cocked the Peacemaker and said, "Move and I kill you."

Abe could not possibly avoid moving because Bud scared the hell out of him. He jerked in his saddle and twisted around to look behind him, finding Bud with his Peacemaker pointed directly at him. He was too close to miss.

As Abe gawked at him, Bud said, "All right, calm down. Get off your horse, and keep your right hand way far up in the air."

Abe sputtered, "Why you bastard, where did you come from? How'd you get back there?" He made no effort to get off the horse.

Shit, do I have to shoot this guy? What the hell is his problem?

Bud tried again. "Mister, I'm not joking. Get off that horse right now, and keep your hand where I can see it. Do it!"

Abe wheeled his horse toward Bud and snarled, "Fuck you, you murderin' bastard!"

Bud pulled the trigger and the heavy bullet struck Abe in the left shoulder, passing through the joint and exploding out through his shoulder blade. Unable to hang on, he fell from the horse.

Bud shooed the horse away and recocked the pistol. Abe was clutching his ruined shoulder, trying to stem the blood.

"What the hell is wrong with you?" Bud shouted. "Why did you make me shoot you? All you had to do was get off the damn horse!"

Abe groaned, "I'll kill you, you bastard…"

Oh. He's crazy.

Bud pulled Abe's gun from its holster and tossed it aside. "I don't want anything from you, mister. I just want to know why you're following me. Hold still, we need to get something in that hole."

He caught Abe's horse and pulled open the saddlebag, dropping the contents on the ground until he found two passably clean shirts. He wadded them up and pressed one into the large exit wound and the other into the smaller entry wound in front. He laid Abe on his back to keep the makeshift bandage pressed into the exit wound.

"Hold still, you're going to make the bleeding worse. Who are you? Why are you following me?"

"You killed my brother, you bastard. Then you stole his gold. I'm going to kill you…"

Killed his brother? Gold?

"I've never killed anyone, mister. And I don't have any gold. Who is your brother?"

"Zack. They told me you killed him, and they brought me his horse."

Bud leaned back, studying the man's face.

Could be.

"Mister," Bud told him, "they lied to you, whoever they are. I've never killed anyone. Who were these men?"

Abe grimaced from the pain, and Bud could tell he was losing enough blood that he could lose consciousness. He might even die without medical attention.

"Uh, Charlie, George, and Roy. I can't remember their last names. They said you shot Zack in Missouri, so I'm going to kill you."

God damn it, Roy and George again. And Charlie...Charlie Jones? How many more?

Bud looked at him apologetically and repeated, "I've never killed anyone. I'm afraid those men lied to you."

"That's what the marshal, Marshal Thomas, said too. Heck said the same thing. But I don't think the boys would lie. You did it. I know you did." Abe groaned, again.

Heck Thomas? Jesus, is this the guy that pointed Thomas at me? Who is this guy?

"Hold still." Abe groaned as Bud pushed more cloth into the wounds. "How do you even know me?"

"The boys brought me to Norman to follow you around … wait for you to lead us to the gold you stole. I'll get Zack's share, then I get to kill you for killing Zack."

"The boys … Charlie, George, and Roy. Mister, I don't know any of those names. I don't even know you. Who are you?"

Abe was getting woozy and disoriented, and Bud could see blood soaking the ground beneath Abe's shoulder. He needed to hurry.

"Never mind, we gotta get you to a doctor. Where are these boys of yours staying? I'll get word to them for you."

"Little saloon on Main Street, just west of the station … Webster's. This ain't gonna keep me from killing you."

Bud sighed and shook his head. "Yes, it is."

Abe groaned loudly as Bud pulled the shirt from the entrance wound, then lifted Abe's ruined shoulder. He pulled the second shirt from the exit wound and was rewarded with a fresh gush of bright red blood.

"You'll feel better in a bit."

Chapter 6

Abe bled out in about twenty minutes as Bud thought about what he'd learned. It was late in the day, just about an hour of daylight left. Bud didn't like to ride at night, but there was no choice this time. He'd need to return to Norman with the corpse immediately and report the whole thing to the sheriff. Then find the boys.

He spent the last of the daylight catching Abe's horse and tying the body across the saddle so it wouldn't fall off. He retrieved his own horse, then went back the way he came, trying to figure when the moon might rise. Until it did, he'd have to pick his way slowly through the dark.

The moon finally rose around ten o'clock and provided enough light to at least trot along the trail. He splashed across the river crossing just after midnight and was pounding on the Cleveland County sheriff's door thirty minutes later.

The sheriff was asleep at home, but there was a deputy handy to wake him up and then fetch the undertaker. The sheriff cut Abe's body loose and eased it to the ground.

"What happened here, Bud?"

"This fellow tried to rob me on the trail, just this side of the new Chickasha post office. I was off my horse and I got the drop on him, told him to get down, but he charged me and I shot him like you see. I don't know if there's any law in Chickasha so I brought him back here."

"Who is he?" the sheriff asked.

"No idea, Sheriff. Never seen him before in my life."

"Another damn outlaw. This is getting out of hand. Chickasha is on Choctaw land, so we'll need to turn it over to the U.S. marshal. I don't expect him to take much interest, though."

The U.S. marshal in charge of the Oklahoma Territory, E.D. Nix, had been appointed during President Cleveland's first term. Nix had no law enforcement experience and had, in fact, been a grocer before the run. A well-connected grocer, it seemed.

Nix traveled to Washington in order to lobby for an appointment to the "plum" position of the new Oklahoma Territory marshal. Despite the fact that Oklahoma was known to be rife with outlaws and criminals of every variety, Nix was inexplicably appointed anyway. His first act was to hire most of his relatives as deputy marshals.

Nix was a hands-off kind of lawman. He rarely left his office, and even then, it was usually for his own benefit. Trips to Washington to increase his budget and hobnob with congressmen or attend the occasional banquet were all he was known for, and he naturally found time to go to the World's Fair and Buffalo Bill's show in Chicago. Both were marvelous.

The sheriff sent Marshal Nix a message about the shooting, and Nix eventually turned up. He asked Bud a few general questions and Bud repeated what he'd told the sheriff earlier. Since no one knew the dead man, and his killer had delivered the body and claimed self-defense, and there was no paper on anyone, Nix decided that justice had been served. Breakfast was waiting.

The undertaker propped up the body on the customary plank and displayed it outside his office while he prepared for the embalming. Much of Norman dropped by to gawk at the corpse and take in the news that Bud Dalton had done the work, defending himself on the trail.

Those in the know looked wisely at each other and nodded. That road leads to the Wichitas, and everyone knows Dalton has business down there. And based on this stranger's condition, it seems Dalton is serious about his business. Don't let that artist act fool you; Dalton is a no-nonsense character and that pistol ain't for show. The stranger on the plank proves that. Oh, yes indeed, you'd best take Mr. Dalton seriously.

***

Charlie had not seen Abe at all the previous day and wanted to make sure he was behaving. He checked Abe's room, the saloons and cafés Abe frequented, but with no luck. As he passed the crowd at the undertaker's, curiosity got the better of him and he edged through the crowd for a look.

Oh, shit. What the hell?

It took all of Charlie's resolve to maintain a disinterested expression as he listened to the story.

"Well, sounds like he had it coming," he said as he pushed his way back into the street.

Maintaining his calm, he managed to get back to his room at Webster's saloon without running or making a scene. Roy's room was next to his, and Charlie banged on the door.

Roy jerked open the door, and was surprised to see Charlie as the source of the racket.

"What's wrong?"

"Bud killed Abe last night. On the trail."

"Trail? The hell you say, what trail?"

"Near Chickasha is what I heard. His body's at the undertakers, shot from about six feet, it looked. Probably bled to death."

"Jesus."

"Gather your gear and get George. We can't run into Bud. We need to move now."

* * *

Bud went straight home after Nix elected to have breakfast. When Bud walked into the house less than twenty-four hours after he left, Angela knew something was horribly wrong. As Bud recounted what happened the previous day, she became appropriately worried.

"Lord, Bud. This is getting out of hand. Janet told everyone in town about the mine and now this guy and the old gang show up looking for the bars. Everyone knows all about us and are just waiting ... for what? What's to keep someone from kicking in the door and ransacking the house? And just leaving us dead?" She shivered at the thought.

"I guess letting everyone think what they want wasn't so good an idea."

"What are we going to do, Bud?"

"We're definitely going to keep a low profile, but I need to find the gang."

"And do what? Shoot them?"

"That's not very low profile. I need to convince them I don't have the bars and don't know where they are. Zack's brother said they told him I have them. He also said they were staying at Webster's. I should be able to find them there. And then I need to get some sleep."

Charlie, George, and Roy had trotted away from Webster's just two minutes before Bud arrived. He checked the register and wasn't surprised to not find any of their names, but the woman at the counter recognized Bud's description of George. He had just checked out; she was surprised Bud hadn't seen him on the way in. Yes, he was with two other men. No, they didn't say where they were going.

Bud went home to get his much-needed sleep. While he was sleeping, the rest of the nation was voting. The date was November 8, 1892, and Grover Cleveland was about to win a rematch of the previous election where he'd lost to Benjamin Harrison. Cleveland was about to become the first president to serve nonconsecutive terms, something no one considered possible. His unexpected victory would rattle the whole nation.

* * *

By itself, Grover Cleveland's election was no reason for alarm. Congress, with the Jerome Commission's help, conjured up quite a bit of it, though.

The Commission had most of an agreement with the Cherokees, and even though they could not agree on a price or get rid of the trespassing whites, they sent the proposal to Congress anyway. Wishing to manufacture some good news, Congress adopted the Commission's proposal with the expectation that the problems would be remedied sometime in the future.

However, there was a small, strange detail which Congress either overlooked or ignored: A mandate that ratification must occur before March 3, 1893 – the day before the next president would be sworn in. Apparently, everyone assumed Harrison would win.

When Cleveland won the election, that small detail suddenly took on outsized significance – Cleveland would not sign anything passed under Harrison's administration, nor could the date be postponed, so Harrison would have to sign it before leaving office. Thus, Congress only had four months to meet the Jerome Commission's date. Congress would have to move uncharacteristically fast, which would be interesting.

Even though the price of the land to be "sold" had not been agreed upon, Congress felt that could be resolved in court after the land was opened, so they moved on to the next problem. That was getting the whites off the land, which meant the army needed to be involved, creating its own legislative challenges. The bottom line, though, was the U.S. would finally begin serious enforcement of the Cherokee's border.

Most believed the hard part was done, but Congress, being Congress, could not agree and time was running out. The mechanism for the opening was to be that year's Indian Appropriations Bill. While the Senate agreed very quickly, there was stiff opposition in the House caused by a rumor that lawyers lobbying for the opening would receive six hundred thousand dollars.

Congress was not the only body keenly aware of the deadline – the whole country knew about it. People were gathering, again, at the Kansas border, anticipating the moment they could claim some of the best land anywhere in America. This gathering was larger than all the previous combined.

One reason was the Cherokee land was not in a remote and unknown place – it was literally yards away from Coffeyville, Arkansas City, Caldwell, and every other border town in Kansas, as well as the northern borders of the Oklahoma Territory.

Another reason was because the date was not fuzzy or debatable, it was written into law and could not be changed. The only question was if the opening would happen or not, and America was not shy about letting their representatives in Congress know its feelings.

As the deadline loomed and with no resolution in sight, Congress became panicky. Representative Samuel Peel, from Arkansas, said on the House floor, "I am receiving telegrams, letters, and petitions praying me for God's sake to do something with the Cherokee Outlet."

Senator Bishop Perkins of Kansas provided a different perspective. Perkins contended it would be impossible to keep settlers off the land after the deadline, and Congress had two choices: a controlled, lawful opening or an armed invasion. The letters he'd received leaned strongly toward invasion.

Back in the House of Representatives another Kansas Congressman, Jeremiah Simpson, had his turn on the floor. Simpson was not concerned with specific dates or prices. His first point was meant to frighten his colleagues in the East, and was prescient:

> *The opening of these lands serve as a safety valve to our Government and perhaps delay for a time the trouble that is sure to arise from the rapid increase of our homeless people. Already we begin to hear the warning cry of an impending panic, when again we will witness the exodus from the great cities. Will it*

not be well, then, to have this country ready for the millions of people that will eventually find homes in this territory?

Simpson piled it higher, focusing away from the people who might come to the Strip to the people who were already there.

And yet another consideration should move you. It is well known that this great vacant territory is a harbor for lawless people, where they flee from justice, where they can issue forth at times to prey upon their neighbors. Open this up and let in the law and light that come with the settlement, with the building of the churches and schoolhouses.

Representative Peel debunked the rumor of lawyers getting rich, and Simpson's points tipped the scales. The bill was ratified at the last possible moment on March 3, 1893, and Harrison's final official act was to sign it.

The next big horse race was going to happen, but as excitement over the Cherokee Strip's opening was building, so was trouble around the Comanche lands.

***

The Wichita Mountains' reputation for hiding gold and silver was ancient, beginning with the Spanish conquistadors reportedly finding both gold and silver there. The range was mostly contained inside the Comanches' land, from Fort Sill westward, all the way to the very edge of the Territory.

But not entirely contained. The North Fork of the Red River was the border between Texas and the Indian Territory, and it ran directly through the westernmost cluster of the Wichita Mountains. Two large complexes, Quartz Mountain and "Navajoe" Mountain, were on the west side of the river in Greer County, Texas, not the Indian Territory. Anyone who wanted to poke around Greer County was free to do so. And they did.

By the time Cleveland was reelected, Greer County was already in the news with reports of rich gold and silver strikes. Something named "The Eureka Mining District" was organized, and a handful of mining companies were founded there.

The *Fort Worth Gazette* enjoyed reporting on the gossip coming from Greer County, so when the miners claimed they had samples that would pay over one hundred dollars per ton, the Gazette dutifully printed it. The *Norman Transcript* picked up on the story, and in the same edition where they reported that a Norman resident had defended himself against an unknown bandit near Chickasha, they fired the next shot in what would become another decade-long land battle:

> *The Boomers claim that the Greer County diggings are only the shadow and that the substance is in the mountains proper, and that there are millions in it. There are those who claim that this district will be the richest gold field in the U.S.*

The story also detailed rumblings of companies organizing in advance of the opening and of threats "to make a rush for the mountains next spring unless the lands are opened to settlement." The fact that the Comanches were nowhere near an agreement with the Jerome Commission meant nothing. "Armed Invasion" was the theme for Indian land everywhere.

Southwest Mineral Interests was one of those companies and was based in Norman. As luck would have it, they shared the same banker as Bud, Sam Deskin. Southwest Mineral had plans for the Kiowa and Comanche lands, especially anything valuable that could be dug out of them.

Deskin had the same suspicions about Bud that the rest of Norman had, and mentioned to Southwest Mineral that he was acquainted with a young man they might be very interested in knowing.

***

Rep. Simpson was proven correct in his predicted economic panic just two months into Cleveland's term. The Reading Railroad had declared bankruptcy weeks before, which had shaken the national markets. Then The National Cordage Company went bankrupt and took the shaky economy with it.

National Cordage produced rope and twine of every sort – from the thin twine farmers used to make bundles of hay to the heavy cables that secure ships' anchors. The company had acquired nearly all its competitors and had taken the bold step of attempting to corner the entire hemp market, which was the raw material used to make rope. National Cordage was immense, larger than many railroads, its products were vital and visible everywhere.

With so many businesses failing, everyone suddenly wanted their money. More railroads failed, and then when banks began to go under, paper money wasn't good enough anymore. Everyone wanted gold.

Unintended consequences emerged. Years before, Congress had passed a bill named The Silver Purchase Act, which obligated the federal government to purchase millions of ounces of silver. The Feds purchased the silver and issued paper certificates against it instead of minting money with it.

Although those certificates were officially backed by silver, they could be redeemed for either silver or gold. After National Cordage went down, the holders of those certificates demanded gold, not silver, and suddenly the gold necessary for the government to back its currency threatened insolvency.

Panic became free-fall, millions of people were out of work, and they were leaving the East as fast as they could.

* * *

As the economy decomposed, Indian land was the center of attention throughout the year, whether it was the "free" Cherokee land about to be given way, or the Comanche land that, according to the papers, was almost certainly littered with gold.

As spring warmed into summer, the government was feverishly preparing for the Cherokee Strip opening but was stumbling over itself at nearly every step. People from across the nation came to wait in Kansas and the Oklahoma Territory for noon on September 16, the date selected for the run.

To prevent the Sooners from repeating their mischief, the inspector general, Alfred Swineford, came up with the idea of registration booths. In order to make a claim, a Boomer would need to register for the run and receive a certificate proving he was a bona fide settler. That should keep the Sooners at bay.

Swineford arrived in June and instantly realized he didn't have enough people, or booths, to register everyone. He cabled Washington, requesting permission to open the booths ten days before the run and to be sent several hundred more clerks to write certificates.

Washington thought about it, and replied, "No." They would not send more staff, nor allow the booths to open ten days in advance. Rather, they would open five and one-half days before the run. A strange number, but Swineford had no choice.

Even as the bureaucrats denied Swineford any help, they admonished him that failure was not an option. Swineford hired the clerical force from the crowd and built registration booths everywhere.

When the booths opened, Swineford was proven correct. The booths were completely overwhelmed and some lines were over a mile long. After five days of furious work, the booths managed to churn out 115,000 certificates.

Three days into the registration, Angela approached Bud.

"Bud, I can't stand it. Let's go watch! Let's go see the run!"

"You don't want to actually run, do you?"

"No, no … the papers say you stand in line for hours to get one of those certificates. I just want to see the people. It's bigger than anything Payne drummed up!"

"All right, why not. Let's go see how these things work."

They packed their wagon and joined the throng headed north to the border. When they finally arrived, Angela was astounded – the whole border, over a hundred miles, was one large camp.

"Bud, we could have gotten rich off these people! There are millions of them!"

"Maybe," he said, gesturing to a man selling pots and pans, "but there seems to be a lot of competition."

They found a decent camping spot and set up their tent to wait with the rest of the Boomers.

When the sun rose on September 16, everyone was ready. The army had been responsible for maintaining security at the line and ensuring no one entered the Territory before the appointed moment. They patrolled and scouted, stationed troops all along the border, and constantly demanded to see documentation of anyone they thought suspicious. They worked diligently and tirelessly to keep the Sooners out.

They failed spectacularly.

Just as in the other openings, men on superb mounts raced deep into the Territory only to discover prime claims held by men on foot, yet in possession of valid certificates. The town of Perry, located eight miles from the border, was somehow inundated with people just seven minutes after the rush began.

Bud and Angela leisurely trotted behind the Boomers, watching the chaos unfold.

As with the previous openings, there were far fewer claims available than there were settlers to claim them. Just forty thousand claims were available to the 115,000 registered settlers, even fewer after the Sooners had completed their mischief.

Bud was delighted. The only thing the land booths had accomplished was to prevent deputies and surveyors from stealing claims, but thousands of other Sooners easily evaded the cavalry and snuck into the Territory days in advance. Bud was certain he could do the same in the Wichitas when his time came.

The deputies and their ilk were very adaptable, however. Since they couldn't take claims outright, they resorted to other methods. It was soon learned that the clerks at the land office were accepting bribes to process, or not process, depending on one's perspective, the paperwork necessary to resolve disputed claims. When it was learned that federal officials were using their influence in the land offices to literally steal claims for their own interests, the entire nation took notice. Finally, it was discovered that some U.S. deputies, unable to simply steal the land, had outrageously demanded payment from settlers to enter or remain in the Outlet.

Neither Marshal Nix nor his deputies were anywhere to be found, even though it was their job to keep the peace in the newly claimed land. The editor of the *State Capital* pointed out the marshal service was virtually invisible, and asked, "Where were the police Saturday?" He then wondered if Marshal Nix "had taken a lot or a claim?"

The corruption surrounding the Cherokee Strip Opening would be investigated and reported for years, but the run's novelty faded and America's attention turned to the Kiowa, Comanche, and Apache lands. Located just south of the Wichitas, those reservations were also enormous. Mostly flat and lush pastureland with grass knee-high, homesteaders eyed it jealously. The reservations also encompassed the mountains so greedily eyed from Greer County, Texas. The sentiment was universal, it was time for those lands to open too.

* * *

The Jerome Commission was on the case. They had come to a basic agreement with the Kiowa and Apache tribes, but there was a problem with the Comanches, and the problem's name was Quanah.

Quanah Parker was the oldest son of Cynthia Ann Parker, a white girl who had been captured by Comanche Indians in June 1836, when she was just nine years old. She was ultimately taken into the tribe and counted as a full member and would marry a prominent Comanche named Peta Nocona.

In December 1860, a detachment of Texas Rangers snuck up on Peta Nocona's camp, who had been conducting raids in Parker County, west of Fort Worth. Ironically, the county had been named after Cynthia Ann's uncle, Isaac Parker. Her husband was raiding her uncle's namesake.

The Rangers attacked and Peta Nocona was killed along with most of the band. Cynthia Ann was recognized as white, and spared, but Quanah and his brother, "Peanut," both escaped to find another band of Comanche and to report what had happened. Cynthia Ann and Quanah never saw each other again.

Quanah grew up to become a superb horseman and eventually a leader of the unsubdued wild Comanches. They refused all truces and peace talks, never signed any treaty, and never set foot on a reservation until the summer before Bud's ride, back in May 1875. The winter of '74 had been brutal and the Comanches were in poor condition, tired of running, and tired of war. Quanah accepted the army's request for a parlay and after two days he was convinced it was time for the Comanche to walk the White Man's Road. Quanah and his Comanches made their way to Fort Sill.

Quanah adapted to the White Man's Road very quickly and walked it better than many white men could. Despite the fact that nothing remotely similar existed in Comanche culture, Quanah grasped the white's notion of "representation." He agreed to speak for the Comanche and to help the army resolve the various "Indian problems" that inevitably arose.

That was the time when Indians across the Territory began making pasture agreements with the cattlemen, and the Comanche were no exception. While the larger, more visible, holdings in the Cherokee Strip would frustrate David Payne and his Boomers for a decade, the Comanche and Kiowa agreements slipped under the radar.

Quanah's Comanche sensibilities helped him intuitively with another white man's idea: corruption. The Comanche in him didn't assign any good or bad, it was simply how it was. As representative between the army and the Comanche, he was the logical person for the cattlemen to turn to for access to the Indians' grassland. When the cattlemen offered something, Quanah simply asked for more – more for his tribe and often more for himself.

As opposed to the northern pasture agreements, which had been handled by the stupendously incompetent Indian agents, Quanah handled the Comanche pasture negotiations directly. He not only secured a fair payment arrangement for his tribe, but he also arranged for a monthly stipend for himself. His relationship with the cattle lobby was so cozy that the cattlemen would finance the construction of Quanah's large house in 1890.

Thus, when the Jerome Commission began their "negotiations" with the Comanche, Quanah was well practiced at their game. He pressed one of the commissioners, Warren Sayre, so hard that Sayre finally admitted he didn't actually know how much the land was worth or even how much there was; they were just guessing.

By the time an agreement was finally reached, Quanah had exposed and negotiated through all the Commission's cheating and swindling. The Comanches, while not getting anything like a good deal, got the best deal they could: The Comanche people would receive two million dollars for the land, would receive 160 acres of land per person, and would select their claims first, before the opening and after the survey.

With the newly opened Cherokee Outlet now safely under white control, the only grassland south of Kansas belonged to the Kiowas, Comanches, and Apaches. Quanah then executed his master stroke: He told his cattlemen friends that if they could hold off Washington, he would make sure the Indians cooperated with their grazing needs. The cattle lobby leapt into action to protect their southern grazing interests.

The cattlemen still had plenty of congressmen in their pockets, and so the ratification of the Kiowa-Comanche-Apache opening was not approved on its first attempt. Or second, third, or fourth. Quanah was walking the White Man's Road very skillfully, indeed.

It would take Bud, and everyone else, quite some time to digest the fact that even though an agreement had been made, the land was not going to open soon. The Commission continued to squabble over details and the cattlemen successfully lobbied to keep the opening on the back burner.

Chapter 7

Bill Dalton was walking a new road too. After burying Grat and Bob and watching Emmett head off to prison, Bill decided to stay in Oklahoma. And, of course, he would not be its leading citizen.

In the spring of 1893, about the time National Cordage was dragging the economy down, Bill tracked down the Dalton Gang's surviving member, Bill Doolin. Dalton eventually made his way to the small town of Ingalls, Oklahoma, where he caught up with Doolin in Ransom's Saloon and proposed forming a new gang.

Doolin wanted to form a gang too. He had sent word to Bitter Creek Newcomb, who was expected at any moment, so Bill's unexpected appearance was a godsend. By the end of the day the Doolin-Dalton Gang had been loosely organized.

The new villains kicked off their summer with a train robbery, then followed up with a bank and several garden-variety robberies. Eventually Doolin and Dalton were both positively identified, and their Ingalls base became so well known that it was often reported in newspapers.

In June Dalton and Doolin openly dared the authorities to try and come arrest them. A group of deputies took them up on their offer but never even made it into town, forced to beat a hasty retreat from a hail of bullets and insults.

The robberies continued through the summer, the gang seemingly immune to any of Nix's cronies. On September 1, two weeks before the massive Cherokee Strip run and as Sooners were sneaking past the army, a group of deputies and posse-men tried to sneak into Ingalls pretending to be Boomers. They entered town in two covered wagons and discreetly spread around the gang's saloon hangout. Surrounded and confronted with greater firepower, the gang would have no choice but to surrender.

Unfortunately, the gang had been tipped off and they were ready. One of the gang members, Arkansas Tom, was not in the saloon but rather in a second-floor room at the hotel across the street.

When the shooting started, the gang fought back briefly, but they were badly outnumbered, which was the only aspect of the law's plan that worked. The gang escaped through the saloon's back door and retreated to a ridge overlooking the town.

While the posse was focused on the saloon, Arkansas Tom carefully began picking off deputies from his hotel room's window. Deputies Speed, Heuston, and Shadley were all killed before the posse realized they were flanked. Panicking, the posse sprinted in every direction, spraying the hotel with bullets as they sought cover.

The hotel was quickly surrounded, but no one was willing to leave whatever shelter they were hiding behind. A lengthy standoff ensued with negotiations shouted back and forth, neither party willing to budge. Arkansas Tom was finally arrested after the deputies threatened to "dynamite the whole damn building." Choosing prison over a coffin, Tom surrendered. He was the only gang member apprehended.

The casualty count was high: six people killed, as well as several horses and mules, with several more wounded, and a lot of property damage from stray bullets. Arkansas Tom was eventually sent to prison, but the Doolin-Dalton Gang had sent a clear message: they were very dangerous.

* * *

Back in Greer County, a man named A.W. Hardtmayer sought permission to mine on the east side of the Red River's North Fork, the Indian Territory side. He claimed that his samples had assayed for the astounding values of $800-$1300 per ton and repeated the claim that the mountains were possibly the richest fields in all America. He was, of course, denied permission, but his wild claims were reported nationwide, as was his desire to mine there.

Just as the Cherokee Outlet had been infested with white trespassers and cattlemen before it was opened, the Kiowa, Comanche, and Apache lands were infested with miners and prospectors. And just as David Payne's Boomers had made claims before the original Unassigned Lands were opened, the prospectors were making claims of their own. The obvious difference was that Boomer claims were on land that was, at that time, in dispute. The miners were making claims on land that belonged, unambiguously, to someone else.

But the owners were just Indians, and it was a foregone conclusion that all the land would eventually be sucked into the Oklahoma Territory, so the prospectors believed their claims would stand. Meanwhile, however, the army was enforcing the treaties and no serious mining activity could be maintained for long. A few shafts were attempted, but they were always discovered and destroyed.

In Norman, the resident expert, through the force of rumor alone, was Bud Dalton. Deskin approached him a few weeks after Bud and Angela had returned from the run. Deskin beat around the bush, asking about the mountains, the quality of the grassland, the availability of water, and so forth. He finally got around to the subject of minerals - did Bud think there were any claims that might be, say, more interesting than others?

Bud was vague, but shared some superficial details about the terrain and resources, and admitted that yes, it was possible some particular locations were likely to be more interesting than others. Certainly, a prospector would be able to eliminate those places that were less interesting.

That seemed to be what Deskin wanted to hear.

"Bud, what would you think about leading a small party down there to formally map the area? I'm acquainted with some businessmen that are intrigued with the region's potential, and you are by far the most experienced man in the Territory. What do you say?"

Bud looked quizzically at the banker and asked, "The army and government must have hundreds of maps. Why go to the trouble to make your own, especially when you could get arrested for trying it?"

"Yes, they have those maps too. What they're interested in knowing are the details the maps don't show. A map might indicate a given creek's course, but it won't give any clue to the geology of the area, for example. Can the creek be navigated? Will it flood? Is there timber?"

Bud nodded, remembering Jesse's map leading them out of Mexico.

"All right, that makes some sense, but why in the world would I do that?"

Deskin replied, "May we speak candidly?"

"Sure."

"There have been rumors of gold and silver in the Wichita Mountains for years, but you are physical proof that it's true. My associates are determined to be on the ground well before the rush and to control the most valuable areas."

"Who says my interest is in the Wichitas?"

"I thought we were speaking candidly?"

"All right, fine. So, they want to buy me out?"

"They might, if you had something to sell, but no. Rather, they are interested in using claims as collateral to capitalize the area's development. Their challenge, of course, is acquiring the right claims."

"Sam, I didn't understand a single word of that except for 'claim.'"

Deskin failed at not appearing exasperated. "They want to get several claims, which, of course, they will acquire for nearly nothing. Their people will take some directly in the run, others they might purchase afterwards. These claims will become very valuable when gold is officially discovered. Your gold. They will then approach a bank, my bank, to borrow money using their now-valuable land as collateral. You understand collateral?"

Bud nodded. "I think so. It's what you'll take if they don't repay you. Speaking of which, I heard your bank was teetering."

"Not like many others. The economy in the rest of the country is still bleak. I'm sure you've read about the strikes and violence?"

"Of course."

"The Cherokee run did a great deal to insulate us from what's happening elsewhere. There was a great deal of commerce leading up to the run, and much of it happened here."

"I noticed."

Sam continued, "Our net deposits actually increased between June and September, and while the rest of the country is struggling, we are sheltered and may even be in a position to expand when the depression finally ends. This enterprise would be an excellent mechanism."

"How so?"

"Railroads, smelters, heavy equipment, and the like. You see, the Comanche opening is going to be much different from all the others. There are no cities, no railroads, and no commerce beyond servicing Fort Sill. That will change after the opening, but when your gold is discovered there will be twenty times the number of people on the land. They will need everything from food to hats, horses, and tools. And unlike the Arapahoe run, this land is known to be desirable."

The next Boomers.

"All right, I understand that."

"Good, but that is just the settlement itself. The gold will require specific businesses to be nearby. The men who run those businesses will become rich. My associates intend to be those men."

"So, what do they want with me?"

"Ultimately, they might want you to join them. In the short term, however, they need better firsthand knowledge of the land. For example, where might a smelter be profitably operated? It needs to be near water and accessible by a good road, which also needs to be built. They want to scout the Territory so they know where to make their claims, and when the time comes they will already be in place and ready to pounce. You are the perfect man to help them do that."

Sam's pretty keen on this.

"So, how does this benefit you? Speaking candidly."

"Right. The bank will finance all of it. First, we will make an excellent profit off the interest from the land loans. All the proposed businesses will house their accounts here, as well. The bank's assets will be considerably larger. Our growth on the heels of a depression could make us the dominant bank in the whole region, perhaps across the entire South."

"So, they're going to build the stuff to mine and process ore before the ore is discovered. When the discovery happens, they will be ready to go before anyone else can even set up their own operation."

"Precisely. They will dominate the economy."

"Tell me, what would happen if gold weren't discovered? What if someone gets the claim I need and puts cows and a garden on it?"

Deskin shook his head. "No, that won't be allowed to happen. Worst case would be for you to purchase the claim, and I assure you the bank will finance that transaction regardless of the cost. Speaking candidly, the Outlet's opening proved beyond doubt that if a man knew which claim he wanted, there's very little the government can do to prevent that man from getting his claim."

I noticed that too.

Bud thought a moment, then said, "I'm trying to see where it could go wrong, but I can't."

"Excellent."

* * *

Bud's mind was racing after his conversation with Deskin. He walked his horse into his yard and was about to dismount when someone called his name.

"Hey, Bud!"

He turned and saw Charlie and George sitting on their horses behind a tree across the street.

I wonder where Roy is.

Bud climbed down and tied up his horse, then strolled across the street. "Hello, Charlie, been a long time. How've you been, George?"

Charlie took the lead. "I think you know what we're here for."

"Well, the last few times I saw George it was about those bars Jesse buried. Nothing's changed, didn't have 'em then, don't have 'em now."

"George says you shot Zack off his horse. What about that?"

So that's how you're going to play it?

"And then his brother, too," Bud replied, "outside Chickasha. What about that?"

"I don't know anything about it."

"You don't, huh? That fool told me everything while he was bleeding to death, and the woman at Webster's told me I missed you by a minute. Quit fucking around, Charlie. What do you want?"

George leaned toward Charlie and told him, "Just do it."

"Shut up, George. Bud, I want money."

"Then go rob a train. Or a bank."

George couldn't stand it anymore and blurted out, "No one cares about Zack or Abe. We just want our share of the bars."

Bud sighed. "Get off your horses so we can talk. Where's Roy?"

"He's watching from a distance to make sure you behave."

"Well, call him in so he can get it all firsthand."

Charlie hesitated for a moment, then looked past Bud and waved. Bud turned around to see Roy step from behind a wagon about a hundred yards away. Charlie waved again and Roy walked over. By the time he got to the group, Charlie and George had dismounted and tied their horses to a bush. The group retreated to the shade beneath the tree.

"Hello, Roy. We were about to chat about the bars and it didn't seem right that you weren't here."

"Appreciated," Roy replied. He spat in the dust and sucked his mustache. "So, what's the word on that?"

Bud looked around the group. "Nothing's changed, Roy. I still don't have them, and I didn't take them."

"What's this about a gold mine in the Wichitas?" Charlie asked.

"Jesus. I know that's what the rumors say, Charlie, but there's no mine. My partner and I found a couple of creeks that show promise, but it's on Comanche land. If we tried to sink a mine either the army or Comanches would find us and that would be the end of it. We work them a little by panning, but that's as far as we can go without getting caught. And I guarantee it doesn't produce enough for my partner to be willing to share any with you."

"How about we take it out of your share?"

Bud scoffed. "Divide it four ways and you'll be robbing trains again in no time."

"So, where does this leave us?" George asked. "What now?"

Well, how about this...

Bud replied, "There's a lot of room in the Wichitas."

"What's that mean?"

"It means when that country is opened then some claims are going to be very, very valuable. And if you get one of those, then your share of the bars will be nothing compared to it. By all means, go find the bars if you can, but I'm attached to this other thing and just don't care about them as much as this."

Roy asked, "Why would you cut us in on that?"

"I'm not cutting you in on anything. It's a free country and if you guys latch on to a gold mine, then that's fine with me. I've already latched on to mine. We can all be rich together."

"How do you know you're going to get your claim?"

"You saw what happened last month – the army can't keep people out, and that was just on the Strip. You think they can handle the Wichitas? They can't. I'll get what I want."

George looked to Roy and Charlie. "I think he's telling the truth. He doesn't have them."

Charlie shrugged. "Maybe not. But maybe so. I think we best keep looking."

Bud interjected, "You find them, you remember my share. I earned it on that damn ride through Texas. Meanwhile I'll hold up my end and point you to some interesting places in the Territory. Now, come on across the street and meet Angela. We can find some real shade and maybe she can rustle up something to drink."

* * *

The arrangements for Southwest Mineral's survey were made. They had identified a handful of potential locations and Bud's job was to be their scout, preventing them from being discovered by either the army or Indians. He told them he was confident about the army, but Indians he couldn't commit to.

Bud studied the maps and came up with a plan that would get them where they wanted to go. He would take them west across the old Cherokee Strip, then sneak south into the Greer County area. They would make their way eastward and examine several sites in what the maps identified as the Otter Creek area, then into the mountains and the valley Bud knew so well. From there, they would slip past Fort Sill and back to Norman. He estimated four weeks if everything went well.

The party would be well mounted, well provisioned, and armed with the best maps they could acquire. They would move quietly and quickly through the selected areas, making measurements and detailed notes of everything they saw, particularly with regard to potential roadways and building sites, water, and timber. They had excellent surveying equipment and intended to create very accurate maps.

There was a lot that needed to be explored and many details to record, but Bud was optimistic. They would leave sometime in the spring.

* * *

Bud and the small team of surveyors returned to Norman in early summer. The surveyors took their measurements and calculations and formed their reports for Southwest Mineral's leaders, who were anxious to meet and discuss the conclusions. Bud was invited to attend.

The overwhelming consensus was that Bud and the surveying team had performed brilliantly. Without being caught by either the army or Indians, they had confirmed the Greer County area was indeed awash in miners and prospectors and was also blessed with the resources to support a considerable industry. The area around Elk and Otter Creeks, near the center of the range, had excellent resources but there was skepticism of their mining prospects. Any location in the east was acceptable and in the central valley near Fort Sill was excellent, perfect for everything from settlement to mining.

While the surveyors were measuring, triangulating, and mapping, Bud had been sketching and adding considerably to his own mental database. The passage through the western half of the Territory and then back along its entire length had been highly educational, and chatting with the professional surveyors had given him a much better appreciation of the entire area's potential.

The surveyors were focused on a few specific qualities – long stretches of relatively level ground for roads, water both for consumption and smelting, timber for rough construction. Bud appreciated that, but he knew that mining was only part of the story. Their close look along East Otter Creek, which the scouting team had blindly dismissed as worthless to their purposes, solidified Bud's belief that every inch of the Indian land was extremely valuable. The fact that the cattle lobby was fighting tooth and nail for every acre of grass was proof that farmers and ranchers could make a living too. When the land run came, Bud was certain it would be huge, possibly dwarfing the Cherokee Strip run.

When Bud arrived at Southwest Mineral's meeting, he discovered that he was already acquainted with two of the company's officers, one from the original Boomer camps and the other from one of his Indian Territory trips.

"Captain" J.B. Cooper was one of David Payne's closest advisers and had been the editor of the Boomer's newspaper, *The Oklahoma Chief*, which they printed from Rock Falls before the army captured them and destroyed their city. Cooper had purchased supplies from Bud and Angela during the original Oklahoma invasions.

Cooper was interesting because he was one of the few Boomers who had made, and successfully defended, a legal claim near Guthrie. He donated part of his land to create the town of Seward, and then sold the rest at an enormous profit. Cooper was hopeful to do it all again in the Kiowa and Comanche lands, but potentially on a much larger scale.

The other acquaintance was none other than Bud's prospector friend, Elmer Kanable. Elmer was one of the major partners in the new venture, along with two men Bud didn't know, Charles Tipton and Thomas Antrim. Elmer had left the mountains with several crates of ore samples, and although none of them showed concentrations of ore that would yield a profit, he was convinced there was gold in paying quantities. It just needed to be found.

Elmer was delighted and amazed that it was Bud who had actually produced the first evidence of gold, and was further delighted when Bud told Elmer that he, after all, was the one who showed Bud how to pan in the first place.

Antrim brought the meeting to order and brought the rest of the members up to speed on Bud, mainly that he had a provable gold strike in the mountains and was validation that their plan would work. The land would be opened, gold would be discovered, and their operations would already be up and running.

After spending the afternoon with Southwest Mineral's partners and listening to their conversations, Bud could finally see his way clearly. While he was confident in Elmer's evaluation about the Wichitas' potential for gold mining, he didn't care. Southwest Mineral was going to create the best cover imaginable for Bud to recover the bars.

He and Angela would grab several claims and then carefully plant some of Angela's gold dust to make those claims appear to be very valuable. They would then sell the claims and the new owners would, of course, mine them. Southwest Mineral would process the ore, and even though no gold would be found in it, the activity itself would justify the smelter's existence.

Once Southwest Mineral's smelter was in operation, he would have it process his ore which, of course, would prove to contain the high gold content Elmer predicted. Bud would then have a perfectly plausible reason to be in possession of many, many gold bars. At which point he could deliver them to a mint without any questions about their origin.

If he could just tie up the few remaining loose ends.

* * *

E.D. Nix was having a bad year. A disagreement between the Rock Island Railroad and two new towns had blown up into a full-fledged shooting war. The deputy he sent to calm the situation, Chris Madsen, just made it worse by simply arresting the mayor and most of the city council.

Between the Ingalls disaster, the marshal service's no-show at the Cherokee Strip run, and now the Railroad War, people began to wonder if Marshal Nix was up for the job. The question was answered a few weeks later when Nix suggested there was an opportunity to negotiate with the Doolin-Dalton Gang. He claimed, and was doubted by many, that he'd been approached by a third party who said the gang would plead guilty, spend two years in prison, and give up thievery forever if the U.S. would agree to the short prison sentences.

The *Norman Transcript's* editor contemptuously wrote:

> *It is a brave US Marshal that Oklahoma has. He wants the Government of the United States to compromise with the Dalton gang. Come off the perch. Go resign. Stick your head in a soak. Go work in a soap factory. Do anything to get out of sight, Mr. Nix.*

The newspapers piled it on, ridiculing the marshals in general and Nix in particular. It was then unearthed, and gleefully reported, that both Madsen and Nix, along with another deputy, Bill Tilghman, had all successfully taken excellent claims in the original '89 land run. Tilghman had been a U.S. deputy then, Madsen was still in the army stationed at Fort Reno, and Nix had materialized in Guthrie at exactly the right moment. All three were obviously Sooners and under investigation for the Cherokee Strip corruption.

No matter who was doing the investigating, the army, attorney general, or inspector general, the name E.D. Nix kept coming up. His expenses did not match his vouchers, his deputies were not where they claimed to be, and some of them were accused of moving settlers off what appeared to be legitimate claims.

Their corruption was so egregious that the *New York Times* suggested statehood might be the only protection Oklahoma residents could find from the federal government.

Complaints rained in from every direction and in December U.S. Attorney Caleb Brooks sent the matter up to the attorney general, officially raising the flag over the Territory's custodians.

> *There is some ugly work going on in the issuing and sale of witness rolls before U.S. Commissioners in this territory, and I have as yet been unable to get onto the facts of just how it is done. It requires considerable ingenuity and time to keep up with the workings of these fellows out here, and I am unable to get the time from court business to give it the attention that it should have. I am of the opinion that there are U.S. Commissioners and Deputy U.S. Marshals interested in buying the witness rolls,*

and making a regular business of it, and I believe they are also speculating in U.S. Grand and Petit Jury fees.

Brooks went on to ask for help in getting to the bottom of it, and to look into a particular judge named W.H. Scott. Brooks was certain there was something shady there, too, but could not quite put his finger on that either.

Something was rotten in the Oklahoma Territory and the authorities were finally going to look into it.

Chapter 8

On May 23, 1894, the bank in Longview, Texas, was robbed. A determined manhunt was initiated which eventually accused Bill Dalton of being the leader and mastermind. Bill was finally cornered in Ardmore, in the Indian Territory, and was killed by the posse hunting the Longview robbers.

Bud was in Seward when he learned of the robbery and Bill's death. Captain Cooper had invited Bud and another prominent Boomer, Judge John Fox, to meet some of Cooper's railroad contacts and hopefully convince them to build routes through the Commanche Territory.

"Bud," Cooper asked, "do you need to head down to Ardmore? I'm sure this can wait."

Bud shook his head and held up the newspaper he was reading. "No, I don't think so. According to this his wife was there and is planning to take him back to California to be buried. They might have even left by now. I don't think there's anything I can do for them."

"I'm very sorry, Bud."

"Thanks, Captain, but you know that's how these stories end … prison or a coffin. I wish Bill had just gone back home and stayed away from Doolin, but that's done now. We need to focus on that land."

Judge Fox was also vocal about opening the Wichitas and had his own plans to exploit whatever he could get. He'd been sneaking around the mountains, quite successfully, for years and was almost as familiar with them as Bud.

Fox, Cooper, and Bud walked their horses back into Norman four weeks later. Fox and Cooper stayed and visited with Angela for a few minutes, then headed to Cooper's place. Fox intended to slip into the mountains and do a bit of prospecting, so Bud invited him to drop by on his way back to talk about what he'd found.

Judge Fox returned to Norman three weeks later and made good on his promise of dropping by and chatting about what he'd seen. His mule was loaded with samples of rocks that the judge believed were very promising. What made them promising was a mystery to Bud, but that was beside the point.

Bud didn't have to pry very hard to get Judge Fox to show him the samples, and one in particular caught Bud's eye. While most of the samples were boxes holding about twenty pounds of assorted rocks, this sample was in a large leather pouch. When Bud opened it, he found coarse sand and some small, smooth stones.

Fox cleared a spot on their table and pulled a handful from the pouch. Rough sand typical of the stream beds from the Wichitas lay on Angela's clean table.

Great. Someone else digging up stream beds.

"A creek?" Bud asked. "How did you decide this one is worth testing?"

"Very good! It's actually those small stones mixed in that caught my eye. As you know, most of the streams are sandy, but some are just stone and others all mud. I thought I'd keep a shovelful of this and see if it shows anything."

Bud pretended to be fascinated and poked at the pebbles, which appeared to be nothing more than bits of stone worn smooth by a zillion years of living in a creek bed. He spread some of the sand on the table and looked closely.

"Yeah, I can see how you'd be interested in this. Did you pan? Does it show any color?"

Judge Fox was delighted. "I did pan! I did not detect any dust, but as you know, the coarse sand does not wash well. Therefore, I kept a larger amount for the assayer. Perhaps some smelting will tell the tale!"

"I agree. Your samples are certainly impressive. Congratulations. I hope you'll share the results?"

"Certainly."

Angela interrupted, "Judge, Bud. It's not too hot this afternoon, and there's a breeze. Perhaps some tea on the porch? It's been steeping on the window all day."

"Why, that would be delightful, my dear," Fox replied.

"All right, you two head out there and I'll tidy up the sand here, and bring out the tea. I won't be a moment. Judge, shall I put the pouch on these other boxes?"

"That would be wonderful, dear. Thank you."

Bud led Fox outside to the porch where Fox lowered himself onto one of the small chairs. Angela could hear them chatting about rocks and the weather as she scraped the sand back into the leather pouch.

This is going to work, she thought. She carried the pouch over to the boxes on the floor and glanced back to make sure she could not be casually seen. Fox could not see her, even by accident.

Angela pulled their pouch with the gold dust from her apron pocket and poured a bit of their gold dust into Fox's sand. She dropped the pouch back into the pocket, closed Fox's large pouch tightly, and turned it over several times to mix the dust in with the sand.

Bud had come up with the vague idea of spiking Fox's samples when they were returning from Seward. Bud had invited the judge to stop by when he returned from his prospecting trip, but he only half-expected the judge to actually show. When he and his rock samples walked into the yard, Bud only had a few moments to get Angela up to speed.

Bud would get the judge to show off his samples, Bud would find one that concealed their dust best, they would lure the judge outside, and Angela would spike the sample. The bag of sand and pebbles was absolutely perfect.

She dropped the bag on the boxes and dusted her hands on her apron, then poured two glasses of tea for the men and another for herself. They spent an hour on the porch before the judge announced that he needed to get to his hotel before they ran out of room.

Bud helped repack the boxes of rock and dirt on the mule and Judge Fox rode across town to his hotel. Bud and Angela were fairly certain they'd hear about the judge sometime soon.

Judge Fox fulfilled Bud's prediction a few weeks later when his sample's assessment was returned and it was impossible for him to keep the results to himself. The newspaper reported that he had returned from the Wichitas with rich samples and the assayer had proven his claims true. The only problem, from the judge's standpoint, was that all his samples had been tested together and he didn't know exactly which location had provided the rich results. But it was out there somewhere.

After the *Transcript* reprinted the article, Angela mentioned how uncomfortable she felt walking around town with everyone staring at her. It was no secret that Bud and Fox had visited Seward together with Cooper, that tidbit dutifully reported in the *Transcript* when they departed, as was their return. And now, barely two months later, they found the same Judge Fox advertising a measurably rich sample from the Wichitas. Coincidence? Norman thought not.

Charlie, Roy, and George were convinced too. They showed up at Bud's door after the *Transcript*'s report with a completely different attitude. Charlie still wanted the bars, but Bud's story now rang true and it seemed that Bud could help them more by choosing claims than finding lost gold bars.

Angela reinforced the idea when she suggested that maybe Bud could help them the same way he helped Judge Fox.

"You know," Bud mused, "that's not a bad idea. I can give you the same kinds of hints I gave the judge."

"Well … all right, I guess. What did you tell that judge fellow?"

"There are a couple of places that I've always thought showed a lot of promise but never got the chance to look into them, and now I don't really need to. I pointed the judge at a couple of them and it looks like one of them might pay. How about I point you fellows at some too. Hell, I'll tell you everything I told the judge."

"What are we gonna do?" Roy laughed. "Pretend to be miners?"

"No," Bud replied. "Prospectors, actually. And you won't be pretending. You think Fox is a miner? He's an old man and he'll never swing a pick any more than I will. Once you have a paying claim you either hire it mined or sell the whole thing. Unless you like moving rocks around."

"How do you know all this?"

"Well, I got lucky, to tell the truth."

Bud told them how he'd met Elmer and Bart, omitting how he'd met them in the Wichitas while he was planning to steal a certain stash of gold bars. He recounted how Elmer had explained how gold washed downstream and was heavier than the sand and gravel, how to pan in the creek beds and work your way upstream looking for the lode. He also explained there could be more gold hidden inside rocks than what you might see, and repeated what Elmer told him about black sand. The boys were clearly incredulous, but Bud laughed and told them he'd looked at all the judge's samples and there wasn't anything golden about any of it. Yet his results had come from somewhere.

When he was through, the boys were convinced that they could be prospectors. Bud laid it on thick, directing them to some gullies he'd sketched around, and to a creek that he recalled having some black sand.

"You're just looking for traces, you're not going to find nuggets so you don't have to spend a lot of time hanging around. You know as well as anyone the army is all over the place, and you'll be doing exactly what they don't want anyone to be doing. Dig down a foot and put all the dirt and rocks in a crate, and move on. Same in the creek—dig down into the bed and dump it all in a box. If it's real sandy you might need some kind of pouch so none of it gets away.

"If you come across a creek that's all black sand, stop and get a shovel or two. Hell, you might know where one is already."

Charlie nodded. "Yeah. I think I might."

"Don't forget about the two kinds of rock; you'll see it everywhere now that you know to look. Creeks and gullies coming off those cliffs have a lot of promise."

George was nearly salivating.

Maybe lightning can strike twice.

"If it were me, I'd leave to the south and go the long way around. If the army sees you with mules and crates full of rocks they'll take it all and probably put you in a cage. And come on back through here and let me see what you find."

Charlie's brow furrowed. "Bud, you trying to get us to do the risky work for you?"

Bud scoffed, "You don't have to tell me where you found it, and you're not gonna leave it here, are you? Shit, you don't even have to tell me what the assayer says. I'm just trying to make good with you boys."

Angela interjected sweetly, "But we'd be happy to stop trying. Just say the word, Charlie."

"Jesus, Charlie, give it a rest," George complained. "Yeah, Bud. We'll come back through here."

"I'd be happy to make you boys a meal," Angela offered. "Y'all like chicken?"

"Well, sure," Roy said. "Chicken is good."

"It's settled, then," Bud told them. "Come for dinner and let's see what you find. You take your crates wherever you want to test them. I figure your chances are as good as the judge's, but if those tests come back with good numbers, then you know I'm not screwing around with you."

Roy looked sheepishly at his boots. "No, Bud, I reckon you're telling the truth. I wasn't sure at first, but I don't see how you could fake this stuff."

"Then I'll see you boys when you come back through. You don't even need to let us know you're coming. Just show up."

The boys finally left Bud and Angela to themselves and Angela busied herself pulling something together for dinner.

"Beans and cornbread all right, Bud?"

"What, no chicken for me?"

Angela wrapped her arms around Bud's neck and slipped into his lap.

"Chicken?" she murmured into his ear. "No, you don't get chicken."

Chapter 9

George and Charlie showed up in Bud's yard a few weeks later. They each had a mule with boxes full of rocks, just like Judge Fox had, but they weren't going to stay for their fried chicken.

"Where's Roy?" Bud asked.

Charlie spat in the dirt and replied, "The dumb bastard got caught by the army."

"Oh, damn!" Bud exclaimed. "Where? Surely not actually digging?"

"Almost. We were trying to leave and he saw a creek coming out of one of them gorges with different layers of rock. So, he stops and climbs down, and gets his sample. He's trying to tie the box onto his mule, but the damn thing wouldn't hold still and he dropped the box right on his foot. The box breaks open and he's hopping up and down on one foot, cussing up a storm. It was funny until a cavalry scout showed up. He shot his pistol in the air, then held down on Roy till the rest of the troop showed up. Apparently, the scout was just over the ridge and heard Roy yelling.

"Anyways, George and I slipped back the way we came, then followed a creek south and hid till night and snuck down about halfway to Texas, and then took the long way here, just like you said."

Charlie paused, then spat again. "I hate this damn mule."

"That's pretty bad luck," Bud replied. "I don't think the army will do anything besides confiscate his gear and run him out of the Territory, but I don't know for sure. I guess we can keep an eye open for him. You got a minute to show off what you found?"

Right on cue, Angela showed up on the porch with a tray of lemonade. "I know you boys are tired and thirsty. Sit for a bit."

George climbed down from his horse with a groan. "Something to drink sounds great."

Charlie dismounted, too, and said, "Well, I guess we can stay for a few minutes."

Bud walked between the horses to examine the mules' cargo. "Do you want to show off what you found?"

"No," Charlie grunted. "We ain't stayin' that long. Just stopped to tell you about Roy."

Bud appeared unconcerned with the rejection. "All right, suit yourself. Let me get some water for these animals, at least."

He walked around the side of the house and returned a few moments later with two wooden buckets of water. He set them on the ground in front of the horses, who began to drink sloppily. When they'd finished, Bud took the buckets back around the house and returned with two more for the mules.

He set the buckets in front of the mules, then knelt to examine Charlie's animal closer. He lifted one of its hooves and said, "This mule doesn't look too good, Charlie."

Charlie swallowed some lemonade and replied, "He's not good. He's stubborn, balky, and brays constantly. I'll be glad to be rid of him"

"Yeah, he's got a bit of a split in this hoof and could definitely use a new shoe. I imagine the rest are no better, that's probably why he's bitching so much."

"Well, he's going to have to make do for a while longer."

Bud dropped the mule's hoof and pulled himself to his feet with a groan, using one of the crates for leverage. He paused for a moment to make sure no one was looking and dribbled a pinch of gold dust into a knothole in the crate's lid. Stretching and groaning again, Bud bent over and picked up the buckets. As he returned from around back Charlie was standing up.

"Well, we need to get on. Thanks for the lemonade."

"You're very welcome," Angela replied. "You sure you can't stay for dinner?"

George clearly wanted to, but Charlie was adamant. "Thanks, but we need to go. Come on, George."

George said his goodbyes to Bud and Angela while Charlie mounted his horse and tried to prompt his mule into motion. He eventually got the animal moving in the right direction, and he and George made their way down the street.

After a minute or two Angela asked, "Any luck?"

Bud shrugged. "I don't know. There was a knothole in the top of one of George's boxes, maybe the size of a dime. I got a pinch in, but not much. Charlie was playing it close, so maybe we'll never know."

Bud and Angela never did know for sure, but a month later the *Transcript* reprinted an article from Guthrie about another rich sample from the Wichitas. No names were mentioned, so Bud had no way of knowing they were reporting on the sample he'd spiked while George was sipping lemonade.

* * *

The Justice Department made its first move against the Territorial Government in January 1895 when they sent an official examiner to investigate. Willoughby Newton was dispatched from Texas to dig through the vouchers and ledgers in order to get a clear picture of what was happening in the Oklahoma Territory. He took the train and was in Guthrie just twenty-four hours after receiving his assignment.

Newton preferred to keep a very low profile. He did not announce his arrival, bring any assistants, or draw any kind of attention to himself at all. He performed his investigation then disappeared without a trace.

Newton had audited the books of the entire district and confirmed that District Attorney Brooks was not imagining things with Oklahoma's courts and marshal service. Judge Scott's expenses were considerably out of line with the other districts and in the final six months of 1894 Scott's court had billed over seven thousand dollars more than the other three districts combined.

Nix didn't slip through the cracks, either. Newton showed that over $250 thousand had been disbursed by the U.S. marshal, but less than $200 thousand could be reconciled with the marshal's expenses and vouchers. A lot of money was missing.

But Judge Scott had powerful friends in Washington and Newton's accusations were just filed away like it had never happened. Marshal Nix, however, did not have the president or senators watching his back. He was unceremoniously removed from his position and replaced by Marshal William Grimes from Kansas.

Unfortunately, all Nix's deputies remained at their posts.

* * *

The army held Roy for two days, then released him with nothing but his horse, saddle, and a summons to explain what he'd been doing in the Comanche lands. His hearing was convened in the Cleveland County Courthouse.

Bud knew all about it, of course, and had coached Roy on how he might respond to particular questions, especially along the lines of "What were you doing there?"

The clerk finally called Roy's name and Roy presented himself to the judge, who read the charges and the army's report of his capture. Roy agreed that all of it was true.

"So," the judge began, "you're confessing to a federal crime?"

"Well, no sir, not exactly," Roy coolly replied. "Everyone knows there's gold out there, and I need money as much as the next man, so I tried to get some. This is how it worked out. I didn't do nuthin' a thousand other men aren't doing right now, sir, and to tell you the truth, prison don't look that bad to me right now. A meal, living indoors... So no, I ain't confessin' to nuthin', but if you want to lock me up I'm not going to slow you down."

"Have you ever been to prison before?"

"No sir. But the army took everything I own when they arrested me and I've been in bad shape since. Got an old tent from a friend, and after a few months like that, prison is worth a try."

The judge scoffed, "You might think differently if you were there, but you're not going to find out. There's no room for the likes of you and, as you so rightly point out, you're just one of many. And since you clearly can't pay a fine, I'm dismissing the charges. Next!"

Roy met Bud outside.

"Thanks, Bud, I thought I was headed to jail for sure."

"I was pretty sure they'd let you go if they thought you didn't have any money."

"That's not far from the truth, really. Charlie's thinking about finding some 'work,' if you know what I mean."

"Hmmm. Well, tell him to be careful."

That would be a huge break.

* * *

Bud would catch no breaks. Charlie indeed found "work" with one of the numerous gangs that E.D. Nix could not catch. Nix's dismissal had the Marshal Service in complete disarray, so Charlie was able to collect a share of several low-profile robberies across Oklahoma and North Texas.

Roy and George assisted in several robberies and collected enough to avoid having to find honest work. Charlie avoided all the mistakes that Bob had made and committed his villainy far from his home base which, to Bud's chagrin, was Norman.

Thankfully, Charlie was wise enough to avoid anything beyond the most casual acquaintance with Bud, but Bud didn't like having Charlie and the others around so much. Not that there was anything to hide, but Bud suspected that Charlie had nagging doubts about the bars.

Quanah's cattlemen were still keeping Washington's bureaucrats tied up, but even though legislation for an official opening could not be passed, most of its preparation could not be prevented. The official survey was underway and a small army of surveyors was carefully measuring and mapping the Territory into townships and sections, dutifully making notes of everything they saw.

Several newspapers began referring to the Kiowa, Comanche, and Apache land as the "Fort Sill Lands," a not-subtle hint that the tribes were not even recognized as the land's legitimate owners anymore.

The newspaper's hint did not go unnoticed. Quanah Parker offered the cattlemen more incentives to further delay the opening. In February 1895, around the time Newton was issuing his official report, the cattlemen's Congressional henchmen pulled off their most impressive legislative stunt.

The House Committee of Indian Affairs officially took up the issue of purchasing the Kiowa, Apache, and Comanche lands. Superficially, it was an enormous step forward – if the committee approved the measure, it would go the House floor for a vote and then to the Senate. After the Senate's inevitable approval, it would be signed into law by the president and the land would open in, perhaps, weeks.

The committee, dominated by the cattlemen's representatives, had something else in mind. Instead of voting on the agreement, they altered its terms, thus requiring it to be sent back to the Indians, namely Quanah Parker, for their approval and agreement.

Under the conditions set by the Jerome Commission, the Indians were allowed two full years to consider and negotiate the changes, and then to push out the opening for another three years after that. It was a brilliant move, and even though everyone knew it was the cattlemen's doing, there was nothing to be done about it. The *Daily Oklahoma State Capital* summed it up perfectly:

The intention, of course, is to tie up the reservation for five years to come.

While it was a rare victory for the Indians, it only delayed the inevitable. Eventually the Indians would have to ratify the changes, the three-year grace period would end, and their land would be distributed.

Bud wasn't concerned, though, because he had become quite busy selling portraits. His work with the fat professor had proven to nearly everyone in Norman that Bud's talent bordered on genius, and Bud was spending hours a day experimenting with anything that he'd heard of or seen in various publications.

His advertising was constant in both the *Norman Transcript* and the new Oklahoma City paper and he had no shortage of potential customers despite the economy. Unless he was working with the university, Bud charged an exorbitant premium and only the relatively wealthy could afford his work.

Bud and Angela quietly watched from the sidelines as Quanah Parker delayed the theft of his land. They could wait.

Part 4

Lottery

1898-1901

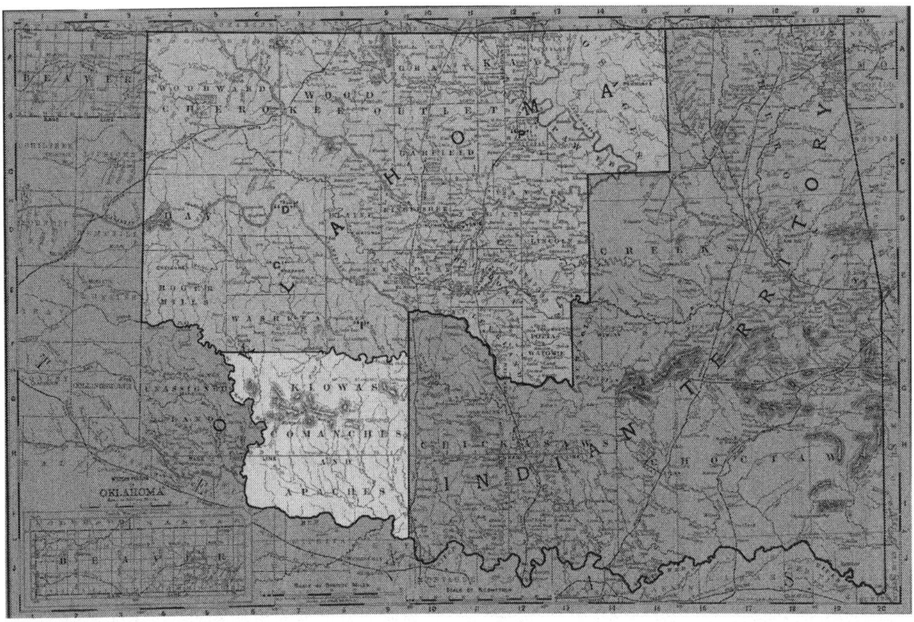

OKLAHOMA
INDIAN TERRITORY
WOODWARD
WOODS
CHEROKEE OUTLET
GRANT
KAY
GARFIELD
DAY
ROGER MILLS
WASHITA
LINCOLN
CREEKS
KIOWAS
COMANCHES
AND
APACHES
CHICKASAWS
BEAVER

Chapter 1

Gold was discovered in Alaska, and a massive rush began. The national economy was still a wreck and even the slightest rumor of work would generate caravans of homeless to go look for it. Millions headed for Dawson, at the mouth of the Klondike River on the Yukon.

Newspapers nationwide implied that gold nuggets were lying about like Easter eggs, but the truth was any paying claim had been scooped up the previous year. That wasn't reported for over a year and the few who managed to get to Dawson were savagely disappointed.

Against the backdrop of the Yukon Gold Rush and the continuing depression, things were happening back in the Lower 48.

Angela received a letter from Arthur, and the news was bad. Sarah's health had declined and she became seriously ill. The local doctor didn't know exactly what was wrong with her, but his prognosis had been dire and Sarah had died in June.

Beyond relaying the bad news, Arthur also wrote that he intended to leave Missouri and by the time Angela had received the letter he would be on his way to Texas. Unfortunately, he would not be passing near Norman or he would have delivered the news in person. He would write when he was settled, wherever that was.

Quanah Parker's cattlemen were running out of moves and legislation involving the Comanche and Apache lands was moving through committees. The survey had been completed and the plat maps of the townships were published. Potential locations for county seats and land offices were analyzed while the railroads threw their weight around, proposing many easements across the Territory.

As far as the prospectors and miners were concerned, however, the Comanche land was already open. They went wherever they wanted, dug shafts wherever they wanted, and made claims wherever they wanted. The entry point, naturally, was from Greer County. Supplies and equipment were readily available and the economic situation made the Wichitas a popular destination to attempt to escape the disaster back east, the possibility of gold closer than Alaska fanning the flames.

Two men from the Greer County invaders stood out. The first was an easterner named Edson Hewes, the second a local named A.J. Meers.

Hewes had drifted to Greer County during the previous years' unrest. Hewes was convinced that the Wichitas held an enormous gold field, larger than the one on the Klondike currently dominating the news. Hewes petitioned daily for the Indian lands to be thrown open so the gold could be taken. He was generally ignored, but he did make himself well-known to the Indian agents.

Not getting his wish, Hewes began organizing and threatening the usual tactic involving Indian land inconveniently in the possession of Indians: armed invasion. Rumors of thousands of armed settlers massing in Greer county earned him a lot of attention from the army.

After a rumored gold strike at the headwater of Otter Creek, just over the line from Greer County but definitely within the Comanche lands, Hewes threatened the secretary of the interior and an Indian agent named Frank Baldwin that there would be bloodshed if the miners' illegal activities were impeded at all.

Agent Baldwin called Hewes's bluff. Baldwin telegraphed the army, who fell upon the illegal camp, destroyed everything, threw the wreckage into the shallow mine shaft, and refilled the hole. Baldwin also instructed the army detachment to remain in the area to keep Hewes under their thumb.

The other man, A.J. Meers, had been a captain in the Confederate Army and had moved to Greer County in 1885. Meers had been prospecting across the area for nearly fifteen years and was actively working several shafts around Quartz Mountain. He was also a surveyor, which gave him the opportunity to legally, sort of, do a little prospecting in areas that were officially off-limits. He had been part of the recent survey of the Comanche lands and he was very intrigued with what he had seen.

Unlike Hewes, Meers didn't make a fuss about anything. He shared Bud's sentiment that a low profile would produce much better results and he simply snuck into whatever area he was interested in. While Hewes kept the army and Agent Baldwin's attention, Meers did whatever he wanted.

Shortly after the army destroyed the mine at Otter Creek, another camp materialized about twenty miles downstream. An illegal town, complete with saloons and whores, sprung up and was dubbed "Wildman" after its founder and the raucous behavior of the miners. It operated for several months before a detachment of cavalry was sent from Fort Sill to arrest everyone and destroy everything left behind. The Wildman miners, despite being dispossessed, were telling anyone who would listen about the rich potential they'd dug out of their shafts. They were clamoring to return, with Hewes's enthusiastic support.

* * *

Gone but not forgotten, ex-Marshal Nix and his crooked deputies, with their bogus expense accounts and Cherokee Strip frauds, were very much on Washington's mind.

A permanent U.S. Marshal, Patrick Nagle, had been appointed to replace Nix. It was quickly apparent that Nagle was caught in an impossible situation and his brief tenure was hell. Nagle had been forced to retain many of Nix's shady deputies and the Justice Department was constantly demanding that Nagle account for their every move.

With every report he wrote and every question he answered, Nagle confirmed what Justice Department's inspectors had suspected: Virtually all of Oklahoma's administration was corrupt, and the deputy U.S. marshals were particularly loathsome. Unfortunately, the Comanche lands had to be opened and the deputy marshals would have to oversee that.

Which was completely unacceptable. Washington was certain, justifiably so, that the deceit and abuses of power so rampant during the Cherokee Strip opening would be repeated on the Kiowa, Comanche, and Apache lands' opening too.

After weeks of back and forth, the idea of a lottery was raised and it only took a few days to nail down the details. To eliminate the Sooners and to keep the deputy marshals out of the equation, the Kiowa-Comanche-Apache opening would be a lottery, not a horse race.

All the 160-acre claims would be plotted on maps, numbered, and then posted for the public to see. Anyone interested in trying for a plot would apply and his name would be dropped into a drum. At the appointed time, names would be randomly drawn from the drum and the lucky winners would select their claim from the map. They would then take their claim documents to the land office and their title would be recorded regardless of who, if anyone, happened to be on the land in advance.

Two cities were designated as registration points. El Reno, the city outside the fort where Bud had recovered from Zack's kick twenty years earlier, was the first registration point. The second would be Lawton, just south of Fort Sill. While El Reno was an actual city, Lawton existed only on paper.

The Indians would select their claims before the lottery and several hundred thousand acres of mountain land was held aside and given to Fort Sill, then another large tract adjacent to Fort Sill was set aside as a forest preserve. The usual processes and paperwork to create towns were deemed suitable, so with all the details safely worked out the only thing missing was the legislation necessary to make it all official.

* * *

Deskin and the principals of Southwest Mineral watched in horror as their foolproof scheme, already delayed for years, melted down completely. It was clear that it would be impossible to steal the necessary claims and the only way to get them would be to purchase them after the lottery, assuming any would be for sale. Or to miraculously win the lottery.

A detailed examination of the new maps threw more wrenches into their works. The entire central valley was included in the area set aside for the forest preserve; nothing could ever be developed there. Equally as bad, their only remaining location for a smelter was now part of Fort Sill's expansion. Bud surreptitiously confirmed his bars were not hidden on reserved land, although they were on a claimable plot dangerously close to Fort Sill's new border.

On top of all that, Southwest Mineral now had a tremendous amount of competition. Wichita Mountain gold and silver was a foregone conclusion by then, and new mining companies were springing up daily. Wildman, it turned out, was the rule and not the exception. Southwest Mineral might be among the first into the country, but there was no chance they would have it to themselves.

No official date had been assigned for the lottery, nor was there any legislation pending that would authorize it, but the government announced that grazing leases would not be renewed and the cattlemen would have to remove their herds. The end of the Indian's grace period was, finally, on the horizon. Southwest Mineral needed a plan B as soon as possible because it was clear that something was about to happen, and it was likely to happen without them. Captain Cooper urged calm.

"Gentlemen, nothing has changed. There is still gold there. It will be discovered. Everything we've been planning will still come about. We simply have to be prepared to do it somewhere else and to purchase the key claims we need. Mr. Dalton's in particular. Yes, there will be competition, but there will be money to be made all round."

Bud said, "Sam and I once discussed a worse-case scenario. Seems we've arrived there."

"Yes," Deskin interjected, "we will certainly finance the acquisition regardless of the price."

Cooper spread his hands and addressed the group, "You see? Merely an additional step. Roads still need to be built, smelters for Mr. Dalton, houses for workers, food, horses, machinery, everything we planned for."

Elmer spoke up, "There's still a problem, Cooper. We need a place to work from. We don't have a place to stage equipment or animals. We were planning to bring them in immediately after the run, but now that's impossible. We need all that crap to be in place immediately, but we can't have any of it. It'll be weeks, maybe months, after the claims are settled before we can even begin."

"And meanwhile, those bastards out in Greer County aren't even waiting," Tipton complained. "Shit, we'll be lucky to get any claims at all, no matter what you think you can buy, Deskin. I'm betting that no one will sell at any price. This is serious."

Cooper nodded and drummed his fingers on the table. "It is indeed," he replied, "but think about this. When Payne founded Rock Falls, his mistake was that it wasn't legally defensible. His entire premise was all of Oklahoma was legally claimable land, but it turned out that Rock Falls wasn't really in 'Oklahoma.' Once the army was given permission to destroy it, they did. You see the same thing happening to the Greer County people now. Getting arrested, their equipment destroyed.

"Even when the Unassigned Lands opened, a claim hardly ever survived. Look what happened to poor Couch, and then his family.

Competing claims, gunfights, court suits. In light of recent events, I think we need a different plan. We need to start with a place that's legally defensible—we cannot afford the risk of building on a place we can't keep. The rest will unfold the way we want it to, and everyone will have the same problems we do with regard to obtaining choice claims. But the claims are really just the excuse to be there, aren't they? The roads, stores, and equipment are key, not the land. Consider Dawson up in the Klondike Territory; we need to be doing the same thing here."

Bud deadpanned, "Actually, Captain, a few of us are very interested in the land. And only the land. I hope you get rich supplying miners, but I need the mine."

"And," Tipton added, "we need Bud's strike to trigger the official rush, assuming someone doesn't do it first."

"Indeed," Cooper hummed. "That is true, isn't it? I don't know how to solve that problem yet. I suppose we will need to rely on Sam to produce enough money to change someone's mind. Meanwhile, we need a home."

"You obviously have something in mind," Elmer snapped. "Out with it."

"I propose forming a town. A legitimate and legal town. Preferably in a dull and uninteresting location that would never provoke any sort of dispute."

Tipton piped up, "You know, that's a damn good idea, Captain. Bud, anything dull and uninteresting jump to mind?"

Bud thought for a moment, then pointed to a map and said, "Yeah actually, something does. Pull that map over here."

He unrolled the map as the others looked on and ran his finger along the western side of the main range. "Yeah, right here on the west side, between East Otter Creek and the mountains. We came through here on the scouting trip, on the way to the top of Medicine Creek. Looks like good, flat land, just farming was all anyone thought it would be good for. I'm no farmer, but from what I could tell anyone would snatch any claim around there. You can't really call it uninteresting."

"True enough," Tipton conceded. "But it ain't gonna be anyone's first choice, especially if they're thinking about mining. But there's nothing wrong with it, is there?"

Elmer was looking at the map. "That location isn't great. It's probably a long way from Bud's claim, wherever it actually is. And no roads anywhere."

"That's true," Cooper agreed. "But it's also directly on the Chisolm Trail and there has to be some value in arriving first, especially if a railroad comes through, and my people hint that it will. Besides, what's the alternative?"

The members mumbled their agreement, and Cooper nodded his own. "It's settled then. Sam, we need to make sure Bud can purchase his claim. Then news of the gold strike should happen as soon as possible."

Deskin nodded too. "Yes, it'll be ready at a moment's notice. Perhaps this will work out after all."

Cooper and the others immediately got to work, pouring over the official territory surveys and augmenting them with the information they'd learned firsthand from their expedition. Cooper finally selected a place in what the maps identified as Section 34. The survey notes indicated there was a small creek running southward and the ground was level, the mountains about two miles to the east. Cooper selected the entire southern half of the section, mainly because it was the easiest way to describe what he wanted. The correct papers were completed, notarized, and submitted to the proper government office.

* * *

Cooper's townsite request was granted in November and the town of Cooperton, Oklahoma Territory, was added to the survey plats. Cooper was forced to endure some good-natured ribbing for naming his town after himself, and then to endure considerably more when it was discovered that his original choice had been "Cooper" but the Post Office had rejected it because there was already a town with that name in the Territory.

In Washington, the appropriate legislation to ratify the Jerome Commission's agreement with the Kiowa, Comanche, and Apache tribes was passed, finally, and the wheels began to turn again. The lottery allotment system was made official, the boundaries of Fort Sill officially detailed, the survey ratified, and the authority to process land claims was granted.

The tension between the illegal miners and virtually everyone else was rising to dangerous levels and the Indians had finally been provoked into quietly killing prospectors they found on their lands. The papers began to mention how prospectors were going into the mountains, but some were not coming out. A particularly grizzly event was reported when a mangled body was discovered near Mt. Scott just a few feet from a claim stake.

The miners insisted that the current mining laws ensured that their claims would prevail and they furiously claimed splotches of land throughout the area—the same land that was about to be distributed or be claimed outright by an Indian.

The Boomers held the opposite view. They were convinced that no claim of any kind could be valid, that was the whole point of the lottery: to prevent these exact sorts of disputes. The miners were nothing more than the latest version of a Sooner. The government provided no guidance and, as usual, the table was set for chaos.

In March 1899 Cooper received permission to lay out his town. He hired a surveyor and a sizable group of people, including Bud, rode southwest to the site of the about-to-exist town of Cooperton.

The surveyor easily found the section's corners, exactly where they were supposed to be, and measured off the new town's boundaries, marking those corners on the halfway points of the section lines. He then began measuring and marking streets, and then town lots between them. Cooper filed the townsite survey and received permission to dispose of the lots by auction. A judge would be named later to validate the land transactions and confirm the new owners had abided by the laws governing townsite claims, a process known as "proving."

Armed for the first time in his life with legal documents permitting him to be on Comanche land, Bud decided to make a scouting trip of his own without having to sneak around or hide from the army. He told the group he'd only be gone for a day and, no, he didn't want any company.

The next morning, with dawn's first rays barely lighting the high ridges two miles to the east, Bud left camp. He was not in a hurry, so when he came to the creek where he thought Jesse had camped the gang on that first ride, he decided to have a look.

Nothing had changed, and it turned out he remembered the correct location. Everything was as he recalled it, and he easily found the gang's campsite location. There were no traces left, naturally, and Bud didn't linger. It was cold and he was really only curious if he remembered correctly. But he was also curious to see if anyone had decided to follow him, and his short detour would allow him to check for followers. There were none.

He finally came to the creek leading to where the James Gang had waited out the blizzard in the cave, and he paused again. He had not been there since he and Angela had discovered the packs, and his horse could use a rest, so he decided one more detour wouldn't hurt anything.

Why not?

The bed was mostly dry, only a trickle of cold water running out into the prairie. The cave was unoccupied, and it seemed to Bud that no one had been there for a long time. He poked around for a few minutes but there wasn't anything to see. Satisfied, he followed the creek bed back to the prairie and checked his back-trail again. He was truly alone.

From there he wasted no time and trotted to his creek and unceremoniously headed upstream to his bars. When he rounded the bend, he was met with an unpleasant surprise: three men, clearly prospectors, were camped on the sand bar where Bud had buried the bars.

They had a small fire heating some coffee, and they were doing a good job of staying hidden. Bud's sudden appearance surprised them as much as they surprised Bud, and he noted that they appeared to be unarmed. Bud acted on impulse, putting his hand on his pistol, loosening it in its holster with his thumb on the hammer.

"What the hell do you think you're doing here?"

Sure enough, one of them reached for something and Bud had his pistol out and cocked, pointing at the miscreant long before he could retrieve whatever he was grabbing. "That's enough of that – get your hands where I can see them, all of you."

They all looked at each other, slowly raising their hands.

The one who'd reached asked, "You stealing our claim, mister? You'll never have it—I'll tell you that much right now."

Bud turned his horse so he could dismount without taking his gun off the prospectors, and did so.

"Claim? What kind of dipshits are y'all? This is Comanche land, and you can't even be here, let alone be trying to claim anything. I guess you must be some of those Greer County assholes, sneaking over from Texas."

"By God, we have every right to make a claim here. And you never mind where we're from, we got as much right to be here as you."

"Actually, you don't," Bud scoffed, patting his breast pocket with his left hand. "I'm here to lay out a town, so you can stuff whatever rights you think you have straight up your ass."

"So, you gonna shoot us?"

"Shoot you? No. Bullets are expensive. I was thinking about having the army send a squad right here to do whatever they do to illegals. Last I heard they destroy equipment and arrest everyone they catch. Oh, you know what would be fun too? Forget the army, maybe I'll find some Comanches. I hear they don't bother with the 'arrest' part too much anymore."

"That's fine, mister, we'll be long gone before that happens. But the claim will still be here. This is the Cache Creek mining district, and there's nothing you can do about that."

Cache Creek. Perfect.

"Well, we'll see about that." Bud went to one of their horses and walked it over to his own, tying the reins to the back of his saddle.

"What the hell do you think you're doing?"

"I'm putting two of you afoot, that's what I'm doing. I reckon you'll be glad to see those soldier-boys when they show up." He finished tying the second horse's reigns next to the first.

"All right now, fellas. On your feet, and keep those hands where I can see them."

"Why?"

"Because I'm not gonna let you shoot me in the back while I ride out of here. Now get on your feet and walk your asses down this creek. I'll tell you when you can stop."

The prospector who had been doing the talking was sputtering and turning red by then. Bud, remembering Abe, was thinking he might have to shoot him. The other two were at least accepting they'd been caught.

One of them spoke up, "Can we at least put on a coat, mister?"

"No, I'm sorry, you can't. Can't take the chance one of you has a little shooter in a pocket somewhere."

"How far are we going, then?"

"Just to the edge of the prairie, a few hundred yards, I guess. Then I'll take the horses to the army and send them back this way, and y'all can figure out how you want to get away after you walk back here."

"Why you doing this to us?"

"Well, truth told, your friend there pissed me off pretty good. Like I said, I'm laying out a town and you chose the wrong creek to squat in. And then he took up an attitude. Frankly, I don't have the patience for it."

Bud motioned with his head back to the west. "If y'all had set up a mile that way we'd have never laid eyes on each other."

The new talker asked, "What if you were to move us there? And we just forgot about all this? Nothing special here, a mile ain't too bad, right guys?"

The red-faced prospector was still unhappy, but clenched his jaws and nodded curtly. The other remained silent, but nodded as well.

Bud wasn't convinced. "What about this Cache Creek horseshit, though? Your friend seems attached to my townsite."

"Mister, we're not attached to anything in this creek. We'll name it something else a mile away. But we can't have the army smashing our stuff, mister. Times are bad, you know it too. We're just trying to get by out here till the Territory opens. Please, mister, we don't want anything to do with your town. Let us go somewhere else and take our chances with the army."

Bud stared at each man in turn, and finally nodded. "All right. You can't be here, but I guess you can go somewhere else. Gather all your gear, right now, and move out. Go find another creek. You don't bother us, we won't bother you."

"You got it, mister. We'll be gone in twenty minutes!"

Bud oversaw their packing and followed them out of the creek.

Pointing west, he said, "I'll wait here for a few hours, I won't even know where you decide to go. That way I can truthfully say I haven't seen anyone in case the army asks. But you best listen hard to this: If I ever find you here again, it's gonna end different. No law, no army. Not even Indians. You understand what I'm telling you?"

They nodded and left in a hurry. Bud watched them rush westward and pondered his next step. It was late enough in the day that he wouldn't make it back to Cooperton before dark, and he still had not been able to spend any time alone in his creek. He had a few hours of daylight left, best use them here and camp overnight. He hadn't anticipated making a camp, but he figured he could make do for one night.

Bud unpacked the few things he'd brought, the most important being a small shovel and a thin, but sturdy, wooden rod about four feet long. He wasn't sure exactly how deep the bars would be, or precisely where they were located, so he would systematically dig shallow holes so that the shovel could perhaps find them. If not, the rod would be used to probe a foot or two further into the sand in each direction around the hole. With luck he would find the cache quickly.

Bud had no luck. With the light about to fail, he dug his twelfth hole, far outside where he'd estimated the bars to lay. The years had widened the bend in the creek, and had deposited more sand, and his estimate was clearly wrong. He felt like the current hole would be well underwater if the creek were running.

His hands were sore from twisting and pushing the wooden rod into the sand, and just as he vowed to bring a mallet next time, the rod struck something solid about a foot down and to the right of his hole.

Probably a rock, with my luck, but let's dig it up and see.

Leaving the rod in place, Bud dug a new hole to expose whatever the rod had found. When his shovel struck it, he knew he'd found the bars. He widened the hole enough to keep sand from falling back in and scraped the sand away to reveal the top of his cache.

He pushed the rod into the sand next to the stash to mark its exact location and went to work filling in the other holes he'd dug. It didn't take long, but by the time he was through he was very tired of the shovel.

He paced off the distance from the rod to the bank. Six paces. He dropped his hat on the top of the bank to mark the spot.

Now I need something permanent, but not obvious. I guess a rock would be best ... wouldn't Jesse be proud of me, now.

He climbed out of the creek and squinted through the gloom, but it was too dark. It would have to wait until morning. He left his hat and the rod where they were and quickly settled down into his camp. He rebuilt the fire the prospectors had lit and set up a small camp. Dinner was some jerky he had in his saddlebag, his horse blanket was his bedroll, and the saddle his pillow. He made one last check on his horse and settled in for what he was sure would be an uncomfortable night.

He was right. It started to drizzle around 3:00 a.m., not that he'd really been sleeping anyway, and soon he was both cold and wet. When the sun finally dribbled some light into the creek bed, Bud was quite ready to leave. Cooperton would at least get him a dry tent and dry clothes.

He saddled his horse and quickly packed his gear while the sun rose, and it wasn't long before he could make out both his hat and the rod.

Time to find a couple of nice rocks and get the hell out of here.

He found a good-sized piece of granite, perhaps forty pounds, and hefted it to where his hat lay. He kicked the hat out of the way and dropped the stone where the hat had been. Then he found a smaller stone, only a few pounds, and placed the smaller rock directly behind the larger, lining up with the rod protruding from the sand.

OK, there you go. Line up the rocks, six paces, dig. Sorry, Jesse, no brass buckets this time. And I'm just going to write it all down in English, like a regular person might.

He stood next to the rod and jotted down the instructions in his sketchbook, then dashed off a quick sketch of the shape of the bend, rocks, and the trees lining the bank, and the landscape in the background, specifically a small crevice in a hillside in the background.

Returning to the hole, he climbed down and pulled a bar from the top and tossed it toward his horse. Groaning as he climbed out of the shallow hole, he unceremoniously pulled the rod from the sand and tossed it next to the bar. The hole was filled five minutes later, the bar hidden in a saddlebag, and Bud was leaving five minutes after that. He was cold and tired and dreaded the ride back to the townsite.

He arrived back at Cooperton just before noon. The men had been concerned when he failed to return the previous evening, but they had no idea where to look for him. Bud recounted his story, leaving out any details about location, and Tipton repeated his belief that those prospectors were going to cause trouble at some point.

"Yeah," Bud replied, "but I have an idea."

Chapter 2

Bud sent a note to Charlie immediately upon his return to Norman. Bud asked him to come at his earliest chance and to bring Roy and George with him.

Angela was still thinking about his story. "Bud, if you hadn't got the drop on them, they might have killed you. I don't think they cared."

"Yeah, I thought about that too. That's where Charlie comes in. I'm gonna get Elmer to hire the three of them to be unofficial regulators."

"What's a regulator?"

"Well, basically an outlaw. Charlie's suited to that, and it seems we might need to fight fire with fire. Tipton is convinced these miners are going to screw the whole thing up, so it should be an easy sell."

It turned out to be a very easy sell. The boys arrived a day later and Bud arranged a meeting with Southwest Minerals. Bud recounted his story and expressed the danger the Greer County prospectors posed. Once Charlie and the boys realized the prospectors would interfere with their own potential claims, they were all very enthusiastic. Roughing up Greer County prospectors was clearly the right thing to do.

Tipton and Elmer were likewise enthusiastic. In less than an hour all three were on the payroll and planning their first "patrol."

Deskin was adamant about one thing, however: "No killing!"

Charlie was noncommittal. "We'll see." The three "regulators" left in September to open yet another violent chapter in the Indian Territory's history.

* * *

A few months of the regulators' harassment began to pay dividends. January 1900 showed the beginning of a spike in violence in the Kiowa and Comanche lands, particularly the area just west of Fort Sill. Charlie could not be blamed for all of it, though, because the Greer County men were starting to turn on each other. The Comanches, Kiowas, and Apaches were doing their part too.

Charlie, George, and Roy raided several small camps and learned that many of the prospectors were indeed armed. If there were more than three or four of them it became too fair a fight for Charlie's liking. After one particularly deadly confrontation with six prospectors, all of whom were killed when they tried to fight back, the regulators reconsidered their strategy.

It turned out that it was easier and safer to simply report the camps to the army. That prevented them from getting shot themselves and allowed them to split up and deal with the Greer County men more efficiently; there were just too many of them. Beyond their numbers, their audacity made it clear that Angela's observation was true: they didn't care about anything at all, and they were perfectly willing to fight.

The raucous Wildman and Greer County miners had organized the "Otter Creek Mining District" and elected A.J. Meers as the recorder. Although every square inch of the "district" was within Indian Territory borders, Meers petitioned to lease two entire townships – just over 46,000 acres – for mining. His petition was rejected and the threat of arrest was reiterated.

Meers responded to the rejection by sneaking to the foot of Mt. Scott, which was not only in the Comanche land but also in the center of the area set aside for the federal preserve. Charlie and George spotted his camp and reported its location to the Indian police who arrived the next day and arrested Meers. After they confiscated his equipment, the police, inexplicably, hauled him to the Indian agent in Anadarko instead of delivering him to the army at Fort Sill.

The Indian agents were responsible for enforcing laws inside Indian reservations, particularly those intended to protect the Indians. Fort Sill was a short ride away, but perhaps the Indian police believed that the Indian agent would hand Meers a more severe punishment than the army.

They were dead wrong. The agent, somehow, was either unaware of the law or decided that the Indian Intercourse Act, the current Kiowa-Comanche Treaty, and 150 years of precedent could not produce a single law allowing him even to hold, never mind to punish, Meers. Meers was released with a healthy finger-wagging by the agent.

That episode turned out to be critical. In June, Congress finally passed an act specifying the Kiowa, Comanche, and Apache lands would be opened by lottery at a time specified by the president. The miners and prospectors took the act to mean they could do what they wanted, roaming the area and staking whatever claims they wished. Meers, naturally, was in the center of it.

* * *

Mountain View was a town that had evolved as most in the Indian Territory had; it was a convenient stop on a well-traveled path. In this case, the path between the old forts built in the 1850s to control the Indians. One of the most dreadful posts in the entire army, Fort Cobb, had been located a few miles to the east. No one had despaired when Fort Cobb was decommissioned in favor of Fort Reno.

One of Meers's friends was a surveyor named Elisha Williams. Williams had surveyed the Arapaho lands for its opening and had lived in Greer County for years. After the Jerome Commission came to terms with Quanah Parker, Williams moved his family to Mountain View on the northern border of the Indian Territory where he could be closer to the action.

In 1900, Mountain View was a still a convenient place to stop and find a bite to eat, which is how Elisha Williams met Bud Dalton and Charles Tipton. Judge Fox had written to Bud about how some of his friends intended to set up mining operations in the Territory and thought perhaps his friends and Bud's friends might be able to help each other. Would they be willing to meet at a more or less central location? Say, Mountain View?

Bud and Tipton rode into town and, at the appointed time, stepped into the small cafe across the street from the livery stable. Williams was already there and sitting with none other than Frank Wildman.

Bud shook Wildman's hand and asked if he was related to the mining camp on Otter Creek that had been removed by the army. Wildman admitted that yes, they had used his name, and Williams commented that Bud was as knowledgeable as the judge had promised.

Tipton broke the ice. "Well, Judge Fox says we all may have some common interests. What can Southwest Mineral do for you?"

Wildman took the lead. "It's no secret that Otter Creek is going to be a huge gold field. It's just a matter of time before pay dirt is struck. Fox says you fellows are onto something good in the east. It seems possible that we could help each other out."

Tipton and Bud glanced at each other, both aware that Southwest Mineral's scouting expedition had produced precisely the opposite conclusion.

Bud put on an apologetic look and asked, "Frank, I hate to seem … indelicate, but have you actually recovered anything?"

"You've seen the assayer's reports, I'm sure."

"I have, and they're impressive. But I haven't seen or heard of anything tangible, and so the question."

Wildman gritted his teeth and shook his head. "No."

Tipton interjected, "Bud, show them?"

Bud was taken aback. "Here?"

"Why not?"

Bud reached into his breast pocket and produced his leather pouch. He surreptitiously pushed it to Wildman and said, "We already have production. Without a bunch of newspaper reports, attention, or the army."

Wildman and Williams peeked into the pouch and then looked at each other. Williams slapped his leg. "I knew it!"

Bud motioned for the pouch to be returned, then humored them. "Right, and there's no doubt that you're going to find a lot all over Otter Creek."

"But you're not interested in a partnership."

Tipton shook his head. "Not right now, no. If you had some production, possibly. Hewes brags weekly about the quality of the ore, but the army is practically camped in his front yard so it's going to be impossible to capitalize until the Territory is officially opened. And Otter Creek is a long way from our interests."

"What would you say," Wildman replied, "if I told you that Elisha and I have our eye on an area on Middle Otter Creek?"

Tipton looked to Bud. "Where's Middle Otter Creek?"

Nowhere, and with the same potential they have now...

Bud shrugged noncommittally. "Well, I don't know that name, but if it's between Otter Creek and East Otter Creek then I have a pretty good idea."

Tipton raised his eyebrows, "And...?"

"It's much closer to town, and possibly a good choice."

Bud turned to Wildman. "If it's where I'm thinking, I assume you're looking at the place where the creek comes out of the gorge? Maybe downstream a bit?"

The shocked look on their faces told Bud he'd hit the bullseye. "Don't worry, like Charles said, we have what we need and we're not interested in looking for more."

Bud turned back to Tipton and lied, "They're on the right track."

"Well, that could change things," Tipton said. "Find a little color and I think we would make a good team."

They spent another ninety minutes eating and talking about mining. Elisha was certain, beyond a doubt, that every mining claim would survive the lottery. Bud wasn't so sure, but kept it to himself along with his doubts about their proposed site.

Williams and Wildman staked their claims a week later. It was only twelve miles from Cooper's townsite and, like Meers, they made no effort to hide their presence. Even though the Indian Territory still belonged to the Indians, sort of, Wildman and Williams's camp became the focus of development in the area. By August a permanent, and illegal, town was built and named, again Wildman. This time, though, the army's hands were tied and unlike Payne's Rock Falls, Wildman would survive.

***

A rumor was circulating among the Greer County men that a detachment from Fort Sill had destroyed a large mining encampment. The rumor said they'd been sent by the Indian agent, and based on what Meers recounted about his own recent encounter, Elisha Williams decided he was ready to act.

On behalf of the mining district, Williams and twenty-six miners brought a lawsuit against Indian Agent James Randlett for damages inflicted by the soldiers. Williams claimed that Randlett had no authority over the mining claims, nor the army any standing to remove the miners.

District Judge C.F. Irwin heard both sides and three days later ruled in favor of the miners. Ignoring the Indian treaties and the Intercourse Act, the judge simply ruled that Randlett had not obeyed the court, presumably referring to the process of disputing a mining claim. The judge ruled that the claims were valid and Randlett had illegally removed their owners. Suddenly, it was indisputably legal to be on an

Indian reservation to make a mining claim. If only Payne had had it so easy.

Tipton had watched the whole affair unfold and when Wildman was unofficially the first city in Indian Territory, he needled Cooper about all the official paperwork necessary to create Cooperton. All he'd needed to do was plant a stake and make a mining claim.

"We'll see," was Captain Cooper's only reply.

The truth, though, was that Wildman now had a substantial lead over everyone wanting to leap into the Kiowa-Comanche-Apache reservations, although Meers was not far behind. Even more disturbing to Southwest Mineral was the fact that Wildman was planning to construct a large commercial smelter. Wildman, not Southwest Mineral, would have the first functional smelter in the mountains.

The entirety of the Wichita range was crawling with miners, and Cooperton's vicinity was not immune. Just two miles away was a wide pass known as Cutthroat Gap. The gap received its name in 1833 when a band of Osage Indians snuck up on a camp of Kiowa Indians. Seeing that the camp contained no warriors, the Osage attacked and killed over 150 women and children, mostly by cutting their throats.

A Greer County miner named William Smiley had set up camp in the Gap and had made several claims there. When Cooperton was being surveyed, he had clearly seen the large camp and had come over to ensure no one planned to interfere with his claims. Cooper replied that as long as Smiley stayed outside the townsite borders there should not be any trouble.

That encounter was being repeated all across the Territory. County seats in Lawton and Hobart were surveyed along with dozens of other townsites, both legal and illegal. There were several conflicts between townsite companies and miners with claims, and court cases were filed on who had rights to the land, even though the Indians still owned it all in real life.

"You watch," Cooper told Bud and Antrim, "these conflicting claims are going to ruin people again, just like before. By the time this is all over, you'll be very glad you weren't involved."

* * *

In order to make a mining claim, a prospector needed only to mark the edges of his claim. Once marked, typically with stakes bearing the name and general description of the claim, the law made considerable allowances for the person who made the claim. Not only was he protected from subsequent claims from later prospectors, he was allowed to tunnel outward up to three thousand feet, even if the tunnel extended beyond his stakes. He had no claim to anything on the surface, but the surface owner had no claim to anything found in the tunnel.

Like the homesteading requirements, the prospector was required to make some kind of improvement on the claim. An "improvement" in this case was a mine, pit, excavation, or the like. The laws did not require the prospector to remain on his claim, which is how Meers could have so many of them. All he had to do was mark the edges of an interesting area, dig a hole, and he would suddenly have considerable legal protections.

That was the basis of the miner's conviction: that their claims would supersede anything that happened to the land's title later. Their miscalculation was that all those laws applied to unallocated federal lands, which the Kiowa, Comanche, and Apache reservations were not. Claims in the new forest preserve, like Meers's, could possibly be worked, the area inside Fort Sill's official boundaries were doubtful, but the Indian selections offered the prospectors no protections. At least they shouldn't have.

Williams's successful suit against Randlett and the government's toleration of Wildman made everything crystal clear for Bud. Being a prospector was the best kind of Sooner.

***

It was September 9, still plenty hot, and Bud was preparing for his third trip to the Wichitas in as many months. He was not enthusiastic to begin with, and looking at the southern sky gave him pause. Rain in September was unusual, but the skies were ominous. His enthusiasm ebbing further, he let Angela talk him into delaying his departure.

The threatened rain began that night, and then intensified. Hard rain and high winds continued through the night and into the next day without letting up. Every creek overflowed its bank, and the South Canadian, usually a wide strip of sand with a shallow red stream meandering through it, was flowing bank-to-bank. Grateful he was still in Norman, Bud and Angela rode out the storm in their small house.

The weather finally broke on the morning of September 11, the storm moving northward into Kansas. As the cleanup commenced, they learned that what they'd just endured was not any regular storm. It was the remains of a tropical hurricane that had ravaged the Caribbean and all of Cuba, then crossed the Gulf of Mexico to wipe Galveston, Texas, completely off the map. Telegraph lines were still down and not a word had been heard from Galveston for two days.

The news from Galveston, when it was finally learned, was horrific. It was feared that six thousand people had died and almost every building in the city was damaged to some extent; the vast majority were completely demolished.

The storm was also a considerable setback for the prospectors in the Wichitas. Nine inches of rainfall had poured out of the clouds and down the mountains; even the tiniest gullies were transformed into raging torrents. They uprooted trees and washed away anything too close to their banks, including wagons, horses, and people. Just as in Norman, every creek overflowed its banks. The winds, over seventy miles per hour, had ripped every tent from the ground, hurling them to points unknown, and no one was spared. When it was all over, the few remaining people looked like survivors of a shipwreck washed onto a particularly inhospitable beach.

Making matters worse, the stakes marking their claims had been washed or blown away. Intended only to establish a prospector's legal rights and not to permanently mark boundaries, no one had put much effort into planting them into the rocky ground. After just a single day, charges of claim-jumping were rippling through every mining district.

It took a week for the water in the South Canadian to retreat to its normal level, and Bud waited several more days before retrying his trip to the mountains. Finally, he loaded the wagon with supplies for several weeks.

Unaware of the trials the prospectors had endured, Bud was delighted to find his creek, and most of the territory for that matter, completely deserted. He drove the wagon along the east bank and made his camp only a few yards from his marker rocks.

He got his tent pitched and tended to the horses, then unloaded much of his gear from the wagon. He had purchased small wooden crates for samples, which he left in the wagon, but everything else went to its place. He then pulled up a large amount of firewood, which was easy because tons of it was littering both sides of the creek.

His camp made, Bud then pulled several long stakes from the wagon and made a claim, pounding a marker into the ground on each side of the creek. He trudged upstream to add more markers, his claim forming a squarish area, about one hundred yards per side with the bars roughly in the middle and the northern side halfway up the two hills on either side of the creek.

All the housekeeping done, he snatched his sketchbook from his pack and climbed down into the creek bed. He turned to the sketch he'd made with the mountain in the background and located the crevice. Lining up the rocks, he took six steps backwards.

Right here.

Three scoops of sand later, the shovel crunched into the bars. He left the pole sticking out of the creek bed to mark the spot, then returned to the wagon to begin the hard work.

Using a pick and shovel, he began to improve his claim. By late afternoon Bud had an excavation about five feet long and a few feet deep and had collected ten boxes of dirt and rocks. Deciding he'd done enough, he dragged one of the empty crates into the shade, fished a piece of jerky from his mess kit, sat down, and called it a day.

He finished his digging the next morning, making a nice square trench running roughly parallel to the creek toward the hill, the excavated dirt and rocks piled tidily alongside. Bud looked down at the hole, then around to the creek and hills, then his stakes marking his claim.

If that's not an "improved" claim, I don't know what is.

He tossed the pick into the wagon, and then climbed down into the creek bed with the shovel to uncover the bars. One by one, he pulled eight bars from the hole and lugged each to the bank and dropped it into an empty box he'd set aside.

He re-covered the stash of bars and climbed out of the creek bed, tossing the wooden rod into the wagon beside the pick. He dumped a shovelful of dirt on top of each bar and nailed the wooden lids onto each crate. The shovel joined the pick and rod and then, with some effort, Bud pushed the boxes with gold bars to the front of the wagon bed. There was not enough dirt in the boxes to justify their weight, and they would never escape a deliberate search. Hopefully, it would never come to that.

He rummaged through his pack, retrieving the leather pouch that held his gold dust. He sprinkled dust liberally into the boxes holding plain dirt, and then mixed them up so the fine dust could not be seen. He nailed the tops onto those boxes, then heaved them into the wagon too.

Anyone looking into those boxes would find exactly what they were: boxes of dirt and stones. Those crates were lashed behind the ones holding the bars so, should anyone look, the first crate of dirt would hopefully dissuade any further examination.

He gathered his gear and loaded it all into the wagon, tying it all on top of the eight boxes behind the seat, the ones hiding bars. He tapped the stakes marking his claim a few more times, just to make sure, and climbed into the wagon to leave.

He let the horses take their time, walking westward back to Wildman, and he figured he'd pull into town about four o'clock.

When he arrived, he made his way to Elisha Williams's main business interest, the Williams Mining and Milling Company. It had been built to service Williams's mine, dubbed the "Lyon Lode," as well as anything a miner was willing to pay to have analyzed.

Bud walked in and asked the clerk how long it would take for them test some samples. The clerk questioned him on how large the sample was that Bud was bringing. About eighty pounds. Oh, yes, that's fine. Did Bud want a complete analysis, or was he looking for something specific? A complete analysis would alert Bud to other valuable minerals like copper, lead, and zinc in addition to gold and silver but would take much longer. Bud elected to limit the testing to just gold and paid the clerk in cash.

He pulled his wagon up to their loading dock and unloaded most of the crates with spiked samples, holding back three. The crates were emptied into a large metal tub on wheels, weighed, then marked with Bud's name. Two workers rolled his sample to the side and told him he could come back in a few days for the analysis and any results his sample yielded.

Curious about what they were going to do with his sample, Bud had one of the clerks explain the process and show him the equipment. Basically, they would grind the sample into a coarse gravel, then dump it all into a coal-burning forge. They would heat the sample until it completely melted, then pour the glowing, red-hot liquid into a cone-shaped iron mold. The heavier gold would settle to the bottom as the lighter molten rock, known as slag, floated above. After cooling, the mold would be inverted and the now-solid, pyramid-shaped contents tapped onto the ground. Any gold would be found at the tip-top of the pyramid and could be removed from the slag with a slight tap of a hammer. The gold would not be pure, but for testing purposes it would be definitive: there would be gold or not, and if so, would provide a rough estimate of the ore's value.

So, Bud killed two days in Wildman, and it was hard to believe he was still in the Indian Territory. Back in Mountain View there was no saloon because of the liquor restrictions detailed in the federal laws. Not so in Wildman; they had a full-fledged saloon right on the street. A few doors away was unmistakable writing on the wall: an official U.S. Post Office somehow standing in an illegal town in the middle of the Indian Territory. Times were definitely changing.

In addition to the post office and saloon there was a newspaper, the *Otter Creek Miner,* and a two-story hotel named the DeRastus, which boasted yet another saloon. Next door was the Meers Mining Exchange Office, another enterprise owned by the omnipresent A. J. Meers.

Bud noticed that while the place was humming with activity, he could not tell that anything was being accomplished. Miners and prospectors scurried about, swapping stories and retelling the latest rumored reports from some sample or another. No one paid for anything with gold, only cash.

Bud waited his two days and finally returned to Williams Milling and asked for his results. It seemed as though they had been waiting for him because both Wildman and Williams were there, along with about eight clerks and workmen. Williams handed Bud the assayer's analysis and Wildman, with a smile, handed Bud two small, triangle-shaped nuggets, each about the size of the end of a match. Bud's samples had proven rich in gold, they estimated similar ore would pay approximately $900 per ton.

"There was never a doubt, Bud," Wildman chuckled. "None at all."

One of the people in attendance was a reporter, probably the only reporter, for the *Otter Creek Miner.* He interviewed Bud, who declined to share his name but agreed the analysis could be shared with the world. That small story was reposted in major newspapers across the Territory.

Bud hauled the last crates with his spiked samples to an assayer near Oklahoma City in mid-November. The assayer reproduced the results Bud had received in Wildman and Bud received his expected pellet of gold and written results. This time, though, Bud was allowed to watch the testing and a hazy notion drifted through his mind.

I wonder if I can do that in reverse.

Chapter 3

"You're gonna do what?"

Bud couldn't help but laugh at Angela's incredulous expression.

"We're gonna melt a couple of these bars and mix it all up with sand and dirt and rocks. Then we're gonna grind all that up with another ton of rocks."

"Bud, are you crazy? Melt?"

He laughed again. "Yep. It'll be much faster than grinding."

* * *

Not at first. Like the Kiowa, Commanche and Apache Land opening, Bud's attempts to melt a bar failed, one after another. They started simply, with a fire burning in a hole dug in the ground, and progressed into more elaborate schemes to contain the heat. One particularly unfortunate episode spewed hot, glowing coals across their back yard, igniting a number of small fires which the wind threatened to spread across town.

Angela had had enough.

"Bud, go buy a cast-iron stove. A big one. Fill it with coal, get it hot, put in the bar. We're going to destroy something pretty soon. Like our house. Or Norman."

A heavy cast-iron stove was delivered from Oklahoma City two weeks later and Bud had it pulled around back. He loaded about twenty pounds of sand and dirt inside, then put one of their bars on top of the dirt. He filled the rest of the stove with coal, and got the fire going. When the coal began to burn, he pumped the bellows he'd set up and eventually the stove was glowing red.

"When do you know it's done?"

Bud shook his head. "No idea, but I can barely get near the thing. Let it burn itself out and we'll see what happened in there."

It took all night for the stove to run out of fuel, and many hours more to cool, but what Bud found inside delighted him. The gold had indeed melted, along with some of the sand and dirt, and seeped together into a weird crusty mixture. The gold could clearly be seen, but it was no longer a bar.

A hammer and chisel were all Bud needed to tear the sand-gold stuff into small enough bits to get out the stove's small door, and then pounded into even smaller bits. They repeated the process with another bar a few days later with the same results.

In March, Bud mixed his fake ore with a hundred pounds of dirt and rocks, then hauled it all to a milling company near Mountain View. The decidedly odd bits mixed in the load went unnoticed and in less than an hour Bud was rewarded with a nicely uniform mix of what, at first glance, appeared to be coarse sand and rough, pea-sized gravel. The results were dumped into their own boxes and their lids were nailed on.

Perfect.

When he got home, he and Angela picked through the results. There were a number of mangled gold chunks and slivers mixed in with the sand and gravel. "Pick out some of the biggest ones," he told her. "I know exactly what to do with them."

***

Anxious to capitalize on the gold fever in Greer County and the Indian lands, one of the railroads had offered to haul ore to the large smelter in Denver where, assuming the ore produced, it could be extracted and sent directly to the mint just a few miles away.

Bud was taking them up on their offer. He could hire a crew to dig, and a freight wagon, capable of hauling several tons of goods, grain, or in this case ore, to carry the load to the station. But first he needed to see Sam Deskin.

Bud walked into Deskin's office unannounced, wearing a large smile.

"Hello, Sam, hope I'm not interrupting."

Deskin looked up from his ledgers and, seeing Bud's huge smile, grinned himself. "Well, you seem to be in a good mood. To what do I owe the pleasure?"

Bud's smile widened, and he told Sam, "I need to show you something. You'll like this."

Deskin spread his hands. "By all means. Please, let me see."

Bud pulled out his leather pouch and carefully dumped the contents onto Deskin's desk. The nuggets he and Angela had picked out along with the small gold buttons he'd received from his spiked samples stared up at Deskin.

Deskin's jaw dropped open and he alternated between looking at Bud and the nuggets for a few seconds. "You found it? You found the source?"

Bud nodded. "Yes! With all the bullshit going on in the Territory we just made a claim and worked it right out in the open. No one knows what the hell's going on, and we're just one of a thousand claims, so no one bothered us. We got a really good sample a few months back that I had tested at Wildman's place."

Bud separated the three symmetrical buttons from the rest and pointed. "That's where these came from. We found the nuggets digging. We're on top of something huge."

Deskin stood up and shook Bud's hand. "Congratulations! What do you need from me?"

"Well, I need money to work the claim properly. Hire men, carry freight, you know. And when it comes to money, you're the first person I think of."

"Quite right!" Deskin exclaimed. "We'll have you set up before the afternoon is out."

Deskin leaned over and called through his office's open door, "Jefferson! Jefferson, in here please. Bring the necessary forms for a letter of credit." Turning back to Bud, he said, "We can easily arrange for several thousand dollars to be made available. Normally I'd insist on valuable collateral, but I'm convinced you have it, even beyond your standing balance. Will ten thousand get you started?"

Bud nodded. "That's more than enough, thanks. I'd like to get a good jump on establishing the claim in case I need to defend it. I'm also going to register for the lottery, of course, but I need to play both hands."

"Absolutely. Let me and Jefferson do our work. I'll have your letter shortly."

* * *

Angela made sure that Norman's gossip network learned that Bud Dalton had found what he was looking for, and the *Transcript* published a brief note about yet another rich find in the Wichitas.

Bud arranged shipping from Texas to the Denver smelter, and alerted the smelter that he would be sending them several tons for processing. The railroad claimed there would be a coal-carrier waiting for Bud and his ore, and the smelter claimed there would be no problem getting the ore from the Denver train station to the smelter itself; there was a narrow-gauge line between the station and the smelter for that exact purpose.

Bud dumped two of the three crates of spiked ore into the freight wagon; the last crate of the gravel would stay in Norman for the time being. All the pieces in place, Bud bounced down to Wildman. His first stop was Meers Mining Exchange.

Bud produced his letter of credit and the gold nuggets he'd shown Deskin. Showing off the nuggets was not necessary, but Bud wanted to produce some excitement and he did. His account was enthusiastically opened and his credit was instantly good everywhere in town.

The next stop was Wildman's place where he said hello and told Frank that he intended to send several tons of ore to Denver and, again, to show off the nuggets. Wildman was impressed, and Bud was certain the hook was set. No one would question anything he credited coming from his claim.

It took no time at all to find a drover with a heavy wagon and team, and then he hired a foreman and six men to work his site. The crew moved out the next morning and they arrived at Bud's claim around mid-day; everything was as Bud had left it.

Bud explained to the foreman that the job was to excavate and level the ground between the existing small hole and the base of the mountain, and then to begin digging a tunnel into the hill. All the diggings would go into the freight wagon where they would be sent to Denver.

The foreman understood perfectly. Three sweaty days later the wagon was full, the dirt and rocks excavated from the claim piled on top of Bud's spiked ore. They broke camp and lumbered back to Wildman.

The diggers were paid, then Bud and the teamster drove the freight wagon to the rail station in Leger, Texas, where there was indeed a hopper car waiting on the station's small siding. Unloading the wagon was a simple chore: the teamster drove the wagon up a ramp and parked it next to the railroad car, then unlatched the sideboard of the wagon. Hinged at the bottom for that very purpose, the sideboard fell open and much of the dirt poured into the open car below. Less than an hour's worth of work with a shovel and the wagon was empty.

Bud paid the teamster and trudged into the station to schedule his car's trip to Denver. The next train would arrive the following day, and his car of ore would be attached at the end. He also learned that there was supposed to be a passenger car on that train, so he could accompany his ore to Denver if he wished. The possibility that he would not be able to accompany the ore had never even occurred to him, so he enthusiastically purchased a seat.

The train arrived on time. It only took a few minutes for his car to be hauled off the siding and attached to the end with a loud clank, and he was off.

The first leg of the train ride was south-westward to Quanah, Texas, where their train was switched onto the Denver, Texas, and Fort Worth rail line. From there it thundered almost non-stop across the Texas Panhandle into New Mexico, then curved northward to Denver, following the Rocky Mountains on the left side of the car.

Bud arrived in Denver just over twenty-four hours after leaving Leger, and he was exhausted. The train car had no facilities, and the wooden benches were very uncomfortable. Being inexperienced with train travel, he had not packed any food, and that particular line did not provide a meal stop. Fortunately, there was a small enclosure at the end of the car where passengers could relieve themselves, if they dared.

Hungry and sleep-deprived, he staggered to the rear of the train to supervise the unhooking of his ore and its removal to the line destined for Denver's state-of-the-art smelter. He showed his receipt to the foreman to prove he belonged there.

"Don't trust us?" the foreman laughed.

"Well," Bud yawned, "let's just say I've never done this before and I'm way too tired to deal with a foul-up."

"Nothing to worry about here, mister. We send stuff like this to the smelter all the time, and your paperwork is all right here." He tapped a wooden box bolted to the front of the coal-carrier. "We'll clamp you into the next one headed there, and I guess it could get pulled out today. I don't know what else might be in line, though. The yardmaster could probably tell you."

Bud yawned again and shook his head. "No, to hell with that. I need some food and sleep. You say it's under control, I'll take your word."

Bud made his way through the station and emerged into the largest city he'd ever seen. Denver stretched, it seemed, all the way to the horizon and suddenly it dawned on him that he would not be able to find anything by simply wandering around.

Several women were nearby, handing out pamphlets advocating women's suffrage. He approached and explained to the woman who appeared to be in charge that he knew nothing about Denver but needed a hotel and meal, as soon as possible. Could she make a recommendation?

The woman pointed to the street directly in front of him and told him to ask for a hack to take him into the opera district, straight down that street southward. He would find what he needed there, just tell the driver. Bud tipped his hat and made his way to the curb where he found several wagons for hire waiting. The driver indeed knew just the place and thirty minutes later Bud had a room at a hotel called the Fairmont.

The hack driver also knew exactly where the smelter was. In fact, everyone knew exactly where it was and if Bud would only look up, he would too. Just a glance around the horizon and Bud got the joke – the smelter's tallest smokestack was enormous and was visible from miles away. Just make your way to the base of the smokestack, and you've found the smelter.

The next day he hired a wagon to take him to the smelter to find out if his ore had arrived and when they would process it. Bud knew this smelter was the destination for millions of tons of silver ore that was still being mined from the mountains to the west, and he was worried that his single carload would get lost in the shuffle.

The smelter was huge and it took him several tries to find the correct place. He was eventually directed to the business office, a small building disconnected from the smelter itself. The clerk consulted a ledger and informed Bud that his hopper car had indeed arrived and they could work it in with the other silver loads.

Bud informed the clerk that any silver taken from his ore would be a happy accident. He was mining gold, not silver.

That got the clerk's attention. He dug around until he found the papers he needed, then scurried off to find his boss. Ten minutes later the clerk returned with the plant foreman, who got right to business.

"Mr. Dalton? I'm the head foreman, Tom Harris. Lawrence here says you've got gold in your ore? Not silver? Are you sure?"

Bud nodded. "Yes, I am. This is from the Indian Territory. We got some good tests from the small smelters around the mine and this is the first real production, so we need a real smelter. If it pays like the samples, I'm expecting about twenty pounds out of my train car."

Harris whistled. "Son of a bitch."

"Is there a problem?"

Harris shook his head. "No. Smelting the ore is nearly the same, but we need to use a different flux and it would probably be best if we didn't squeeze your load into a million pounds of silver ore. We would have figured it out, but Lawrence here just saved you some time and trouble. Plus, your load is very small. It's probably best to work you in earlier and get it out of the way."

"My load is small? I figure it's six to eight tons."

"No offense, Mr. Dalton, but we have jobs of several dozen train cars just like yours. Eight tons is small."

He turned to Lawrence. "Let's get Mr. Dalton's car hauled to bed number one. I'll walk the order over myself."

Harris turned back to Bud. "Do you know if your ore contains a lot of sulfur?"

Bud shrugged. "No idea. No one mentioned it in the samples."

"Indian Territory, you say? Maybe there isn't. Most of the ore around here does, so we'll bake it, just in case."

"When will we know anything?"

"Oh, just a few hours. Bed number one's furnace is up and ready. We'll bake your carload for a while and if it doesn't smell like burning shit we'll mix it with some coke and limestone and dump it in the furnace."

"Coke and limestone?"

Harris was already headed for the door. "Yeah, we call it 'flux.' The shit you don't want sticks to it and the silver, err … gold, separates easier. See you this afternoon, Mr. Dalton."

Harris left Bud and Lawrence standing in the office.

"Come back around three o'clock, Mr. Dalton. Oh, how would you like to pay?"

"With gold, hopefully."

* * *

With five hours to kill, Bud elected to walk back into Denver proper. The smelter and its huge smokestack were only about a mile from Union Station, and Bud recalled there seemed to be plenty going on around there. A saloon seemed possible.

Sure enough, saloons were as thick in Denver as they were in Joplin. Bud had lunch, and by one o'clock he was officially bored. He decided he could wait at the smelter as easily as anywhere else and set off toward the smokestack.

Lawrence looked up when Bud came in, then looked at the clock.

"I think you're a little early, Mr. Dalton."

"Yes, but I've seen all of Denver I need for one day. Do you mind me waiting here?"

"Not at all."

Forty-five minutes with Lawrence taught Bud that he had no idea what real boredom was. Lawrence worked at his ledger and papers in silence, the Regulator clock in the corner providing the only sound aside from an occasional scratch from Lawrence's pencil.

Thankfully, Harris banged through the door a short time later.

"Ah, Mr. Dalton, already here. Good. The bake was uneventful and we did indeed get a good pour out of your carload. About three hundred ounces, a pound or two under your estimate, but congratulations."

Bud could feel his heart pounding in his chest and was certain that both Harris and Lawrence could hear it too. He discreetly looked down to make sure the front of his shirt and coat weren't jumping about madly.

I can't believe this actually worked.

Bud swallowed and tried to act like everything was normal. "That's great news. What now?"

"We sent your pour to the refinery where they'll get your gold pure enough to send to the mint; that's where Lawrence saved you the time. Purifying gold isn't quite the same as silver."

"So, tomorrow?"

"Oh, no. Two hours more, maybe three. They'll pour it into ingot molds and they're all yours. They'll still be warm, but you can have them."

* * *

Refining took place in a separate building that looked like a small version of the larger one. It had its own furnace and smokestack, but was responsible for much more than simply melting rocks. The refining process used cyanide and strong acids to separate silver from a dizzying array of other compounds trapped in the mix, but gold was refined using a process developed by a British assayer named Francis Bowyer Miller.

Using Miller's process, the metal was remelted in a furnace and chlorine gas forced into and through the melted gold. The chlorine would react with any impurities remaining in the metal to form different materials that, like before, would separate from the gold. The resulting metal was very, very pure.

Bud didn't understand any of it beyond "melting," and he was disappointed that he could not watch the refining process. Harris explained that the fumes that came out of the crucible were deadly, so Bud would need to wait with Lawrence. Time crawled, but two hours later Bud was presented with three small, brightly gleaming ingots, each weighing just over six pounds. Into the top of each ingot the letters "OG" were deeply imprinted.

"What's 'OG'?"

Lawrence looked up from his ledger, "It stands for 'Omaha Grant.' That's the smelter's real name. It tells the mint that those ingots were refined here and that we vouch for their purity. The mint will trust them and take them on weight alone."

"What if I have the next load processed somewhere else?"

"Then your ingots will have whatever mark that refiner uses."

"And the mint needs that mark?"

"Yes." Lawrence was getting impatient. "You can't just haul ingots to the mint and expect them to exchange them without an assurance. They must have a known mark."

Known mark? My bars don't have marks at all...

Bud thought for a moment. "There's a big smelter being built in the Territory, but I haven't heard anything about refining. Can I bring metal from there and have you refine it? That would be a lot cheaper than hauling half a mountain across the country."

"Yes, we can do that. I'm not sure how wise it would be to travel with that much gold, but that's your affair."

Bud's wheels were turning.

* * *

The smelter loaded Bud's ingots into a small box, then loaded the box into a heavy, and heavily armed, wagon along with more boxes containing several tons of silver ingots. The wagon was joined with two similarly loaded wagons and escorted straight through town to the mint, less than three miles to the south. The mint was located, conveniently, a few hundred yards from Bud's hotel.

Bud walked in, not knowing what to expect. The smelter provided him some papers identifying the box his gold had been delivered in as well as a manifest of the box's contents. He was directed to the Exchange Desk, which wasn't a desk at all but rather a room containing three large wooden tables. The clerk took his paperwork and left through a rear door, returning a few minutes later pushing a flat cart loaded with Bud's small box.

The clerk hefted the box onto one of the tables and confirmed the number on the box matched Bud's paperwork. Then he opened the box and confirmed the contents matched what was listed on the manifest. The clerk examined the marks on the ingots, then consulted his papers which apparently detailed each ingot's exact weight.

Everything being in order, the clerk initialed and stamped one of the pages and handed it to Bud.

"Your receipt, Mr. Dalton."

"Receipt?"

"Yes. This acknowledges that we've taken possession of your gold and accounted for its value. Keep track of that. How would you like your exchange?"

"Exchange?"

The clerk looked at Bud as if he was a dolt. "Yes. We can provide coinage or a letter of deposit. Or both. This is a mint, after all."

"Oh, all right, I understand. I need twenty 10-dollar coins and a letter for the rest. I assume my banker will know what to do with it?"

"Yes, he should. I'll be back shortly."

The clerk made some notes and returned the box to the cart and pushed it back through the rear door. He kept Bud waiting for about forty-five minutes, but he finally returned carrying a wooden tray holding a leather pouch and another stack of papers.

He set down the tray and carefully dumped the contents of the pouch on the table, counting and arranging twenty gold coins into stacks of five each. Bud then signed a paper confirming that he'd received the two hundred dollars, then another confirming he'd received his letter of deposit for the balance, which the clerk handed over in a waxed envelope.

Back in his hotel room, Bud looked at the letter carefully. It was very straightforward, stating that the bearer of that document held a credit of just under six thousand dollars with the Denver Mint. The letter was signed and stamped and looked very official.

Bud gathered his luggage and arranged all the papers from both the smelter and the refinery, the letter in particular, safely in his case. He then went to the train station and purchased a return ticket to Leger.

Chapter 4

Being experienced now with train travel, Bud purchased a loaf of bread, some cured ham, and a small block of cheese so he would have something to eat along the way. He also purchased a canteen, nearly identical to the one he carried with his trail gear, and filled it with water. Armed with his food and drink, he lugged his now-heavy case through the train station to the correct platform.

The trip back was the same as the one out – long and exhausting. The train stopped in Quanah, just for Bud, where he found a shabby room to wait and recover from the journey.

The train finally arrived and Bud boarded it for the two-hour ride north. He climbed down from the train car and made his way directly to the livery barn where he'd housed his horse and buckboard. He hurried back to Wildman, his last stop before getting back to Angela in Norman.

He arrived just before dinnertime, his timing perfect. Bud installed the horse and wagon into the livery's corral, then took a room in the DeRastus where he stashed most of the gold coins and the papers he'd received in Denver. He slipped the smelter report into his pocket, along with several gold coins, and headed down to the saloon.

This is it … it'll either work or it won't.

The barroom had about twenty people lounging around, talking about the weather, latest gossip, and of course the progress of the many shafts sunk in the area. Bud walked directly up to the bar and slapped down one of the gold coins with a loud smack.

"Set up a round for the house!"

The bartender, as well as everyone else in the room, looked over and Bud held another coin in the air. "I just got back from Denver and this here is part of what they took out of my load! I want to celebrate! Set 'em up!"

The small crowd cheered and swarmed around Bud, slapping him on the back while the bartender poured beer and whiskey. Bud tossed the second coin to him and yelled, "And keep 'em coming!"

The crowd cheered again, and people began to come into the saloon wondering what the noise was about. They quickly learned that a rich claim had proved out and the news spread like a prairie fire. Soon the saloon was packed, everyone wanting to have a drink on the house and to hear the story.

Bud climbed onto a chair and told the crowd his "story" from the beginning. Back in the late '70s, when Bud was just a kid, he'd met some prospectors who told him there was almost certainly gold, at the very least, in the Wichitas.

The crowd murmured its agreement and Bud continued.

The prospectors shared a few hints with him, and a few years later he snuck back into the Territory and had a little luck. But the damn army and the damn Indians made it impossible to do any real work – couldn't dig a shaft or pile up tailings, couldn't pan in the open, hell, couldn't even light a damn fire!

The crowd roared its agreement and Bud continued.

Well, he'd kept sneaking into the mountains and was careful to keep out of sight. He still got caught by the army once or twice, but he always traveled light and his location was never found. He eventually found the place where his shaft should be dug. He'd been taking respectable color out of a creek …

"Which creek?" a voice called out.

The crowd laughed uproariously, and Bud laughed too. "Oh, it's out there somewhere. Everyone will know all about it pretty soon!"

So, anyway, he was getting color but the damn politicians kept the Territory closed. Finally, just a few months ago, things started to happen and he could put some work into his claim and get some real samples. He brought them right here to Wildman and, by God, one of them produced! Bud pointed toward Williams's small test smelter

Right there in that smelter!

The crowd roared again.

The railroad offered to haul ore to Denver, so Bud took them up on it. Two weeks ago he'd hauled—Bud consulted the paper he'd been waving as he spoke—just over seven tons of ore to Denver. Just one little carload. That load produced—consulting the paper again—nearly nine hundred dollars per ton!

He reached into his pocket and produced a third gold coin. "Barkeep! Another round for Wildman! The new Dawson and the heart of the greatest gold field America has ever seen!"

That produced the loudest roar yet, and Bud tossed the coin to the barman. Wildman and Williams were both in the saloon by then, and they shouldered their way through the crowd to offer Bud their congratulations and to offer some more words to the crowd.

Bud stayed for another hour or so, then slipped up the back stairs to his room and let the party continue without him. Thirty dollars would buy many, many drinks, and he suspected the festivities might still be going the next morning, but he needed to get back to Norman. He'd done what he'd hoped to do, and it had worked beyond his wildest hopes. He'd successfully tricked the world into believing what it wanted to believe: that the Wichita Mountains held vast gold deposits and that he had a producing mine there.

* * *

Bud's plan worked spectacularly. He'd thrown his party in Wildman on May 15, 1901, and the miner's irrational rumor mill did the rest. By the twenty-first, the story of Bud's strike had morphed into a legend of its own and every sample sent to any test smelter was reported to pay anywhere from $80 to $1,200 per ton of ore. What the ore was really worth was anyone's guess, but probably much closer to zero.

On June 6, the Jerome Commission's agreement with the Kiowa, Comanche, and Apache tribes was, finally, officially ratified in Congress. Claims from mountain tops to creek beds were feverishly staked and supplies of every sort poured into the Territory. Hundreds more illegal camps erupted across an area larger than the state of Connecticut, and absurd reports of outrageous discoveries hit the newspapers, easily surpassing the lies conjured from the Klondike.

The Indians began selecting their allotments first, either in a single 160-acre chunk or, if they preferred, in up to four distributed 40-acre selections. Problems immediately commenced when prospectors refused to abandon claims situated on an Indian selection. The prospectors were adamantly defending their shaky interpretation of the mining laws for public lands.

On July 4, President McKinley signed the proclamation declaring that the Kiowa, Comanche, and Apache lands would be opened by lottery on August 6 and registrations at Lawton and El Reno would commence immediately. The proclamation also served the prospectors their first, albeit limited, setback. The Jerome Commission's treaty specified that the Indian allotments would be held in trust by the U.S. government for twenty years, and thus were immune from the mining laws. Indian claims were superior to mining claims. But that was just on the Indian allotments, and Indian Agent Randlett estimated that over eighty thousand prospectors were afoot in the Wichitas and surrounding lands.

The July 4 proclamation also triggered the birth of a legitimate tent city, namely the city of Lawton. Lawton's status was in a very grey area. The town's streets and lots had been laid out, but none were claimable

– those lots would be sold at auction after the lottery. But even though neither Lawton or the land around it was open, Lawton had been designated as a registration point and anyone who came to Lawton was assumed to have legitimate business there.

Thus, the tent city was a "wide open" town, which meant that anything was tolerated. Tents housing saloons, prostitutes, gambling, and every other vice were in ready supply, but law enforcement wasn't. Lawton wasn't officially a city yet, the land was still technically part of the Indian Territory, so the U.S. marshal and his deputies would need to keep order.

No chance there. The U.S. marshal was only concerned with making sure the registration process and lottery went according to plan. What the contestants did in the meantime was not the marshal's concern; order would be maintained when Lawton became a real town with whatever police force it could muster. Things were getting rowdy.

"It's time," Bud told Angela. "Pack up, we're going to Denver."

* * *

After he had thrown his party back in May, he took his letter of deposit to Deskin, who explained that it was basically the same as cash and Bud's account would be credited accordingly. They settled up the loan Bud had taken with the letter of credit, netting Bud between four and five thousand dollars into his account.

As Lawton was erupting into its rambunctious existence, Bud gathered the remaining six bars he'd smuggled out of the Indian Territory and locked them into a strongbox, which he then secured into a nondescript crate claiming to contain farming equipment.

The crate was hauled to Norman's train station where Bud purchased tickets to Denver for Angela and himself, along with shipping for the crate. Bud was a little nervous that his bars were unceremoniously left at the end of the platform along with a half-dozen other items that were going somewhere else. Anyone who stole the heavy crate marked "harrow parts" would be delighted with what they found inside, but that was the risk Bud's ruse forced upon him.

Norman's station was part of the Santa Fe railroad system, which was connected to the other large railroad systems that crisscrossed America. Unlike Bud's previous train ride, both his origination and destination were on major rail lines and there would be very little waiting. Another difference from the previous trip was the opportunity to purchase a compartment on one of George Pullman's sleeper cars, which they did.

Their passenger car was composed of several sections – a large open area in the middle with two seats, facing each other, on either side and a pull-down berth above where one could lie down and sleep in relative comfort. There were toilet facilities at either end, one for women and another for men, and a communal drawing room where passengers could sit in traditional chairs or play cards around a table. Between the toilets and the common area were private compartments that used the same seat and berth arrangement but provided some privacy with a thin wall.

All the seats were padded and the floor was carpeted, gas lights provided adjustable lighting for each set of seats, and there was even a water supply. Her baggage stowed, Angela slipped into one of the seats and looked around approvingly.

"I don't see what you were complaining about," she teased. "This is lovely. You must be getting old."

Their train pulled out of Norman, heading northward to Salina, Kansas, but stopping frequently. When they got to Salina they would change trains and get onto a similar passenger car belonging to the Union Pacific railway. From there they would head nearly due west to Denver without stopping.

They arrived in Denver, well rested and alert, on July 18, just a day and a half after leaving Norman.

I'll never ride in a regular passenger car again.

The only other train ride Angela had ever taken was when they'd left Missouri on the relatively short ride from Joplin down to Norman, and most of that had been in the dark. She found the ride to Denver exhilarating, although the seemingly blazing speed of the train coupled with the amazing distances containing nothing but prairie left her a little dizzy. Apparently, America was huge.

She wrote in her journal:

> *I cannot believe what I've seen over the last day. The train is a miracle, it is so fast and is so comfortable it's no wonder the railroads are so important. The conductor showed me a map of our path to Denver, the distance is so small compared to the rest of the country. He says that it's possible to go from San Francisco to Boston in less than a week, perhaps Bud will take me to those places, too.*

Denver was huge too. Norman's train station was just a platform with a building where people waited, but Denver's train station was a palace. Platforms for a dozen trains, all covered, with hundreds of people coming and going. Bud pointed out the gigantic chimney violating the horizon and told her that's where they turned dirt, sand, and rocks into gold and silver bars.

Speaking of which, he needed to retrieve his crate. He found his way to the shipping platform and, after producing his shipping receipt, was directed to the place where his train's freight had been staged. He found the crate and, after producing the receipt again, was allowed to claim it, at which point he asked if he could hire a wagon to carry it from the station. A boy raced away, returning two minutes later riding on the promised wagon. Bud retrieved his still-awed wife and their luggage, which was loaded next to the ostensible crate of harrow parts.

Bud directed the driver to the same hotel he'd used before, the Fairmont, and had him wait while Angela's luggage was hauled up to their room. The crate could go to its destination after they were officially checked in.

Bud and Angela returned to the wagon about twenty minutes later, but now Bud was wearing his Peacemaker. The driver was a little startled.

"You expecting trouble, mister?"

"No," Bud answered. "But you can never be too sure. We need to head over to the smelter."

"The smelter?" The driver glanced back at the crate in the wagon. "For that little thing? Why? What the hell do you have in there?"

Bud put his hand on the big pistol's grip, but Angela stopped him and leaned conspiratorially over toward the driver. In the sweetest voice she could muster, she told the driver, "Now, honey, that's just how trouble starts. Let's all sneak over there and everything will be fine."

The driver gaped a little and looked back to Bud, who just nodded toward the smokestack.

"Yes, ma'am."

They made the short ride in silence. When they arrived, Bud directed the driver around to Lawrence and the business office. Bud told the driver to wait; Angela would wait with him.

Bud walked into the office and immediately caused a commotion.

Angela heard someone inside yell, "Hells bells! You can't have that in here. What the hell's wrong with you?"

Bud staggered backwards through the door he'd just entered, his hands in front of him, exclaiming, "Whoa, easy!"

Three men burst through the door, all yelling at Bud who kept yelling back, "Whoa! It's all right, hang on!"

The wagon driver snorted and laughed until his eyes watered.

Angela looked at him. "Did you know this was going to happen?"

The driver smiled broadly, sniffling and wiping his eyes. "No weapons allowed at the smelter."

By then Bud was backed against the wagon's rear wheel, the three men still yelling at him about wearing a pistol at the smelter. Angela stood up and yelled, "Excuse me! Please!"

The men looked up and stopped yelling, giving Bud a chance.

"Harris! Lawrence! It's me, Bud Dalton. I was here a couple of months back. The guy with gold?"

Harris and Lawrence squinted at him, Lawrence exclaiming, "Oh, I remember you. What are you doing and why do you have a gun?"

Bud didn't let the opportunity escape. "I have another load," he gasped. "Do you remember what I said about refining another smelter's metal? Well, here I am."

Lawrence sputtered that he certainly did not remember anything of the sort, but Harris understood.

"Jesus Christ! Are you telling us that you brought raw metal directly here?"

Bud nodded and looked at the crate in the back of the wagon. Everyone else looked at the crate too.

"That's why I have the pistol."

Harris was dumbfounded. He reached into the back of the wagon and tried to pull the crate toward him but it wouldn't budge. "Great God almighty."

Harris looked at Lawrence and told him, "I think we need security and at least one bean-counter. Go."

He looked at the third man. "Mr. Goodrich, I think we might need to postpone for a while. We have an unusual situation here."

Goodrich replied, "You do indeed. I wouldn't miss this for the world."

Harris turned to Bud and pointed at the crate. "What's in there? Not harrow parts, whatever that is."

"A harrow is a sort of plow," Goodrich added helpfully over Harris's shoulder.

Bud shook his head. "About a hundred and fifty pounds of unrefined gold."

Harris pulled his hand back as if it burned and the wagon driver gasped.

"All right." Harris pointed at Angela and the driver. "Mister, you and the lady need to get out of the wagon."

The driver secured the brake and hopped down while Bud helped Angela down from the other side. Harris motioned to Angela and asked, "And this is…?"

"My wife."

Goodrich gaped. "Your wife? You brought your wife to guard forty thousand dollars in gold?"

"No," Bud replied. "She's guarding harrow parts. I'm guarding the gold."

"Dalton, you are sincerely crazy. But it looks like you pulled it off. It would probably be best for you to take off the pistol before the guards get here; that box isn't going anywhere."

Bud took off the holster and wrapped the belt around the pistol and put it into the wagon bed. Two minutes later Lawrence and three other men, two with rifles and one with a book, came bursting out of the business office. Harris calmed everyone down and explained that Bud had brought unrefined gold across the country so they could refine it and send it to the mint. It was in that crate and it would need to be documented, weighed, and the appropriate paperwork begun.

Harris dismissed the two guards, but they, like Goodrich, wanted to watch. The crate was taken apart, and Bud opened the strongbox inside it. One by one, each bar was removed and lined up on the wagon's bed. The accountant tied a tag to each and numbered it, then everything was taken to the refining office. The bars were each precisely weighed, and each recorded in the accountant's ledger.

Finally, Bud was given a receipt for his bars. Harris told him, "Your smelter did a good job with those; their weights are very consistent."

"How long until you can get to them?"

"Tomorrow at the very earliest. Day after is more likely. Where are you staying? I can have the final paperwork sent over and ship the bars directly to the mint if you like."

"That's fine. We're staying at the Fairmont. You know where that is?" Harris nodded and Bud continued, "Now, all this is going to happen again in a few months, maybe sooner. How should I get these bars up here without making a big scene or getting robbed along the way?"

"We can arrange safe shipping from the rail station, and the railroad understands how to safely ship valuable cargo. You certainly should not be smuggling these things across the country. And when you get here, leave the pistol in your hotel. For the love of God, don't take it to the mint when you go there."

Bud wasn't going to wear his gun to the mint, but he doubted the railroad could really protect anything, particularly if it was valuable. Outlaws of every variety had been stopping trains for the last fifty years and, much more recently, Butch Cassidy's Wild Bunch had been robbing Union Pacific trains in Colorado, Utah, and Wyoming, and doing so with spectacular success. They used explosives liberally, going straight for the express cars and dynamiting every safe or strongbox they found, which was the main reason Bud had employed the diversion he'd used. If the train had been stopped, it didn't seem likely any robbers would be interested in a box of "harrow parts" randomly shipped in a freight car when there were safes locked in the express car just begging to be blown open. Bud thought his way was better, but he would let the smelter handle the leg from the station to the refinery next time.

He kept all that to himself and said his goodbyes to Harris and, finally, returned to the now-impatient wagon driver. Bud handed him four silver dollar coins and said, "Sorry about the wasted day. This should make up for it."

The money changed the driver's attitude instantly. "No problem, mister. It was definitely something new."

* * *

Bud and Angela explored Denver all the next day, which is to say Angela went shopping. The fancy new fabrics and new styled dresses were irresistible, as were three hats and two pairs of gloves. There were fancy restaurants where she could taste fancy foods, and fancy tea-rooms to try fancy teas. The entire trip was a huge adventure for her and it made Bud happy to see her so happy. And besides, they would be legitimately rich at any moment.

Shit, if I'd known this was all I had to do, I'd have done it ten years ago instead of grinding that damn bar into dust and fucking around with Charlie and Elmer. And I damn sure wouldn't have screwed around with trying to melt gold bars. What a mess that was, and unnecessary in the long run.

Bud sighed to himself and wondered if he could get the rest of the bars out before the lottery. Angela was happily examining yet another hat.

When they finally returned to their hotel, there was an envelope waiting for Bud at the front desk. It contained the refining results and the paperwork Bud would need at the mint. He was not surprised to learn that the bars had refined into one hundred and fifty pounds of pure gold, worth just under fifty thousand dollars after refining fees and costs.

The next morning, they packed up Angela's new acquisitions for the train ride home, then went down the street to the mint. Bud was turned over his paperwork and they were shown into the same room Bud had used before. Bud informed the clerk that he didn't need to see the bars; as long as the paperwork was in order, a letter of deposit for the balance would be sufficient.

The clerk returned with the letter after a half-hour wait.

Bud told Angela, "That's all there is to it."

"We should have done this a long time ago. Remind me why we nearly set fire to the town?"

"Yeah, I was thinking that very thing yesterday. In my defense, I didn't know about the refining marks until I got here."

"Well, we know now, don't we?"

Chapter 5

August was approaching and Quanah Parker's hard work came, finally, to an end. Hundreds of thousands of people had registered for the lottery, their cards and numbers carefully saved for the big day. Many went home to await the drawing results, but tens of thousands stayed to watch the drawing at Fort Reno. On August 1, in full view of the public, the registration tickets were dropped into two giant hoppers, and the hoppers were turned for a full fifteen minutes.

In order to avoid even the tiniest hint of cheating, two children were selected at random from the crowd to pull the first tickets. The drawings continued for three days and, ticket by ticket, the last of the Indian Territory disappeared.

When a ticket was drawn, the person with the corresponding receipt had to appear and select the parcel he or she wanted from the land map. The selections had to be made in order and if the winner didn't show he lost his place and forfeited his claim. The winner's names were listed in the papers, and people began flooding into the Territory to stand in yet another endlessly long line.

Hundreds of towns, like Cooperton, were waiting to be born once the drawings were completed. Town lots were to be auctioned off, and the better the location, the more they would sell for. The proceeds were to cover the administrative costs of distributing the property.

Cooper still had friends. On August 3, one of Guthrie's papers printed a brief article about Cooperton and all its promise. While the *Daily Oklahoma State Capital* never actually mentioned the name of the town, they did mention Cooper and where his town was located. They also hinted that everyone should hurry.

> *SEWARD, O.T, AUG. 3 –(Special)– Capt. Geo. Cooper the famous Kiowa and Comanche boomer has a townsite reserved twenty miles southeast of Hobart at the foot of the Wichita mountains.*
>
> *This is a promising site for a town, a fine agricultural region to the north and west of it. An ever-flowing spring on the site. Above all the picturesque Wichita mountains on the southeast whose towering peaks rise from 1,000 to 3,000 feet above the sea level. These mountains are glittering with precious metals. A great rush is anticipated for possession of these valuable mineral claims. Capt. Cooper has an organized townsite association of 500 men ready to make settlement on the new townsite, as soon as it is opened for settlement which will not be later than August 6th.*

Cooperton's day turned out to be the same day the article was printed, August 3. Elmer and Antrim brought a long train of equipment, men, and animals, and purchased the three lots each they'd selected in advance. While the rest of the lots were being auctioned off, Elmer and Antrim's crews were erecting tents, unloading wagons, and tending to animals. No one was wasting any time and Antrim was already saddling up to advertise his freight service to every mining camp, town, and rail yard within twenty miles.

Antrim had printed up hundreds of flyers and convinced Charlie to use his knowledge of the area and the locations of the mining camps to advertise. Houses needed to be built, equipment hauled, goods sold, and there was no time to lose. A little honest work wouldn't harm Charlie's reputation.

Charles Tipton would sell real estate and insurance, and would deal with the mountains of paperwork that would surely engulf them all. He took a nice lot on Cooperton's north side, as far as he could get from Antrim's animals, and quickly set up shop. He was certain that there would soon be people everywhere.

Tipton was right; the final barrier had been lifted. Even if a person didn't win a claim or purchase a lot, they could still travel the Territory as they could anywhere else in America.

Lottery winners, businessmen, speculators like Southwest Mineral, the ever-present prospectors, newspaper reporters, railroad men, office-seekers, and the merely curious were simply everywhere. The period between the lottery's initiation in August and when land claims could officially be filed in January 1902 was near chaos in the new counties.

Lucky lottery winners were not the only people clogging the land offices; the prospectors were too. Over 20,000 mining claims were officially recorded in Kiowa and Comanche counties within weeks of the counties' creation. Confrontations between prospectors and settlers commenced immediately

* * *

Bud and Angela wasted no time once they returned from Denver. Bud took the new letter to Deskin who cheerfully credited Bud's account, making him and Angela officially rich. Angela unpacked all her fancy new clothes and hats, then repacked for an extended stay in a tent somewhere near Bud's claim.

They pulled into Lawton a few days before the lottery and what they found shocked them both.

Angela's last experience there had been fifteen years earlier when she and Bud had snuck into what was now the forest preserve and quietly camped for several days. She recalled being enthralled with the area and was excited to return. What she found was the equivalent of one of the Kansas border towns from Payne's days, except without any of the order or restraint that Payne had preached.

The "city" had evolved, as most do, into areas dominated by a particular theme – much of a particular area was dedicated to simply living, another to the selling of the items people needed on a day-to-day basis – food, firewood, hay for horses, tools of every sort. Another strip, dubbed "Main Street," housed much of what one would expect to find on any Main Street – insurance, lawyers, assayers, surveyors, map makers and so forth. Facilities for livestock such as corrals, blacksmiths, and water troughs were scattered throughout it all.

Intersecting Main Street, near the edge of town, was Goo Goo Avenue, and that was the place where gambling, money lending, drinking, and every other kind of debauchery dwelled. The street had been named for a particular saloon singer who repeatedly sang "Just Because She Made Those Goo Goo Eyes" in such a high and piercing voice that she could be heard hundreds of yards away.

During the daylight hours there were some legitimate reasons to come to Goo Goo Avenue, though. Water was in relatively short supply at that moment, and some men had set up an operation selling it. Goo Goo Avenue was the natural place for them to do it.

As the sun set, though, people did what people do when they have too much time on their hands and no boundaries on any behavior. The whiskey and beer joints opened up, the gambling tents got louder, and the confidence men and swindlers mixed in with their marks. Anyone looking for trouble could find it on Goo Goo Avenue, and even if one wasn't looking for it, it could be found accidentally.

"Jesus, Bud, this is worse than Joplin ever was."

And she was right; at least there was some law in Joplin, occasionally. There was almost none in Rag-Town, Lawton's unofficial and entirely accurate nickname. The residential area was somewhat self-policing, the typical resident there anxious to keep trouble at least at arm's length. No one really cared what happened on Goo Goo Avenue as long as it happened there, and not outside their tent.

The man officially responsible for keeping order in Lawton was Deputy Marshal Bill Fossett. Deputy Fossett liked to keep a low profile, however, and no one could remember him making a single arrest for anything that occurred in Lawton.

Lawton was to be a temporary stop for Fossett, though. He had his eye on the U.S. marshal's job and when he officially announced his intentions, the newspaper in Chandler questioned Fossett's assertion that he'd kept good order in Lawton, the editor wondering what "bad order" would have looked like.

Bud and Angela drove their wagon through the throng, pushing on to Bud's claim to set up camp. At no time during the ten-mile trip from Lawton to the claim were they alone. The road was full, horses and wagons moving in both directions. Every creek was lined with people camping and, sure enough, Bud's creek was no different.

By the time they got their camp set up on the claim, they were hot and tired, the temperature still well north of ninety-five degrees. They sat in the shade, resting, while they watched their neighbors' young children playing in the narrow stream of water running through the creek bed.

If that kid starts digging, he might get rich.

Angela climbed to her feet and went over to introduce herself and get to know their neighbors. They were from different places, but they all had the same story: They had registered for the lottery weeks ago and were waiting for their names to be drawn at El Reno next week.

After she returned to their camp, she told Bud, "It might be quite a while before we get any privacy."

People, usually individuals and but sometimes in groups, turned up every day. They usually moved on, but some liked that spot on that creek, and elected to stay and set up their own camps. The number of squatters' camps around Bud, not counting Bud and Angela themselves, had grown to ten by the time the drawing was held.

None of the squatters' envelopes were drawn. Most of them packed up and moved on, but one elected to stay, hoping the plot's owner would miss his filing and they could contest the claim.

Those hopes were dashed when Leon Wright arrived. Wright's name had been drawn on the third day and he had selected the quarter section where Bud and his neighbors were camped. He was there to start proving up his claim, and none of the present occupants were welcome.

Disposing of the squatters was easy. Wright simply told them that he was that quarter's new owner, he had filed, and they needed to leave. Right away, before there was trouble. They reluctantly packed up their camp and promised to be gone immediately. Disposing of Bud was a different matter.

Bud and Angela were sitting outside and saw him coming. Even though Bud couldn't hear what Wright had said to the squatters, he surmised that the new arrival was the land's owner and he was evicting everyone. That was fine; there had been far too many people in the area for far too long, in Bud's view.

Wright dismounted and tied his horse to a nearby tree, then took a few steps toward them. He put his hands on his hips and looked around, noting the excavated area and the poles marking Bud's claim site, including the two barely visible across the creek. He shook his head.

"Nope. Y'all need to pack up and go. I've claimed this quarter and won't have you here."

Bud didn't respond immediately, observing Wright's body language and noting the fact that he was unarmed.

"That's all well and good," Bud replied, "but I was here first. I don't care much what you do with the rest of it, but this little bit here and that little bit over there and the creek in between is already claimed. We don't want trouble, but this is a legal claim, and you know it."

"I don't know anything of the sort. I know that I've selected this quarter section and I don't have to share it with anyone. Pack all your shit, put it in your wagon, and go somewhere else. Any direction you want, just a quarter mile, and you'll be someone else's problem. If you stay here there's going to be trouble. You say you don't want any, so move along."

Bud stood up. "Mister, I know the law, and the law says mining claims are superior to all others. Meaning the shitty little one you pulled out of a drum too."

Wright was about to say something, but Angela cut in and motioned Bud to sit back down. "Let's not start out this way. My name is Angela, and this is Bud. What's your name?"

Bud slowly sank back down onto the box he was using for a chair while Wright looked Angela over.

He finally replied, "My name's Leon Wright."

"We're pleased to meet you, aren't we, Bud?"

"Pleasure's mine." It clearly wasn't.

Angela continued, "We really don't want any trouble, Mr. Wright. We really want to figure out how all of us can be neighbors. Friendly ones, at that. We won't bother your cattle, or horses, or crops, or whatever, but I think Bud is right that you know about mineral claims. You know this is legal."

"Ma'am, I've heard that but I don't believe it. Eventually the law is going to make you leave."

Bud nodded and added, "Maybe, but only if the claim doesn't produce. If there's paying ore here, we'll prove it before you and I ever stand in front of a judge, and there's no doubt how that will come down. Besides, look at it this way: If we're right, there's likely gold outside our claim and it's all yours. If we're wrong then we're going to leave anyway."

Wright stared at them for a moment, then asked, "Do you really believe there's gold here?"

Bud nodded. "Yes. The only question is if it'll pay enough to produce."

Gesturing toward the shallow hole in the mountain, Wright asked, "And when will you know about this? How long will that take?"

Angela took over. "We've been ready to take samples out to Wildman for weeks now, but were afraid to leave the claim. You just chased away the squatters, so I think we could go right away. Right, Bud?"

"Yup. And one way or the other, it'll all be over in a week or two."

Wright stood there for another moment and said, "All right, I'll be neighborly for a week or so. Then either you'll be gone, or we'll let the law work it out when the time comes."

He pointed at one of Bud's marking stakes and continued, "And when I come back, I'm going to start building a barn right there."

Bud shrugged. "Yeah, well, we'll see what happens."

They watched him walk his horse back to the squatters who apparently were not breaking camp fast enough for his liking, even though it had barely been fifteen minutes since he'd first met them. Wright spent a few minutes there, gesturing both at the squatters' location and Bud's, clearly telling them that everyone had been evicted.

"Well," Angela said, "what are we going to do in a week?"

"We are going to do exactly what I told that asshole. He chased away every reason we had for waiting, so we're going to collect our things and when he comes back in a week we'll be long gone. Turns out this claim isn't so good after all."

They made a show of gathering their belongings and moving the wagon around so it looked like they were about to break camp.

The squatters pulled out the next day. Bud and Angela took down their tent and any casual observer would have rightly believed they were leaving too.

It should only take a little while, no more than an hour, to extract as many bars as the wagon could carry. Then they would leave, blending in with the other failed homesteaders slowly making their way somewhere else.

Chapter 6

Charlie had spent August hunting down mining camps while Antrim was racing to every townsite in the new counties. In the weeks following the drawing Charlie had found over a hundred camps and had left Antrim's flyers at each. He had a standard speech, explaining how he hoped they all struck it rich and how the new shipping company would deliver any and all equipment, supplies, or animals they would need. Antrim would pick up from anywhere and deliver anywhere.

He'd begun just east of Cooperton, slowly working his way south along the face of the mountains. By the time the lottery was completed he'd reached the southern edge of the range. Wildman was a relatively short distance to the northwest, Lawton a little farther due east. Between him and Lawton was a heavy concentration of Comanche claims that he could safely ignore, but there were also plenty of areas on the southern edge that had potential. He decided to head toward Lawton for a day or so before returning to Cooperton and waiting for Antrim to turn up again so he could get paid.

He trudged about halfway to Lawton, the first of the useless Comanche claims just a few miles to the south. Lawton was much more convenient for anyone around there to purchase anything, and there were plenty of shipping companies there already. There was little reason to go much farther.

Another creek crossed his path, and Charlie paused, debating if it was worth any more effort. He was about to turn around when he realized where he was.

Pretty sure that's where I found the packs. What the hell, let's have a look.

He turned his horse up the creek, then took the left fork into the canyon and found yet another group of prospectors camped in front of the little cave. Their equipment and mules were everywhere, and it appeared they'd been there for many weeks.

Charlie stopped short of their camp and called out. He dismounted and gave his speech, and handed out a few of Antrim's flyers. He'd already decided to return to Cooperton, but automatically asked if they knew of other camps in the vicinity. Yes, they were pretty sure there was another camp about a mile to the east.

Another mile, Charlie sighed to himself. He looked up, gauging the sun's position in the sky.

Nearly noon, I reckon. All right, one more.

Charlie made his way the last mile, then walked his horse up the creek bed, taking his time in the heat. His horse paused for a moment, pricking up its ears and sniffing the air, then offering a short whinny. Charlie knew his horse had just smelled another horse, probably a filly if that whinny was what he thought it was.

Sure enough, he rounded a short bend in the creek and there was a man digging a hole near the eastern bank. The hole wasn't deep, a bit deeper than his knees. He'd apparently found something because he'd just hefted it out of it of the hole and dropped it into the sand. Charlie reined in and called out his normal greeting.

The man whirled around in the hole, obviously startled. Six gold bars were lying in the sand, gleaming in the sun.

It took Charlie a second to realize that he was looking at Bud Dalton, and then another to register what Bud had just dropped. The dots connected and Charlie suddenly understood everything.

"You son of a bitch!" Charlie instinctively reached for his pistol, forgetting that he wasn't wearing it because nothing created a scene like an unexpected and armed visitor at a potentially illegal mining camp. Bud, working in the creek bed, obviously wasn't wearing his pistol, either. Unfortunately for Bud, Charlie had packed his Winchester.

***

Bud heard Charlie's greeting and whirled around, horrified to see Charlie sitting on a horse fifty feet away. He didn't even have a chance to move before Charlie pulled out his rifle and Bud knew he only had seconds before Charlie began sending bullets his way. At that range they would tear him to pieces. Abe's destroyed shoulder flickered through his mind.

And that was just a pistol.

He lunged out of the hole and rolled to his right, away from Angela and the wagon. He'd made it to his feet and only taken a single step toward the creek's far bank when the first shot rang out. He simultaneously heard and felt the bullet pass behind his head to kick up sand in the creek bed, to his right. He knew the next shot would be coming in about a second, and put everything he had into lunging behind the nearest tree which was, unfortunately, at least ten steps away.

Bud heard Charlie working the rifle's lever, jacking another round into the chamber.

Dodge.

He angled his step to his right, upstream and away from Charlie and his rifle. He felt his left boot sinking and sliding in the deep sand and knew he was about to fall.

* * *

Charlie saw his first shot kick up the sand beyond Bud, barely missing behind. He operated the rifle's lever without thinking, already looking for his next shot. Bud stumbled just as he pulled the trigger and Charlie knew he'd scored a hit, but wasn't sure how solid it was.

Doesn't matter, this one will do it.

* * *

Bud was face down in the sand and heard Charlie work the rifle's lever again, and he knew he was dead. He'd felt the last shot hit his back and push him down, into the sand. He couldn't tell how bad it was, but it didn't matter. He exhaled into the sand and waited for the end. He heard the rifle shot, but didn't feel the bullet strike.

He missed? Jesus, move!

His right shoulder screamed as he tried to lurch to his feet and scramble to the bank. Bud's only thought was to get out of the creek bed, but he was only halfway to his feet when the next shot rang out, followed immediately by another.

Christ, Charlie can shoot fast.

Bud risked a glance at Charlie, just in time to see him fall off his horse.

* * *

Angela had heard Charlie's horse whinny and had seen both of her horses looking over their shoulders, downstream toward the prairie. Someone was coming up the creek, and the timing could not have been worse. She found her rifle just as she heard someone shout, "Son of a bitch!"

Her heart pounded in her ears and she was barely aware that she had operated the lever on her own rifle. She hurried around the back of the wagon, trying to see through the bushes and what was going on. She saw a man on his horse, pulling out his rifle, and Bud diving out of the hole, trying to run. She managed to get her own rifle stabilized on the wagon's side just as the intruder took his first shot at Bud.

She was still aiming as he cocked his rifle and shot again, all seemingly in one motion.

Angela saw Bud go down and knew he'd been hit.

She felt panic washing over her, adrenalin flooding into her bloodstream. Hurrying, but trying to be steady, she aimed her rifle at the intruder.

Charlie was angled slightly away from her, and was already operating the lever for his next shot. She had the bead of her front sight squarely in the center of his back and she pulled the trigger before he could shoot Bud again. She saw him lurch in the saddle and knew she'd scored a hit of her own.

He didn't fall, though. Instead, he turned toward her, looking for whoever had just shot him. Charlie saw the bluish cloud of gun smoke drifting through the leaves on the bank and Angela knew he'd have her in a moment. She feverishly worked the action on her rifle as Charlie peered at the bushes, searching for his target. Her heart was pounding unbelievably, and she could hear nothing but roaring in her ears.

Charlie saw her. He steadied his aim and fired, but just missed high. Angela had not moved the rifle from where she'd rested it, using the wagon to hold the stock steady. When Charlie turned to shoot at her, he put the center of his chest in the center of her sights. Charlie's bullet tore through the leaves eight inches above Angela's head as she gently squeezed the trigger.

The man fell that time, sliding off his horse into the sandy bed. Angela sprinted around the wagon, running to Bud and calling to him as she leaped into the creek.

"Bud! My God, Bud! Are you all right? Who was that? Are you shot? Let me see you! Bud, say something!"

Bud could feel his shoulder now, throbbing, and knew he was not seriously wounded. Angela skidded to a stop and frantically began looking him over, pulling at his shirt and feeling all over his shoulders and chest. There was a trickle of blood dripping off his hand and when she looked at his back, she saw the wound.

Charlie's shot had grazed the back of Bud's shoulder, gouging a deep, perfectly straight, furrow just beneath his shoulder blade. The wound was about a foot long and was bleeding freely.

"Oh, thank God, it's a flesh wound! It's deep but just a bad scratch! Bud, I thought he'd killed you! Oh, God, Bud, I was so scared!"

She looked over at the man she'd shot, lying in the sand next to his horse. Hands trembling, Angela let the rifle slip from her grasp. She shuddered and sank to her knees.

"Who is that? Why was he shooting at you? Oh, my God, did I kill him? Is he dead? Bud, I can't breathe…" She leaned forward onto her hands and knees and vomited into the sand next to her rifle.

Bud felt the same way, but needed to make sure that Charlie was really dead. His back burned furiously, but he could still function. He picked up Angela's rifle and walked over to Charlie, jacking a new round into the chamber as he went.

Charlie should have been dead, but wasn't quite. He was lying on his side with his back to Bud, and Bud could clearly see where Angela's first shot had hit him. It had entered just below Charlie's left shoulder blade, and unlike Bud's flesh wound, Angela's bullet had penetrated. There was an exit wound under Charlie's armpit.

Bud rolled Charlie onto his back and Charlie let out a low groan. Angela's second shot had missed his heart, but not by much. He whispered, "You bastard. I knew it…"

Bud told him, "I didn't want it to come to this. I'm sorry."

Charlie tried to blow the sand out of his mouth, but couldn't manage enough pressure and that turned out to be his final breath. His eyes widened and his mouth opened like he was gasping for air, then he went completely limp, eyes unfocused and glazed.

Bud called over to Angela, who was spitting into the creek bed, wiping bile from her mouth with the back of her hand. "It's Charlie. He's dead."

"Charlie? Our Charlie?"

"Yeah. I don't know what he's doing here, but he saw me with the bars and I guess he figured it all out and started shooting. Thank God you were there. He had me cold—I was dead as yesterday's dinner. You saved my life, hon."

Angela hacked and spat more bile into the sand, then asked, "Bud, do you think anyone heard the shooting?"

He was collecting Charlie's horse and replied, "Oh, yeah, no way it wasn't heard, and five shots at that. Someone will be along pretty quick."

"What should we do?"

He thought quickly, and said, "OK, I'm going to use Charlie's horse to drag his body upstream a bit, out of sight. If anyone comes toward the camp, you play dumb – make a lot of noise about hearing shooting and ask whoever it is if they did it. Ask them what they want, and act really scared and hysterical."

She spat into the sand again. "No problem there."

"Right, and get my pistol and wave it around, tell them to stay away. I should only be gone a few minutes, meanwhile get me out a clean shirt, I don't want to look like I was just in a gunfight."

There was a rope on Charlie's saddle. He looped the end around one of Charlie's legs, then climbed into the saddle and cinched the rope around the saddle horn. Bud dragged Charlie's body to a downed tree about a hundred yards upstream. It would conceal the body until it was safe to hide it properly.

He rode back to the camp, grateful that no one had shown up yet. He stripped off his shirt and Angela used it to clean up the still-bleeding gash. Bud gasped as Angela pushed the cloth into the wound.

"Hopefully that will slow the bleeding. Here's your shirt." She had to help him put it on.

Bud's heart was still pounding. "OK, good. I'm gonna ride out and see if anyone's looking around. Toss some sand on top of the bars there. Don't worry about the hole. You might cover up that bloodstain in the sand, though. Whew, OK. I'll be right back."

He climbed into Charlie's saddle and walked the horse out to the edge of the prairie. Sure enough, two men galloped up to him.

"You all right, mister? Was that you doing the shooting?"

Bud shook his head. "No, I heard it too, and come out to see what's happening. Did someone get robbed?"

"Don't know yet. Who all's down there?"

"Just me and the wife. We were squatting till the owner showed up and ran us off. Seems his paperwork is in order … We were packing up when we heard the shots."

"Where did the shots come from? What direction?"

"Well," Bud said, "sounded to me like they came from right here. I was expecting to find quite a mess."

Another man came galloping up from the east and breathlessly announced, "False alarm! There's a couple of fellows hunting in the hills back there. We think it was them."

The first man seemed relieved. "All right, good. That's a relief."

Bud was now genuinely puzzled. "What on earth are y'all worried about?"

The recent arrival looked at Bud, then looked at his friends with a puzzled expression.

"Squatter."

"Ohhh," the new arrival droned. "Right, you wouldn't know. The new lottery has made a lot of problems with the miners and settlers, and a lot of people are talking about a range war."

Bud snorted. "Well, it's a damn good time to be leaving, then. Good luck to you."

"And you too. Be wary." The three men turned back toward Lawton at a trot.

Bud watched for a minute and rode back to Angela.

* * *

There was no time to rest. Angela was put to work pulling the gold bars out of the creek bed and into the wagon while Bud disposed of Charlie's corpse. By then the adrenaline had worn off and Bud was in pain. He was sweating, covered in sand, and working a shovel made the gash burn horribly. He dug a shallow trench next to the body, then went through Charlie's pockets to make sure there was nothing to identify the body.

Bud took his boots and pocket watch, then rolled the body into the shallow grave and painfully shoveled the sand back into it.

Tough break, Charlie. So long.

By the time Bud met her back at the camp, Angela had lugged the bars scattered around the hole to the bank. She had been working as hard she could, her clothes were completely soaked with sweat and Bud had never seen her so disheveled and dirty. Bud joined her, painfully pulling another fifteen bars from the hole and lugging them to the wagon.

Looking at the crates, Bud told her, "I think it's overloaded already. I'm worried that if we take a hard bounce it'll break through the boards in the bed."

"But it's only half full."

"I think we need to be happy with what we have." Bud looked at the sun and continued, "We have to get out of here, anyway."

Bud reburied the remaining bars and trudged up the bank. Charlie's horse was tied behind the wagon, his saddle tossed into the back with their gear. He pulled his last clean clothes from his pack and pulled off his boots, followed by the rest of his clothes which he wadded up and tossed into the back of the wagon too. He left the clean clothes on the bank and gingerly made his way to the stream.

"Bud," Angela asked, "what are you doing?"

"Rinsing off. I need to get out whatever's in the gash, it's killing me. Besides, if I look anything like you do everyone will think we killed someone and stole their wagon."

Angela picked at her hair and looked down at her filthy, sweat-soaked dress, and nodded.

She got out some clean clothes of her own and stripped off the sweat-soaked ones, then joined Bud in the stream. He was kneeling in the shallow water, splashing it on his face and trying to rinse off his back. She knelt behind him and tended to his wound. There was indeed sand in it and Bud gasped as she tried to brush it out.

"I'm sorry," she told him. "I don't know what to do."

"Keep doing it, just clean it as best you can, we need to hurry. Sure as God made little green apples someone else is gonna turn up and find you naked in the creek."

She splashed one last scoop of water over the wound, then quickly rinsed herself off too. It only took a few minutes to dry off in the heat, and the clean clothes made her feel and look much better. After she'd tied her hair back and put on her hat, she appeared almost normal.

"What are we going to do with Charlie's stuff?" Angela asked.

"We're taking it to Lawton and getting rid of it. Then we head back to Norman and get ready for another trip to Denver."

"What about the rest in the creek?"

"You remember that last box of fake ore we have? I'm gonna take it to Wildman and have it tested, then give Wright the bad news. I'll pull out the rest of the bars when I can, then hightail it back home."

They sold Charlie's horse and saddle for almost nothing on Goo Goo Avenue and continued the short distance north to Medicine Park, the community attached to Fort Sill. By then it was getting dark, and both were mentally and physically exhausted. Neither had eaten anything since breakfast, so Bud elected to make a full camp, complete with a campfire and tent.

They lingered before making their way back to Norman, recuperating as much as possible. Bud's wound was not dangerous, but it hurt like hell and was prone to bleeding if he moved too much. Unfortunately, Bud didn't see any rest in his future.

Chapter 7

They arrived in Norman to find a letter from Arthur in their mail. Angela learned that he was to be married in December and his soon-to-be brother- and sister-in-law had gone to Oklahoma for the lottery. The letter was over a month old, so there was no indication on how that had worked out for them.

Bud took his spiked sample to Wildman a few days later and got the results he was expecting. He only tested half the box; the rest he dumped into the hole at the claim, just in case someone tried to test their own sample from Bud's site.

Bud hadn't been there a full day before Wright stomped into camp, demanding that he leave. It was obvious that Bud was working the claim, and Bud showed Wright the test results and the small button of gold that had come out of the test smelter.

"So, are we going to work something out, or are we going to be at each other's throats?" Bud asked him. Bud was wearing his pistol this time.

Wright was clearly torn because, as with every other opening, there were conflicts everywhere. If a judge saw that assayer's report and the tiny golden pyramid, it was almost certain that Bud's claim would stand. At the same time, though, Wright was going to prove his claim and take deed to the entire quarter section, including Bud's mining claim, which Wright may or may not actually own. Assuming a judge could rule in the next year, which was also questionable.

Leon Wright's brain was not built to deal with problems like those, and Bud could see that Wright was evaluating the costs and benefits of being at each other's throats. Having just barely survived a gunfight and the gash on his back still prone to bleeding, Bud decided to try a little honey instead of vinegar.

"Listen, Wright, I really don't want anything from you, or to cause you any trouble. I just want to dig that hole and try to make some money."

And to be left the hell alone for just a couple of days. Christ, why does this have to be so hard?

Bud continued, "Come on, drag that box over and sit down. Have some coffee and let's work something out. Tell me what you need and if I can give it to you, you can have it."

That seemed to disarm Wright a little. He sat down and said, "All right. Here's my problem."

He pointed to a flat spot about ten yards away. "I want to build a house right there. The mountain blocks the north wind, the creek seems to run most of the time, so a well should always have water." He gestured out toward the prairie. "Lots of grass for stock, and I don't see why food wouldn't grow."

Wright looked directly at Bud and continued, "So, you see why I'm not crazy about the thought of your loud-ass mules, broke-down wagons, and beat-up tent sitting in my yard and scaring my chickens. How you gonna fix that? What are we gonna work out?"

He has a point there.

Bud nodded. "All right, we're getting somewhere. I wouldn't want that either. Here's the thing, I don't have a crew or a lot of animals or equipment. It's just me and my wife, which means mostly me. No mules, just this wagon and those two horses. I don't think I can do anything about the tent. Maybe pitch it somewhere else, I guess. What I'm trying to tell you is that I'm not gonna scare your chickens. And like I told you before, when this is played out, I'm gonna leave. Or sell it."

Wright snorted. "When's that gonna be?"

"Well, every time you show up, I have to stop everything I'm doing and argue with you. How about you leave me alone and let me work? Build your house, I don't care. I just want to take a few thousand dollars out of the hole, if it'll produce, then sell it. The more you let me be, the sooner I'll be gone."

* * *

Wright went back to Lawton, leaving Bud to himself, finally. He spent the rest of the day loading twenty more bars into small crates, and started home the next day.

He finally pulled the wagon into their back yard. Angela met him to see how he was and what had gone wrong this time. Bud told her about Wright, and that he'd pulled out another twenty bars. The plan was to get a heavy wagon and make one last trip after they'd sent the bars they already had to Denver.

Angela nodded. "So, how do we get all these to Denver?"

"Same as last time. I think we'll need to ship eight or nine boxes this time."

"Harrow parts again?"

"Something like that, yes."

* * *

Bud bought seven crates and had them all labeled "Lakeside Iron Works" in large letters and "Scrap" in smaller letters beneath. He bolted a smaller crate inside each of the larger ones, put seven bars inside each small crate, then nailed their tops on. He dumped a few pounds of actual scrap in with the small crates so they would rattle and clank, then nailed the large tops on.

He went to the train station and arranged for a freight shipment to Denver, as well as two more tickets in a sleeper car, for a train scheduled two days later. Then he telegraphed the smelter and informed them that they needed to arrange transportation for just under one half ton of "material" that would arrive at Denver's station four days hence. He would meet them at the station and accompany the shipment. They telegraphed back the next day, confirming the arrangements.

The trip to Denver went smoothly, Angela feeling like an experienced world traveler on her second trip in just a few months. When they arrived, Bud tracked down his crates and watched them get loaded onto a small freight car destined for the smelter. Everything was accounted for, and the paperwork was in order, so Bud gathered Angela's baggage and took her to the hotel to unpack.

Their wagon waited for them, then they leisurely rode to the smelter where Lawrence confirmed the crates arrived and all the paperwork started. He gave Bud his receipt and asked where they were staying.

"The Fairmont again. Can you have the paperwork sent to me there?"

"Certainly. Wasn't this easier than last time?"

"It was. Thank you, Lawrence."

"Would you like to keep the junk you shipped with them?"

"No, thank you. That's all yours."

* * *

Bud and Angela had to hang around Denver for two days, to Angela's delight. When the paperwork showed up at their hotel, Bud booked return travel to Norman and then took the papers to the mint. Once he had the certificate he took it to the Colorado National Bank, which catered to mining companies in Denver, and opened a new account with the staggering sum of over three hundred and fifty thousand dollars.

"Sam can't have it?" Angela asked.

"No, Sam doesn't need to know about any of this. I think we're almost done. One last big load will do the job."

* * *

When Wright left Bud and the claim, gold fever began to consume him. By the time he'd returned to Lawton he'd convinced himself that Bud's gold was not limited to the claim. He discovered that testing a sample was as easy as taking twenty pounds of dirt and rocks to one of the test smelters dotting the area and decided he would do just that.

As Bud was boxing up his crates bound for Denver, Wright returned to the claim. Delighted that Bud was absent, Wright entered the small excavation and shoveled the spiked soil Bud had left for him, just in case. Wright took the sample to Meers's new test smelter and was rewarded with his own tiny golden pyramid.

The results accelerated his mania. He had no trouble finding a speculator in Lawton who, upon seeing the sample results, offered to purchase Wright's claim on the spot. Wright declined, but that cemented his desire to get Bud and his claim off his quarter-section.

Bud turned up three weeks later, in November, looking haggard and driving a heavy freight wagon, which convinced Wright that Bud intended to exploit the claim. Bud hadn't even climbed down when Wright came stomping up.

"Dalton, I have a proposal for you. Climb down and let's talk about it."

Bud climbed off the wagon. "Well, here I am. What's on your mind?"

"I want to buy you out. Right now."

This is interesting…

"All right, let's hear it. What do you offer?"

"Well," Wright said, "you mentioned before that you wanted to take a few thousand out of the hole if it will produce, then sell. Right?"

Bud nodded.

"And what were the estimates from your samples?"

"About three hundred per ton."

"I'll give you two thousand dollars, right now. About seven tons of good ore you don't have to dig, haul, or test. And that's what you were looking for anyway, right?"

Bud paused. He'd intended to bring out the rest of the bars, but everything was going wrong. The freight wagon had broken down once already, so in addition to being frustratingly slow Bud didn't really trust it. The weather was acting like it was about to produce a cold rain, which beyond making him miserable could potentially get the creek flowing. The wound from Charlie's bullet itched madly, and now, there was Wright, waiting for him and forcing him to keep up the charade of mining. As long as Wright remained, Bud could not retrieve anything. His resolution was fading, the bars weren't going anywhere, and Wright's offer was tempting.

Wright saw Bud's hesitation and sweetened the offer. "I'll go up to twenty-five hundred, but it has to be right now. Otherwise, it's you and me here together, all winter long."

That did it; the thought of weeks, perhaps months, of waiting for Wright to leave him alone was too much to bear. He nodded his head.

"All right, done. One thing, though. You pay in gold."

Wright snorted. "I knew you'd say that. Follow me."

Wright led Bud to his tent where he retrieved a heavy strongbox. He opened it and pulled out a leather bag and handed it to Bud.

"That's eighty double eagles. Go ahead and count. I'll get you the last twenty and you can get the hell off my land."

"You had this waiting? Damn, Wright, you must think this is gonna pay good. But for twenty-five hundred you can have it."

Bud dropped the additional coins into the heavy bag and returned to the freight wagon.

Enjoy your hole.

"Good luck to you, Wright. Goodbye."

Wright pulled out all the stakes marking Bud's claim. He stood in front of the excavation for a moment, pondering the hole in the side of the mountain. He looked up the slope, then down into the creek.

I'm going to be rich.

* * *

Bud returned to Norman far too soon, so Angela assumed the worst.

"Bud, what happened? Why are you back so soon?"

"Well," he replied, "Wright was waiting for me. He offered to buy me out and threatened to never leave if I didn't take his offer. So I took it."

"How much?"

"Twenty-five hundred."

"That's a lot of money, but what now? We wait for him to give up?"

"Maybe. We'll need to see what happens."

Part 5

The Legend of Jesse's Gold

1902-1905

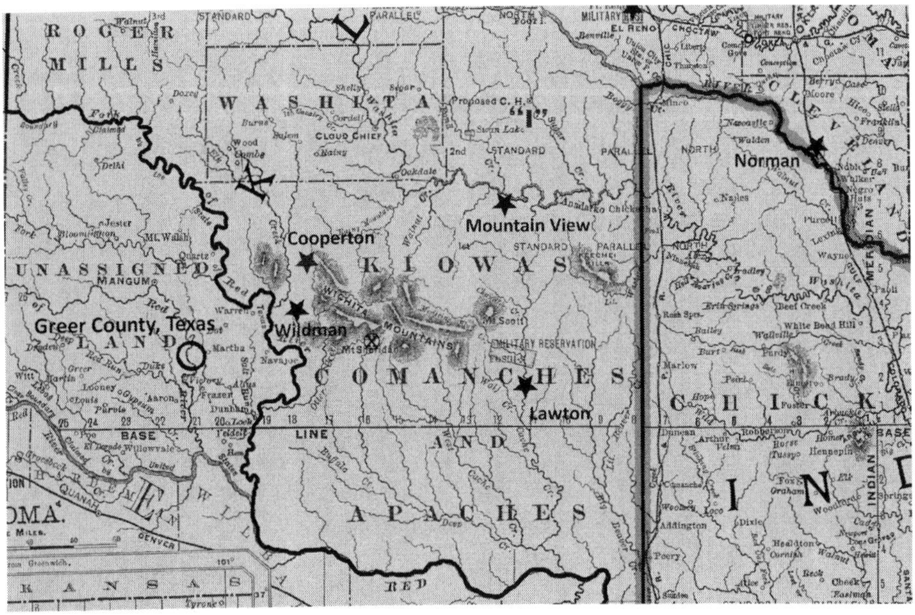
Cooperton
Mountain View
Norman
Greer County, Texas
Wildman
Lawton
ROGER MILLS
WASHITA
KIOWAS
WICHITA MOUNTAINS
COMANCHES
AND
APACHES
UNASSIGNED
MANGUM
MILITARY RESERVATION
EL RENO
CLOUD CHIEF
STANDARD
PARALLEL
QUANAH
DENVER
Mt. Scott
Marlow
Duncan
Addington
Norman

Chapter 1

All across the New Territory, settlers and miners were embracing the approach Bud and Wright had elected to avoid: They were at each other's throats. Captain Cooper and the rest of his town had a bird's-eye view of one of the more dramatic episodes anywhere in the New Territory.

The prospector who had staked his claims in Cutthroat Gap, William Smiley, had moved his wife onto one of his claims and built a small cabin. That quarter-section was selected in the lottery by a settler named Alex Wynn. Wynn's brother, Ed, had also had his envelope drawn and the two had somehow managed to select adjoining quarter-sections.

Smiley and Wynn were at odds immediately. Wynn, like Leon Wright, believed his deed was superior to all other claims and he worked dutifully to prove up his claim. The official proving was completed in March 1902, and Wynn promptly sued to have Smiley evicted from his land. Smiley countered that his mining claims could not be touched.

They went to court in May and, despite his assayer reports, his improvements, and his prior presence, Smiley was found guilty of trespassing and was ordered to vacate the property. Even though Wynn had won in court, it was still Oklahoma so Smiley simply ignored the order. Wynn's cattle were falling into Smiley's holes two months later.

They finally came to blows in August. The Wynns, along with their neighbor, Ed Eurey, confronted Smiley, his wife, and E.M. Dixon, Smiley's partner, at Smiley's cabin. The Wynns were armed and demanded the miners leave right then. The miners refused, and the shooting, heard clearly in Cooperton, began.

When the smoke cleared, Wynn's brother was dead and Wynn was injured. Smiley and his wife tore away to the south, leaving Dixon afoot to be captured by the six men from Cooperton who covered the two short miles in just a few minutes. The posse listened to Wynn's and Eurey's story and then roughly hauled Dixon to Hobart and turned him over to Sheriff Hobbs.

Smiley and his wife found refuge in the small mining town of Oreanna, just a few miles to the south where they received food and shelter for several days. The Smileys then headed to Wildman where they were certain they would be protected, and they were.

Since nothing could be kept quiet, the law learned where the Smileys were hiding and a Lawton deputy sheriff, Ed Chapman, was dispatched to serve the warrant and fetch the murderers back to Lawton. That couldn't be kept quiet either, and by the time the deputy approached Wildman, a large crowd of well-armed miners was there to meet him.

Chapman was not intimidated. He explained to the mob that if they interfered at all with him doing his duty or, God forbid, shot at him, the army would return and burn the town to the ground, for good this time. It wasn't the Indian Territory anymore and the law was going to be served.

The miners consulted for a moment and demanded that a group of them be allowed to protect Smiley during the trip to Lawton. Chapman shrugged. "It's a free country." The deputy collected Smiley and his wife, shackling both, and took them to Lawton. Eight miners followed along to "protect" the Smileys.

Mrs. Smiley was released in Lawton, everyone assuming that she had taken no part in the actual shooting. Dixon was retrieved from Hobart and the pair were sent to the federal prison in Guthrie to await their trial and would be found guilty. They only served one year in prison, the governor granting them clemency after several mining districts lobbied on their behalf.

Years later it was revealed that Mrs. Smiley had not only taken part in the shooting, but had fired the shot that killed Ed Wynn, executing him as he lay on the ground.

* * *

Back in Wildman, things were going downhill. The town, illegal to start with, partially occupied two quarter-sections that had been selected in the lottery. The settlers who owned those quarters had become increasingly hostile toward the town, and their neighbors were perfectly willing to help Wildman, both the man and the town, disappear as soon as possible.

It started simply enough. Rifle shots began to hit buildings and kick up dirt in the streets. Then a few outlying buildings were burned. Wildman and Williams were hanged in effigy. Heavy rocks began to fall into pits while miners were working them, and several shafts were intentionally collapsed. When their post office was forced to close, Williams and Wildman petitioned the governor for help.

Williams warned that the tensions between the miners and the settlers was so high that any event could "break forth into wholesale slaughter." The governor had bigger fish to fry, and he passed the issue to someone else to ignore. He replied that he had notified the Kiowa County sheriff and had ordered him to protect the miners and prevent bloodshed until the Department of the Interior settled the question. Until then, the locals would have to behave themselves.

* * *

As the new counties worked themselves into a frenzy, Angela and Bud quickly realized that they would not be recovering the remaining bars any time soon, and possibly not at all. If, Bud pointed out, the prospectors struck gold, then it would be virtually impossible to dig up the stash without getting caught. Even if no gold was found, Wright now owned that quarter-section and Bud was pretty sure he would not let them hang around for a couple of days.

"Then," Angela asked, "we're done? It's over?"

"I think so, yeah."

"I can live with that."

With nothing more than a passing interest in the Comanche lands and the unfolding chaos in every corner, Bud returned to painting. Angela made it real when she gossiped to Janet Monroe that Bud's partners had bought him out and whatever was going to happen in the Wichitas was going to happen without Bud.

Janet was so successful in feeding Norman's ever-growing rumor mill that a few weeks later Deskin approached Bud, surprised that Bud was out so early. Everything down there was going gangbusters; why did Bud exit?

"They made me an excellent offer, Sam. Between that and what we took out before, I think Angela and I are set."

"Well," Deskin droned, "you're probably right. I don't typically watch my depositor's balances, but we've done so much business I have to confess I do keep an eye on yours. I hate you leaving anything on the table, but you and Angela should never have financial problems. You've done well."

Bud nodded. "Thanks"

If you only knew what's in Denver.

"So," Sam asked, "what now?"

"I'm going to spend some time drawing, Sam. It'll be nice to focus on something quiet and safe. My biggest risk will be staining my shirts."

* * *

Angela took the opportunity to write Arthur and catch up with him. The last she'd heard he was somewhere in Texas, about to be married, and some of the new in-laws had been eyeing Oklahoma.

She got a letter back a few weeks later. He was married to a nice young woman named Zenie Gilbreath and they were living in Dublin, Texas. Zenie's sister and her husband had purchased a town lot in a place named Gotebo.

"Bud," Angela called, "you ever heard of Gotebo?"

"Never heard of Gotebo. What is it?"

"Town in Kiowa County, somewhere. A big help you are, Mr. Oklahoma expert..."

Zenie's family, the Gilbreaths, were entranced by the idea of Oklahoma, and several of Zenie's siblings had gone to visit and see for themselves. They returned determined to emigrate; town lots were available everywhere in the new counties. Arthur wrote that he and Zenie planned to join them.

A few months later, in March 1903, Angela received another letter. One of Zenie's brothers had gone north and Arthur was ready to go too, but Zenie was pregnant. They would stay for a while longer. That December Arthur wrote again, Angela had become an aunt in October, but Zenie had "somehow" gotten pregnant again. Maybe next year.

"Jesus," Bud exclaimed, "give the poor girl a chance to catch her breath. I thought my parents were bad..."

The next spring, Bud surprised Angela. She'd been to Denver; what did she think about visiting San Francisco?

Once the squealing stopped, Bud explained that he'd been contacted by an art gallery there who was interested in "provincial" work—Indians, deserts, and so on. Bud's name had surfaced; would he be willing to come out and show his work? Angela made the decision for him.

They purchased tickets to Omaha, then San Francisco, returning by way of Los Angeles, El Paso, Fort Worth and, finally, Norman. Bud estimated they would be gone for two months.

They returned home in August, Angela's journals full of her amazed descriptions of San Francisco, the Pacific Ocean, the wild California coastline, and the astounding fortress that was the Rocky Mountains – How had they built the railroad at all??

Also waiting was a letter from Arthur. Angela was an aunt again, and Arthur and Zenie were headed to Oklahoma too. A place named Cooperton.

"Wait, Cooperton? Bud, isn't Cooperton Captain Cooper's town?"

"Yes. Why?"

She handed him the letter and said, "It really is a small world. My brother is moving to Cooperton. Says he wants to open a store there."

"I'll be damned. Well, I guess you're going to want to go visit, right?"

"You better believe it. I haven't seen Arthur in years and I want to meet his wife. And I definitely want to see those babies. Just because we can't have children doesn't mean I can't enjoy my brother's."

* * *

It was February 1905 when Angela received the letter informing her that Arthur and his family were installed in Cooperton. Angela instructed Bud to finish up anything he was working on; they were going to visit that summer.

Bud and Angela dragged their luggage off the train at the Fort Sill station on June 12, 1905. They hired a wagon to take them to the livery stable where they could get a wagon to haul their luggage to Cooperton.

Bud approached the livery's office just as another man was opening the door to leave. He was tall with a bushy mustache and large felt hat, not different from anyone else, so Bud didn't pay much attention to him.

The tall man, however, took one look at Bud and said, "Hello, Mr. Dalton. You look well." The man held out his hand for Bud to shake.

Surprised, Bud looked closely at him and suddenly realized that he was standing with Heck Thomas.

"Deputy Thomas, I'm sorry, I didn't recognize you. I didn't expect to meet anyone I know here." Bud shook the large hand and asked, "What brings you to Lawton?"

"I live here. I was made police chief after the lottery. How about you?"

"Visiting my wife's family out in Cooperton. We'll probably stay a week or two. I was about to get a wagon and team."

"All right, good to have you in town."

Thomas opened the door he'd just exited and called back into the office, "Hey, Frank."

Bud heard, "Yes, Chief?" float through the open door.

"Take good care of Mr. Dalton here, please."

"You bet, Chief!"

Thomas nodded to Bud, then tipped his hat to Angela, who was approaching, as he passed.

Angela did a double take and looked back at Thomas, then asked Bud, "Was that Deputy Thomas?"

"Chief Thomas, now. It seems he's the chief of police here."

"Well, I hope he's cleaned this place up. It was intolerable last time."

Bud loaded their wagon and pulled out of the livery yard. They headed through Lawton to join the road leading west to the Cooperton Valley.

As they made their way through town it was clear that Heck Thomas had made no progress in cleaning up anything. Dozens of ordinances, orders, and edicts had been announced over the previous four years, none of which had any effect. Gambling, carrying guns, and prostitution were all supposed to be illegal, but all were in abundant supply. Soldiers from Fort Sill were a source of ready cash for all the banned activities, and the Indians were a new, completely unanticipated, complication.

After the Indians had selected their land allotments, they continued to receive the cash payments they were owed from previous treaties – the Jerome Commission had the power to take their land, it seemed, but not their money. Each month, the Indians surrounding Lawton would collect their payments and bring their cash into town, which was now part of the Oklahoma Territory.

Being in Oklahoma meant the old Indian Intercourse Act was null and void. The Indians could legally purchase all the whiskey they wanted and gamble whatever they pleased, and it was perfectly legal to sell them whatever they could pay for. The amount of money the Indians pushed into Goo-Goo Avenue was considerable – one hundred thousand dollars per month.

The Lawton police had no public support to end the filth; the only time they were alerted was, typically, after the fact. Drunk or disorderly people were dealt with, but that was the extent of the cleanup—no effort was made to remove the brothels or gambling tents. Between the Indians and the soldiers there was just too much money.

"Looks the same to me," Angela remarked. "Humph."

When they came to the creek leading to their old claim, and the bars, Bud hesitated. "Let's go see."

Angela objected, but Bud was determined and he turned the wagon up a now well-defined road to the camp. They found a large mining operation, the tunnel pushed fifty feet into the side of the mountain. They were looking around when a man hurried over.

"Hey, this is private property. You can't be here! You lost?" the man asked. "This is a working mine, no place for women," he continued, looking Angela up and down. "What do you want?"

"Nothing, really. I used to own this and was curious what happened to it. I guess it produced after all."

The man spat and shook his head. “Oh, is that right? Well, it produced a little at first, and then petered out fast. We’ve been looking over a year now, but nothing is coming back from the assayer.”

“Well,” Bud declared, “now we’ve seen it, I guess. Good luck.” Bud turned the team around and headed back to the trail.

“So,” Angela asked, “if someone knew where to look and could have a few hours alone…”

Bud snorted. “To hell with that. It took forever to get rid of Wright, and that bunch has too much in it. They’ll never leave.”

Chapter 2

Between Cooper, Antrim, and Tipton, Bud and Angela had plenty of places to stay in Cooperton, and everyone was delighted to see them again. They had been told the same tale that Angela had spread in Norman, that Bud had sold out early and done well.

Bud and Angela told stories of Denver and California, and remarked at how Cooperton, and all the Indian Territory, had grown.

Arthur and Zenie were healthy but haggard. A two-year-old and a toddler appeared to be quite a bit of work. Adding in making a new home and getting a business on solid footing, the couple was justifiably weary.

Bud and Angela spent ten days in Cooperton getting to know Zenie and her sister and husband, the Atkinsons from Gotebo, and catching up with Captain Cooper. His town had become far more than he'd ever expected, and Bud learned that while the lottery system had prevented the deputy marshals from lining their pockets, that was about all it did. Cooper was still bitter about it, but at the same time a bit proud of himself – he'd managed to extract a pound of flesh.

Cooper told Bud the whole story. The county probate judge, Harrison Finley, had assigned the proving commissioners right after the lottery. They showed up, collected all the documentation they needed, inspected all the lots, and brought it all back to Finley.

Cooper's Boomers filled out their deed applications, and dutifully filed them with the county.

Then the Boomers received the invoices for the proving commissioner's fees and expenses – over ten times what had been promised. Finley pleaded ignorance, claiming he was only obeying the law: The commissioners had fees and expenses and he, as probate judge, was obligated to collect them. Want that deed filed? Pay up.

Captain Cooper cried foul immediately and filed his complaint, one of the first filed against Finley, it turned out. Cooperton was small potatoes in Finley's extortion scheme, and all three of the new judges were the subjects of investigations. But Finley, Cooper laughed, became the first victim when Cooper exposed the fact that one of Cooperton's crooked commissioners was Finley's own son.

It got better when eight thousand dollars went missing for another town's proving and one of those commissioners turned out to be Finley's son-in-law. When the investigation began to turn up real dirt, Finley's son-in-law resigned and pointed the finger at his father-in-law, claiming in the papers that he "could not be part of that sort of corruption."

Finley doggedly stuck to his earlier claim, that he was only following the law. The attorney general then educated Finley on a bit of law he should have been aware of, pointing out that probate judges were only entitled to their salary, nothing more. Since Finley had not missed a paycheck, he was obligated to turn over all the money he'd collected, regardless of where it came from.

Finley gave up his pretense of respectability and refused to turn over anything he'd collected. That was a mistake because the governor who'd appointed him had just been removed for, among other things, his sketchy appointments in the new territory. The new temporary governor was none other than William Grimes, the same man who'd been assigned E.D. Nix's remaining term after his dismissal.

Grimes had no patience for the likes of Finley and threw him to the wolves. Finley was dismissed, then convicted a few months later. The crooked judges in the other counties suffered the same fate.

Cooper chuckled. "Elmer gave me a rash of shit about this town, but it was still the right move, even after paying off that bastard Finley and all his kids. I hope he rots in prison for a long time."

Talk turned to the gold rush that seemed about to bust.

"Bud," Cooper began, "when I heard you'd sold out early I couldn't believe it. But it looks like you did the right thing."

"Captain, I have to tell you, when the first tests came back we were disappointed with them. We thought they should have been much richer, especially after everything we got out of the creek. That got us thinking that maybe it was just a placer after all, and the vein was farther uphill, so when they offered to buy, we sold."

"Can I ask you what your share of the sale was?"

"My part came to ten thousand. I figured that would set us up for the rest of our lives, plus we still have plenty from the gold itself. Angela and I won't ever be hurting."

"Good for you, my boy, good for you!"

"I read about a lot of promising tests, almost every day it seems. Has anyone produced anything?"

"Nope," Cooper replied. "Lots of talk, especially from that mining paper in Lawton. Have you heard from George or Roy? Or Charlie for that matter? He ran out on Antrim just after the lottery. At first we figured he fell into a good claim at one of those camps, but now it seems likely that he just rode away."

"No, I haven't. I don't know where to find any of them."

Except Charlie.

"Well, I know where George is. He's down in Mountain Park, just south of Wildman. He made a claim down there, and I think I recall him marrying. You should ride down and call on them. It's not too far."

"That's not a bad idea, Captain. Zenie and Arthur are taking the kids up to Gotebo tomorrow and Angela wants to go, too, so maybe I'll ride down and see George. I'll stop in Wildman and see how things are going with Frank. Probably not too good if what you say is true."

"Give my best to George, and tell him not to be a stranger. Hell, invite him out here. Let's have a shindig!"

* * *

Bud rode south to visit George. Mountain Park was situated six miles south of Wildman on a picturesque bend in the creek. Needing directions, he stopped at a small store and asked the clerk if he knew where George Overton lived. Mountain Park was about the same size as Cooperton, so it was no surprise that the clerk knew exactly where George's place was.

Bud knocked on the door, which was opened by a woman who eyed Bud suspiciously. Bud explained that he'd known George for years and was in the area. Was George there? No, he was working his claim. She reluctantly gave Bud directions, and he made his way there.

The town was located between East and West Otter Creeks, about four miles north from where the two streams converged. West Otter Creek had carved a deep gorge between two low mountain peaks near Mountain Park and five miles farther upstream lay Wildman, itself at the base of a gorge. Between the two gorges the creek was dotted with dozens of mining claims. George's claim was located nearest to Mountain Park.

Bud remembered the area from his scouting mission for Southwest Mineral, and recalled that Elmer's engineers had not been impressed with its potential.

Bud found George's claim and looked around. The creek was about twenty feet wide at that point, the gorge beginning to form a few dozen yards upstream. Bud could see that farther upstream the canyon was at least a hundred feet deep and perhaps two hundred feet between the ridges. Unlike the place where Bud had hidden the bars, there was almost no sand in the creek bed. It appeared to Bud to be solid rock.

I wonder why anyone thinks this is a good place?

George didn't notice Bud's arrival; he was distracted in repairing something.

Bud dismounted and called out, "Hello, George."

George looked around, then dropped the broken shovel. "Bud Dalton! It's good to see you. How'd you happen along this way?"

"Well," Bud began, "Angela's family moved up to Captain Cooper's town and so we came to visit. Cooper said you'd married and were in Mountain Park. The fellow at the store sent me to your house, and your wife sent me here. So here I am." Bud motioned around. "You having any luck with this?"

George shook his head, "Nah, not at all. There's a lot of talk upstream, but nothing here yet. How about you?"

Bud edged into the shade of one of the trees bordering the creek. "I sold out a few years back, a little after the lottery. Digging is damned hard work, figured I'd leave it to someone else. How about Roy and Charlie? They take claims too? How're they getting on?"

George slid into the shade, too, and plopped down into a thin patch of grass growing there. "Charlie was working for one of Cooper's guys, uh, Antrim. The one with the freight outfit. He went out one day and never came back. Everyone figured he found something better and just quit. You know how Charlie is, not one to hesitate for long. No one's seen him since.

"Roy did like you, he made a claim and sold it, I guess about three years back. He got five hundred dollars and headed south to Texas. Haven't heard from him since, either."

"And you got married somewhere in there."

"Yeah. Met Martha in Wildman just before the lottery, and we were able to get that place in Mountain Park when they couldn't sell all the lots. I'd like to sell this, but I don't know who'd buy it. I'm about ready to walk away from it."

George and Bud talked for an hour, catching up and reminiscing. Bud relayed Cooper's invitation to come up to Cooperton before Bud and Angela returned to Denver. George agreed and promised to ride up in a few days.

Bud finally left and made his way upstream to Wildman. A mile south of town he found Wildman's huge mill and paused to gawk at it. The tramway was hauling a huge steel bin of ore slowly up the hill to be dumped into the mill, and there was activity everywhere. A large sign on the building's roof proclaimed it to be the "Gold Bells M. & M. Co."

Bud asked for Wildman, but was told he wasn't there; Bud could find him up in town. Bud nudged the horse into a trot and was in town fifteen minutes later. Wildman was in his office and Bud was sent back, which Bud found interesting – Wildman liked to keep people waiting.

Bud rapped on the rickety door and stepped in. "Hello, Frank. I just rode past your mill. Pretty impressive."

Wildman rose and extended his hand over the desk. "Well, Bud! Been a few years, I think. How are you? You look good."

Bud shook his hand and looked around for a place to sit. He spotted a chair and lowered himself into it.

"Angela and I are making out pretty well. Some of her family moved to Cooperton and we came to visit a while. Since I'm in the neighborhood, I thought I'd say hello."

"Glad you did. How's your claim working? I recall you were in tall cotton, lots of potential."

Bud replied, "I sold out. I'm painting full-time now."

"Well, I'm glad to hear someone's capitalized. It's been hit and miss out this way, generally miss. Lots of good signs, teasing mostly, but no major strike. The only thing that mill needs is some good ore to grind. We'll find it eventually."

"I've been talking with some other fellows," Bud replied, "and they seem to be losing faith. One said he would be happy to sell his claim for anything at all, another guy sold his for just a few hundred and moved to Texas. A big outfit near Lawton was complaining that production had stopped completely. I sold mine, like I said, but it was at least producing a little.

"But I'll tell you, Frank, it wasn't producing like it should've been and the tests were getting worse … I'm glad I sold when I could because I'm not sure I wouldn't be in the same boat."

Wildman sighed and nodded his head. "Yeah, it's hard to hang onto a claim that doesn't pay; you just run out of money. Can't eat, buy anything you need, pay for tests … pretty soon you have to give up. I'm seeing that all over, too, and I'd say a third of the claims are abandoned now. Everyone's betting on their best site, but it's hard to even find someone to grubstake you now. Not sure how much longer these fellows can hang on."

"You're all right, though, right, Frank? That mill back there just screams money, and the mine is right there. It sure looks impressive."

"Oh, yeah, we're fine. We borrowed against the mine's production to build the mill. We just need the production. It'll happen, just a matter of time, but some good tests would certainly cheer things up around here."

Bud grinned, and said, "Shit, Frank, you know how to make a good test. Toss a gold coin into one of those grinders you have and mix it into a few hundred pounds of ore. That'll get them off your back till you make your strike!"

Wildman laughed. "It's not quite that bad yet."

Yet.

Changing the subject, Wildman asked, "How long will you be around?"

"Maybe another week. Angela hasn't seen her brother in a long time and is getting on pretty well with his wife. Doesn't seem to be in a hurry to get back home. And that's fine—gives me a chance to catch up with old friends around here..."

Bud chatted with Wildman for another half hour, then excused himself so he could get back to Cooperton before it got too dark. As he trotted back, Bud considered everything he'd heard over the previous week. The common theme was "Nothing yet," and Wildman had him wondering how much longer the miners could hang on.

Not long, I bet.

Chapter 3

George was true to his word and brought his wife, Martha, to Cooperton four days later, and the Atkinsons came down from Gotebo. Elmer's brother was visiting from Colorado, so everyone went over to the Arthur and Zenie's place, and the large group enjoyed an afternoon lounging in the shade and telling stories.

One of the topics was the destruction caused by a massive tornado a month earlier. The town of Snyder, just two miles south of Mountain Park, suffered a direct hit from the mile-wide storm. A staggering ninety-seven people were killed with another dozen still missing. George had a clear view of the monster as it passed just east of his place. The storm had lifted by the time it reached Cooperton, but had scared everyone badly as it flew overhead just a few hundred yards to the east.

Bud mentioned how much the area had changed and George, with a mischievous look, asked him, "Do you remember the first time we were here, Bud? When was that?"

Cooper had known Bud for nearly twenty years, but didn't know exactly how Bud had so much experience in the Oklahoma Territory before there was even an Oklahoma. George obviously knew, it was a nice day for a long story, so Cooper bit.

"That sounds like an interesting tale, George," Cooper said. "Let's hear it. I don't know a thing about Bud before Payne's Boomers."

George looked over to Bud and raised his eyebrows, and Bud shrugged in return. "What the hell. It's quite a story, and was a long time ago."

Everyone was officially interested and George began, "Well, Bud and I first met in … when was it, Bud?"

"Fall of '75, if I recall."

"Yeah, that sounds right. Bud and I were riding with a group of fellows that had quite a reputation. We were both just pups back then and these fellows let us join, I don't know why."

Bud snorted. "Hell, I practically kidnapped them. I had been pestering Cole for years, and when they turned up I was on them like a chicken on a june-bug. I think Jesse just wanted to shut me up."

Cooper leaned forward and gaped. "Jesse and Cole? Reputation? Lord, do you mean Jesse James? And Cole Younger? The outlaws?"

"Yup." Bud nodded. "That's them. Charlie was with us, too, and so was Roy. Frank, of course, he, Cole, and Jesse were in charge. Quite a time."

"How in the world did you two get tied up with them?"

"I was just a kid," Bud replied, "and I met Jesse and Frank after the war. They knew my Pa through my mother—Cole Younger is my first cousin. The only thing I ever wanted was to ride with Cole and Jesse, and when the chance came up, I jumped on it."

"Same here," George said. "My big brothers all rode with Jesse in the war, so when Jesse sent for Will I just went with him. No one chased me off, so there I was."

Martha was staring at her husband, her mouth slack. "George, why didn't you tell me about this? Good God, George, did you kill anyone?"

Bud and George glanced at each other, and George said, "Well, neither Bud or I shot anyone, but Jesse was, well, he was Jesse. Some of the others were a little rough, too, but no, I never shot anyone. Besides, all we wanted to do was to head south and lure the Pinkertons away from our families in Missouri. We rode right through this valley on our way to Texas. Hell, we might have ridden over this exact spot."

"So, Captain," Bud said, "that was the first time I came through here, headed south. If not right here, within a mile."

George continued, "We kept on into Texas, till Jesse turned west to New Mexico. By then we'd been on the trail for a few weeks and the weather was getting cold, so when we found Roswell we stopped. We stayed long enough to get some mail."

"And get your horse stolen," Bud interjected.

"Yeah, that was fun. Anyway, Jesse learned that the Pinkertons had chased us to Texas, then left Missouri alone. So, we didn't really have anything to do. We drifted south to Mexico, and that's where the fun started. We stumbled on some Mexicans pushing some mules north. One of the Mexicans pissed Jesse off, which was not very hard to do, and Jesse...uh…robbed them. He, err, well, a few Mexicans got shot, but two got away. We learned they were Mexican soldiers later, but we grabbed the mules and hauled ass."

The whole group was listening intently, the only people uninterested were Zenie's children, playing in the thin grass of the yard. "Well?" Zenie demanded, "what did they have? What was it?"

"You won't believe it," George said. "They were hauling gold bars."

The group collectively gasped, then Martha asked, "Gold bars? Why are we so damn poor, then? What the heck did you do with them?"

Angela grinned inwardly, remembering asking Bud almost the same question years ago in Missouri.

"Well," Bud replied, "we hauled them across Texas with a Mexican posse on our tail."

George gestured toward the mountains. "Jesse was making for the Wichitas, but the weather turned on us, and then, just as we arrived, a blizzard hit full force. Everyone was spent, including our horses, so we hid in a canyon and rode it out. We buried the bars the next day and let the mules go. When the weather cleared, we scattered and went home."

Bud was glad George elected to omit the part about his fight with Zack, and Bud figured it was time for the story to end anyway. The group, however, was very excited and Atkinson asked the obvious question, "Jesus, man, where is it? Can't we dig it up right now?"

"Well," Bud said, "that's the problem…it's not that simple. Jesse and Frank and Cole got shot up in Minnesota and the truth is they were the ones that knew where we buried it. Like George said, we were all wasted and the weather was horrible … we couldn't find them.

"I spent years down here looking, which is how I came to know the area, Captain, but no luck. That's when I first met Elmer too. He was prospecting and shared a little of what he knows with me."

Angela had been doing a superb job of appearing as if she was hearing the story for the first time when she saw George look up sharply at Bud mentioning looking for the bars. Bud had just been caught in an old lie, and Angela wondered how many pieces George would be able assemble.

Bud didn't notice and continued, "So, Jesse James's Mexican gold is buried out there, somewhere, and me and George were there when it happened. I guess someday it'll get found, and I reckon it's gonna be finders-keepers."

The group babbled excitedly, and both Bud and George had to spend a while answering questions about the James Gang and where they thought the bars might be. Bud and George both had to confirm, without doubt, that neither of them had shot anyone. Neither mentioned anything about the bars already having been moved or the drama of trailing Bud, and Bud certainly didn't mention killing either Zack or his brother.

The out-of-town guests finally began to gather their things for their ride home when George approached Bud.

"Bud. You never told us that you'd looked for the bars. For years, you said."

Caught off guard, all Bud could manage was, "Huh?"

"The bars, when did you look for them? Where?" George pressed. "I recall you being pretty firm that you wouldn't go with Zack, and that the bucket didn't make any sense to you. But now you're saying you did go, more than once, and before I turned up, I'll warrant.

"And then you wouldn't come along … Was that because you'd already moved them? And then shot Zack because he had it right when he called you out?"

Bud recovered quickly. He lowered his voice to make sure they were not overheard. "No, everything I told you was true. There was no way I was going to ride with Zack, and I shot the bastard because he had it coming.

"So, yeah, I looked, but I couldn't find them. Then Payne and his Boomers showed up, Angela and I got married, and I didn't care so much. Plus, I'd met Elmer and stumbled onto a creek that I could find any time I wanted. You know all about that.

"So, if Zack thought he could find the bars, then good for him, but he'd have to do it without me."

Bud paused as Angela walked up. "You two look serious."

"George didn't know I'd hunted for the bars, and he's a bit angry."

"Well," George barked, "all I know is you looked when you said you didn't, then we found empty packs in the creek, then you shot Zack, now it seems like maybe your mine is a distraction. Zack had it right—you were the one playing us for fools. I want my share of the bars, Bud."

Bud shook his head. "I never said I didn't look, I told you I wouldn't go. And you know I don't have them. If I did, I wouldn't be standing here with you arguing about it … I'd have shot you when Zack got his."

Angela interrupted, putting her hand on Bud's arm and leaning into their conversation. "Bud, George, this isn't the time or place to talk about this. Bud, let's tell George the whole story, just not here."

"Whole story?" George growled.

"Lower your voice, George," Angela hissed. "It's not what you think."

Bud rubbed his eyes and shook his head. "All right, fine. George, can you meet us in Lawton in a few days? We need a place we can talk. There's a few things you should know."

George eyed them angrily, but said, "All right, where?"

"How about First Bank of Lawton on Main Street? Say, noon in three days?"

"All right, fine. I'll see you then and you can tell me what the hell you've done."

Martha and George left for Mountain Park, and the Atkinsons for Gotebo. Zenie was trying to get the kids to eat, so Bud and Angela wandered away from the house as the twilight deepened.

"All right, I give," Bud started. "What are we going to tell George?"

"Everything. Tell him where the bars are, let them be his problem. You got your share; he can get his if he can figure out how. Now, we leave. We're done here."

* * *

Bud and Angela said their goodbyes three days later. They rode to Lawton where they returned the wagon and horses and hired a hack to take them to the train station. They purchased tickets to Norman later that afternoon, then walked to the bank.

George kept them waiting, finally turning up at one o'clock. Angela was not happy about being forced to stand around in the bright sunlight on one of the longest and hottest days of the year. When George finally turned up, she was brusque.

Pointing at a saloon across the street, she said, "There. This won't take long." She walked away without waiting for either of the men.

It was hot in the saloon, too, but at least it was in the shade. They sat at a table in the back and got started.

"Well," George said, "what do I need to know?"

Bud replied, "That you're right, it's exactly what you think. I got to the bars first and moved them; my mistake was leaving the packs. I've taken my share already. I'll tell you where the rest is and you can take your share too."

"You son of a bitch."

Everyone keeps calling me that...

"Say what you want, but you should be grateful. We're out of this clean and I don't have to tell you shit."

"What are you going to do when I show up with Charlie and Roy?"

"You're not going to show up with Charlie."

George stared at Bud, who didn't blink.

"Bastard. And your gold mine?"

Bud snickered. "Yeah, that was a hell of a thing, wasn't it? Got out of that just in time too. This gold rush is about to bust. But it served its purpose."

George stared at Bud for another full minute, then asked, "Why? Why did you go to all this trouble if you weren't going to keep it all? Hell, we would have helped you...we offered to help you."

"Yeah, you did. But you were with Zack. If you'd shown up by yourself it all might have happened different. You're a good guy, and so is your brother. When it comes right down to it, I don't mind sharing with you. I wish Cole could get his, but fuck all the rest of them. Especially Jesse and Zack. And, by the way, the only reason we're talking at all is because I couldn't get all of it. I'd have been done and gone years ago if it weren't for that damn Quanah Parker.

"Speaking of Zack," Bud continued, "how did his brother get involved? What the hell was that all about? How did he get mixed up in this?"

George's face colored a little. "After you shot Zack, we took his horse and saddle like we said we would. I'm not sure how it all happened, but Abe talked to a deputy marshal named Thomas and told him how you'd shot his brother. At the same time, we did like we said, we found some of the boys, that's how Charlie got involved. He told us that he was the one that dug up the packs, and so it all pointed back to you.

"We were watching you both, waiting for some idea where you'd left the bars when Abe turned up in a saloon asking for you. He was hell-bent to shoot you, but we sent him back home. Then you gave us the slip when you moved to Norman. We picked up your trail again after your brothers were shot in Coffeyville. You didn't know Abe and we needed someone to trail you around Norman. We wanted clues to the bars, but he still wanted to kill you and then tried for you on the trail."

Angela had been listening closely. "George, you said Charlie dug up the packs?"

George nodded.

"Good thing Bud got there first then, otherwise you'd have nothing. Right? I'm pretty sure Charlie wasn't going to deliver your share."

"No, he said he was gonna take them to Texas."

"Uh-huh. And then Zack's plan was…what? Deliver Bud's share to Bud? You all were going to split it all up fair and square? Wasn't Zack talking about hanging and such?"

George colored more and began to squirm in his chair. "Well, yeah. I guess."

"And Bud is a son of a bitch? You have some nerve."

"Hmmmm," Bud pondered. "We met Thomas. Did you know he's the chief of police here now? Anyhow, he was tracking my brothers and came to ask us about them, but then he asked about Zack. I never figured out how they connected, but you told Abe about me, and he told Thomas. So, it must have been you, Roy, and Charlie that went through our place in Joplin, then?"

George finished turning red and nodded. "Yeah, I didn't know you knew about that."

"It was you?" Angela exploded. "George Overton, you are the son of a bitch here! You picked through my things! My house! You dug through our barn! It wasn't the Pinkerton agents looking for Grat! It was you all along! You bastard! You … you …"

All she could do was sputter; Bud had never seen her so furious. He saw her reliving her feelings of being violated, their panicked departure from Joplin, and the horrible winter in the Sibley tent. She'd sold all her belongings and fled, and the reason had been George, not Bud's outlaw brothers or the law-men hunting them.

Angela visibly tried to calm herself, but could not get the image of George pawing through her belongings out of her mind. "Bud, let's get on with this and get out of here. I never want to see him again."

"Right. George, can you find the original creek again? With the cave?"

"Yes."

"From there, go east one mile, there's another creek. It's pretty good sized, you can't really miss it. Go upstream maybe a few hundred yards at most and the creek makes a slight bend. There's a sand bar on the right, and that's where they're buried. About ten paces from the eastern bank."

"That's it?"

"That's it. All yours."

"What are you going to do?"

"None of your business," Angela barked. "Let's go, Bud."

* * *

Bud and Angela went directly to the train station, Angela forced to wait in the heat again. George, naturally, went out to the bars' location and was very disappointed to discover an active mine operating just a few yards away. He watched discreetly from the opposite bank for about an hour before concluding that it would be impossible to search for the bars, never mind to remove them inconspicuously.

That's why Bud couldn't get them all. Time's on my side, though.

By the time George finished spying on Bud's old mine, Bud and Angela were headed home. Angela still wanted to claw out George's eyes, but was calm enough to have a conversation.

"So," Bud began, "we leave everything to George and ...?"

"Do not start with me. You know as well as I do that it's all over. We have all we're going to get. And it's a lot, but if you're right, and the rush is a bust, then eventually someone is going to ask how Bud

Dalton made out so well and everyone else didn't. Now George knows the answer to that, so it's best we're nowhere to be found."

"Yeah. How does Denver sound? Far enough?"

Angela brightened noticeably. "Oh, that sounds marvelous. When can we leave?"

"How about tomorrow?"

Chapter 4

After George confronted Bud in Cooperton, he had been forced to endure Martha all the way back to Mountain Park. The new and unexpected knowledge that her husband had ridden with the James Gang and had helped bury Mexican gold had her in a tizzy. She was certain that George could find the gold again, with the right prodding and encouragement.

Martha detected a change in George when he returned from his meeting with Bud in Lawton. There was a glimmer in his eye and she just knew he'd learned something good. She also knew that a good dinner and an invitation to bed would pry it all out of him, whatever it was.

George told Martha nearly everything: the gunfight in Mexico, he and Zack learning of the pursuit, the savage trip across Texas, the blizzard, the creek, and, of course, burying the bars in it. He did not tell her about Bud, beyond Bud being in the gang too. He didn't tell her that Bud had moved the bars or that Bud had killed Zack, or how George and Charlie had stalked Bud for years. She only knew that Bud and George had met after all those years and now George knew where to find the bars.

When the pillow talk was done, she could barely contain herself, fantasizing about how they would spend their … thousands? However much it was, she certainly needed it, and perhaps there would be enough for them to move to the city, away from the bugs, heat, and tornados.

She managed to keep her mouth shut for just under a week before she confided to her friend, Freida, that her husband was really an ex-outlaw who had ridden with the James Gang and had buried some stolen Mexican gold in one of the Wichita's creeks. Freida didn't even try to keep her mouth shut and she told everyone she knew.

* * *

As the summer of 1905 dragged on, the gold rush busted. Nothing was producing, no one had any money, little food, and the remaining prospectors were beyond desperate. As the rumor of buried Mexican gold spread, it was accepted as certain truth. When Freida dropped George's name, the rumor became as tangible as the original rumors of the Klondike had been.

George Overton was a real person, with a real claim, and he had been there when the gold was hidden. He was the key. And that was how four men concluded that the bars must be on Overton's claim – why else would he have claimed that spot? It was on a creek in the Wichita Mountains, just like the bars in the story, and he was one of the original thieves. It was obvious to anyone with two eyes and the "facts."

The men snuck up to George's claim before noon on July 10. George was in the creek with a pick, trying to dislodge a good-sized rock with the hope that perhaps some color had collected beneath it. He'd almost got it out when they surprised him by calling him out of the creek.

They demanded he tell them where the Mexican gold was, and the very shocked George Overton sputtered that he didn't know what they were talking about. The apparent leader informed George about the rumor and his role in it, then demanded again. Not sure what to do, he pointed westward at the mountains on the horizon. "Well, it's over there."

"Bullshit, mister. It's right here. Why else would you pick this shitty spot? Tell us and you'll come to no harm."

George recalled Bud's response. "Listen, if I had a lot of gold, would I be trying to dig up a fucking boulder in the middle of the creek? No, I'd be eating and drinking in San Francisco. We buried it over there somewhere, in a creek running south out of the mountains somewhere west of Cache. Can't find it."

One of the bandits pulled a pistol from his pocket and cocked it. "We'll let you keep some, but if we can't have any then neither can you. Come on, mister, you don't want to die for nothing."

"I promise you, if it were here, I'd have taken it already. Hell, you're welcome to dig around all you want. Keep whatever you find, and good luck to you."

"Last chance. Give it up."

George spread his arms. "I don't have it."

The gunman tried to make a show of a sending a warning shot past George's left side, but he wasn't much of a gunman. His casual attempt struck George in the pelvis, just above the ball and socket of his left hip, spinning him around and dropping him into the rocky creek bed.

The gun was a small caliber. The bullet broke off a small crescent-shaped piece of bone and forced it into the socket, the bullet itself wedged just above, in George's hip bone.

The wound was not fatal, but was agonizingly painful. George screamed when the bullet hit, then again when he fell into the creek, his left leg grinding the piece of bone into his hip's socket. He tried to get to his feet but moving the injured hip simply didn't work anymore and he was rewarded with another savage bolt of pain. He tumbled back onto the hot rocks, screaming again.

The would-be claim jumpers panicked and scattered, none of them capable of more than bravado at best, mayhem at worst. George heard them shouting at each other as they ran and knew they weren't going to shoot him again. He gingerly explored the wound, relieved that at least it wasn't bleeding too much, yet. Unfortunately, any attempt to move resulted in more blinding, nauseating pain.

George lay on the rocks, trying to figure out what to do. The sun was directly overhead, and if nothing else he needed to get into some shade. Hopefully someone heard the shot and would come to investigate.

But no one did, and he had to concede he'd need to move himself out of the creek. But he could barely make a foot at a time. If he carefully used his arms and right leg to take most of his bodyweight, he could drag himself backwards. The rocks were hot and sharp, and anything that manipulated his left hip, like dragging its attached leg over the rocks, brought on more agony.

After nearly an hour of dragging and screaming, George finally got to the bank. It was only a foot high, but George thought it might as well be twenty. He painfully scooted his way over, his back against the rocky bank. He would use his arms and good leg to hoist himself up and, hopefully, topple backwards out of the creek. George assumed he would pass out from the pain.

Just sitting up was bad, but as he heaved with his arms and pushed up with his right leg, the agony was complete. He screamed as he stood, his final thought to lean backwards so as to fall into the dirt outside the creek bed. He was certain that if he fell back into the creek he would never get out.

He regained consciousness sometime later; he wasn't sure how long. The sun was still overhead, so perhaps it was only a few minutes. His mouth was dry and his lips cracked, so maybe longer. His canteen was fifteen agonizing feet away, and he steeled himself for the first gentle push.

The grass and dirt were much easier to navigate than the creek bed, and George got to his canteen, and the shade, in just a few painful minutes. He took a long drink, and poured a little over his head to cool off.

I wonder how long it'll take for Martha to miss me?

He could not get a good look at the wound, but he knew it was bleeding, although not too badly. He laid back, preventing as much movement of his hip as possible. His only idea was to shout if he heard someone, but that seemed a remote possibility.

The hours wore on, the shadows lengthening until dusk covered the camp. Martha should have missed him by then, the house just a few miles away. Hopefully help was on the way.

Dusk deepened into full-fledged night, but no one arrived. George called into the dark, hoping that someone was nearby. Nothing but the whine of mosquitoes, a new and unwelcome misery arriving on the scene.

At least I won't freeze.

George wished he'd frozen by the time dawn arrived. He had not slept at all, the bugs tormenting him and each accidental movement bringing a new flash of pain. It was impossible to believe that Martha hadn't noticed his absence, and by dawn he was angry.

About an hour later George heard his name, a faint shout from a distance.

"Here! I'm over here! At the creek! Help!"

Another minute of yelling and Marshal Charles Hook, accompanied by a man George didn't know, burst through the scrub into his camp.

"Meadows!" Hook called. "Get the others and bring the doc. Make sure they know right where we are. And bring a wagon!"

Hook looked George over. "What happened, Overton? Can you talk?"

George nodded. "Water?"

The marshal retrieved a canteen from his saddlebag and gave it to George, who drank deeply. "Thanks."

"You keep that," Hook replied. "Now tell me what happened. Who shot you?"

"I don't know. They wanted my claim, then shot me and ran away. There were four of them. I've never seen them before."

"That's going to make them hard to find. Meanwhile let's have a look at this."

Hook gently picked at the bloody fabric around the bullet hole, George wincing as he did.

"Pretty bad luck, Overton. It hits three inches to the left and you only have a flesh wound. Six and he misses you completely," Hook told him. "You're gonna live, though."

"Why did it take so long to find me? Been laying here since noon yesterday."

"Your wife didn't tell anyone you were missing until after dark. We started this way at dawn, got here as fast as we could."

The wagon and doctor arrived a few minutes later, accompanied by three additional men. The doctor cut three long slits outward from the bullet hole in George's pants, then folded back the fabric so he could get a good look at the wound.

"This is going to hurt," he told George seriously. "I'm sorry."

George screamed again as the doctor probed around the wound, feeling for the ball that should be lodged in George's hip.

"All right, I found it. I won't do that again. The gunshot wound is not serious by itself, but I'm worried about the leg. We need to get that bullet out, and hopefully we can save it. I think you're going to have a limp, though." To the others, he said, "All right, let's get him into the wagon. Gently, please."

The ride back to Mountain Park was misery and George passed out from the pain halfway there. He woke up in the doctor's office, groggy, his left hip throbbing painfully. Martha saw him moving and ran out to get the doctor.

The doctor explained that even though he'd found the bullet, he could not remove it. They would need to send to Hobart for a surgeon who had the skills and equipment to remove a bullet embedded in a vital bone. If it were an arm or leg they would have just cut it off already, but in this case he'd need to hold on for another day. They had sent for the surgeon, and the doctor had a supply of laudanum that would dull the pain until he arrived, so George should just try to rest.

The surgeon arrived the next day, two full days after George had been shot. He got to work immediately, soaking a rag in something called chloroform. He told George to relax and slowly breath in the fumes, it would smell sweet and make him dizzy. That was normal and he should not be worried, he just needed to breath normally.

The chloroform did its work and George was under in just a minute. The surgeon quickly exposed the wound and found the bullet. He cut the skin and muscle and used what appeared to be a pair of needle-nosed pliers to wrestle the ball out of George's hip as the nurse sopped up the blood.

The bullet came out with a crunch, then the surgeon removed the bone fragment. He cauterized the bleeding vessels and when he was satisfied, he used a needle and silk thread to sew up the wound.

George woke up ten minutes later, and it took another twenty for him to become coherent. The surgeon explained that he'd removed the ball along with a piece of bone wedged in the joint. There was a lot of damage, but he didn't think George would lose the leg. A limp was definite, but he should recover.

The doctor sent him home and gave Martha instructions on how to change the bandages and clean the wound, along with a small amount of laudanum and strict instructions on how to give it to George. Martha nodded dutifully, then took George home.

Martha didn't like the sight of blood, and changing George's bandages made her nauseous, so she didn't change them as she'd promised, merely giving her husband some more laudanum. All George knew was that his hip hurt all the time and the laudanum helped, so he didn't really notice that the bandages were not getting changed.

On the few occasions that Martha did change them, she ignored the greenish-yellow tinge and covered the wound with fresh bandages without tending the wound. The first hint that something was wrong was when George began to run a fever. Martha got him cool rags for his head, but still never checked the bandages. By the time the doctor was called and the wound inspected, they discovered the worst – gangrene had set in and the flesh was dying.

The doctor scraped and cut away as much of the decayed flesh as he dared, but it was clear that the infection had traced all the way down the incision and would get into his bloodstream, if it hadn't already. He was far too weak to fight for long, and George died without regaining consciousness two days later.

Martha's negligence wasn't entirely to blame, although if George had received help earlier it might have turned out better for him. The wound was filthy and wasn't cleaned for a full day, then the surgeon's cauterization caused more opportunity for infection. Martha's failed attempt at care ensured that nature took its course. George never had much of a chance.

* * *

Martha stayed in Mountain Park for another year, trying to organize search parties for Jesse's gold. No one took Martha seriously, but it was a good story and fun to retell, making her the butt of jokes. By the time Martha left Oklahoma, George Overton wasn't even a faint memory anywhere in the Territory.

The only thing George left behind was the legend of Jesse James's buried Mexican gold.

Afterward: The Final Dot, 1986

The Wichita Mountain Gold Rush busted in the summer of 1905. Some organizations and a few prospectors hung on doggedly, but it was hopeless. The gold that everyone was so certain must be waiting was never there at all.

Frank Wildman finally took Bud's advice and closed the circle in 1906. On a warm day in June he told his workers to take the day off and go relax with their families; it was just too damn hot. After they left, he took down his shotgun and went into the shaft, by then over a hundred feet deep. With rags stuffed into his ears, Wildman loaded the shotgun with the shells he'd specially made the day before, replacing the bird shot with the filings and dust he'd made by dropping a ten-dollar gold piece into his milling machine.

He fired the shotgun shells into the back of the mine shaft, the concussions making him dizzy, the thick powder smoke in the confined space making him nauseous. Four shots, spread across the mineshaft's face. He pulled the rags from his ears and staggered out of the mine, finding a shady spot to sit and let his head clear.

He was trying to sell both the mine and mill, and he expected the prospective investors to require their own sample. Their results should come back positive and artificially inflate the value of his pile of dirt and rocks.

His investors did exactly as Wildman had hoped, and he was able to unload his worthless mine and plant to several unsuspecting businessmen from Kansas. Wildman and his town were both gone within a year. The Kansas businessmen would also give up, abandoning The Gold Bells Mill in 1910.

In 1907 the Oklahoma Territory and the remaining Indian Territory were combined to create the forty-sixth state admitted to the U.S. Only the Arizona Territory and New Mexico Territory remained unadmitted.

Arthur and Zenie Wood had another daughter, Lottie Pauline, on June 9, 1915. Arthur ran his general store in Cooperton until his death in 1931. Zenie remained in Cooperton until she moved to Roosevelt in the 1940s and lived there until her death in 1974.

Bud and Angela lived happily in Denver until 1929 when the stock market's crash erased much of their wealth. Both were in their 70s and their banker gave them the bad news in late October. They were not poor by any means, but they no longer enjoyed unlimited funds.

Bud and Angela returned to Cooperton in 1931 for Arthur's funeral. They were able to take the train from Denver all the way to Hobart, changing trains only once. Bud was amazed at the small city that Cooperton had become, although compared to Denver it was, in Angela's words, "primitive."

"Someone's gotten soft," Bud teased. "I bet just one night under the wagon would kill an old woman like you."

They returned to Denver after the funeral where, two years later, Bud died in his sleep. After his funeral Angela, despondent, wrote in her diary:

> *I don't see a way through. I've never known loneliness before, this is the most dreadful feeling anyone could ever have. What can be worse than this? I am so sad, I miss Bud so much, I can't stop crying. I am completely alone now and there is no future. I'm done. I won't go on. I wouldn't change anything except losing Bud like that. I wish I'd gone with him, but I'll see him soon.*

That was Angela's final entry. She stopped eating or drinking and followed Bud four days later.

Their lawyer and banker were left to figure out what to do. Bud and Angela had no children, and Bud's will left everything to Angela. Angela also had an old will, but had not thought to update it after Arthur's death and she had designated him as her heir if both she and Bud were gone.

The lawyer arranged for everything to be liquidated and had Angela buried next to Bud with a large service and matching headstone. He billed the estate handsomely, the banker doing the same. By the time their thievery was complete and the expenses paid, there was very little cash and just a small handful of personal effects that could not be sold. The lawyer tracked down Zenie and informed her that she, as Arthur's heir, would receive those effects.

A week later, two large trunks were delivered to Zenie in Cooperton. She opened them and found they contained Bud's sketchbooks and Angela's diaries, all carefully numbered and dated. Being related to neither Bud nor Angela, Zenie was tempted to throw them away and keep the luggage, but curiosity got the better of her and she began picking through the books. Second thoughts intruded as she leafed through the pages.

Bud's books contained an uncountable stock of drawings and rough sketches. There were hundreds, perhaps thousands, of portraits, many of Angela throughout her life but also hundreds of others whom Zenie could never recognize. There were landscapes, some that Zenie did recognize and she compared Bud's sketch of Cutthroat Gap to the real thing clearly visible just a few miles away. There were sketches of everything: people, animals, rocks and leaves, sunrise and sunset, maps and personal notes.

Lottie, sixteen years old, was looking over Zenie's shoulder and asked, "Mama, what are all these?"

Zenie handed Lottie the sketchbook and opened one of Angela's journals at random; the entry was from June 1881 and described how she'd met a boy named Bud. She flipped forward to 1883; the entry told how Arthur had thrown their father out of the shack and that he had been killed later that night.

Arthur never talked about his father...

An entry from 1890 had Angela wondering why she could not get pregnant; another from 1897 told of Bud goofing around with her one afternoon, how he'd made her laugh and how she loved him so very much.

"They belonged to your aunt and her husband. Do you remember Bud and Angela from your daddy's funeral?"

Lottie nodded.

"Well, he would draw and your Pa said Angela would write down everything she saw, heard, or thought about." Zenie thought for a moment, trying to come up with something that might make sense to both Lottie and herself.

"Do you know what an autobiography is?"

Lottie nodded again. "That's when someone writes their own story. They were old, weren't they? There are a lot of books here, Mama. It must be a long story."

Zenie nodded, reading Angela's final entry and wondering to herself how that must have felt, at the very end, to decide to be out of time. And to be glad of it.

She glanced down at all of Bud's sketchbooks, and recalled Bud's and George's story of Jesse James and Mexican gold, the stories of his outlaw brothers and cousins, Oklahoma's chaotic birth, and the fact that her sister-in-law had been at the center of all of it. And had written it down.

Lottie's right—the whole story is right here. I wonder if there's a picture of Jesse James in there somewhere? Arthur might be in there too ... If I throw these out, it will be gone forever, after everything that's happened. After all they did and saw. Everything in there will be gone, like it never happened.

In an unusual moment of introspection, Zenie wondered if it was all for nothing. If, at the end of your life, there's nothing left behind, then you're completely gone. Worse, maybe you never existed.

Lottie brought Zenie back to the moment. "Mama?"

"I'm sorry, dear, I was just thinking. Yes, it must be a very long story." Zenie replaced Angela's last journal and closed the trunk.

"Help me put these in the attic over the carriage. We'll read their story someday."

***

As with so many things, once Bud and Angela's trunks were stored away, they were forgotten. When Zenie moved to Roosevelt, the two old anonymous trunks were moved without a thought. When Zenie died, they returned to Lottie along with a few belongings Zenie had left her youngest daughter.

Lottie vaguely recalled them, but was living her own life by then. Married, four grown children, a platoon of grandchildren, and living in a small farmhouse in the Cooperton Valley would never permit her the spare time to peruse the trunk's contents, even if she were inclined to explore them. Which she wasn't.

Sad from her mother's death and nostalgic for anything that belonged to her, Lottie inadvertently copied Zenie's decision to have them stored away. They were hauled up into the attic above the garage where they would be out of the way and relatively safe.

I was a little kid then, but I remember when Zenie died. I definitely remember my brother and I being admonished to stay away from the things Zenie had left my grandmother, her tone warning us that any harm that came to them would create sincere hardship for the perpetrator. The days were long on the farm, and there was no shortage of unpleasant work. We took the hint.

When the chores were done, my brother and I were often banished outside. Our favorite thing was to dig through the old things we found everywhere – old farm equipment and tools in the barn, bridles, saddles, parts from tractors we'd never seen; there was stuff everywhere. Our favorite place, though, was in the attic above the garage.

We noticed the trunks instantly, but were hesitant to mess with them. These were clearly Zenie's, and our grandmother's warning was fresh in our minds. But if they were so important, then why were they up here and not down in the house? They were probably full of old papers and the crap that grown-ups seemed to love to keep.

Worse, they were full of books. We spent a few minutes picking through them, being careful not to damage any because they were really old. I read the name "Bud Dalton" on the inside cover of one I'd randomly pulled from the closest trunk, and wondered who he was. If the book was any hint, the guy had been an artist.

Bud Dalton … I was instantly fixated on him – who was he? Was he famous?

It was hot in the attic and I was sweating. I'll never forget the droplet of sweat that ran down my forehead and right off the end of my nose, straight onto the ancient page I was staring at. The paper absorbed the water and instantly smudged the jawline of the woman staring back at me.

Visions of hauling hay and chopping cotton for the rest of my miserable life replaced the picture and I carefully closed and returned the book, fervently hoping my grandmother never opened it. I could feel the next droplet forming; it was time to go.

Bud Dalton. No one had heard of him, Grandma was vague—her mother's brother-in-law or something like that, not family. She didn't know anything about him, but she knew we'd been messing with those trunks.

"Stay out of those!"

Absolutely. Probably. Actually… no, definitely not. I kept that to myself.

I discreetly perused Bud's sketchbooks when I could. We generally stayed with my grandparents during the summer because Mom didn't have an elementary school to keep an eye on us, so my opportunities were limited. The heat of the summer, darkness of the attic, and the never-ending supply of work limited my sessions with Bud, but I spent enough time with his books that I felt like I got to know him.

The books in the other trunk were a diary, probably his wife's. To be honest, I could never really stand to read them … it was like overhearing the girls at school gossiping between classes. No thanks.

Over the years, I scrutinized Bud's drawings closely. They were amazing and I could barely draw a straight line so, to me, Bud was a mystery of the universe. Like gravity. Not meant to be known or understood, simply acknowledged.

Crazy things happen. Dots connect that should not even be on the same page, but they connect nonetheless. Years passed. I was in college at the University of Oklahoma, researching a paper. I was in the library, scanning an old newspaper article on the micro-fiche when the words "Bud Dalton" crept past in the adjacent article.

What the hell?

A name, scratched onto a brass bucket. From the Wichitas. The dots connected.

And that's when crazy started.

Real Dots
Notes, Acknowledgements, and Gaps

The Wichita Mountains are a low, very rugged mountain range that rise abruptly from the plains in southwestern Oklahoma and run generally northwestward from Lawton. While none of the mountains are tall, they feature steep cliffs, narrow canyons, thousands of springs, and uncounted rock outcrops and boulder fields.

The mountains were formed over the course of hundreds of millions of years when seismic forces created a depression near the center of the inland sea that covered what are now the central plains. The depression was relatively weak and cracks formed as the bedrock was pulled in different directions. Volcanic rock and magma were forced into the cracks and formed huge masses of granite and basalt beneath the surface. The land ultimately was forced back together, and the mountains were formed when the enormous slabs of rock were pushed upwards to eventually protrude above the surface of the shallow sea. Wave terraces are still visible at Quartz Mountain on the western edge of the range.

The sea eventually drained and erosion went to work on the mountains. Layers of softer rock were broken up and washed away to form gravel deposits and sand bars in the multitude of creeks that run from and between the peaks. The dramatic cliffs and ridges seen today are the result of the erosion, which was also responsible for exposing the different colors of stone and black sand that so thoroughly fooled the prospectors for decades.

The plains Indians were naturally attracted to the mountains for the cover, water, and abundant game. They also believed it to be the perfect site from which to raid settlers in Texas and Kansas, and they did so with abandon. In 1852 Captain Randolph Marcy agreed with the Indians and recommended a post be constructed on the eastern edge of the range so the army could at least start from the same place the Indians did. General Philip Sheridan founded the post in 1869 and named it Fort Sill after his West Point friend Joshua Sill who was killed in the Civil War.

By the time the post was founded, things were getting dicey. The Indians had become more aggressive in their attempts to keep the white man at bay, but the end of the Civil War allowed the army to actually put a garrison at Fort Sill. Settlers were pushing westward, relentlessly, and the army was tasked with protecting them.

The end of the Civil War also spelled unemployment for hundreds of former militias in Missouri. Just as the Indians regarded the new Texans' cattle, horses, and scalps as their own, some of the dispossessed militia regarded the new banks, pay wagons, and trains in Texas the same way. And just like the Indians, the outlaws found the mountains in the lawless Indian Territory an ideal place to escape into.

The James Gang was known to have raided in Texas and escaped back into the Wichita Mountains more than once. Sometimes they were forced to hide their loot in order to complete their escape, and the mountains were absolutely perfect for that purpose.

Jesse liked to hide loot in impossibly difficult places and then draw intricate and complicated maps that only he could understand. Given his mania for obscurity and his relatively short life, it is a virtual certainty that some of the caches are still undiscovered, both inside the Wichitas and elsewhere.

Some caches have been discovered by accident. In 1913 (according to Steve Wilson in *Oklahoma Treasures and Treasure Tales*), a laborer uncovered over $13,000 in $20 gold coins while digging a trench for an oil pipeline.

The legend of the James Gang's Mexican gold really is common knowledge and Wilson's book includes a well-written version: Frank and Jesse conducted a raid in the mid-1870s and hit pay dirt beyond their wildest dreams. They somehow highjacked a mule train loaded with Mexican gold and hightailed it back through Texas. With a posse hot on their trail and a blizzard threatening, they escaped into the Wichita Mountains to hide. They released the mules and buried the gold until they could safely retrieve it.

Six months later Frank and Jesse's luck turned sour in Northfield, Minnesota. The gang was destroyed and Jesse would never return to the Wichitas before he was killed in Missouri.

Frank apparently attempted to recover some of his hidden loot. Once his outlaw days were behind him, Frank moved into a farmhouse outside of Lawton and, although he did absolutely no farming, he did ride around the countryside nearly every day and night.

Rumors flew that Frank was retrieving his old treasure caches, and Wilson presents evidence that he actually recovered some of them. It was also rumored that he was looking for one cache in particular, but could never find it. The rumors flared again when he was visited in Lawton by his old outlaw buddy, Cole Younger, after his release from prison. Frank finally left Lawton and drifted from job to job, generally in north Texas, until his death 1915.

A man named Joe Hunter allegedly acquired some of Jesse's cryptic maps. Hunter began looking for Frank's caches, seemingly with more success than Frank had. Not only did Hunter track down two major finds that Frank overlooked, but in February 1948 he produced an old brass bucket he claimed he'd found on Tarbone Mountain in the Wichitas.

The bucket contained instructions, a date, and a reference to "this gold" scratched roughly into the surface along with the names Frank and Jesse James, Cole Younger, George and Will Overton, Frank Miller,

Rub Busse, George Payne, Roy Baxter, Charlie Jones, Zack Smith, and our own Bud Dalton. Lawton was electrified by the possibility of a tremendous gold cache just outside of town.

Later the same year the *Lawton Constitution*'s headlines screamed, "Jesse James is Alive! In Lawton!" A man named J. Frank Dalton had materialized and claimed to be Jesse James. Dalton, under intense scrutiny, was indeed able to produce information that was known to be true, but not well publicized, about the James brothers. Unfortunately, he was also completely unaware of other well-known facts about Jesse and Frank (Frank's full name, for example). The consensus was that Dalton might have known Jesse at one time but was certainly not Jesse James. It seems likely the publicity surrounding Hunter's finds attracted Dalton to Lawton.

Dalton continued traveling around claiming to be Jesse until his death in Granbury, Texas, three years later. Claiming to be related to the Dalton Gang was a cottage industry in the 1940s. Nancy B. Samuelson (in *The Dalton Gang Story: Lawmen to Outlaws*) details numerous "Daltons" and gives particular attention to J. Frank. Was this the "Bud Dalton" scratched onto Hunter's bucket?

Almost certainly not. J. Frank Dalton had a reputation as a swindler and Jesse's surviving relatives at the time laughed at Dalton's claim. They were well aware of him and pointed out that J. Frank turned up every few years with a new spin. Indeed, his picture was published twice in 1948 commemorating his 100th birthday. Once in March, then again in a different town and newspaper in May. J. Frank was a sketchy character no matter who tells the story.

Dalton is a common name. The 1880 census shows over 430 male entries named "Dalton" in Missouri, and thousands nationwide. "Bud" was (and still is) a common nickname with no base name – literally anyone could be a "Bud."

The closest "Bud Dalton" I could find was a man named Elmer Bud Dalton (the "Elmer" is a complete coincidence) who was killed in a car accident in 1948. "Bud Dalton" was also a character in a 1915 movie played by Joseph Flores, even less tangible than Hunter's bucket. In the context of Jesse James, Hunter's bucket is the only documentation that anyone named "Bud Dalton" ever existed.

The Bud Dalton in this story is, obviously, fictitious. Adeline and Lewis never had a son named Bud – the Daltons were well documented in the census – but the James, Dalton, and Doolin gangs were real, the events in the late 1800s were real, and Oklahoma is certainly real. So, what if Bud had been real?

What if Bud Dalton was a real person, the gold legend was true, and Hunter's bucket was the proof? What might that story be, and how might it fit into the events that unfolded in the real world? Can the dots be connected to make an interesting story?

Maybe. Most of the people, places, and events in this book are (generally, mostly) accurate representations of what happened in the big picture. A grain of salt is necessary in the details, however … actually, many, many grains are necessary. I had to make some of my own dots.

For instance, the description of where the James Gang waited out the blizzard is a fictionalized description of a place called "the Narrows" in the Wichita Mountains. There is, however, no safe place in the Wichitas to ride out a blizzard, and trying to do so in the Narrows would certainly be fatal. The blizzard is a key detail in the legend of the James Gang's Mexican gold, though, and thus part of Bud's adventure. It's also a pretty good indication of why the legend is probably false.

It is nearly impossible to get a consistent account of almost any event of that period. Newspaper accounts differ according to the editor's politics and opinions, then whole articles would be reprinted in other papers without credit to the original. Even photographs have been altered – you can find the same photograph of the dead Daltons with contradictory notations and labels. Bill Doolin's death is another example: In the days following Doolin's shooting, newspapers across the state credited every member of the posse with the fatal shot. One story claimed that Doolin had died of natural causes and the deputies shot the body after it was discovered so as to get credit for the kill.

Small details thwart us too. The Smiley and Wynn episode really occurred, but some newspapers spelled Wynn's name "Winn." That is a constant in newspapers across the Territory; people and place names spelled and misspelled in different ways between papers. The town "Oreanna" (Wilson claims the name was made by combining "ore" with the local postmistress "anna") was also referred to as "Arena," but was briefly called "Park City" first. Whatever its name and history, it's gone and left no remains aside from its location on old maps.

We can't lay it all at the newspaper's feet, though. Many of the people used as primary sources of the time were unreliable. E.D. Nix's deputy Chris Madsen was notorious for telling different versions of a particular lie and then those lies were recorded and treated as fact. Another deputy, Bill Tilghman, was no better, and Nancy Samuelson mentions in her notes in *Shoot from the Lip: The Lives, Legends & Lies of the Three Guardsmen of Oklahoma & U. S. Marshal Nix* that nothing Marshal Nix ever recorded should be viewed as reliable.

Thus, inserting a completely fictitious person into a vague history is going to be hard on the truth, and in this case it's very hard on the real Daltons. Anyone familiar with the Dalton history will instantly see that Bud's story only vaguely resembles what the real Daltons (probably) did in real life: Dates and places are skewed throughout this story. Lewis Dalton is one victim here – almost everything up to and including his death is fabricated and intended to fit into the storyline. And it gets worse – several events in my story are almost certainly false. For example, Bob Dalton (probably) did not kill Cochran's son, rather he only shot the horse ... although Emmet (who wasn't present) claimed it happened as presented here. Perhaps I'm not the only one making his own dots.

What to do? When there were conflicting versions, the one I found most convenient was the one I selected. Thus, a dead boy instead of just a dead horse.

Another possibly innocent victim here is Bill Dalton, who deserves some attention. Samuelson (in *The Dalton Gang Story*) makes a good argument that Bill's criminal activities are very likely overstated. Bill got on the wrong side of the newspapers and was blamed for every criminal activity from Chicago to North Texas, and his location was often reported in multiple places at the same time. He was finally hunted down and killed after being blamed for a bank robbery in Longview, Texas, which Samuelson convincingly shows he had no part of. Two years after Bill was killed, all the deputies involved were indicted for Bill's murder, but nothing can be found regarding the subsequent trial, and Samuelson notes, quite rightly, how very odd that is.

But alas, this story needed desperadoes and not innocent victims. Unfortunately for Bill, he's forced into the villain's role and no mention is made of his potential innocence. My sincere apologies to Nancy Samuelson and all other Dalton historians.

Chris Madsen, Bill Tilghman, Heck Thomas, and E.D. Nix were also real people. The deputies were dubbed "The Three Guardsmen" and had reputations as the best of the best. Samuelson debunks that in *Shoot from the Lip* and documents the gory details fully. I can't (won't) disregard her research, so I've accepted her interpretation of those miscreants here. The exception might be Heck Thomas who appears to have been a capable deputy. Emmett Dalton supposedly said that Heck Thomas was the only deputy that the Daltons actually feared, and Thomas was known to have been on the Dalton's trail, so, maybe.

E.D. Nix was an embarrassment to Oklahoma and the United States in general. Sadly, not the last. Early Oklahoma politics is a fascinating topic in a sad, how-was-this-allowed-to-happen sort of way. Actually, it's pretty clear how it happened: After the land was stolen from the Indians, an anything-goes attitude prevailed. From the Sooners to Nix's corrupt deputies, to crooked judges and commissioners across the Territories, it's no mystery as to why Oklahoma was still part of the Wild West well into the twentieth century.

David Payne was a real person who was vital to opening the Unassigned Lands. Carl Coke Rister's *Land Hunger: David L. Payne And The Oklahoma Boomers* was my primary source for Payne and

Couch's adventures and is mandatory reading for anyone seriously interested in Oklahoma's story. I've attempted to keep the time frame and activities of this tiny sliver in line with what Rister documented – the truth of that story is better than any fiction.

Cooperton is a real place, at least what's left of it is. Its remains lie on State Highway 54 about two miles northwest of Cutthroat Gap (also a real place). Unfortunately, the box containing Cooperton's founding documents is apparently misfiled in the National Archives and can't be found, which seems to be typical of everything "Oklahoma." The township Cooperton resides in is listed in the census documents as "Cooper" Township (which is accurate), but all the entries for those residents are recorded as residing in "Cooper, Kiowa County, Oklahoma" – a place that never existed. It gets worse: many of Oklahoma's Township names are duplicated across the state and "Cooper" is one of them. The other "Cooper" Township was in Kingfisher County.

I envision Cooperton's box being filed away in the same manner as the crate in the final scene of *Raiders of the Lost Ark*.

Further complicating Cooperton's genesis is some ambiguity around who actually founded the town. The Oklahoma Archives was able to produce a copy of the Articles of Incorporation for the Cooperton Townsite Corporation. The officers listed on that document do not match any people mentioned in newspaper articles surrounding the drama of the town's "proving out." And in typical fashion the newspapers are also contradictory with ambiguous references to a different town named "Cooper," which is near Guthrie. Rister mentions "Captain Cooper" being one of Payne's closest associates, and a news article refers to a "Capt. Cooper" as the "town father," along with other articles referring to "Captain" and "J.B." Cooper being a close associate of David Payne, and there's solid evidence that he was an original Boomer with Payne at Rock Falls. I've chosen that version.

Also worth noting is that I elected to ignore the "Cooperton" entry from the Oklahoma Historical Society's outstanding website (see

"Cooperton," *The Encyclopedia of Oklahoma History and Culture,* https://www.okhistory.org/publications/enc/entry.php?entry=-CO055, by Ethel Crisp Taylor). That article attributes the founding to a man named "Frank Cooper," mentions the naming problem, and attributes the town's location to a filing error. There was indeed a Frank Cooper who, like Captain Cooper, was from Seward and was a teacher there. My research indicates that Frank Cooper was still a teacher in Seward well after the lottery and well into Cooperton's proving difficulties, when simultaneous articles mention "Capt. Cooper" in Kiowa County. It seems unlikely that Frank Cooper had anything to do with the town, although it seems very likely that the Coopers could have been related.

The article mentions the town's naming problem, but also brings up the possibility of the town being laid out in the wrong place. That seems impossible to me and would have been discovered well before the lottery. However, like the newspapers, the maps of the day were also full of errors and Cooperton is a victim. For example, Geo. F. Cram's 1902 version of *The New Survey Map of Oklahoma and Indian Territory* places Cooperton in the northwest quadrant of Township 5, which is false. Cooperton unambiguously resides in Section 34, part of Township 5's southern border. I can't speak to the whole map, but that part is very misleading and perhaps Ms. Taylor was a victim. Or perhaps I am, but all things considered I like my research better and went in that direction.

In any event, there are oral histories, memories, and some newspapers. I've heard some of these personally from my grandparents and father, but it would have been nice to see something legitimate on paper. The Territory newspapers reported on much of Cooperton's early trials and events, so those will have to do.

The gold rush that occurred during the Kiowa-Commanche opening was real, too, and worked out how it's described here. There had been persistent rumors of gold in the mountains and creeks all around the area for many years (Colonel W. S. Nye records this in *Carbine and*

Lance: The Story of Old Fort Sill and John W. Morris documents how the rumors began in *Drill Bits, Picks, and Shovels*) and there are still remnants of mines and smelters across the area. The foundation steps and water tank from the Gold Bells Mill are easily found just a few miles north of Mountain Park.

A reporter named W.R. Draper published several stories, one in the *New York Times* about gold fields in the Wichitas and claimed to have interviewed miners. Draper also claimed to be present at the 1901 lottery and his published account meshes with other accounts. He also mentions meeting Heck Thomas, who is known to have been in Lawton during and after the lottery, and interviewing speculators for a mining outfit from Denver.

There was, of course, no gold, even if Draper didn't know it, but at this point we're long past believing anything a reporter writes. The "Cold Lode Mine" was an actual claim and was located in the vicinity of where Bud's claim is described and, according to Wilson, was sold in 1903 for $10 thousand. It was just one of many claims in the area between present-day Cache and the mountains, and none produced anything. But someone has to be responsible for that mess, which is where Bud shines.

Even if there could be gold hidden in the Wichita Mountains, there's little point in searching (although many people do search for Jesse's gold bars). Much of the area is now part of the Fort Sill Artillery School and, aside from being off-limits, is peppered with unexploded ordnance. Anything hidden inside the base perimeter is truly gone forever. Many of the canyons and gorges that would have been excellent hiding places were dammed in the 1930s and are now small lakes. Finally, much of the area is part of the Wichita Mountain Wildlife Refuge and is home to buffalo and long-horn cattle but is off-limits to regular people. Even so, people still ponder the clues and wonder about Jesse's Mexican gold. What if . . . ?

There is treasure in those mountains. The refuge is worth a visit (there's an old mine not far from the Narrows, and the remains of John

Pearson's mill are easily accessible), and Fort Sill's history is fascinating in its own right. (Colonel Nye's book mentioned earlier is outstanding). The terrain is stupendously beautiful, and if you approach from the south, through the Big Pasture (north of Chattanooga headed toward Cache), you'll see what Bud might have seen as he rode north, pushing a mule train as fast as it could go.